T0285286

ESCAPE TO PUMPKIN COTTAGE

By Anna and Jacqui Burns

Poles Apart
Escape to Pumpkin Cottage

ESCAPE TO
PUMPKIN COTTAGE

ANNA AND JACQUI BURNS

Allison & Busby Limited
11 Wardour Mews
London W1F 8AN
allisonandbusby.com

First published in Great Britain by Allison & Busby in 2024.

A CIP catalogue record for this book is available from
the British Library.

First Edition

ISBN 978-0-7490-3195-4

Typeset in 11/16 pt Adobe Garamond Pro by
Allison & Busby Ltd.

By choosing this product, you help take care of the world's forests.
Learn more: www.fsc.org.

Printed and bound by
CPI Group (UK) Ltd, Croydon, CR0 4YY

For Carole
We miss you every day.

Chapter One

Pippa

Pippa lets out an involuntary shriek as she spots the sign. 'Welcome to Riverdean.' She has arrived!

She follows the road as it bends sharply to the right, and her Audi is plunged under a canopy of trees. The brilliant blue of the sky peeks through the green and mustard leaves, as though even the sky is promising good times to come. And boy, does Pippa need good times. It's been one hell of a year, filled with grief, job stress and break-up angst.

Pippa is ready for a fresh start. To stand on her own feet. The months of preparation, staying up late after work to plan, nights filled with worry and doubt, all seem worth it now she's here.

She's waiting for her first glimpse of the village. The Google images promised her chalet-style cottages in vibrant reds and greens, all with views of the sparkling river, scenes not unlike the Swiss Alps. The magic her mum spoke about all those years ago, wistful tales about her childhood spent in the idyllic Wye Valley. It sounded like a fairy tale to Pippa's ears, compared to the constant bustle of London.

She spots one cabin, almost hidden from the road amongst the trees, spellbinding with fairy lights wrapped around the porch and ivy growing either side of the door. It's all starting to feel real. The fairy tale might actually come true. Pippa can't wait.

She rounds one more bend and is dazzled by the sun glinting off the river, ripples of babbling waters, just like the pictures. She thinks of lowering the window to hear the rush of water, but before she can, Pippa nearly barrels into the car in front of her.

She brakes just in time, gasping and yanking the seat belt away from crushing her chest.

The road has narrowed to a single track and, ahead, cars are stopped as far as Pippa can see.

A traffic jam in Riverdean? That's not part of the plan.

She notices the car in front of her has its doors open and a man is leaning against it. He's obviously been here some time. Pippa presses a few buttons on her car touchscreen, willing the satnav to work its magic.

'Searching for alternate route . . .' the robotic voice tells her. 'No route found.'

Pippa repeats this a few times with the same outcome and sighs. She opens the car door herself, and shouts to the man.

'Excuse me, do you know if there are any other routes into Riverdean?'

He turns round, surprised to be spoken to. 'Tough luck,' a Welsh accent tells her. 'One road in, one road out. Probably some van up ahead blocking everyone's way.'

'Oh,' Pippa says, her good mood starting to fail her.

'I'd settle in if I were you. All part of Riverdean's charm.'

She gets back in the car, shutting the door with a huff. She still has half an hour before she's arranged to meet the local handyman at the house. She guessed he was the real deal when he told her he could only fit her in for ten minutes on Tuesday for a quote.

The river seems to be taunting her now, as do the roofs of cottages up ahead. So close and yet . . .

Pippa takes a sip of the pumpkin-spiced latte she picked up in Hereford. It's her yearly tradition on the first of September, a way to mark the start of her favourite season. There's the prospect of getting her coats out of hibernation, of taking long bubble baths with hot chocolates, the heat of the London Underground turning from unbearable to almost tolerable. Not that she'll be seeing much of the city any more. Autumn in Riverdean seems a much more favourable option, if slightly terrifying. There is a sign advertising the 'Riverdean Harvest Festival' on the side of the road, complete with hand-painted gourds. *This is more like it*, Pippa thinks.

Pippa had driven from London to Hereford this morning, getting to the estate agents just after opening time to pick up the keys.

The keys to her very own B&B.

Something she's dreamt of since she was a teenager. The white envelope on her passenger seat feels pregnant with future possibilities, the keys to her new venture. She can't quite believe it's hers. Can't believe she no longer has to work on the reception desk of a hotel chain any more, trilling 'Welcome to Mallory's. Checking in?' hundreds of times a day, drafting staff rotas and cajoling teenagers into cleaning rooms. She gets to be her own boss, set her own rules.

Pippa has wanted this ever since she stayed in a B&B in Scotland with her mother when she was about thirteen. She'd had a tough week in school and was feeling down.

'We haven't left the city for far too long,' her mother had said, sensing her unhappiness. They'd driven up, spur of the moment, on a dark and dreary Friday night. The hotel was an old castle, and Pippa vividly remembers the owner passing her a cup of coffee as she curled up in front of the stone fireplace. She remembers feeling so grown up. How that weekend had felt more like home than any of their flats in London. How she and her mother had giggled, chatted and relaxed in the countryside. They'd left the B&B only to go for walks and had been greeted with warm biscuits and blankets on their return. Pippa wanted to create that atmosphere for other people. She wanted to curate her own slice of it in Riverdean.

And now all her belongings are crammed into the Audi, ready to get started. It's depressing to think this junk filled her flat in Clapham, but barely reaches the roof of her car now. She thinks she had more possessions when she went off to uni to study Hospitality and Tourism. Then again, after uni, she shared so much stuff with Ben, the flotsam and jetsam of couple-life accumulated over their five years together. She couldn't bear to see it any more after they broke up. And so, a few sad boxes are all she has. Some possessions of her mother's. Cushions and a duvet. A box of photo albums.

Pippa blinks. She's becoming maudlin now. This is an opportunity to buy new things. To fill her B&B with modern and quirky items that will keep her guests coming back for years to come. She already has three Pinterest boards dedicated to ideas for different themes. Scandinavian cosiness is her favourite at the moment, but she will decide when she sees the building she's bought.

If she ever sees it.

Suddenly, there is noise. Car doors slamming shut. Engines turning on. The car in front lurches ahead and she trundles after it. She can see the reason for the hold-up as a box van is waiting, two-wheels perched on someone's driveway, letting others pass.

Does this seriously count as a road? It's ridiculous, Pippa thinks, as she's forced to edge off the road to get past the van, her wheels practically dancing over the drop to the river. She takes another gulp of pumpkin latte to bolster her confidence as though it contains alcohol, and nearly misses her turning.

The B&B is down a steep incline, and another sharp bend. She'll have to warn guests about this when she updates the website, Pippa realises. Maybe she can have a map and a recommendation for parking. At the moment it's just a white screen, with the words '*Pumpkin Cottage B&B. Coming Soon . . .*' in black cursive letters, aptly named for the most scenic season in Riverdean.

God, how do people in this village get around? The opportunities for dropping into the river seem all too possible. She needs the nerves of a moped driver on the Amalfi coast to navigate this road. Pippa's brakes make an uncomfortable noise as she inches downwards, bunny-hopping her way towards the bottom. Where the hell is this place?

Finally, she spots the right building. There are only two other cottages on this road, which runs parallel to the river, with the B&B right at the end. It's familiar from afar, similar in shape to the estate agent's pictures, but up close is another story.

Is this really the 'Charming B&B in need of updating' they advertised? 'Updating' seems the understatement of the millennium. This looks as if it needs tearing down and starting again. She sees the crumbling brickwork, the faded paint on the door and windows, the weed-ridden front driveway, and water damage reaching over a foot up the front wall.

'Bloody hell,' Pippa sighs, turning the car engine off. What has she let herself in for?

She gets out of the car and walks around to the house. It has an odd layout, Pippa can tell even from the outside. 'Higgledy-piggledy perfection,' Pippa remembers the estate agent brochure saying. There was clearly a main house built at some point, but the building has been extended and extended, in various clashing styles of architecture, to form a real mishmash. She wonders where her dwelling will be. Hopefully she can find some corner tucked away from her guests, so she can have her own privacy.

Pippa's Hunter Wellington boots sink into the muddy drive. This will be the first speck of mud they've seen since she purchased them in London years ago. They were a payday present to herself, representing her countryside dream, and she thought today would be the perfect day to get them out of the box. Pippa thought she'd fit right in with her Barbour jacket, Mango sweater, and wellies, but she suddenly feels like an alien. What is she doing? Buying a B&B like this, without even having seen it? No one she knows to help her?

This is new territory for Pippa and, despite her doubts, she's determined to make a go of this on her own.

She walks up to the front door and inserts the key, although the door is in such a crumbling state Pippa wouldn't be surprised if it fell open at the touch of her hand. Stepping immediately into a kitchen, she's greeted by the enormous kitchen island, although that's where the modern luxuries end, as the kitchen itself is an ode to pine. The pine cabinets blend into the pine-panelled walls so well, that the only giveaway to where the counters are is the lurid green work surface. The previous owner clearly had a love affair with china ornaments and net curtains, and the whole room seems dark, weighed down with the clutter, and lingering smells of greasy breakfasts. In need of updating is too right. Probably more than that, if the sagging damp patch in the centre of the ceiling is anything to go by.

And then Pippa sees it. The Aga. Standing proudly in the heart of the kitchen. If it was a Farrow & Ball colour, it would be named 'heritage green', Pippa thinks. She closes her eyes, imagining the current pine hideousness replaced by oak countertops, repainted cupboards, and a Belfast sink. Yes. The Aga would fit in quite nicely. She just needs to learn how the hell to use it.

The rest of the main building is in a similar state. Swirly-patterned brown carpets, corduroy furniture and Artex-covered walls abound. Just when Pippa's feeling really disheartened, her gaze is pulled to movement outside the window. A flash of colour. She moves to look out of the communal living room window, and her heart soars. The view really is breathtaking. Nothing but the blue of the river, and verdant green of the trees opposite creeping up the other side of the valley. It feels as though the living room is suspended over the water. The flash of colour was a passing kayak, and Pippa watches as a group of them whizz past, a flurry of red plastic and the foamy spray of water.

'Okay, so it has potential,' Pippa says aloud, needing to hear her voice, to make sure this is all reality, not a far-off dream. She's really here and this is really her B&B. This mess.

The doorbell rings and Pippa bolts to answer it.

'You must be Grant,' she says.

The man, in his early forties, is sullen and his creased forehead suggests this is his habitual expression. He raises an eyebrow, as if to say *durr?* The splattered overalls and dirty fingernails confirm she has the right man.

'I'm Pippa. Come in,' she offers, although he is already squeezing past her in the doorway, stepping on the cigarette he's just stubbed out in the process. Okay, so she and Grant aren't exactly going to hit it off.

'Feel free to take a look around,' Pippa says.

'No, s'alright,' he says in one word. 'My grandma used to own this place. I know it like the back of my hand.'

'Oh,' Pippa says, unsure of herself. She recovers, reminds herself she is in charge. 'Then you'll know there's quite a lot of water damage, some damp that needs fixing. I'm hoping to replace the render, maybe have some of the building cladded. Then a new kitchen, obviously. Replaster and paint throughout. I'll source the materials.'

She nods, happy that she sounded confident, and fairly competent. Grant says nothing, but crosses his arms and walks past her so she's forced to follow him. She notices his glance at her boots, the doubtful look on his face. Oh God, he knows she is a fraud.

'I want the wall knocking down to the smallest bedroom too, open it up. I assume that'll need planning permission?'

'Should be fine,' Grant shrugs. 'I wouldn't bother.' Pippa frowns. She'll have to check that.

'I need this doing by the end of the month.' She wants to get her first bookings in for October.

At this, Grant puffs out a breath. Pippa tries to keep her voice even. She's used to dealing with builders, in fact prided herself on her ability to interact with them in Mallory's. Whether she was chatting with decorators or schmoozing VIP guests, Pippa could mould herself into whatever was needed. A social chameleon. So why are her skills failing her now? She suddenly feels very tired. The early start. The drive. The exhaustion of finding herself here. Has this all been a mistake?

'What do you think?'

Grant is silent again, and Pippa wishes he'd say something to ease her discomfort. She wishes she had someone she could call and complain to. Her mother. Maybe even Ben.

Grant turns to her suddenly. 'Should be doable,' he nods. 'I've got a young lad that helps me out if it's a big job. It'll cost, though. I hope you've brought your chequebook.'

Chapter Two

Jenny

Realising the door's locked, Jenny drops the shopping bags at her feet and sighs. She presses the bell, becoming more impatient with each unanswered ring.

'Phil! Phil!' she calls. It's hopeless. She decides to go around the back. As soon as she touches the handle, she realises the back door is locked too. Peering through the window, she can see Phil at the table, his back to her.

'Phil, open up!' she shouts. The man's deaf, she thinks, annoyed.

Then, as if he has all the time in the world, he gets up and unlocks the door. 'Sorry, I didn't realise I'd locked it.'

'What on earth are you doing, anyway?'

'Finishing that jigsaw. I'm almost done.'

Jenny rolls her eyes. She glances at the picture of Puzzlewood in the Forest of Dean, a local tourist spot, and the gigantic roots of an ancient oak, its moss-covered limbs stretching out on a carpet of gold leaves. Like a fairy wood. She can just imagine Titania and Oberon arguing in the clearing. 'Ooh, well done. That bird is upside down, though.'

'It's not.' Phil pauses and squints at it. 'Perhaps you're right.'

'I'm always right,' she grins, bringing the shopping bags into the kitchen and plonking them down in front of the fridge.

'Town was absolutely heaving this afternoon. Seemed to be lots of families getting the last bits of school uniform before the kiddies return next week. I had to drive around the car park for ten minutes before I spotted a space.'

'Shall I get the kettle on?'

'I'll get it now,' Jenny says. 'Thank God I checked we had enough bacon in. We've got ten in tonight. Nothing would have been right in the morning if we couldn't give our guests their fry-ups.' She shudders, 'Can you imagine? Aw, Phil, you didn't eat the cheese sandwiches I made for your lunch. You must be starving. I put your favourite onion chutney in, too.'

Phil looks at her sheepishly. 'I forgot. I'll have them now.'

'Well, don't have all of them. It's gone four o'clock. You won't want dinner later,' she says, trying to keep the irritation from her voice.

'Ahem!' There's a polite knock at the kitchen door. A young couple is standing there. Room Eight. Darren and Zoe Hall from the Midlands. Jenny makes a point of memorising all of her guests' names, even if they are only staying one night.

'Everything okay?' Jenny asks.

'We were wondering if you can recommend a good place to eat tonight. We were hoping to eat at The Trout, but it's fully booked.'

'Yes, it's a popular place that,' Jenny commiserates. 'You've got to book in advance for Fridays and Saturdays. Greenbrook, the village opposite the river, has a couple of nice pubs. There's the White Swan and The Anchor. You'll have to take the car. Or you could order a taxi.' The fridge lets out its irritating beep warning the door has been open too long. Jenny closes it. 'My son Jake could take you. It's only a fifteen-minute drive, but he'll be having a couple at The Trout himself later.'

'Oh no, we couldn't impose,' Darren says, shaking his head.

'Jake won't mind. You'll have to have a taxi back. Do you want me to try and book one of the pubs in Greenbrook for you?'

'That's okay,' Zoe says.

After Jenny has taken their order for breakfast in the morning and they leave the kitche, she smiles. She loves helping her guests out and she knows she'll have a great review from them. Good reviews are everything in this day and age of social media. They can make or break you. In the fifteen years since Jenny and Phil opened Riverside Lodge, guests had returned year after year, for the prime location of the ten-roomed bed and breakfast and the excellent hospitality they received. The review left on the website last week was glowing:

> Riverside Lodge is a lovely place, situated on the banks of the Wye River with its romantic weeping willows. There are terrific walks in Riverdean and a smattering of lively pubs in the village and Greenbrook opposite. The host Jenny Foster couldn't do enough for us. The beds were comfortable and the breakfast was superb. It felt a real home from home. We'll be back.

Jenny was still basking in the compliments, even if Jake put on a silly Arnold Schwarzenegger voice from *The Terminator* when he repeated the last sentence. It's true the summer season is coming to a close, but Jenny knows they will have guests throughout the year, flocking to the treasures this area of the country offers. Ramblers, families, even the odd hen or stag party, although the latter are very rare these days as Riverdean is a rather tame place for those seeking lively nightclubs or raucous company. Mind you, The Trout could be as noisy and boisterous as any pub in Hereford, Ross or Monmouth. Brett and Shaun, the pub landlords, usually had something going on every night with quizzes, karaoke, live music and open mic nights. Their honest pub grub, roaring fire in winter and fairy-light-festooned garden in the summer saw standing room only on many nights. The pub is also a magnet for Jake, especially since he's been single.

Talk of the devil, Jenny thinks, hearing the clattering in the shed. She sees Jake wrestling with the red kayak as he puts it away for the evening.

'Hi Jakey. Good day?' she asks, as he enters the kitchen.

'Beautiful,' he grins. 'The river was like a millpond. Crowds out today. Always the same in the good weather.' He kisses Jenny on the cheek. 'How's Ma, then? The hostess with the mostest! The best landlady in the Wye Valley.'

Jenny laughs. 'Can you ever be serious? I've just got in from town. Can you be a love tonight and give a lift to that lovely couple in Room Eight. Only to Greenbrook. They'll have a taxi back.'

'What's in it for me, then?' he teases. Jenny looks up at her handsome son, all six foot four of him. He's a catch, that's for sure, with his angular jaw, blonde hair and muscular frame from all the exercise he takes.

'Well, I have made a steak and kidney pie for dinner tonight, which I believe is your favourite,' Jenny says and then frowns. 'Phil, you've eaten all those sandwiches. You'll never eat your dinner later.'

'Leave him alone, Ma. You'll eat tonight, won't you, Dad?'

'Yes, leave him alone, Ma,' Phil repeats.

'Oh, well, if you're both ganging up on me,' Jenny says, good-humouredly. 'Anyway, I need a cup of tea before I do anything else.'

The three sit down in companionable silence as Jenny pours them tea. 'Is there anything better than tea from a proper china teapot?' she asks, realising she says this rather a lot.

'I see nothing wrong with dipping a teabag into a cup once in a while,' Jake winks. 'By the way, I passed Pumpkin Cottage earlier and could see life in there. Some mug has been tricked into buying that place, by the looks of it.'

'It's a lovely position that cottage. Right on the river. I thought that place might have been perfect for you when . . .' Jenny pauses, 'when you came back to Riverdean.' Of course, they all know exactly what Jenny was going to say – when Jake and Amber split up. It's like a sore spot, though – you avoided touching it at all costs.

Jenny had never liked Amber when Jake brought her to visit them when they started going out years ago. Amber was far too into her looks, Jenny thought at the time, with her bright red fingernails, her perfectly arched eyebrows and those four-inch heels totally inappropriate for Riverdean. And totally not right for Jake. Outdoorsy Jake. Kind, uncomplicated, salt of the earth. And so it proved, but not before Amber had got pregnant and they had Lola to complicate matters. Adorable Lola. And now poor old Jake was having to face being a part-time dad.

'Yeh, but it's in a right state. I wouldn't touch it with a barge pole. Too much work to make it habitable. A lot of water damage after the flood and it's designed in such a topsy-turvy way.'

'Any idea who's got it? Someone local?'

Jake shakes his head. 'Don't know. I saw Grant go in there, so he's obviously going to start work on it.'

'That miserable so-and-so. He's got a face that could curdle milk, that man. I've never seen him smile. And he's certainly not the fastest worker. Too slow to catch a cold.'

'You've almost finished the jigsaw, Dad,' Jake says, changing the subject. 'Impressive! Fancy coming to the pub tonight, then?'

Phil sips his tea, looks at Jenny as if for approval.

'You boys go and enjoy yourselves. There's a good film on tonight.' She mouths to Jake, 'Are you sure?'

Jake nods, 'I won't have a late one. I'm picking Lola up in the morning for a dad and daughter day.'

Although Phil isn't Jake's real father, you would never know. They have such a special rapport between them.

'That's lovely,' Jenny says. 'What are you going to do?'

'I promised her we'd look for conkers and have a game. I might take her on the river later.'

'Be careful. She's only five.' Jenny berates herself inwardly, knowing Jake is a protective father.

'She loves it, you know that. I wouldn't let anything happen to her,' he says defensively.

'I know,' Jenny nods.

Later, as she loads the dishwasher, she thinks about all the jobs she has to do tonight. She's got a few booked in for tomorrow night and she'll have to set up Rooms Five and Six. There's never any let up. She can hear *Pointless* blasting on the telly in the living room. Phil has the volume up too loud. She has to think about the guests. When you run a B&B, you sacrifice the privacy and freedom of normal family life. She wouldn't have it any other way, though. It allows her to work from home and she loves meeting new people and hearing their stories. She's just a nosy person, and loves the buzz of having the house full. It would be nice now and again if Phil could help out. It was their dream for so many years. No use thinking of that now.

'Have you seen my checked shirt, Mum?'

'The one you left on your bedroom floor all crumpled yesterday?'

He grins. 'That would be the one.'

'It's in the airing cupboard. Honestly, it's like having a teenager in the house.' She rolls her eyes but she loves having him home. At twenty-eight, she knows he must be desperate to find his own place. He's keeping himself busy, though. He runs Riverdean's kayaking club, has his own boat for trips down the river. He's even started orienteering expeditions for school groups. Then there's his craft ciders and ales. Like Jenny, Jake's always on the go. All he needs is a nice young woman to settle down with. Perhaps buy a place of his own close by.

'Do us a favour, Jake, and turn that telly down. It's driving me mad. I don't know why he watches it. He can never answer any of the questions.'

Jake shrugs, 'It's harmless. He enjoys it.'

'He locked the doors again this afternoon. Better that than he goes wandering off. I worry something terrible will happen to him when I'm not here.'

'He's okay, though,' Jake insists. 'We're managing.'

'Are we? He will get worse. It's inevitable. What happens then?'

'Take each day as it comes. Isn't that what the doctor said? Try not to think too far ahead.'

'Easier said than done when you're not living with it.'

'I know,' Jake says. 'I'll help as much as I can.'

'You've got your own life, Jake. It's not fair for you to be saddled with this.'

'He's my dad,' he says simply. Jenny's so grateful that Jake sees him this way. She married Phil when Jake was seven and he's been more of a father than his real one, that feckless idiot. He went off to live in America and hasn't bothered with Jake since.

'The dementia nurse is coming for a visit Monday. At bloody last. It's nearly three months now since we got the diagnosis.'

'What will she do, then?

'Assess our needs, apparently. Look at aids we can have at home to help him. See what support we're entitled to. Anything will be a help.' Jenny shoulders sag in exhaustion.

'Hello?' A young woman stands at the door, looking awkward.

'Eve? Is there a problem?'

'Sorry to be an absolute pain. I think I left the key in my room this morning. I can't find it anywhere. We're locked out.'

Jenny smiles. 'Room Two, isn't it? It happens all the time, don't worry. I've got spares. I'll let you in now.' This is one problem she can solve, she thinks, as she goes into the cabinet in the hallway to get the spare key.

Chapter Three

Pippa

Pippa rubs the expensive oil into her hair, cherishing the smell of rose and sandalwood. She's been in Riverdean a week now, and she'll need to get round to finding the nearest salon. There certainly isn't one in Riverdean, nor Greenbrook, and Pippa wonders if going furniture shopping in Hereford is enough of an excuse to pop in and have her roots retouched whilst she's there. Her hair certainly needs it, restoring the golden and honey tones to her otherwise mousy natural colour.

She slips a dressing gown around her shoulders, tying it just in time as she spots a crowd outside her bedroom window. Teenagers, all in brightly coloured cagoules, are congregating on the lane outside her bedroom. They crowd around a map, frowning and pointing in various directions.

Pippa spies the familiar rucksacks, heavy with Duke of Edinburgh supplies. She remembers her DofE days, using the two-day camping trip as an excuse to stay up late with friends, talking about boys and drinking the premixed cocktails in lurid colours that they'd sneaked in their rucksacks amongst balled-up socks. These teenagers seem much more hard core, not put off by the rain currently pelting Riverdean, and trampling onwards with the help of their compasses. Maybe Pippa should have concentrated a bit more when she did it; it might have stood her in better stead for life in the countryside.

Her phone rings and Pippa spots Hannah's name on the screen, one of her buddies from those schooldays.

'Hellooo,' she answers, hoping she sounds upbeat and cheerful.

'Just checking in on my country bumpkin.' Hannah's face appears on the FaceTime screen. Pippa can see she's wearing a blouse and faded lipstick, probably calling in on her way to her magazine editor job in London. 'How's it going there? Are you planning on spending the morning picking vegetables, mucking out horses, rolling around in the hay?'

'Such a cliché,' Pippa laughs. 'You know I'm in a village, not on a farm. Try moaning at the builder and washing plaster dust out of my hair.'

'The renovation not going well?'

'It's going . . . it's going slowly, that's all I can say. Grant keeps finding problem after problem. A rotten ceiling beam was yesterday's issue. "*That'll add another grand on to the bill and if you want like for like, I'll order the beam from Germany.*"' Pippa mimics his sallow expression and downbeat tone.

'Are you sure he's not hot? He sounds hot,' Hannah says.

'Definitely not hot,' Pippa says firmly, though keeping her voice low as she can hear Grant crashing his way through another room in the house. 'Besides, you know I'm not in the market for a guy at the moment.'

'Doesn't hurt to look,' Hannah reminds her, grinning wickedly. 'You might find a sexy farmer.'

'It seems to me that everyone in this village is over fifty years old. Which is fine by me, by the way. I need to focus on nothing but getting this B&B into shape.'

'Please tell me you're doing something other than work?' Hannah groans.

'Yes, I am,' Pippa lies. 'There's loads to do here, walking, kayaking, climbing . . .'

'All things I've never heard you interested in,' Hannah says, incredulously.

'Well, I had broadband installed yesterday, so now it's back to online shopping for decor,' Pippa grins.

'Okay, now I can imagine what you're up to,' Hannah smirks. 'And that explains why you haven't been replying to my WhatsApp. Seriously, did you have to move to the back of beyond?'

'You know this village was very special to my mother,' Pippa says, serious now.

'So serious she never took you there before she died?' Hannah says.

Pippa bristles. 'There was a reason for that.' Though what the reason was, Pippa doesn't know. Her mother had talked about Riverdean, the village where she grew up, so fondly, yet never seemed to want to return. As much as Pippa asked, her mother never talked about why she left, and what was keeping her away. A part of her hopes that by being here she might get to the bottom of it.

'I'm sorry,' Hannah says, softening. 'I just miss you, that's all. And I'm trying to understand why you moved so far away from me. And to somewhere with no train station. It's not fair I have to lose my best friend.'

'You'll understand when you see the village. It's so beautiful here, it's like another world. Completely different from the bustle of the city. You'll love it.' Although Pippa doubts Hannah will love anywhere without a sushi restaurant and a 24-hour gym.

'You'd better invite me down soon,' Hannah teases. 'Anyway,

enough about you, I have big big news. Huge!'

'And we've been blabbing on about me this whole time!'

'Last night, Louis was late coming home and I decided to do a bit of reorganising,' Hannah begins.

'As you do.' Pippa knows Hannah's flat is organised with military precision, the whole place Marie Kondo-ed on a fortnightly basis.

'I was going through his pants drawer and guess what I found . . .'

'I really don't want to guess what he keeps in there,' Pippa jokes.

'A ring box.' Hannah's eyes widen. 'He's going to propose!'

'A ring box,' Pippa repeats, hoping her expression is convincing enough. 'That's amazing news!'

This isn't exactly news to Pippa; in fact, she helped her best friend's boyfriend pick out the ring as one of the last things she did in London. 'You didn't look inside it, did you?'

'I was tempted but I thought I'd let the man have one surprise for me,' Hannah says excitedly. 'I wonder when he's going to do it.'

Pippa could answer that, knowing Louis has plans to take Hannah to the top of the Shard on her birthday in a week's time, but really hopes her poker face is convincing enough. She'd warned Louis to keep the ring in his car. Was there really an inch of that apartment that Hannah wasn't going to clean regularly?

'That's incredible, Han! I'm so happy for you both.'

'I know! I can't believe I'm getting engaged,' Hannah beams.

'You'll have to keep this a secret from Louis,' Pippa warns.

'Durr! Luckily, I'm a lot better at keeping things secret than he is. We just need to get you a man now, too,' Hannah says.

'Okay, I'm happy for you but I'm going to hang up so I can join the real world where I don't need a man,' Pippa jokes.

'I'm sorry, I'm sorry. Just be happy for me! Shit, is that the time? I'm late,' Hannah says, blowing air kisses at the screen.

'You go,' Pippa waves. 'I'm missing you, too. Bye!'

She hangs up, and instead of moving to dry her hair at the ancient dressing table, she flops back onto the bed. Speaking to Hannah is a reminder of everything she's left behind in London. Pippa felt lonely enough after her mum passed away at the start of the year, and now she's left her social life, her old colleagues, everyone she knows and loves behind to start over somewhere completely new. Was it a crazy decision?

She remembers getting the phone call from her mother, asking if she could come round. Pippa could hear in her voice that there was a problem. She couldn't have imagined what she was about to be told. Pancreatic cancer. There was more to explain the few weeks of tiredness and loss of appetite her mother had experienced than they could have predicted. Pippa still hasn't quite digested how quickly her mum was taken from her. There one minute, walking around Winter Wonderland in Hyde Park with her, drinking hot chocolates and dragging Pippa ice skating, to lying in a hospital bed weeks later. Praying for a miracle. The unfairness of it all still has the ability to wind Pippa.

She realises she's tracing her mother's necklace with her finger, sliding the gold star pendant from side to side on its chain. Pippa is glad she's here in Riverdean, even if it is the most dramatic life change she's ever made. If she's learnt anything this year, it's that life is too short to spend a second of it wasting time, sitting back, waiting for the future you want to come and find you. She might have stayed in that Mallory's job for ever, getting more and more stuck in her career. It's time to chase her dreams now.

She hears a crash from the next room again, and Grant mutter a long drawn-out, 'Fuuuuck.'

Pippa decides she'd better face the music now.

* * *

The air in Riverdean smells heavy with woodsmoke, and leaf mulch. Pippa loves how you can always smell autumn approaching, almost before any leaves change. The whole village is surrounded by a canopy of trees, interrupted only by roofs with smoking chimneys and the rush of the River Wye. She can't wait to be crunching mustard leaves underfoot as she walks around the village. It will be a nice change to dodging puddles of vomit and broken bottles on her way to work in London.

She unzips her jacket as she steps off the gravel driveway, knowing it will be too hot once she's walked around a little. The heat of the summer is still lingering in the September air. She starts up the road leading away from Pumpkin Cottage and towards the centre of Riverdean. It's only minutes before she's sweating and breathing heavily. It's been far too long since she's done a Pilates class, Pippa curses.

Now it makes sense to her why everyone in Riverdean looks so lean and healthy – even Grant, despite the chain smoking he's partial to at lunchtimes. You need the thighs of an Everest climber to get up the various slopes and hills that lead around the village.

As Pippa reaches a bend in the road, she gasps at the view around the next corner, as more of the River Wye snakes into view. The water looks so active today, agitated and frothing against the banks on either side. She's noticed the river has looked different every day since she's been here, from serene in the sunshine to a few brooding rainy days. The hill continues to climb, and Pippa gets her phone out to check she's going in the right direction for the post office, forgetting of course that the village of Riverdean has not been blessed with a strong phone signal. Dammit, why didn't she check when she had Wi-Fi? Still, there seems to be only one path she can take, and that's onwards and upwards.

'Afternoon.' Two walkers pass her quickly as if demonstrating how much fitter they are.

'Good afternoon,' she puffs, then pretends to tie her bootlace while she gets her breath back. She notices a child's doll on the other side of the road. It looks too nice to be purposefully abandoned, barely a speck of dirt on it. Pippa goes to pick it up and perches it on top of a nearby hedge. Hopefully, someone will find it and the rain won't get heavier.

She plods on up the hill, hoping the post office will be at the top of it. If only bloody Grant hadn't missed answering the door yesterday when she was out, she wouldn't need to be making this collection. He'd pretended he didn't hear it, but she can well imagine him ignoring the doorbell. Probably didn't think it was in his job description. Still, picking up the new chenille curtains she's ordered for the guest rooms is exciting enough to keep Pippa walking up the hill. She's chosen neutral colours, creams and buffs, wanting to keep calm and cosy vibes in the rooms, but has opted for floor-length for a bit of drama. She's ordered some textured fabrics online that's she's planning to use to reupholster the old headboards. A combination of velvets and pinstripes that she hopes will give the rooms personality. She will try and make matching cushions for the beds and armchairs. The views of the river speak for themselves, so she's decided to keep the rooms relatively simple. Simple, cosy, luxurious.

Pippa's distracted by footsteps up ahead as a young girl of about five or six comes running towards her, her face tomato red and tear-stained. Is she on her own? She stops behind Pippa before letting out a guttural wail, that seems to originate all the way from her pink trainers.

'Are . . . are you okay?' Pippa asks, realising how redundant the question is. She can't simply ignore this child. What if she's gone missing? There has to be someone looking for her.

The girl ignores Pippa and continues her scream-wail of a cry. Pippa feels utterly panicked now. She has no idea what to do in this scenario.

'What's wrong?' She approaches the girl, who seems to see her for the first time and takes several steps backwards.

Luckily, Pippa hears heavier footsteps coming down the hill, just as fast and panicked as the little girl's.

'There you are. Thank God for that,' a man says, stopping next to them. He bends down, takes the girl by her shoulders and says very seriously, 'You are never ever to run away from your dad like that again. Ever. Do you understand me?'

The girl continues crying and he hugs her to him, seemingly oblivious to Pippa's presence. And why is she present exactly, she asks herself.

'You scared the life out of Daddy. Now, come on.'

'But I can't find her,' the girl says between sobs.

'Maybe you left her in the car?'

'No!'

Something clicks inside Pippa's mind now. 'Are you looking for a doll?'

The man and the girl both look at her at the same time, hopeful.

'I just found her on the ground. She's back . . . here.' Pippa jogs down the hill, locating the doll.

The girl whips the doll from her hands, hugging her to her chest. It seems joy is restored, as she promptly falls to her knees and instantly starts checking the doll over.

'You've saved the day,' the man says. It's only now Pippa realises how attractive he is. Tall, blonde. Muscular beneath a faded old T-shirt. He looks like he's stepped out of the pages of some activewear catalogue.

'No problem,' she smiles, suddenly embarrassed. She should not be checking out fathers and husbands.

'Thank you so much,' he beams. 'You've saved me from an afternoon of pain and tears. Not all of them hers.' He indicates the girl.

'No problem,' she repeats. 'Well, have a nice day.' Pippa moves away, although has the distinct feeling of his eyes on her, that he wanted her to stay and talk.

No, that's ridiculous.

She walks up the hill with a smile now, though. That's her good deed done for the day. Maybe not everyone in Riverdean is a miserable sod like Grant. Hannah's right, she needs to get out and actually meet people in the village. She can start by going to The Trout soon for food. It seems popular, if the full car park and muffled music at night is anything to go by. And the Harvest Festival is in one week. Surely the whole village will be going to that.

Pippa can't stay holed up in Pumpkin Cottage forever, as appealing as that sounds. And who knows who she'll meet?

Chapter Four

Jenny

'Take your time,' says Maeve, the dementia nurse, a warm, compassionate woman with curly red hair. Jenny knew she'd like her as soon as she opened the door to her earlier. She has no airs and graces and seems intuitively to know how Jenny is feeling.

Jenny is making a cup of tea, putting scones on a plate, with a little jar of blackberry jam and clotted cream, while Phil tries to draw the hands and numbers on a clock face.

Phil drops the pen in frustration. Jenny wants to put her arms around him, run away from everything. He doesn't have to do this. They can pretend it's not happening if they don't say the words out loud.

'That's okay, my love,' Maeve says, placing a reassuring hand on his arm. 'Can you remember that name I told you earlier?'

Phil shakes his head.

'Jason,' she prompts.

'Brown,' Phil smiles in relief.

'That's right. Now what about the address?'

'Uh,' he says, face twisting in concentration, 'Something street?' Phil asks.

'Yes, good. Victoria Street. And the number?'

Phil shakes his head. He's obviously distressed. Jenny swallows a lump in her throat. The doctor had gone through a similar series of tests six weeks ago. Maeve had told her, though, that she just needed to confirm the diagnosis, see what stage he's at. The worst thing is seeing his frustration.

When Phil retreats to the living room, his face is drawn with tiredness. Maeve sips the rest of her tea, a half-eaten scone in front of her.

'Well?' Jenny asks.

'Yes.' She pauses. 'As you suspected, I'm sure. He has short-term memory loss. It's a classic sign of Alzheimer's.'

It makes Jenny's heart freeze, even though she's known the diagnosis for a few weeks. 'So, what happens now?' Jenny looks through the kitchen window, watches the river, green and murky today in the gloomy weather. Usually, it's a reassuring presence.

'I'll go through some things with you about the support you can have, the allowances you're entitled to. There's lots of practical things you can do to help with everyday tasks. I can see you have lists everywhere and that helps.' She nods to the whiteboard above the kettle and Jenny's instructions on making a cup of tea:

'1. Make sure there is water in the kettle and switch it on. 2. Put a teabag in the cup . . .'

'It's not the end of your lives together, you know. Try not to see it like that. Things will be different, of course, but you have to try and stay positive, Jenny.'

Jenny nods and Maeve hands her a clutch of leaflets about Alzheimer's.

'I am always on the end of the phone if things get too much. You will need to take care of yourself. You can't neglect your own needs, Jenny.'

'I know. I've been reading all these stories about carers.'

'Everyone's journey is different, though. Do you have any help? You've got a son, haven't you?'

'Yes, Jake. He's twenty-eight. He lives with us at the moment and he does what he can. But he's busy working and he has a young daughter, Lola.'

Maeve smiles. 'You are entitled to some respite, too. You'll need it. How are you managing with the business?'

'It's difficult. I tell the guests when they arrive. Just in case he decides to walk around in his underpants.' Jenny manages a small smile. 'We're coping at the moment.'

'Well, when things change, we can look at more support.' Jenny notices she says *when*, not *if*. Maeve nibbles the rest of the scone.

'At first, I actually thought he was having an affair,' Jenny says, desperate to share this with someone who understands her guilt. 'He seemed to have become so detached from us, almost bored, uninterested. I was hurt by his behaviour. Angry with him.'

Maeve nods and lets Jenny speak.

'It slowly dawned on me that it was more than that. He left for work one day. I kissed him as usual. An ordinary day. And then I looked out the window. It must have been about fifteen minutes later, and he was still sitting in the car in the drive. He told me he didn't know how to start the car.'

'What work did he do?'

'He was a deputy headteacher – a school in Ross. He was such an intelligent, clever man.' Angry tears suddenly spill down her cheeks. 'It's cruel to see the essence of him just ebb away like this.'

'Many call it a long goodbye,' Maeve says.

Jenny likes the fact Maeve doesn't try to tell her everything will be okay. She doesn't offer false hope. She's just there, understanding. When she leaves, Jake returns and Jenny is desperate to get out of the house.

'I'm taking Archie for a walk,' she calls to Jake. Their little rusty Labradoodle pricks up his ears in response as Jenny grabs the lead from the dresser. 'Come on, boy. You've been very patient today.' He tilts his head to the side as if he understands her.

Outside, Jenny inhales deeply, thankful to take lungfuls of the chilly autumn morning. Archie tugs on the lead in his enthusiasm to be outside. The sky is leaden and brooding, matching Jenny's gloomy mood.

'No, Archie, you can't go down to the river.' It's a constant battle to keep him from wading in. He's magnetically drawn to it. The path is so familiar to her; she knows it like the back of her hand. God, the plans she and Phil had when they moved in. It was around this time of year. Jake was thirteen and he was thrilled there were other boys in the village his age. The bed and breakfast was a new adventure. Jenny's dream more than Phil's. And she still loves it, but now she wonders how on earth she can go on running it and seeing to Phil.

'Well, hi, Jen.' Paula gives her a warm smile of greeting. She's lived in the village a few years and has a little shepherd's hut selling arts and crafts and souvenirs. It's very cute with its gingham curtains and pastel-coloured bunting. Tourists can't resist calling in to buy her jewellery, scarves, notebooks and home-made truffles.

'Hello, Paula. It's unlike you to be out and about this time,' Jenny says. 'Who's holding the fort?'

'Abi's over with the baby. I had to pop out to post a letter.' Paula and her daughter are like two peas in a pod, with the same tousled hair and nose rings. 'Did you hear that someone's moved into Pumpkin Cottage?' Paula doesn't give Jenny a chance to answer. 'I saw a girl go in there earlier. I didn't see her man. There's a lot of work to do there before that place is straight.'

'Well, we'll soon find out all about it, no doubt. You know

what Riverdean's like.' Jenny's in no mood for idle gossip. 'I'd love to chat but I'm trying to get this one walked before the rain comes in.'

As if on cue, big, fat droplets splash their polka dots on the path. Paula hurries off, resting a paper on her head. With dismay, Jenny realises she hasn't got an umbrella.

'Come on, Archie, let's run to The Trout.'

By the time Jenny reaches the porch of the pub, she's soaked through and Archie is shivering. 'Me and my bright ideas, eh, Archie?'

Inside, Jenny sees there's a few tourists and locals about and Brett and Shaun have lit the wood burner, creating a warm, cosy feel. With its mismatched tables, bright scatter cushions and wooden floor, it's like a welcoming old friend. No wonder the place is so popular.

'You're like a drowned rat!' Brett laughs. 'Come on in, Jen, and sit by the fire. What can I get you? Whisky? It's never too early for mulled wine.' He hands Jenny a biscuit for Archie.

'Hot chocolate,' Jenny says, 'but without any of that nonsense you put on the top.'

'Nonsense like marshmallows and whipped cream? That's what I like about you, Jenny Foster. You know how to live.'

Suddenly, Jenny feels tears prick her eyes.

'Go and sit down. I'll bring it to you.'

Archie snaffles his biscuit as soon as Jenny is seated. The dining room, adjacent to the bar, looks out onto the river and Jenny watches the rain battering the window. Her nose is running and she reaches for a tissue from her pocket, resorting to using the back of her hand.

'Here you are,' Brett says, handing her a tissue and laying the hot chocolate down on the table. 'Hot chocolate, straight up and no frills. On the house.' He pulls up a chair next to her and sits down. 'Now, are you going to tell Uncle Brett what this is all about?'

'The dementia nurse called this morning.'

'Oh, darling,' Brett rubs her arm.

'Don't be nice to me or I'll cry again,' Jenny says.

'Okay. Drink up and haul your arse out of here as soon as you can,' he teases.

'She didn't tell me anything I don't know,' she sniffs. 'He can't drive, he can't work. And day by day, he's becoming a shell of the man I used to know.' Brett says nothing, puts his arm around her and pulls her into his shoulder. 'I'm scared, Brett. I don't know how I'll cope when he can't do anything for himself.'

'Take each day as it comes,' Brett says. 'If anyone will cope, you will. You're like a lemon sherbet. All hard and sour on the outside and then soft and squidgy – well, powdery – on the inside.'

'God, that's a terrible analogy,' Jenny says, lifting her head up.

'I hope you haven't left snot on my best shirt,' Brett says, wiping his shoulder. 'This is a Hugo Boss and cost a fortune. Well, so Shaun told me.'

'Where is Shaun, then?'

'He's gone to the Cash and Carry in Hereford to get supplies. He talked about some Jo Malone candles.'

'For the pub?'

'Good grief, no. Have you seen the prices? That's for our private use.' He suddenly has a glint in his eye. 'Can you keep a secret?'

Jenny nods, grateful for the distraction.

'I think he's going to propose.'

'How do you know?'

'He's transparent, darling. He can't keep anything secret. He was using my laptop recently and now I keep getting adverts for rings and proposal ideas. The difficulty will be acting surprised.'

'That's fantastic news!' Jenny says, genuinely pleased. 'When's he going to do it?'

'That I don't know. Perhaps during the Harvest Festival. In the pub one night. God only knows.' He rolls his eyes. 'He'd better hurry up. I want to have a say in all these plans of his. I don't want a honeymoon in Bognor Regis or Swansea.'

'Will you have a big wedding, do you think?'

'Honey, do you not know us at all? I do nothing by halves!'

Jenny sips her hot chocolate. 'Well, I hope we'll get an invite.'

'The whole of Riverdean will have an invite!' The door to The Trout swings open, bringing a gust of rain inside. 'Oh, here he is.' Brett rises to greet Shaun. 'The wanderer returns at last! I was going to send out a search party.' He kisses his cheek. 'You're like a wet sheepdog. Go and get changed before you put our customers off.'

'Come on, Archie,' Jenny says, getting to her feet. 'Let's get home.' She thinks about all the beds she has to make and then lunch before the new guests arrive for the afternoon.

'Take one of the umbrellas,' Brett calls out to her. 'I hope you're coming to the quiz night tomorrow.' He mimics zipping his mouth. 'Keep shtum about what I told you earlier.'

'I'm all discretion,' she promises, smiling properly for the first time that morning.

Chapter Five

Pippa

Pippa scrolls nervously through the pictures on her phone, even though she's seen the string of photos a hundred times before. Her B&B blog and booking system is now live, the one finished room available to reserve, and Pippa has taken a handful of shots herself to advertise the room on her website. She will hire a professional photographer once the entire B&B is finished, hopefully making her website more polished, but she wants to get cracking on taking bookings with what she has. And, more importantly, she needs the money.

Her first customers are due to arrive in the next hour – an older couple from Devon – and Pippa doesn't think she's ever been so nervous. Especially as Grant and his helper young boy Joel are continuing to work in the next room, and she hopes Grant's intermittent clattering and near-constant swearing won't put them off. She has already warned them of the building work in an email, of course, and offered a fifty per cent discount off future bookings if they give her a Tripadvisor review. Grant is attaching some wooden panelling in the next room, which Pippa is planning to paint an olive green.

Pippa decides to do one more sweep of the completed room. She takes the brass key off the ledge next to her reception desk and heads down the corridor. The room's really been opened up since Grant's knocked the wall through. With her tight time frame, she had to take his word for the lack of planning approval. He's been doing this for years and has done a professional job.

She's named this one the Willow Room, after the enormous willow tree outside the window, which offers glimpses of the Wye River between its elegant fronds. Pippa's tried to pick up the willow pattern in the cushions and curtains of the room, and has opted for a neutral scheme in here, with touches of sage green and lemon. The whole effect is very calming, and she feels a fizz of butterflies in her tummy imagining what her guests will think of it.

The tray is well stocked with herbal teas, artisan coffees, and shortbread biscuits – lavender and poppy seed – home-made that morning. The welcome booklet is perched on the dressing table. The room is bijou but has the cutest little window seat which Pippa has lined with cushions and second-hand books. Grant might have cursed her when she asked him to fashion the curved bench to fit in the window, but the overall look is worth it, she thinks. She gives the toilet in the en-suite a flush, just to double-check, and is hit by a waft of lavender air freshener.

It's all good to go.

Pippa locks the room after her and promptly steps back onto an eight-inch drill bit, lying in the middle of the corridor. The twisted metal cuts into her socked foot.

'Shit.' Pippa mutters, stumbling back. *Bloody Grant.* Pippa's of half a mind to storm next door and show him some swearing to match his own. Back when she worked in Mallory's, she often had to be stern with workers, and Pippa had learnt to switch on her no-nonsense side when she needed to. But pissing off the only workman in a five-mile radius while he is working on her cottage probably isn't the best plan.

'Grant, I think you've left some things in the corridor,' she says now through gritted teeth, as she opens the door to the next room. The window is wide open and Grant is hanging out, smoking a cigarette. Joel is measuring some wood in the opposite corner of the room. Oh God, she hopes Grant finishes smoking before the guests arrive, or else it won't be the best first impression of Pumpkin Cottage.

'I found this.' She goes to pass him the drill bit, but Grant simply looks at her blankly, and goes back to smoking. 'Usually it's fine, but I really need to be tidy today with the guests arriving.'

Wordlessly, Grant throws the stub outside. Pippa makes a mental note to retrieve it from her driveway later. Honestly, the sooner he finishes, the better.

'Just out of curiosity, what time are you finishing today?' For once, Pippa hopes he isn't staying late and will leave her guests in peace.

'Four-ish.' He shrugs again. 'Quiz night at The Trout.'

'I didn't know you were much of a quizzer?' Pippa's surprised.

'Sometimes.' He's becoming less and less of a talker by the minute.

'Right . . .' Pippa looks around. 'Good conversation. I'll let you get back to work.' She shouldn't be sarcastic but with Grant she can't resist.

The doorbell rings and Pippa feels her heart thudding with adrenaline. They're here. Her first guests are here.

She races towards the door, wishing she had time to put on slippers. Pippa flings the door open, grinning maniacally.

'Mr and Mrs Wilson?'

'That's us,' a middle-aged man says. 'Although we prefer Bob and Sandra.'

'Well, Bob and Sandra, welcome to Pumpkin Cottage,' Pippa

gestures them inside. 'I'm Pippa, and I'm very excited as you're our first guests.' She doesn't know why she's used the word *our*, when Pumpkin Cottage is very much just *her*. 'I hope you've had a good journey from . . . ?'

'Ilfracombe,' Sandra fills in, stopping in the kitchen to take in the room. Pippa feels a swell of pride. In all fairness to Grant, the kitchen does look dramatically different now to when Pippa first arrived. Out with the pine and in with the Shaker-style cabinets in duck-egg blue, the light oak worktops, and expansive island. The perfect country kitchen for her perfect country cottage.

She leads the couple to the reception desk. 'Ilfracombe's gorgeous enough, I'm surprised you need a night away! Is it your first time in Riverdean?'

'Goodness, no. My sister, Paula, has lived in Riverdean for over twenty years now. She owns the little shepherd's hut in the village centre selling souvenirs and knick-knacks.'

'Oh, how lovely, I don't think I've been in there yet. I'll have to stop by. I can always recommend it to my guests in future,' Pippa says. She passes them a registration form and a pen, and Bob gets scribbling away while Sandra chats.

'Marvellous,' Sandra says in that lovely West Country accent. 'We're very different, my sister and I, like two peas in opposite ends of the field, our mother used to say. Her shop is beautiful, though.'

'We usually stay in Riverside Lodge, at the other end of the village,' Bob chips in.

'But we've been coming so long, it's nice to mix it up. When we saw there was a new B&B opening in the village, I said *Let's book it!*'

'Thank you so much,' Pippa beams. 'I hope you'll have a great stay here. And as my official guinea pigs, I'm counting on you for feedback. Anything you think I can do differently or should think about in future, please let me know.' She feels a swell of satisfaction. In Mallory's there was essentially a reception desk script, which you weren't allowed to stray from, especially if management were within earshot. It's nice to give a more personal service, get to know her guests.

'Oh, we will do,' Sandra smiles.

'And that includes my builder,' Pippa lowers her voice conspiratorially. 'As mentioned in my email, he's still working on the room next door, but he can be a bit grumpy. Let me know if you have any trouble.'

'That sounds like Grant to me,' Bob says now, looking up.

'Paula had a thing with him years ago,' Sandra chuckles. 'We're well used to Grant's charms.'

'Oh,' Pippa feels dismayed, hoping she hasn't put her foot in it. It's hard to imagine Grant ever having a partner. Is there anyone on this planet that would put up with him?

'All in the past now, thank goodness,' Bob winks, sensing her discomfort.

'Right, I'll show you to your room,' Pippa leads the couple to the Willow Room, beaming when they make the appropriate 'ooh' and 'aah' noises.

'I would recommend a few places for dinner, but I think you probably know more than I do,' Pippa says.

'You can't go wrong with The Trout.'

'Especially on quiz night,' they tell her.

'I might see you there, then,' Pippa says. She's chickened out of going to The Trout so far. It seems to be a village favourite, and Pippa has a horrible premonition of her walking in the door to gaping mouths and stares at the outsider. She supposes they have enough tourists here, the residents must be used to new blood. But Pippa still feels a stranger here, as though she still has one foot in her old life and one very tentative toe in her new one.

After bidding farewell to the Wilsons and noting their preferred breakfast order, gluten free for Sandra, Pippa sits at the kitchen island, feeling at a loose end. She wondered if she would feel odd having strangers stay in her cottage, but this has been her plan for such a long time. Tomorrow she will have bedding to change and paperwork to do, but now she feels a bit flat. Maybe she will just go to The Trout tonight.

The Trout is the picture of charm, an olde-worlde, timber-framed building that is deceptive, hiding a modern interior and enormous log fireplace inside. And it's busy. Really busy.

Pippa thought that arriving at 5 p.m. for dinner would mean she didn't have to jostle for space at the bar but could order food and a drink in peace.

That's clearly not going to happen. The little pub is packed to the rafters, the noise of chattering carrying well beyond the River Wye.

Although no one stares, Pippa does feel a little out of place. She squeezes past a busy table to get to the bar, at the same time as someone gets up from their seat, shoving it straight into Pippa's side. The offender looks at her as though it is her fault, and Pippa wonders if she's made a mistake coming here tonight. Coming to Riverdean at all.

As she waits in the queue for the bar, Pippa spots Sandra and Bob in the corner, sitting at a table with a woman wearing wispy scarves and colourful corduroy, who she guesses must be Paula, and a younger woman carrying a baby. They are chatting animatedly, pausing only to laugh and make silly faces at the baby.

The cosy family scene makes Pippa's heart hurt. She has no family left herself, this village the last connection to her mother that she has. She looks away, blinking back tears.

'Are you all right?'

Pippa hasn't noticed the man behind the bar, watching her. He's serving someone else but his encouraging smile makes Pippa want to cry even more.

'I'm fine,' she says, then decides that there's no harm in being honest with this stranger. 'I've just moved here and feel a bit of an outsider.'

'I thought the only people that moved here were retirees and ramblers, and you seem to be neither. You look fabulous!'

'Thank you,' she smiles. He moves away to hand another customer two drinks in tall cocktail glasses.

'Listen, moving to Riverdean can be hard for outsiders. I've been through it myself when I moved here to be with my boyfriend,' the man says. Pippa had guessed he was gay from the platonic compliment on her image.

'How long ago was that?'

'Ten years now. It's such a close-knit community, it can take a while before you really start to feel like part of the village. Riverdean residents can be a bit suspicious of newcomers. Greenbrook is a bit friendlier, but who wants to live there? Riverdean is the best by far!' He moves around the bar with frenetic energy.

Pippa laughs. 'Well, Riverdean has the best pub for a start.' She guesses he's a manager or landlord from his command of the bar.

'I'm Shaun.' He offers a hand in between pouring drinks. 'My partner Brett is around here somewhere. You usually hear him before you see him.'

'Pippa,' she grins. 'I've bought Pumpkin Cottage down the lane.'

'Oh, that's you, is it? We heard someone had bought it and was making a new B&B. It's about time we have some new blood in there.'

Pippa feels her heart warm.

'You'll have to come and have a nosy round,' she says.

'Music to my ears.' Shaun places another of the tall cocktails in front of her. 'It's a Trout special. Lethal alcohol content and certain diabetes, but I think you'll like it.'

'I think I will too, Shaun,' Pippa grins.

'On the house. Now go and find yourself a seat somewhere for the quiz.'

'Thank you.' She collects her drink, feeling buoyed by the interaction. She takes a sip of the clear liquid and nearly splutters most of it out. Shaun isn't wrong, it is lethal. Maybe alcohol is the solution to her woes, that is as long as she keeps her wits about her and can make Bob and Sandra breakfast tomorrow.

She peers around the corner from the bar, spotting no empty tables, but a few empty seats. Hmm, she needs a bigger gulp of the cocktail for this.

Pippa looks at the sea of unfamiliar faces in their gangs and groups. She thinks she's seen a few of the people before, particularly when she spies one very attractive head. It takes her a second to recognise the dad from her walk last week, with the crying daughter. He's sitting with a few guys of the same age. No sign of his wife tonight, she thinks.

Pippa feels incredibly awkward again, and pauses to lean against a wall, hoping no one else can tell how uncomfortable she is. She wishes she had Hannah with her, although knowing Hannah, she'd force her to go and speak to the hot dad, using some engineered excuse like asking for a spare chair or 'accidentally' spilling her drink near him. She told Hannah she's fine on her own, and tonight she needs to prove it to herself.

Then Pippa spots a table for two in the corner that's vacant, squeezed in next to a bigger table. She rushes over to the seat, plonking herself down before it can be taken.

This pub really is the heart of the village, and it seems everyone has congregated here for the quiz. She tries to listen in to a few conversations around her but is interrupted.

'Are you on your own?'

A friendly-looking woman asks in heavily accented English. She's sitting at the bigger table with her family, and Pippa is surprised to be spoken to, particularly following Shaun's comment about Riverdean's residents being hard to crack.

'I am. It's my first time at a quiz night.'

'You should join our team. We're called the Uk-brainians.'

'Oh,' Pippa says, not getting the joke.

'Because we're from Ukraine.' The man sitting on the other side of the woman laughs uproariously.

'You don't want me to join, I'm terrible at quizzing,' she says, shyly. She doesn't want them to offer a stranger to join just out of pity.

'We're terrible too. I guarantee it. And we need English representation,' the woman says, already pulling a chair over.

'What do we win?'

'About thirty pounds,' the man explains, 'and your picture on the quiz board.' He points to a blackboard across the room, featuring a picture of a group of men cheering triumphantly. It's the hot dad, Pippa thinks.

'Well, then. We have to win, don't we?' she says now, shuffling across to join the table. 'I'm Pippa.'

'I'm Petro,' the man says. 'This is my wife Maryska, and our daughter Inna.'

Inna smiles, fiddling with a strand of hair, a typical nervous teenager.

'How long have you been in Riverdean?' Pippa asks.

'About twelve months,' Maryska explains. 'We're from Kyiv and moved in the war.'

'Oh, that's terrible,' Pippa wonders what the right thing to say in this scenario is. She guesses there isn't a right thing.

'We still have family there, so we are very worried. But we were lucky to come here.'

'I don't know if anything about it is lucky,' Pippa says, surprised at how jovially Petro and Maryska speak about it.

'We're . . . how you say . . . making the best of a bad situation?' Pippa smiles in encouragement.

'Inna misses her boyfriend, though. He's still in Kyiv.'

'That must be hard,' Pippa sympathises. 'Are you working over here?'

'Petro has a job in the supermarket.'

'I own a bakery in Kyiv,' he explains. 'But I couldn't find a job here where I can bake.'

'So, all of his baking is at home now,' Maryska shrugs.

Pippa's face lights up. 'I'd love to have some fresh home-made bread for the B&B,' she says, explaining about Pumpkin Cottage and her business venture. It doesn't seem fair that this family can't get the right work after such a momentous move. She wants to help, even if in a tiny way. 'Could I maybe buy a loaf from you for breakfasts in the B&B?' That would be a real selling point for her, too. Guests love home-made touches.

'Ukrainian bread is . . .' He makes a chef's kiss gesture. 'Of course. Let me know how much you need. We always have some in the house.'

'Great,' Pippa grins.

'We hope to move back to Ukraine soon,' Maryska says solemnly now, 'but Riverdean is a great place to live. You will be happy here, Pippa, I think.'

'I hope so.' She really does. 'And before that, I know what we need to do . . .'

'What?' Petro looks quizzical.

'Win this quiz!'

Chapter Six

Jenny

'You've got a right old builder's bum on you there, Jake,' Jenny laughs. 'Have you no shame?' Jake has been pottering in the shed, bringing in the bottles to take to The Trout later.

'If you've got it, flaunt it!' he grins. 'Do you know, I think this is the best crop yet.'

Jenny shakes her head. Jake's obsessed with the craft cider he's been brewing in time for Riverdean's Harvest Festival. There's a small orchard at the back of Riverside Lodge and he's been handpicking the crop of apples and pears and producing his wild-fermented ciders and perry. 'Well, you can't leave all those bottles there. I've got guests in later.'

'Wait 'til you taste it, Mum. So crisp and tangy with a sweet note right at the end.' He smacks his lips.

'I'm surprised you can face any alcohol after last night. I could hear you trip over your old boots as you came in and I swear I could have got drunk from the fumes across the breakfast table.'

'I was celebrating. Another resounding win for the Wye-ipedias,' Jake laughs again at the silly name the boys invented for their team. 'It was a close one this time, too. The Ukrainians had a secret weapon. Some woman with them – I think I've seen her in the village. She was getting all the answers right until Brett got to the sports section. It was game over then.'

'I'd love to have seen you win. Again!' she says, teasing, before her face clouds over. 'Your dad was all agitated last night. You know what he's like in the evening. Sundowning, they call it. That's what Maeve, the dementia nurse, told me. It's quite common, but it should settle in time. It was only when we sat down after dinner, and I dimmed the lights that he calmed down.'

'You should have called me, Mum. You know I'd come right over.'

'I know, but I managed. I don't want to be calling you for every little thing.' She slips her apron ties over her head. 'Anyway, I'm taking my apple cake up to the church hall. Can you keep an eye on your father while I'm gone?'

Jake stands back to admire the cake his mother has placed in a box on the counter. Her maple, apple and pecan cake with its soft, creamy, iced topping.

'You've outdone yourself there, Ma. First prize again this year, I reckon,' he says. 'What with me and the quizzes and your cakes, well, Jenny Foster and Jake Taylor are an unbeatable team.'

Jenny smiles but brushes off the compliment. She has won first prize for the last two years running. It's nice to have something positive to focus on. Besides, it's given her a good excuse to flick through Paul Hollywood's latest baking book. A man with impossibly blue eyes and he can cook!

'I hope you've made an extra one for us tonight,' Jake says, reaching out to dip his finger in the icing.

'You wouldn't dare, Jake Taylor. I've spent the entire morning getting this right. I have made another, as it happens, but let's just say it's more rustic than this one.' Jenny grabs her coat. 'I'll take Archie with me. I shouldn't be too long.'

The early afternoon is unseasonably warm and inviting. Jenny has a protective arm around the cake box. 'Careful, Archie,' she warns as he tugs on the lead. The river gurgles down below. She loves this time of year, when the Wye Valley is at its best, and the trees are dressed in their autumn palette. The church is at the top of the hill, beyond the post office. The views are beautiful from up there.

Jenny tucks herself into the side of the path as a couple, walking hand in hand, pass her. Pulling on Archie's lead, she looks up.

'Bob, Sandra, I didn't know you were in Riverdean.'

Sandra gives her an awkward smile, before Bob mumbles, 'A flying visit. Unplanned, really.'

'A last-minute thing,' Sandra says.

Jenny is puzzled. 'Don't say I missed your call. I'm not full this week.'

'Oh, dear,' Bob begins, coughs.

'Are you staying with Paula? It must be a tight squeeze. I know Abi and the baby are there this week.'

'Uh, we're, uh, not staying with Paula,' Bob stutters.

'Oh, for heaven's sake. We're staying at the new B&B – Pumpkin Cottage,' Sandra blurts out. 'It's no reflection on you, Jenny. We love staying at Riverside Lodge, but we just fancied a change this time.'

'Pumpkin Cottage? I thought that was just a residential property. And there's so much work to be done on it. Surely it can't be fit for any guests.'

'Well, just one room is ready. Grant is working on the rest of it. And it was quite dusty and a bit noisy,' Bob says diplomatically.

'Tell the truth, Bob,' Sandra says. 'It was delightful. Very cute with a gorgeous window seat in the bedroom overlooking the river. And Pippa is lovely.'

'But Riverside Lodge has bay windows. And we're higher up

than the cottage. Our views are fantastic.'

'Well, of course, that goes without saying, Jenny,' Bob nods.

'We're staying with you next time,' Sandra insists.

'Don't bother,' Jenny says. 'We're fully booked.'

'Fully booked? But you don't know when we'll be needing it.'

'If you'll excuse me,' Jenny says, tugging on Archie's lead, just as he's squatting to do his business. His little legs tremble as Jenny gives another tug. 'Archie!' she calls sharply, and he follows obediently behind. Jenny dithers about picking up his deposit. It really is difficult to make a dramatic exit when you've got a black sack in your hand and you're picking up dog poo, then tying a knot at the top. Bob and Sandra are still watching her from the path as Jenny holds the little bag away from her cake box.

'There really are not enough bins in Riverdean,' Jenny says. 'I shall write another letter to the council.' She sweeps off without looking back.

The path meanders downwards towards the river before taking a trajectory up the slope towards the post office and there, nestled in the bank, is Pumpkin Cottage, all higgledy-piggledy. Jenny pauses outside, wishing she could take a peek in the window. She can hear the sound of drilling and the radio blasting from the open front door, Meatloaf's 'Bat Out of Hell'. That will be Grant Campbell for you, no consideration for anyone. It must be freezing in there with that door wide open.

There's a lot going on inside and Jenny spots the slate sign with Pumpkin Cottage and an orange gourd painted on it. What a ridiculous name, she thinks.

'Grant, will you lower that din! Pleeease! The whole of Riverdean can hear the music,' a voice calls from inside.

Suddenly, she can see a petite figure walk down the hallway towards the open front door. Archie barks and spins around.

Worried, she'll be caught gawping, Jenny turns in the opposite direction to Archie, his lead encircling her ankle. The cake box tips precariously on its side, almost falling from Jenny's arms. She manages to retrieve it and her heart thumps in her chest.

'You silly sausage!' she warns Archie. 'What on earth are you barking for?'

By the time Jenny reaches Riverdean's parish church at the top of the hill, she is out of breath. From the apex, she can see right across to Greenbrook, the village opposite the river, with its milky cottages idling in the warm afternoon. She can see passengers on the hand-pulled ferry halfway across the river. George is the skipper today, a ruddy-cheeked, benign man with a comb-over that lifts gently in the breeze. The ferry has been crossing the river for at least two hundred years and Jenny likes to imagine what life would have been like then. Less complicated, perhaps, not so many demands on people's time.

'Hello, daydreamer. Penny for your thoughts.'

'Hi, Fi. Yes, I was far away then,' Jenny admits, turning to see Fi Clark, who runs the paper shop, emerging from the hall by the side of the church. 'Is it busy in there?'

'Packed. I've just been helping set up the tables for the festival. Apple cake is a strong category this year,' she teases. 'I think the trophy will still be yours, Jen. Let's take a look, then.'

'Oh, I didn't spend long on it this time. Just an hour,' Jenny fibs, opening the box. Fi glances inside the box and her look of shock is evident.

'What happened?' she asks.

Jenny looks inside to see the lopsided cake, her pride and joy, absolutely ruined. The creamy topping has drifted to the side, smearing the inside of the box, leaving gaps of bare sponge beneath. 'It's ruined,' she says, looking down at Archie. 'I almost tripped over his bloody lead on the path up here.' Gazing at the cake, Jenny contemplates smudging the topping to disguise the bare bits.

'It's only the harvest festival,' Fi commiserates. 'There are far more important things to worry about.'

Jenny nods, but feels tears prick her eyes. How ridiculous. It's just everything seems to be going wrong for her these days. Phil, Pumpkin Cottage and now the cake. She shakes herself, realising that smudged icing is nowhere near on a par with her husband's dementia. She will give herself a stern talking to later.

Back at home, Jenny sits at the computer in the little office adjacent to the conservatory, where Phil is snoozing in the armchair. Googling Pumpkin Cottage in Riverdean, it takes her directly to the website. Images of the cottage and its owner, Pippa Mason, fill the screen. She's the one Jenny saw earlier in the hallway shouting to Grant. She has blonde, curly hair framing a pretty oval face and she smiles with even, white teeth. Jenny guesses she's about twenty-seven, twenty-eight. There are links to her Instagram page and her blog, *My journey to running my very own bed and breakfast alongside the enchanting River Wye!* Jenny scans the page, reading the first entry.

Hi everyone. Welcome to Pumpkin Cottage, my little piece of heaven, or at least it will be when I finish with it. I bought this ramshackle, rundown, topsy-turvy cottage in the village where my mother grew up.

Jenny wonders if she knows Pippa's mother, but she knows no one by the name of Mason. She reads on.

It was an impulsive buy – I am prone to these. After all, you only live once. Anyway, there's loads of work to do and I mean loads. I want to turn it into my dream bed and breakfast destination. I know exactly in my head how I want it to look – a cross between a fairy-tale cottage and a boutique hotel. Each bedroom will have a bespoke design and its own character. The Willow Room is the first room finished and tonight I welcome my very first guests . . .

Jenny groans inwardly. Then she looks at the before and after photographs of the bedroom. Begrudgingly, she admits Pippa Mason has done a good job. The bedroom manages to look tranquil, fresh and cosy all at once, with coordinated soft-furnishings and pastel shades. Very different to Jenny's traditional rooms, with their tartan armchairs, grey accent walls and dramatic navy bedding. Grey is still in, isn't it? It was only four years ago she had some of the rooms updated and she'd invested in those silver decorated stag heads from Next. She was chuffed to bits with those at the time. Still is.

There are other pictures of the kitchen at Pumpkin Cottage. One of those country modern affairs with an enormous island in the middle. Jenny's always wanted an island. She glances through the conservatory at her own kitchen. The dark pine units really look dated, but she just doesn't have the time to even consider changing them and all the disruption it would cause.

On the island, Pippa has some of the breakfast fare she'll be serving her guests. Just as Jenny suspected. All that trendy stuff you see nowadays. Avocado, pancakes, shakshuka. Pfft! Pippa Mason should know that most people prefer a hearty cooked breakfast and Jenny serves the best. Fried bread, Wye Valley bacon from the butchers in town, mushrooms, beans and eggs sunny-side up.

Jake comes into the conservatory, all flushed from a day on the river taking groups of kayakers downstream.

'Mum, I won't have dinner tonight. I'm off into Hereford with the boys.'

'Did you know that Pumpkin Cottage has opened as a bed and breakfast?' she asks him.

Wiping his hands on the towel, he comes in and looks over her shoulder at the computer screen.

'You're not worried, are you? It's only a small place. Surely, they can't have more than three or four bedrooms there.'

'Not worried, no,' Jenny says, unconvincingly. 'Although Bob and Sandra Wilson stayed there last night.'

'They're more trouble than they're worth, those two. Bob snores so loudly, I could feel the floor vibrating the last time they stayed. And Sandra always asks for gluten-free bread, doesn't she?'

Jenny nods. Jake knows exactly the right things to say at times.

'Don't be too late tonight. You promised to take your father to the dentist in the morning. I've got a lot in tonight, so I'll be busy making breakfasts in the morning.'

'I'm twenty-eight,' Jake moans loudly. 'I'll be in when I like.'

Phil suddenly opens his eyes and sits upright.

'Thank you very much, Jake. Now, you've gone and woken your poor father up.'

'I wasn't sleeping,' says Phil. 'I was just resting my eyes. Is the food on yet?'

No rest for the wicked, Jenny thinks, closing the laptop with a sigh.

Chapter Seven

Pippa

Pippa checks the time on her smartwatch and feels a rising sense of panic. Despite working flat out since eight this morning, she's still behind.

Bob and Sandra seemed pleased with their breakfast. Bob opted for the maple pancakes with bacon, although Pippa could have guessed he'd choose that, men never passed up the opportunity for bacon. Sandra raved about the avocado on her gluten-free sourdough. Pippa bets it will taste even better on Petro's Ukrainian bread, and he's promised to drop off several loaves for her next week.

Since breakfast, it's been a non-stop frenzy of dishes, laundry, cleaning, resetting the tea tray, updating the website, and today's the day she's spray-painting some furniture for the new bedrooms. Grant is taking down some of the plastic sheeting in two more of the rooms tomorrow, and it's a good opportunity to do the messy task without needing to protect the surfaces herself.

In an effort to save money, Pippa's decided to repurpose some of the old wooden dressing tables and wardrobes herself. The days of Pumpkin Cottage's affinity with pine are long gone now, she thinks, as she covers the last bare inch of ugly orange wood with her chalk paint in antique white. Grant's music continues to blare from the room next door.

It's late September and the light is starting to fade from the day, that telltale sign that autumn is taking its grip. Pippa had better get moving. She loves the idea of a harvest festival. It's exactly the kind of thing she dreamt of when she moved out of London. She might even get some snaps for Pumpkin Cottage's Instagram page. The pictures of the Willow Room got her a number of new followers, and she hopes that will translate to sales in the coming months, especially as her booking calendar is sparse at the moment.

Pippa checks her appearance in the mirror in her own room and has a fright. Smudged make-up, messy hair tied back in a bun, and paint-splattered clothes. Not ideal, and Pippa definitely can't go out like this, even though Riverdean seems to favour a dressed-down vibe. She felt a little dressed up for the pub in her high-heeled boots and leather jacket the other night. Maybe the harvest festival will be a little dressier; it is a festival, after all.

It seems like a lifetime has passed since Pippa went to real music festivals. She loved them for a while, stepping in her mother's party-girl shoes in her student days. She walked past a man in the supermarket last week who smelt of BO, and the smell took her right back to standing in a field with thousands of people who hadn't showered in three days. It's funny how you can get sentimental about the strangest of things, she'd thought.

After she got the job in Mallory's she had to rein in her drinking and partying, adopt a more controlled lifestyle where she couldn't turn up to work with dark shadows under her eyes holding the ghosts of drunken weekends. She'd had to cover up a lot of her real self in Mallory's, to become the kind of softly spoken clone the revered hotel wanted their guests to be greeted with. Her social life had to become more regimented, coffee dates with her friends and mother squeezed in around her long shifts. What she wouldn't give to meet her mother one more time in their favourite little coffee spot in Clapham . . .

Pippa puts powder under her eyes and opts for a classic pillar box red on her lips. That's enough to give anyone a more polished look, and she needs it after a day of painting. She wears a thin green jumper and pulls a long grey coatigan around her. The messy bun in her hair will have to stay in lieu of more time to wash it.

Pippa's out of breath by the time she gets to the top of the hill, sounds of a guitar and multiple voices spilling out of the red-brick village hall.

'We have time for one more song from the Riverdean Rockers before it's time to put on your jackets and join us outside for the great pumpkin toss,' a microphoned voice calls from inside.

'I'd better limber up,' a man in a flannel shirt says to his friends outside the hall, pretending to stretch side-to-side in a warm-up. His friends laugh, and he flings his arms out to the sides, just knocking Pippa off balance. She manages to regain her footing without going flying.

'Woah,' he says as his hand accidentally makes contact with her chest region. Pippa feels her cheeks flare red, at the same time as she realises it's the man from the pub the other night. The hot one, with the child.

'Sorry,' Pippa apologises in that terrible British tendency, even though she hasn't done anything wrong. She scuttles off before she can be embarrassed any further.

The hall is heaving inside, hundreds of people chatting and clinking glasses. Pippa circles the room, past several tables set around the perimeter. There is a table selling leaf-shaped biscuits in auburns and greens. Then one selling mini cups of hot chocolate, complete with marshmallows and clouds of whipped cream, for the children.

Pippa finally spots a stall she is interested in. 'Jake's home-brewed ciders,' the sign tells her.

Several mini barrels of cider line the table, each with a different sign, from 'Pear and Blueberry Cider' to 'Sour Apple Cider'. Pippa makes a face, imagining how it would taste.

'Which of these has the highest alcohol percentage?' she asks a woman behind the table.

'That would be the usual apple variety. Fifteen per cent, so it is pretty strong.'

'I'll take it,' Pippa says, reaching for her purse.

'It's on the house,' the woman says. 'Jake's experimenting with new flavours this year so he's using the harvest festival as his live human trial.'

Pippa laughs. 'I'm happy to be a guinea pig,' she says, taking a sip of the cider, then wincing. 'That's strong stuff.'

'Burns the back of your throat.'

It really does. Pippa's left with an unpleasantly strong aftertaste that makes her wince again.

'I'm guessing you're not Jake, then?'

'I'm Monica,' the woman holds out a hand. She's slim, around Pippa's age, and very smiley. 'Jake's my friend. We grew up together. He's outside somewhere, probably preparing for the great pumpkin toss. He does it every year.'

'And you've offered to help for the free booze?'

'So I can get quietly hammered on apple cider, that's correct,' Monica giggles.

'I might need to sign up next year,' Pippa grins. 'I'm Pippa.'

'I haven't seen you around Riverdean before?'

'I'm a newbie,' Pippa explains. 'Moved here at the start of the month for work.'

'Excellent. I like new blood here. Especially young people.

61

Riverdean's started to look like a retirement home.'

'Do you work here too?'

'I teach at the primary school in Greenbrook, but I live in Riverdean.'

'I thought Greenbrook was a dirty word around here,' Pippa laughs, having noticed the rivalry and sneers around the village at any mention of Greenbrook. Pippa doesn't know why, the village looks beautiful perched across the river. She feels the alcohol loosening her tongue already.

'It is, but I think I'm forgiven as I'm handing out free cider.'

'Cheers!' Pippa bashes her plastic cup against Monica's.

'So, if it's your first harvest festival you need to go to the cake tasting, and do it quickly. After the pumpkin toss, everyone's hands are all pumpkin-y and gross, and people go digging into the cakes.'

Pippa laughs again. 'Okay, noted. I'll go and check it out. Any tips?'

'Well, there's war this year. Jenny Foster at the Riverside Lodge usually wins but,' Monica glances to each side at this and lowers her voice, 'she's turned in a bit of a stinker this year. The whole village is talking about it. Petro's handed in some cinnamon-y, apple-y honey creation that's hands-down the best, in my opinion.'

'Say no more,' Pippa says. 'I'm there.'

'You get to taste what you want and vote for the best.'

'Maybe we could go for a drink or something. When you're not serving cider, of course?' Pippa asks, emboldened by alcohol. 'I'm trying to meet more people here.'

'Definitely.'

Pippa takes Monica's number and has a few more sour swigs of cider. She could definitely get used to Riverdean life if it's all about free cake and cider, Pippa thinks.

On Monica's advice, Pippa heads to the table under a large

sign proclaiming 'Riverdean Cake Competition.' Small samples are being cut from a plethora of cakes, each with a name card beneath. Pippa spots the one labelled Jenny Foster, which looks a little sad with its smudged icing and toppled structure.

'Petro's is clearly the best,' Pippa overhears a woman whispering next to her.

'Jenny won't be happy,' another says, 'but it's not up to her usual standard.'

'Maybe it's something to do with her husband . . . having you-know-what.'

Pippa tries not to lean in to village gossip. At the moment she needs everyone to be on her side, especially if she's looking for new business for the B&B.

'Can I try some of Petro's honey cake?' Pippa asks one of the people working behind the table.

'You're lucky there's any left,' the woman tells her, handing her a miniature plate with a cube of cake on it. Pippa can already tell from the smell that it will taste divine. She lets the soft texture melt in her mouth, leaving behind the sweet taste of honey and cinnamon. It's so good, Pippa has to close her eyes. She sends Monica a thumbs-up when she spots her watching.

'Let's give a big round of applause for the Riverdean Rockers!' the microphoned voice booms from the front of the hall. 'Now, if everyone wants to congregate outside for this year's great pumpkin toss. We're now closed to sign-ups so everyone that has been given a number, please pick your pumpkin and join us on the starting line.'

Bemused, Pippa follows the crowd as they pour out of the hall and on to the lawn outside. She finds herself jostled along to stand just behind the starting line, where a number of men are assessing pumpkins in a wheelbarrow.

'This looks more aerodynamic to me,' she hears one man say.

'Nah, forget about aerodynamics, it's all about weight in the pumpkin toss.'

'And you're the expert, are you?'

'Last year's champion!' It's the flannel-shirted man from outside. He seems to spy Pippa at the same time as she sees him. 'Excuse me, I need your help. As a sorry for bumping into you earlier, can you help me pick a pumpkin?'

'Me?' Pippa asks, surprised.

'Why not? Your quiz knowledge was impressive the other night. It might give me good luck picking a pumpkin.'

'Okay,' Pippa smiles, secretly pleased that he's remembered her. 'This one.' She opts for a green and white knobbly pumpkin, balancing precariously amongst the orange ones.

'That one? Seriously?'

'What's wrong with it?' she asks, faux-innocently.

'It's . . . a bit of an odd shape.' He hoists it in the air, and Pippa sees how lopsided it is, almost boomerang shaped. As he spins it in the air, bobbing up and down to feel the weight of it, Pippa notices he's not wearing a wedding ring. Maybe he's not married, then?

'The best things come in unusual shapes,' she says. 'I stand by my choice.'

He shakes his head. 'I might be about to lose my record, but here we go.'

Pippa laughs. 'So, you win the pub quizzes and the pumpkin toss. Who do you bribe around this village? To win all the pointless competitions, I mean?'

'Oh, pointless competitions, is it?' He smiles again, his blue eyes dancing in the light of the lanterns strung around the lawn. 'I'd like to see you have a go at the pumpkin toss.'

'I would, but not tonight. Not after that cider,' Pippa pulls a face. 'Have you tried them?'

'Which ciders?'

'Jake's,' Pippa nods. 'I've only had one, but I reckon one more and I'll have to roll home down the hill.'

The man laughs, although an odd look passes his face. 'Are they nice ciders?'

'The apple one was all right,' Pippa shrugs. 'Nothing special. Nice if getting rat-arsed is what you're looking for.'

'What's your name?' he asks, suddenly changing the conversation.

'I'm Pippa.' She holds her hand out to him. He takes it, dwarfing her palm with the warmth and size of his. It sends shivers up Pippa's spine.

'I'm Jake.'

'Jake,' she repeats, frowning. He pauses, letting her figure it out. Realisation dawns. 'Oh God.'

'So, what were you saying about the ciders?'

'I'm so sorry,' Pippa says, mortified. 'I had no idea. They were lovely. Really lovely. I'm just not used to such strong drinks.' She's tying herself in knots, digging a bigger hole for herself by the second. And Jake isn't helping, with a face like thunder.

'Nothing special, eh?' he says, before breaking into a grin. 'Don't worry. It's okay. I brew them as a bit of a passion project. I know they're a bit sharp. Riverdean doesn't really have a choice but to serve them.'

'They're not . . . sharp,' Pippa says, unconvincingly. 'Okay, maybe a bit.'

Jake lets out a bark of laughter. 'It's a good thing my livelihood doesn't depend on selling cider, clearly.'

Pippa hits his arm gently, then wonders where that move came from. She's not flirting, is she? Pippa hasn't flirted for such a long time she's forgotten what it feels like. To stand so close to a man. To hear him laugh at her jokes. It feels good.

'What do you do, Pippa?' he asks, nodding to someone who passes.

'Spend all day shouting at a builder, at the moment,' she says. 'But soon, hopefully, I'll be opening my B&B. I've bought Pumpkin Cottage, down by the river. How about you?'

'Grant's not so bad,' Jake says now. Pippa curses herself again. She keeps forgetting how incestuous this village is.

'Please don't tell me you're his brother,' Pippa jokes, although she knows the two aren't related. There's no way the surly Grant shares any genetic material with the golden and muscly Jake.

'Definitely not,' Jake shakes his head. 'I own an adventure company based in Riverdean. We do kayaking, rock climbing, that sort of stuff around the valley.'

That makes sense, Pippa thinks. He looks so athletic. Has the complexion of a person who's never spent a day inside sofa-slobbing in pyjamas.

'Pumpkin tossers, get ready on the starting line,' a voice calls out.

'I'd better let you get back to . . . um . . . tossing.'

'You enjoyed that a bit too much,' Jake grins.

'Maybe,' Pippa feels her cheeks flush.

'Maybe we could get a drink afterwards?' Jake asks. 'Something that isn't cider? Especially seeing as I'm destined to lose this.' He gestures with the pumpkin.

Pippa pretends to think. Can hear Hannah's voice in her mind, urging her to accept. 'Sounds good . . . I'll make you a deal. We can have a drink, but only if you win, of course.'

Chapter Eight

Jenny

Riverside Lodge is in a terrific location, with incredible views over the River Wye. Jenny is a superb host and can't do enough for her guests. The breakfast was substantial, to say the least, and my husband and I didn't eat lunch that day. We'll definitely return to the Lodge sometime soon. Donna and Steve.

Smiling benignly, Jenny sips her coffee. That is definitely that nice couple from Winchester. They were exuberant in their praise when they left a few days ago. This is her weekly Monday morning ritual – to read the reviews posted on Tripadvisor. They're often glowing, and it gives her goosebumps when she gets a particularly good one. Her eyes flick over the dozen or so on there since last week. She encourages her guests to post knowing full well that good reviews can make your business.

Riverside Lodge is in a grate location . . . the next one begins. Jenny winces at the bad spelling. *There are lots of places to visit close by and the views from the bed and breakfast are excelent. The beds were comfy but the rooms are stuck in a time warp – all heavy furniture and checked curtains. Jenny was very friendly and helpful and serves up a full cooked English. It was disappointing there was no other choices as my wife wanted poached egg and smoked samon or avocado on toast but it wasn't availabel. Won't stay there again. Mick.*

Who on earth is that? Her mind races. Well, he can hardly string a sentence together or spell for that matter. One bad review doesn't panic her.

Absolutely perfect property and location for our needs. Very clean and comfortable. The decor's all a bit 1980s for our liking. Huge breakfast but very average. Host is friendly and welcoming. Rhoda and Eric.

Jenny takes a gulp of her coffee. She glances at the television past Phil's head. The presenter on the sofa is interviewing a soap actor and giggling and spluttering. It annoys the hell out of Jenny. Phil watches, his face inscrutable. He never used to watch television like he does now. He used to be scornful of daytime TV. Chewing gum telly, he called it. He would have told her to take no notice of reviews like this. She can hear him say it in her head, 'Take it with a pinch of salt, Jen. What do they know? Talking through their arse!' Jenny smiles. What she wouldn't give to hear his advice now.

Rhoda and Eric? Jenny wonders if they're real names. Some people use fake ones for bad reviews. She can't help but feel disconcerted, though. That's two in a week. On top of her loss at the harvest festival. It's not great with the new B&B opening. Pumpkin Cottage is small and unfinished at the moment and surely can't pose too much of a threat to Riverside Lodge.

Typing in Pumpkin Cottage, Jenny scans the three reviews posted on Tripadvisor.

What an absolute gem! Fantastic location, right on the banks of the River Wye. Sooo many little things thought about,

from the pack of home-made truffles left in our room to the
fresh flowers on the bedside table. I cannot recommend this
place highly enough. We have stayed in many b&bs, cottages,
apartments etc. and this one is by far the most amazing place
we have visted!

Jenny slams the laptop shut in frustration.

'Come on, Phil. Let's take Archie for a walk.' She hands him his coat and scarf. Archie, having heard the magic words, emerges from under the kitchen table, his ears pricked in anticipation.

'Where are we going?' Phil asks.

'Taking Archie out to do his business. We can call in The Trout and have a coffee. What do you think?'

Jenny is desperate to get out of the house, to see familiar faces, friends. The morning is grey and cold and the air catches her throat. The river is a muddy brown and rushes by swiftly, the soundtrack to everyone's lives in Riverdean and Greenbrook. Archie sniffs around happily, his tail in the air. They head downwards on the steep path towards The Trout, passing some ramblers on the way. Jenny gazes at the sheep in the field on the opposite side of the river, red smit marks on their coats, and their heads down nibbling the grass.

'Good morning, George,' Jenny says to the hand-ferryman on the river's edge. 'Busy one today, by the looks of it.'

He looks up and smiles, 'I hope so. Well, good morning, Phil. It's lovely to see you out and about.'

Jenny feels proud that Phil is so well-liked. He always had lots of friends and they still visit now and again, George being one of them. It's hard, though, as Phil's lucid moments are becoming rarer.

Archie barks at a little terrier with the couple on the ferry.

Jenny tugs his lead, 'Come on, you noisy thing. He's doing nothing to you.'

When they enter The Trout, Jenny can see that there's about half a dozen in there already. She marvels that the pub can have customers on a Monday morning. There's an open fire in the bar area and some empty armchairs around it.

'Go and sit by the fire with Archie, Phil. I'll get us a coffee.'

'Well, hello, Jen,' Brett says, smiling warmly. 'The pub on a Monday morning. I do like your style.'

'Don't get ahead of yourself, we're only in for a coffee.'

'The last of the big spenders, eh?' Brett grins. 'You coming along to our open mic night on Saturday?'

'I don't know. We've got Lola staying with us at the end of the week. Amber is going away for the weekend. I'll probably be babysitting.'

As Jenny leans on the bar, she spots some business cards. Very ornate writing on them and that familiar pumpkin logo. She picks one up and reads it. 'Newly opened, boutique bed and breakfast. Enjoy a cosy and luxurious break in an idyllic riverside cottage. Contact Pippa Mason' and then her telephone number. Jenny turns over the little card in her hand.

'How could you, Brett?'

'What do you mean?'

'Advertising Pumpkin Cottage is what I mean. I can't believe it. Do you know how many times we advertise The Trout to our guests? I don't think you have any idea, because if you did, you wouldn't advertise a rival place.' Jenny's voice is rising and she can feel her cheeks flushing. Other customers turn around, aware there is some sort of kerfuffle going on. Oblivious, Phil is sitting by the fire, playing with Archie's ears.

'Come on, now, Jen. You're overreacting. We advertise lots

of businesses here,' Brett says, placing the coffees down on the counter.

Jenny throws a ten-pound note onto the counter. 'Take this, but we shan't be needing these. I honestly thought of you and Shaun as our friends.'

As if on cue, Shaun enters the bar with some logs for the fire.

'Hiya, Jen, it's good to see you in here.'

'Hmm,' is all Jenny can say in acknowledgement. 'Come on, Phil, we're leaving. Now!'

Brett rolls his eyes as Phil gets up awkwardly, Archie trotting behind him.

Jenny has had time to calm down when Amber and Lola arrive late Friday afternoon. Jake isn't back from work yet.

'Nanny!' Lola yells, her pigtails bouncing as she runs into Jenny's arms.

'Hello, my darling.'

'Grandpa!' she says, releasing herself and running into Phil's lap. This is the first proper smile that Jenny has seen him give this week.

Amber stands awkwardly in the doorway. 'Where's Jake?'

'Some group he's taking out was late arriving. Broke down on the M50, apparently. He shouldn't be too long. Why don't you have a cuppa?' Jenny offers.

Amber nods, steps into the kitchen and drops Lola's holdall, decorated with characters from *Frozen*, onto the floor. She flops into the kitchen chair. She's wearing a leopard print blazer over jeans and a black crop top, baring an implausibly golden-brown midriff. Red, spiked ankle-boots complete the look. Totally inappropriate for the chilly October weather. Typical Amber. It still amazes Jenny that Jake and Amber were ever together – the outdoorsy, chilled, good-humoured Jake and Amber – so into her looks. It was obviously lust and then Lola came along.

'So, Jake says you're going away, Amber?'

She taps a long talon against her whitened teeth. 'Yes, Ethan and I are off to Amsterdam,' she says. 'I'm so excited!'

Lola looks over to her mother, clearly not as excited at the prospect of her absence.

'You're going to stay with Daddy,' Jenny tells her, 'and Nanny and Grandpa. Daddy's got lots of things planned for you. He's taking you to Wizard Wood tomorrow.'

Lola goes back to combing her doll's hair as she sits on Phil's lap. The doll is dressed in a black mini dress with silver chains around her neck.

'She loves that Kim Kardashian doll, even sleeps with it.' Amber rolls her eyes. Jenny shudders at the messages it sends. Amber lowers her voice, 'How is Phil? Jake told me that he's struggling. How are you coping?'

Jenny is grateful for her concern. She doesn't question the fact that she can tolerate Amber now that she's not with Jake. 'Jake's right. He's finding it hard when he can't remember things. Gets frustrated sometimes and quite angry.'

'God, that must be so tough with guests here.' She flicks her hair over her shoulder.

'Well, he's been started on medication. Donepezil. It's for moderate Alzheimer's. Maeve, the dementia nurse, saw him a few weeks ago and she said his symptoms are typical of patients with a moderate level of the disease.'

'Has it helped?'

Jenny nods, 'I think so. He gets really agitated at night. It's horrible to see. It's like he's tortured or something. Anyway, Maeve told me that can happen, and it usually subsides. I think it is lessening. It's not going to happen overnight, though.'

'Poor you,' Amber says, and she places a hand over Jenny's. Jenny notices she has at least ten different bracelets on her wrist.

'Look at him,' Jenny says, nodding to Phil. Lola is sucking her thumb and clutching Kim Kardashian in the other hand. Phil is resting his head on Lola's. 'He's happy as Larry.'

'She's doing really well in school,' Amber says proudly. 'She was Star of the Week last week.'

'That's my girl,' Jenny says. 'How does she get on with Ethan's daughter?'

'Riley? Good,' Amber nods. 'She gets a bit jealous sometimes if I make a fuss of Riley. It's complicated. She doesn't understand. There's only a year between them. Ethan would like us to have one of our own.'

Poor Lola, Jenny thinks. She'll make an extra fuss of her this weekend. 'What about you?'

'Well, I suppose if I'm going to have another one, I don't want to leave it too long. I'm only part-time at the beauty salon and I don't know if we can afford for me to give up entirely. And child care, well, it costs a fortune.' She shrugs.

'If it comes to it, perhaps I could pick Lola up from school for you. The mornings would be difficult, though.'

Amber smiles, 'Thanks, Jen, but you've got enough on your plate, haven't you?' They both turn to look at Phil. Lola has closed her eyes. 'God, she'll never sleep tonight if she has a nap now.'

Suddenly, Jake fills the doorway and, as if by magic, Lola rouses immediately. 'Daddy! Daddy!' she yells.

'Come here, Tinker!'

She jumps into his arms, the doll abandoned on the armchair next to Phil. Jake nods awkwardly to Amber.

'You smell, Daddy!'

'Do I now? Is that what you say to your daddy who has been working hard on the river all day?'

Amber snorts, the tension from their break-up still there between them, and the energy Jake put into his business was one of the many sticking points towards the end.

'When are you flying?' he asks her.

'Ten tonight. I'd better make tracks. We're flying from Bristol. You'll take her into school on Monday? My mum will be there to pick her up.'

'I said I would, didn't I?' Jake says, an unfamiliar sharp edge to his voice.

'Don't go, Mummy,' Amber pleads.

Jake bounces Lola in his arms. 'Wait until you see the den I've built in the garden for you, Lola-Cola. You're going to love it.' Lola squeals.

'I'd better go,' Amber mouths and Jenny breathes a sigh of relief. She wishes the two would get on. Things between Jake and Amber have got frostier lately and Jenny has no idea why.

Chapter Nine

Pippa

'Pumpkin-spiced gin for you, and toffee apple sour for you.' Brett places two lurid-coloured drinks in front of Pippa and Monica. Their first meet-up and second drink of the night.

'Thanks, Brett,' Monica says, before holding her glass up for a cheers.

'Cheers!' Pippa clinks her glass, careful not to spill any of her toffee apple concoction. 'And I'm in awe of you having another double gin and tonic . . . that's like a quadruple gin anywhere else.'

'Brett and Shaun always give generous measures,' Monica says. 'It's one of the reasons why The Trout is so popular.'

'I think I'm just used to London measures. These cocktails would be eighteen quid in the city.'

'I could never live in London.' Monica makes a face. 'Too much traffic and too many crowds. Every time I've visited, I couldn't wait to get out again.'

'You've never been tempted to move out of Riverdean?' Pippa asks, hoping she doesn't sound too judgemental. The village is clearly beautiful, although she can't help but think that if she grew up here, she'd need to escape every now and then to see different faces, a different pace of life.

'Maybe a little.' Monica takes a sip, thinking. 'There's not exactly much of a social life round here.'

Pippa opens her mouth to protest but Monica interrupts, 'Until you came along, of course.'

'What about a dating life?' Pippa asks. Monica grimaces again.

'Dire, as you can probably imagine. I had a long-term boyfriend once. High school sweethearts.'

'Did he live in Riverdean too?'

'Greenbrook. We stayed together for a few years after school before he got itchy feet. And an itchy penis.'

'Disgusting,' Pippa laughs.

'He was cheating on me with someone in Monmouth. The whole village was whispering about it before I'd even found out. Apparently, they were walking around Greenbrook together, blatantly flaunting the affair. Arsehole.'

'Ouch,' Pippa groans.

'That's the problem with village life. Gossip spreads faster than flu in winter. I actually found out from Shaun! I remember him asking how I was feeling, with these big sympathetic eyes. He clammed up when he realised I had no idea what was going on. The truth came tumbling out, though.' Monica rolls her eyes at the memory. 'Getting over a break-up is hard enough without being cheated on. And harder again when you can't walk down the road without being asked how you're holding up. They all mean well, though.'

'I bet.' Pippa winces at the toffee apple sour. 'You've not had anyone since?'

'I can't really face the drama again. Besides, I went to school with all the men around here under the age of forty. There's no one I'm interested in.' She shakes her head.

'Too right.' Pippa sips her drink again but wonders if there's more to Monica's hesitation on the dating scene.

'What about you?' She turns the heat on Pippa. 'Please tell me dating is much more glamorous in London?'

'God, no.' Pippa laughs a bit too loudly. 'I've had my fair share of shockers too. I was with my last boyfriend, Ben, for three years. He was a chef so we both worked such long hours we couldn't really spend much time together. Our relationship crawled along at a snail's pace.'

'Why did you split up? I hope I'm not being too pushy. I blame the quadruple gin.' Monica smiles.

'He didn't *cheat* cheat on me, but he was looking for it. I found dating apps on his phone. He'd been messaging other women throughout our relationship.'

Monica gasps.

'I know. I'm not even sure if he was planning to cheat on me, but he was looking for other options. Seeing if there was anything better out there. That's the problem with a big city. Men have too many options. They can't just settle and appreciate what they have. There's always the possibility of something better.'

'Okay, now it's making sense why you've moved to Riverdean. I thought you were nuts when we first met.'

'It's partly that,' Pippa says. Then, when she realises Monica is waiting for more, she explains, 'I was getting sick of being just another anonymous face in the crowd. My mum died last year. About a month before I found out about Ben. She was all I had in the world and I felt lost without her. I could go on being miserable in London, having no roots, no one who really cared about me, or I could move.' She hopes she hasn't brought the tone of the night down.

'You poor thing,' Monica says, with genuine sympathy. 'I get wanting to move, but why Riverdean?'

'It's . . . complicated,' Pippa says. 'My mum was from here, and she talked about it so fondly. I think I wanted to feel closer to her. Closer to family.'

Monica smiles. 'That's lovely.'

Pippa nods. She doesn't tell Monica the rest of the story. That she wants to know why her mum left and never went back. Why she never spoke about it. Why she's never told Pippa about her father.

'I hope so.'

'Well, I'm glad you've moved,' Monica grins. 'I finally have someone new to talk to.'

'And I finally have a drinking buddy in Riverdean.' Pippa cheers again.

'Anyway, it doesn't seem like *you're* going to be single for long in Riverdean,' Monica says, slyly.

'I have no idea what you mean.' Pippa tries to keep a straight face.

'Don't be coy. I saw you talking to Jake the other night. At the harvest festival. Before he won the pumpkin toss.'

'Jake . . . Jake who?' Pippa feigns indifference.

'You don't fool me!'

'He is pretty good-looking,' Pippa says, then quickly adds, 'not that I'm in the market for a relationship. It's the last thing I need right now. I should be focusing on my B&B.'

'There's no harm in enjoying yourself, though,' Monica says.

'We had a nice drink at the festival,' Pippa concedes. 'But that's all there is to it. We swapped numbers but we haven't made any plans yet.'

'You certainly looked close to me,' Monica says. Pippa doesn't know her well enough yet, but she can tell Monica's enjoying her squirming.

'We haven't even messaged each other.' Pippa tries to sound firm. 'Besides, he's got a daughter. There's got to be baggage there?' She's prying now, hoping Monica knows more about Jake's situation.

'A daughter and an ex-partner. They see each other but Jake doesn't really talk about her much,' Monica says. 'Jake's a good guy. He won't mess you around.'

'Okay,' Pippa nods. 'Nothing's going to happen anyway.'

'I'm sure,' Monica raises a sceptical eyebrow. 'Just be careful. If you get together, you'll be the talk of the town. And if things go tits up, then the gossip gets even worse. Take it from someone who knows.'

Even though Monica's smiling, Pippa decides to take her warning seriously. She's trying to establish a successful business, make a name for herself. The last thing she wants is village gossip. A relationship in the spotlight. An unnecessary complication.

And Pippa's learnt that men aren't to be trusted. She's sure underneath all the flannel and muscle that country men are just the same as city men.

But she does need some enjoyment in her life, doesn't she?

'Another drink?' Pippa asks, knocking her current one back.

The sky is darkening as Monica and Pippa leave The Trout.

'I didn't realise it was raining,' Pippa says, horrified.

'Riverdean has its own microclimate. You can never predict what's going to happen – sun one second, storms the next.' Monica shrugs on her coat.

'I didn't bring an umbrella,' Pippa pouts.

'Are you sure you don't want dinner at mine?' Monica asks.

'No, I'd better go and check on the B&B,' Pippa says. 'Thank you, though. Dinner at mine next week?'

'Sounds good. Just text me.'

'I will.' Pippa waves her off. Why didn't she wear a coat with a hood? She holds a futile hand above her head and starts a fast walk up the lane from The Trout. It's not far to Pumpkin Cottage but Pippa's already drenched and the rain is cold against her skin, soaking through her denim-ed legs.

As Pippa begins to turn the corner down the lane to Pumpkin Cottage, she spots a tall fair head that is unmistakeably Jake.

'Shit,' she mutters. It's typical of her to run into him now, when she's wet through and slightly drunk. He couldn't have seen her earlier when she was fully made up for her drink with Monica?

She hopes her make-up hasn't run, Joker-style, down her cheeks.

As she's about to brave it and step out ahead of Jake, she sees he's with someone else. A woman. And his daughter. Although she's in full Wellingtons and a raincoat, Pippa recognises her blonde curls. But who is this woman? Is this Jake's ex? She should have been brave and asked Monica more about her.

Pippa wants to get a better look but she can't without being seen. And she definitely doesn't want to be seen by Jake now. She makes a U-turn and darts back up the lane until she sees a parked car. Pippa stops behind it, ready for the most prolonged shoelace tying she's ever done.

She prays they don't see her as they pass by, painfully slowly. Jake and his ex walk in step while his daughter skips ahead, splashing in puddles as she goes. The adults seem to be walking very closely together.

As they pass, Pippa slowly rises to her feet, hoping she's not seen. She risks stopping to watch them walk off. They are huddled under one umbrella, not touching but not exactly keeping their distance. Did Monica have it all wrong? Is there unfinished business between them? There's definitely tension, Pippa can hear it in their voices.

Pippa doesn't know why she feels so disappointed. Jake clearly isn't as free and single as he made out. Baggage is the last thing Pippa needs now.

She walks towards Pumpkin Cottage again feeling deflated. The afternoon started full of promise. At least Pippa has a friend in Riverdean now. She can cope without a flirtation in the village too.

The rain is tempered by the time she reaches her cottage, and she notices Grant's van still in the driveway. Grant's meant to finish this week, meaning Pippa can open all four rooms of her B&B and really get bookings underway. But Grant working until any time after three o'clock is not a good sign.

'Grant!' she shouts, after opening the front door and shaking herself off like a dog. She puts her jacket, dripping wet, over a kitchen chair next to the radiator. 'Grant?'

When there's no answer, she walks down the corridor to find him bent over in one of the bedrooms, peering into the corner.

'Grant?'

'Just what I thought,' he says, not looking at Pippa. 'Over here.' She edges closer, noticing a damp, fetid smell in the air.

'What's up now?'

'I took the floor up today to attach the underlay, but do you see this?'

Pippa's scared to move closer but squints into the corner where Grant is. 'Those black marks?' There are hundreds of minute markings on the wood of the skirting and floorboards.

'Yep,' Grant confirms, before going silent again.

'What are they?' Pippa guesses it's not good news, but it seems that's par for the course with Grant.

'Droppings.' He stands up now, shaking his head. 'Cockroaches. You've got a nest under here.'

Pippa's legs instantly carry her backwards. She has to force herself to be an adult over this. 'Cockroaches?'

'Big ones,' Grant says. 'And little ones. And eggs. Hundreds under here. It's dark under the window, see, and warm by the radiator. They love that.'

'Have you seen cockroach . . . infestations before?'

'A few.' He folds his arms.

'Please tell me it's easy to solve.'

'Easy for pest controllers, yes. But they don't come cheap. Or fast.'

'Right,' Pippa says, blinking back the urge to cry. She will not cry. She won't.

'There's a bloke in Hereford, I think.'

Pippa takes his number, then Grant leaves. She slams the door to the offending room, then still feeling unsafe, grabs an old scarf to stuff in the gap under the door. Just in case.

Now she's alone, the tears come thick and fast. Why is it that everything one step foward in Riverdean is followed by ten steps backwards?

Chapter Ten

Jenny

Jenny hurriedly cleans the bathroom in Room Six, spraying the mirror and wiping away the smudges. The bin is overflowing with tissues, an empty shampoo bottle and biscuit wrappers. Damp, used towels are heaped on the floor. This is quite neat compared to most. Sometimes the things people leave in their rooms surprises Jenny; there's the usual phone chargers and books, underwear, but once someone left a prosthetic leg and last year a woman left an urn with her father's ashes. It's just as well Jenny isn't squeamish. Gloves on, she pours bleach down the loo and wipes around the toilet bowl, not breathing in the fumes, as Radio Four plays *Woman's Hour* in the background. Today, Anita Rani is talking about the menopause and Jenny mentally ticks off all her symptoms. She had a rough night last night and was awake at three and couldn't get back to sleep. It's in the darkness that she worries the most about Phil and the future, when Jake isn't there to reassure her that they'll cope.

It's all hands on deck this morning and Abigail, Paula's daughter, is working in Rooms One to Four. She's a bit slower than Jenny but she gets stuck in and her two hours every morning really help. This afternoon, the British Alpaca Society has block-booked rooms and arrive in convoy. They do it every year when members visit the Wye Valley and a farm breeding two hundred of the strange-looking creatures. Jenny loves the enthusiasm and quirky habits of these devotees. Mary brings with her a silk cushion embroidered with alpacas, and rosettes from her prize-winning alpacas decorate her weekend holdall.

That's one advantage she has over Pumpkin Cottage, the parking space for at least a dozen cars. New guests always complain about the hairy drive to reach Riverside Lodge, a single-track road with more zigzag twists and hairpin bends than the Monaco Grand Prix. You're pretty much stuffed if you meet something coming from the opposite direction, but many park their cars in Riverside Lodge and leave them there for their stay.

'I think someone's nabbed the towels in Room Three,' Abi says, peeping into Jenny's room. 'The two bath towels are missing.'

'Again!' Jenny sighs. 'That will be the Allens. I didn't like him. Shifty eyes. Oh well, nothing we can do about it now.'

'It's not right, though, Jenny,' Abi sympathises, tucking a lilac curl back that's escaped from her ponytail.

'Everything okay?' Jenny asks. 'The baby okay?'

'Well, she's teething at the moment and she's being an absolute nightmare. I was up three times last night.'

'Look, you finish in Room Three and I'll do the last of yours.'

'No way. You've got enough to do.'

Jenny smiles. She wasn't sure about Paula and Abi when they first moved into the village, with their piercings and implausibly coloured hair. It just shows how wrong you can be.

Jenny takes a step back as she finishes Room Six, feeling satisfied at a job well done. Everything is sparkling and spick and span. Buttery sunlight spills on the thick beige carpet and tartan bedspread. Is it old-fashioned, she wonders? What did those reviews say, 'stuck in a time warp' and 'outdated.' She always liked the silver stag heads above the bed. Gives the room a country feel, Balmoral chic, perhaps. They're not in a big city here. People come to escape the rat-race, a few days of tranquillity. Whatever. She certainly can't afford to refurbish or reupholster anything at the moment, not with Phil the way he is and his salary no longer coming in. He has his pension but it's nowhere near what he used to earn. Years ago, they'd planned to do a bit of travelling when they retired, see New Zealand, Japan. She tries not to dwell on what could have been. It's now that's important. There are glimpses of the real Phil now and again. His sense of humour, his kindness. A palimpsest of the man he was. Enough to keep Jenny going for now.

After she finishes the bedroom, she makes some shortbread biscuits in the shape of alpacas. She did it last year and the guests were so pleased with them, she vowed to make them again. She just has time before Jake and Phil return from walking Archie. No doubt they've called for a pint at The Trout.

'Well, Ma, you've been baking,' Jake says coming in, spotting the biscuits on the kitchen counter.

'Keep your hands off, Jake Taylor. They're not for you.'

'What are they? Aliens? Rhinos?'

'Very droll, Jake.' She turns to Phil, 'Nice walk, darling?' Jenny asks, as he kisses her on the cheek.

'We didn't go to The Trout,' Phil says, giving the game away. Jake rolls his eyes.

'And I suppose those aren't beer fumes you're breathing all over me.'

'There's no harm in it,' Jake says defensively. 'It was just one pint.'

'Well, he's not supposed to drink alcohol with his medication.' Jenny decides to let it go. 'I'll get the kettle on. You've got that school group in an hour, haven't you?'

'Yes, from Hereford. I'll be out all afternoon I should think. The weather's ideal by the looks of it,' he says, gazing out of the kitchen window. 'Cold, though.'

'I'll be making dinner early tonight,' Jenny announces. 'Your father and I are going to that choir in Ross.' She's careful not to say dementia choir.

'I don't want to go,' Phil says firmly.

'Don't be like that. Maeve suggested it. It'll be good for you. It's good to socialise rather than be stuck here all the time.'

'I don't want to mix with all those doolally people. I don't like singing.'

'Don't call them that. Besides, you loved singing. I couldn't stop you half the time. In the shower. And then when you got the ukulele, you were playing The Beatles.' Jenny remembers him playing 'I Want to Hold Your Hand' and how touched she was that he learnt it.

'Well, I'm not going,' Phil says. 'And you can't make me.'

Jenny realises there's no talking him around for the moment. 'Well, I'm making food early, Jake, so I'll plate one for you.'

As Phil retreats to the conservatory, Jake places an arm around her shoulder. 'Don't push now. He might change his mind later.'

'I know. He hates new things, that's what it is. Go on, have an alien,' Jenny grins.

The hall is flooded with light and Jenny can see bodies moving inside. The car engine is switched off and Phil sits next to her, his arms crossed.

'Come on, Phil, just try it this once. What harm can it do?'

He has retreated into his shell and has barely spoken a word since they got here. It's been a rush to make the choir, too. Mary and her friends from the British Alpaca Society arrived later than they planned, but they greeted Jenny like an old friend.

'Oh, my goodness!' Mary had said. 'I forget how lovely it is here. And you've made biscuits,' she gasped. 'Look, girls, Jenny has made biscuits again.'

'The rooms are all ready,' Jenny told them. She helped carry some of their bags.

Mary told her all about her plans to visit the farm and how some of the group had arranged a trip to Orangeville in Canada for the Easter holidays and the alpaca convention that takes place there. By the time Jenny got in the kitchen to make their sausage and mash dinner, they'd barely had time to eat it. And now this! She feels overwhelmed.

'Right, well, I'd better get in and tell the choir leader we won't be able to make it this week.' She glances at Phil pleadingly, but there's a blank look in his eye and he feels further away from her than he's ever been, stranded on a faraway shore she can't reach.

Inside, there's someone playing the piano and the hall is filled with light and good-humoured chatter. People are wearing green sweatshirts with Wye Valley Choristers emblazoned on them. It's difficult to tell who are the carers and who are those with dementia, which cheers Jenny. A woman, who Jenny assumes is Angela, is greeting everyone and waving song sheets. Her voice is loud and she has a ready laugh.

Jenny stands next to her, hesitant. 'Umm, are you Angela?'

The woman turns around. 'Call me, Angie, love. Everyone does.' She smiles, waiting for Jenny to speak. She wears bright red lipstick, and a pink and brown paisley pashmina is wrapped around her shoulders.

'I was supposed to bring my husband Phil here tonight. We spoke earlier in the week on the phone. Well, he's here, but he won't get out of the car and it's hopeless, really. . .' Jenny trails off.

'Don't worry yourself, darling. This often happens. He'll come around. Perhaps for the first couple of weeks, he can just sit at the back and watch what's going on. Before long, he won't be able to resist joining in. Trust me.'

'Angie's right,' says a woman, moving from behind Jenny. 'Mark refused to come in with me at first. I had to leave him in the car. It was embarrassing. It took a month before I actually got him inside the hall. I'm Louise, by the way.'

Jenny smiles and Louise gives her a hug. 'You'll need this place as much as he does. It's a tonic, honestly. We've been coming for six months now, and we both really look forward to it. I'm guessing your husband is young like mine. Well, young for dementia.' Jenny nods at this.

Angie smiles sympathetically. 'It takes as long as it takes, Jenny. My father had dementia and I know exactly what it's like. Bring your husband along next week. Don't push it today. Take these with you and talk to him about it.' Angie gives her leaflets on dementia and singing. Jenny takes them but she's already read all the literature on the positive impact of music on the well-being of dementia patients.

'See you next week, hopefully,' Louise says.

Jenny leaves the hall feeling uplifted, the rousing piano music drifting outside into the car park. She swallows the sadness of seeing Phil's lonely silhouette in the car. She lifts her face to the sky, gazes at the stars pinpricking the black above them. She can't allow herself to be swamped with self-pity or to ask why it's happened to them. Besides, going to that choir, even if it was just stepping inside the doors, has made her feel less alone.

Back at Riverside Lodge, Jenny can see the lights on in the guest bedrooms. The alpaca crowd hasn't gone out yet. It's still early – not even eight o'clock – and they're off to The Trout.

When Jenny and Phil enter the kitchen, they can see Jake in the little office next to the conservatory. Phil goes in to watch television.

'So, he refused to go in, then?' Jake asks.

'Afraid so. I'm not giving up, though. I'll try again next week. What are you up to?' she asks, standing in the doorway.

'Just sorting out a few bookings for kayaking. I've applied for a stall to sell my craft cider in some of the Christmas markets in the area.'

'You don't stop, Jake,' Jenny says, smiling.

'Got to keep the cash coming in.'

'Oh God, he's got some game show on. I was hoping to put my feet up and watch *Line of Duty* tonight.' She takes off her coat in the hall and stands in the doorway again. 'You need to find a new woman, Jake. Have a bit of fun.'

'Oh, I have my fair share of fun,' he says, flashing an enigmatic smile. 'I'm not sure I trust the female sex, anyway.' Jenny detects a bitter tone in his voice.

'Everything okay with you and Amber?' She asks nervously, knowing Jake doesn't usually like to talk about it.

He shrugs. 'A couple of weeks ago she told me that she and Ethan are talking about moving to France. His family's got a holiday home there. In Brittany. And Riley loves it there. I'll never see Lola if she does that.'

'Oh, Jake,' is all Jenny can manage.

'It's not fair. I don't get a say in all this. We got into a bit of an argument when we went for a walk the other day. She kept saying it was her choice and it was for a better life.' Jake looks up from the computer. 'Whose life is it better for, though? Lola? She won't have her father around.'

'What does Lola say?'

'She doesn't understand. It's just some adventure for her.'

'You'll see her, Jake. We'll make it work. Brittany is not that far.' Jenny puts an arm around him. 'Is it definite?'

'Not yet. But Amber is all excited about it and it makes me bloody mad.' He gets up. 'I think I'll have one in The Trout,' he says, grabbing his coat.

Jenny watches from the kitchen window as Jake leaves, the music blaring from the living room. Life can be so bloody complicated sometimes, she thinks, switching on the kettle.

Chapter Eleven

Pippa

Pippa spots a tall, fair head at the bottom of the driveway leading to The Trout. She feels her heart rate speed up, like a teenager. Pathetic, she thinks. She's had her outfit planned for days – a scarlet jumper, jeans and brand-new boots that cost more than the entire outfit. They look outdoorsy but Pippa's only worn them around the B&B, and she can already tell they are going to be uncomfortable by the end of the day, a little too tight around her left ankle. Her blonde hair is blow-dried and curled, and she has a new coat of purple nail varnish on. This would be on the side of casual for a date in London, but Pippa already feels too made-up when she spies Jake's muddy boots, the dog yipping at his ankles.

It's a sunny, but cold day in early October. The river sparkles a brilliant blue amongst the burnt umber leaves either side of the valley. Riverdean is bustling with tourists, The Trout car park is full with people carriers and minibuses. Pippa has two rooms booked tonight. A quick turnaround from the weird alpaca lovers who stayed a few days ago. Pippa made the mistake of referring to them as llamas when she was greeting her guests, and watched a woman's lips shrivel with disgust, before launching into a ten-minute explanation of the differences between them. Apparently, it's all in the size and the coats, with llamas having a thicker, coarser wool.

Pippa will never make *that* mistake again.

Jake turns round just as she is about to reach him. That man is six feet of total gorgeousness, she thinks. His eyes crease at the corners with a smile as he sees Pippa.

'Hello you,' he says. Pippa pauses just opposite him, and there is an awkward moment where they don't know how best to greet each other. A hug? A kiss? Definitely not a handshake. Eventually she steps closer and they share an awkward one-armed hug. The dog, on noticing this, takes an interest in Pippa and starts circling her.

'Hi,' she says, bending down.

'This is Archie,' Jake introduces.

'Hello, Archie.' Pippa extends a hand to pat the dog's head but Archie takes the encouragement a step too far, and before Pippa can do anything about it, Archie's up on his hind legs, planting two very muddy paws on Pippa's jeans.

'Shit, no,' Jake says, noticing far too late. 'Archie,' he scolds, grabbing the dog by the collar.

'It's okay,' Pippa says, inspecting the damage. She now has two very fetching mud patches above her knees. She tries to brush herself off but the mud is wet and has already seeped through the material.

'I'll get you a tissue,' Jake says.

'No, it's fine,' Pippa paints on a smile. 'It'll come out in the wash, I'm sure.' She hopes that's true. Archie gives her an apologetic look.

She stands up and there is another awkward moment between them.

'Not a great start,' Jake acknowledges. 'Archie's just excited. He doesn't get out much with attractive women.'

'That's a bit of a cheesy line,' Pippa says.

'Sorry. It's clearly me who doesn't get out much.' Pippa wants to contradict him as he was out and about with his ex last week.

'I was surprised you're not working today,' she says instead, noticing his fleece has the logo 'Jake's Adventures' on it.

'We have one team-building adventure booked this weekend, but I've done enough of those recently so my colleague, Adam, is doing it. Taking them rafting.'

'Team building rafting adventure,' Pippa shudders. 'Sounds like hell.' She remembers the one she did in Mallory's. A conference room in Slough with motivational talks and bonding exercises until six pm. The highlight of the day was the sandwiches – a few pieces of grated cheese and a thin slather of mayonnaise cut into a triangle, with weak orange squash and a packet of crisps.

'You're not a fan of rafting?'

'Never tried it,' Pippa shrugs. 'And I don't intend to . . . unless you've planned a surprise for today?'

'Not today,' Jake laughs. 'But you'll need to do it for the rafting competition next month. Riverdean versus Greenbrook, from Bobbin Bridge all the way past the village. It's great fun. Plus, Riverdean smashes them every year.'

'I don't get this weird rivalry with Greenbrook,' Pippa huffs. 'I think I'd better leave the rafting to you.'

'How do you feel about a more sedate pace across the river?' Jake leads her towards where the little hand-pulled boat is waiting.

'As long as there's no chance of falling in, I'm happy,' Pippa nods.

'Good,' Jake nudges her with his elbow and Pippa smiles. Tourists are being let on the boat six at a time.

'Room for two more!' a man shouts, whilst counting cash and allowing a family of four on board. Pippa and Jake get to skip the queue of bigger families in front, and step into the little vessel at the edge of the river. Pippa's stomach lurches at the unpleasant rocking sensation of the boat, and sits down as quickly as she can. Archie looks questioningly up at her, before deciding it's probably best not to attack her jeans again, and hops up on Jake's lap for the journey.

'I haven't done this for a while,' Jake says. 'My daughter loves it.' They watch the hand-ferryman as the boat is tugged along on what looks like a washing line, but Pippa hopes is a lot more sturdy.

'How old is your daughter?' Pippa asks.

'Lola's five this year. She's growing up far too quickly. Every time I see her, she's like a whole new person.' He goes quiet for a second.

'I'm guessing she doesn't live with you, then?' Pippa says. She wants to probe about his ex, what the whole situation is. The image of Jake huddling close to her under that umbrella is still vivid in her mind.

'Amber and I split up when she was three. They live about an hour away now in Cardiff with Amber's new partner.'

That settles that then, Pippa thinks with relief.

'How often do you get to see her?'

Jake frowns. 'Lola? About once a fortnight. More if Amber needs babysitting. My mum loves looking after Lola. She calls her Lola Lolly.'

The boat slowly moves across the water as two kayakers go past in fluorescent helmets.

'Do you get on with Amber?' Pippa realises she sounds a bit forward in asking this question, but Jake doesn't seem to mind.

'Amber . . . it's complicated.' He pauses and Pippa hopes he's not just going to leave it hanging there. What does complicated mean? 'We can be civil and friendly, although she can also wind me up like no one else. Depends what mood she's in.'

'Right,' Pippa wants to ask more, but can't. 'And do you live on your own now?'

Jake huffs out a breath. 'This is the question I try to avoid answering . . . Please say you won't go home if I tell you I live with my parents?' He winces and Pippa laughs.

'Oh no, I might have to consider this. Is this why you've got me on a boat in the middle of the river before telling me?'

'It's a temporary arrangement only. Amber and I were saving up for a house, but I've obviously had to save more since the break-up, and it was just easier with my parents. Plus, houses don't come up to rent very often in Riverdean.'

'Excuses, excuses,' Pippa says, teasing.

'Hopefully I'll be out in a few months. Some nights I sleep at the office — there's a little lodge on the way into Riverdean where we run Jake's Adventures and it's got a bedroom. But . . . I'd be lying if I said Mum's cooking wasn't a factor.'

'Don't tell me it's like a hotel there,' Pippa grins.

'Funny you should say—Oh no, Archie, get back.' The little dog seems intent on dangling as far out of the boat as possible. 'I swear this dog hasn't got the memo that he can't swim.'

'Well, living in a B&B isn't all it's cracked up to be,' Pippa says, once the dog is tugged safely back inside.

'It's not?' Jake asks, an odd look on his face.

'I own this cottage but only one room is really mine – the bedroom. I have to make sure I'm dressed and looking presentable before going in to my kitchen and living room. I didn't really think that through before buying it. Luckily the bedroom's pretty big, I've got my own little sofa area.' Why is she talking about her bedroom? Pippa scolds herself. 'Maybe I can extend it one day, if Pumpkin Cottage is successful enough.'

'Mmm,' Jake says. He looks deep in thought. 'It's going well so far?'

'I've had . . . setbacks. The cockroach infestation was particularly unpleasant but luckily confined to one room. The bookings I have had seem really happy. One woman said she'll never stay in Riverside Lodge again! Oh look, we're here now.'

With a bump the boat moors on the Greenbrook side of the river, and the family get out ahead of them. Pippa, Jake and Archie follow behind, walking up the slope to the village. Pippa shivers as the sun passes behind a cloud.

'See, this is typical of Greenbrook,' Jake shakes his head.

'It's one cloud,' Pippa laughs.

'Yes, but it's just not as nice, is it?'

'You're mad,' Pippa thinks the village looks identical, the mirror image of Riverdean. The village pub, The Swan, even has a similar menu to The Trout as they pass.

'The walks around here are great, though, I will admit that,' Jake says, leading Pippa to a path that looks like it opens into a field. There is a large muddy puddle on the way that Jake happily ploughs straight through as though it is nothing. Pippa looks down at her new boots and takes a gulp of air. There's no way out of this. She tries to delicately splash her way through the edge of the puddle but realises the mud is deeper there as one of her boots sinks in with a large squelch. Jake turns round and she tries to smooth the frown on her face.

'Are you up for a muddy walk? I can't imagine you did many in London,' he says.

'I resent the implication,' Pippa says, although it's true. 'I love a muddy walk.'

'Those boots aren't new, are they?'

'These old things!' Pippa shakes her head, feeling the mud seep around the ankle of her boot and under her sock.

She follows as Jake jumps over a stile easily, using one hand for balance. There's really no way she can make this look attractive as

Pippa goes for the one-leg-over-before-the-other approach.

'So, I bet your family are pretty proud of you, being a B&B owner,' Jake says once he's lifted Archie over the fence.

'Err,' Pippa fiddles with a strand of her hair as they walk. 'I don't really have much family. My mum raised me on her own. We don't have many relatives.'

'No siblings?'

She shakes her head.

'Me neither. I used to wish for a brother growing up. Someone to play with, fight with, scheme with.'

'I bet you were a handful all on your own,' Pippa says. 'I was happy being an only child. It felt special just Mum and me. I used to hate when she'd have boyfriends, not that it ever lasted long. She even got married a few times.'

'What about your dad?'

'I don't know anything about him,' Pippa says frankly. 'Mum rarely talked about him. She said he didn't want to be a father. All I know is she moved away from Riverdean when she was twenty-one and pregnant with me. She never really explained why.'

'I didn't know your mum came from Riverdean. I wonder if your dad was local as well.'

'I don't even know his name,' Pippa says. 'I'm not trying to find him or anything and he clearly wasn't father material. I just wanted to feel closer to my mum. So much of who we are seems tied up in places, especially where we grew up.'

'I agree,' Jake says, walking in step with her. 'My dad has early-onset Alzheimer's. It's okay. Hard to watch, and so hard for my mum. She puts a brave face on it but seeing his personality slip away . . . anyway, he goes from not knowing how to use the TV remote one minute and putting mayonnaise in a cup of tea, to completely with it when we're out. It's like seeing the landmarks of Riverdean, the places he's grown up in, ignites something in his brain. One minute outside the primary school and he's back to cracking jokes, reciting memories of his youth. It's bizarre. That's why I take him out every day for a walk. I don't know if it's slowing anything down but . . . I need that time with him as well.'

Pippa nods. Jake is a good person, she decides.

'That's nice,' Pippa teases, 'in between torturing people on team building days and poisoning others with your crap cider.'

'Ouch,' Jake yells, but laughs. 'Come on, there's a really good pub on the other side of this field.'

The field slopes to the riverside, with dramatic views of Riverdean. Pippa spots Pumpkin Cottage over there, Grant's van is parked outside. Archie barks at a few sheep hanging about. Pippa looks at Jake and how at ease he is in the outdoors with his scruffy dog. This might be new territory for her, but maybe she should embrace all the parts of moving to Riverdean.

Chapter Twelve

Jenny

The hall is filled with light and a frisson of excitement. Jenny and Phil sidle in and take a seat at the back. This is progress. This is better than last week. Jenny has managed to get Phil through the doors by promising he will not have to stand with the choir at the front and can just observe.

She had phoned Angela and explained the situation.

'Honestly, it's not a problem. I won't draw attention to him, but I bet within ten minutes he'll be singing along to one of the songs.' She bursts into laughter at this point. 'You'll see.'

Jenny very much doubted it, but didn't contradict Angela, who seemed to think that Jenny needed convincing of its benefits.

'Psychologists have shown how singing reduces stress and anxiety and helps dementia patients maintain speech and language.'

'Yes, but . . .'

'It'll be good for you too, Jenny. A lifeline. I wish we'd had classes like this when my father was alive. He loved music and could remember lyrics to songs from decades ago, yet couldn't remember how to tie his shoelaces or turn the shower on.'

'Yes, I've read about it all and I know—'

Angela spoke over Jenny, 'You'll have seen that Vicky McClure documentary about people living with dementia? I just knew this was something I could contribute to. Did I tell you I'm a music teacher?'

'No, I don't think you did . . .'

'Bring him on Friday and just let him watch,' she said again, leaving Jenny feeling she had got totally the wrong end of the stick. It wasn't that she needed convincing to take Phil. He was the one refusing.

Louise, the woman Jenny met last week, and her husband Mark are sitting in the second row and she turns around to wave at Jenny and Phil. Angela, or Angie, as she likes to be called, is standing at the front now, chatting to everyone as they come in like they're old friends. Her laughter travels to the back of the hall. She's wearing an emerald green jumper and huge, oval drop earrings to match, which bounce as she laughs at some joke she's made. The man who was playing the piano last week stands next to her rather awkwardly.

Suddenly, Angie claps her hands. 'Good evening, all of you. Welcome to all my songbirds, old and new. I'm Angie and this is Jude, who most of you know by now, and he'll be playing songs on the piano for us tonight. We're going to be singing some old favourites and a couple of new ones, just to keep you all on your toes.'

Jenny picks up the song sheets on the empty seat next to her with the playlist of songs for the evening. 'Singing in the Rain'. 'You Are My Sunshine'. 'Moon River'. Sinatra's 'You Make Me Feel So Young'. Jenny's heart sinks. Will these be the type of songs Phil will like? She can't help worrying that perhaps most of the dementia patients here are two decades older than him. Phil used to love U2 and Billy Idol, Annie Lennox. Always favoured singers or bands with a slight edge. This all seems a bit tame for him. He'll know the music, though, she thinks.

Jude takes his seat at the piano, folding his long legs under the stool. He pushes his glasses up the bridge of his nose and stares at the music sheet in front of him.

'Now, I want everyone, and I mean everyone, to join in,' Angie says, smiling broadly.

Jenny glances surreptitiously to Phil. His arms are folded and he rolls his eyes. She braces herself for the car crash. Jude plays the opening bars of 'You Are My Sunshine' and, tentatively, people start singing along.

Ignoring Phil's sighs, Jenny joins in, self-consciously. She knows the lyrics for the first verse but has to put on her reading glasses to read the rest of them on the song sheet. Phil continues to sit there, unmoving, his arms determinedly folded across his chest. He looks ridiculous, she thinks, and sniggers.

At the end of the song, the ice is truly broken and everyone chatters at once.

'Did you enjoy that?' Angie asks. 'My father always sang that song for me as a child and for a long time when he was ill, he stopped singing. When he heard that song again, it gladdened my heart to hear him sing it and remember all those long-forgotten words.'

Jenny warms to Angie with her openness and willingness to share her story about her father. It doesn't seem to matter what genre of music you're into, Angie has chosen these songs with care. They put a smile on your face.

When Jude starts playing The Beatles' 'I Want to Hold Your Hand', everyone is joining in and she notices Phil's left foot is tapping ever so slightly, although his arms are still resolutely unmoving. The singing is uneven, Jenny thinks. There are one or two good voices, but the overall sound is slightly jarring, people singing lyrics at a beat later than others. The Wye Valley Choristers are unlikely to be appearing in the Albert Hall anytime soon. It's beginning to irritate her that Phil is not even trying like the rest of them.

'You are a miserable old bugger,' she tells him, just as the music stops. She can tell people have heard her as some turn around to look at her. She gazes intently at the song sheet, her cheeks flushing.

There's a break halfway through and everyone has a cup of tea and nibbles custard creams.

Louise makes her way to her. 'Are you enjoying it?' she asks them.

'Well, I am,' Jenny says. 'I'm not sure about Phil.'

She nudges Mark, who looks about Phil's age. 'Do you remember you were exactly the same, Mark. You hated it at first. Now I can't keep him away.'

'I didn't,' he protests and Louise rolls her eyes.

'Angie's great, mind you,' Louise says. 'She's such a vibrant character. She's got a real way with her. Last week we ended up jigging along on our feet. I felt really lifted at the end of it.'

'Hmm,' Jenny says, feeling some dread if Phil refuses to play ball. This could be embarrassing.

Inhibitions seem to have disappeared in the second half and everyone is on their feet and clapping along to Queen's 'Another One Bites the Dust'. With the song sheets on the chairs, the lyrics are largely lost, but it doesn't seem to bother anyone. Phil is sitting there, the only one, the picture of misery in the moat of happy singers around him. Jenny grabs him by the arm, 'Come on, Phil, you love this song.'

She can see by the end of the song, he's mouthing the lyrics under his breath, hiding it from Jenny.

The hour passes quickly and Jenny feels energised by the enthusiasm around her. For the first time in ages, she doesn't feel swamped by the permanent feeling of impending doom. Phil, if he let himself admit it, seems to have enjoyed himself too.

Angie calls out as they leave, 'See you next week Jenny, Phil.'

'Oh, we'll be here,' Jenny says as they head out to the car park.

When they get home, Jake asks them expectantly, 'So, how did it go?'

'Marvellous,' says Jenny.

'S'okay,' says Phil at the same time.

'High praise, indeed,' Jenny shrugs, taking off her shoes. How irritating can one person be!

Jenny wakes feeling more positive. Phil can't help being the way he is. She has to remember that. The reason he was so reluctant to join in last night was his fear. He really hates going to different places, new places. She glances over at him next to her in bed. His hair is thinning and falls over his forehead. She knows every crinkle in that face, that mole beneath his right eye, that strong jaw, softening now. When he's sleeping like this, she likes to imagine that nothing is wrong, that his mind isn't the fragile, unpredictable thing it seems to be these days.

When his eyes open, she kisses him on the lips. 'Morning, handsome. Did you sleep well?'

He shakes his head, 'No, I did not. Jakey cried all night. Why did you hide his elephant? He loves that elephant.'

And just like that, the spell is broken. 'Jake hasn't slept with that elephant since he was a child. He's twenty-eight now. Perhaps it was a bad dream,' she says gently.

'I saw you hide it yesterday. I saw you, woman.'

Jenny ignores him. She finds the best way to deal with these moments of paranoia is to distract him. 'Jake is talking about going fishing tomorrow. Do you fancy it? Just you and him.' She gets out of bed and senses the mood has shifted slightly. 'I'd better get those breakfasts on. I'll help you dress first.'

Six rooms are occupied and Jenny dispatches the breakfasts in no time. She can make these with her eyes closed. After she's loaded the dishwasher, she decides she'll take Archie for his morning walk before she tackles the bedrooms and Abi arrives. Jake is making coffee in the kitchen, his dressing gown draped casually over his boxers and T-shirt.

'Planning on giving the guests an eyeful,' she teases him.

Spreading Marmite on his toast, he grins. 'Thought I'd show the old biddies what they've been missing.'

'Old biddies, indeed. The Walker sisters in Room Two can't be much past forty.'

Jake rolls back his dressing gown sleeve and twitches his biceps, 'Bet they'd love to get their hands on a real man. None of these namby-pambies from London.'

'Cheeky. Honestly, Jake, your head is getting so big these days, you'll hardly fit through the door.' Jenny laughs. 'I'm taking Archie out for a quick walk. Keep an eye on your father.'

A watery sun greets her as she makes her way down the path from Riverside Lodge. The river gurgles below and Archie trots ahead, excitedly sniffing everything in his path and stopping to lift his leg at a fence post. Jenny makes a mental list of a few things she needs in the post office and grocery shop – stamps, dishwasher tablets if they have any. She's running low. As she turns down into the dip past Pumpkin Cottage, she sees someone coming out of the door. She can't turn around and avoid meeting her. It will look odd. Perhaps if she speeds up, she might look as if she's in a rush to go somewhere.

She tugs on Archie's lead, 'Come on, boy.'

Pippa Mason stops in the middle of the path, obviously not in a hurry to go anywhere and keen to stop and chat.

'Lovely morning for a walk,' she smiles. Her blonde curls spill out of her bobble hat and her hands are tucked in her coat pocket. 'Chilly, though. Are you local?'

Jenny nods, 'I am.'

'I'm Pippa. I've just moved in, well, a few weeks ago.' She waves her arm behind her. 'Pumpkin Cottage. A new B&B.' There's an awkward silence and Pippa seems to give Archie a puzzled look. 'There's a gorgeous dog.' Archie wags his tail and yaps happily at the attention. Traitor!

'Do you live in Riverdean or Greenbrook?' Pippa asks. There's something about her eyes, brilliant grey, that seem familiar to Jenny.

'Riverdean,' Jenny says. 'I'm not sure we need another bed and breakfast here, to be frank. And I certainly wouldn't have bought *that* cottage. It's damp and liable to flooding.'

Pippa looks startled for a moment and flushes. She seems at a loss as to what to say next. 'Well, I'm having some work done on it.' Then she thrusts her chin up. 'And I think there is plenty of room for another bed and breakfast, *to be perfectly frank*. There's always room for a cosy, riverside cottage and I've had lots of bookings so far.'

'Hmm, the novelty, no doubt. Anyway, I must be off,' Jenny says, walking on and not looking back. As she reaches the top of the hill, she begins to feel guilty. She was a bit mean, but really the smugness of the girl was very irritating. Was she honestly expected to congratulate this Pippa Mason when she was starting up a rival business? Hearing that some of the alpaca crowd had stayed at Pumpkin Cottage when Jenny had enough room to accommodate them all at Riverside Lodge just about put the tin hat on it.

The confidence of youth. She has no idea how difficult it is running a B&B. There are fire regulations, food hygiene standards, all sorts of legal requirements. Jenny bets that Pippa hasn't the foggiest what she's got herself into. And if she is transgressing all sorts of laws, well, then, Jenny will have to, in all conscience, do something about it. Maybe a phone call to find out wouldn't harm.

'Come on, Archie. We've got some work to do,' she says, pulling on his lead.

Chapter Thirteen

Pippa

Pippa stares up the lane, too gobsmacked to move. She knew villages could sometimes be close-knit and unwelcoming to new members, but this is the first openly hostile interaction she's had. And with a total stranger.

What had that woman said? *I'm not sure we need another B&B in Riverdean.* Something about her bookings being *a novelty, no doubt.* Pippa had been too shocked to retaliate, but now she feels fired up, a thousand possible responses coming to the surface. It was always the same after a conflict. She'd felt powerless in the heat of the moment, but now she is angry.

What right does that woman have, whoever she is, to insult Pippa's business? To be so openly horrible? It just doesn't make sense. Everyone she's met in Riverdean so far has been lovely to her. Maybe this woman is from Greenbrook and Jake is right about the differences between the two.

She will show her. She will make this business a success. And if Pippa ever sees that woman again, she will rub it in her face. What a cheek!

Pippa carries on walking up the lane to the village shop, hoping she isn't too late before they close for lunch. She'd been surprised the first time when she'd seen the sign in the window 'Closed for lunch break. Back at 2.' She glances at her watch. Who has a two-hour lunch break? It's like something from Italy or France.

Thoughts of the stranger and her dog continue to whizz round Pippa's mind. Her dog had looked similar to Jake's. At least this one didn't try to mount her like Jake's did. The mud hadn't fully washed out of her jeans, especially where it was caked around the ankles after their walk. No, this ambush was all the strange woman's.

The date had been fun, mud and aching thighs aside. The three blisters on her left foot from the definitely-too-tight boots were worth it. Jake was a charmer. They'd giggled and flirted all day, chatting about everything from cider to box sets. Jake is extremely attractive, Pippa has to admit, in a kind of rough-around-the-edges, countryside way. And she'd dreamt every night about those enormous hands on her waist, sinking into his arms while her lips press against his . . .

But they have nothing in common. Jake is the kind of uncomplicated outdoorsy soul that's known nothing other than Riverdean his whole life. Happiest spending his time in the fresh air, pumping his muscles while hiking or trail running or kayaking. He'd talked through their whole walk without breaking a sweat. Probably never worn a suit in his life.

Pippa is altogether different. She's moved from house to house her whole life and while she might have done a good job of pretending to be outdoorsy, Pippa is happiest with a bottle of wine and a hot water bottle on the sofa. Anything beyond a walk is completely out of her comfort zone. She'd done the occasional Pilates class in London, the odd jog now and again, but pounding the pavements isn't a possibility in Riverdean where the paths slope and curve so ridiculously. The line chalk and cheese comes to mind.

No, they will never work in the long run. Having a relationship with Jake will just lead to disaster and awkwardness around the village, exactly as Monica had warned her. It is best to just keep things casual between them. The question is how long Pippa can stay casual when he looks so damn good, those eyes sparkling at her across the log fire in the pub. Luckily she'd had to leave early to greet her guests or else a kiss would have been irresistible.

Thankfully, the shop is still open, and Pippa manages to stock up her wine collection. She throws a jumbo bag of Doritos and a few dips into her basket, as well as some smoked salmon and crème fraîche for the morning. The recipe for a great night in with her friend.

Just time to skip home and get changed out of her scruffy painting clothes.

'Pips!'

She hears the screech before Hannah has opened the car door.

'Thank you so much for coming!' She runs around to the driver's door of the black Mercedes, which Hannah has parked badly, crossing two spaces. Surely Grant will have something to say about this later when it comes to getting his van out.

'It's beautiful here,' Hannah says while they are still hugging. 'But how the hell do you get around? I feel sick from all the bends, and I thought my car was going to roll into the river on that lane.'

'It's not so bad,' Pippa laughs at her friend's exaggeration. 'You get used to it.'

'Tell me about it,' Hannah says, 'you even look like a local as well.'

'Cheeky cow! What's that supposed to mean?' Pippa laughs.

'You look different. Not bad, though!'

'It's the lack of a decent hairdresser,' Pippa says. 'I haven't had my roots done in six weeks.'

Hannah has clearly had her roots done, and looks impossibly glamorous, Pippa thinks, her dark, sleek hair shining in the autumn sunlight. She leads Hannah into the house, helping her carry some bags and a dress in a dry-cleaning bag. Pippa doesn't remember feeling so short around Hannah, but she sees Hannah's in heeled boots. They were together when she bought them in Camden Market. Pippa smiles at the memory, how tipsy they'd been walking back along the canal.

'So, what do you think?' Pippa asks when they get to the kitchen of Pumpkin Cottage.

'It's perfect,' Hannah's smile lights up. 'Like something on Instagram. And that view!' She moves to the window. 'Are you sure that's not green screen?'

'It's called countryside,' Pippa knows Hannah is winding her up. She grew up on a farm in Berkshire, after all, although Hannah insists she had the wrong upbringing. She moved to London at the age of eighteen and only went back home for holidays, moaning about it no end whenever she returned.

'Well done, Pips. I love it! Who wouldn't want to stay here?' Hannah inspects every aspect of the kitchen, peering out of the window again. Pippa's mind again turns to the woman this morning and her mean words. She hopes Hannah is right and it isn't just novelty, as that woman said, that's got her bookings thus far. Her words had played right into Pippa's insecurities and doubts about the B&B.

'Everything all right?' Hannah asks.

'Yes,' Pippa says, a half-truth. 'I just miss you.'

'Of course you do,' Hannah laughs, then gives Pippa a hug. 'I miss you too. I'm devastated having to tell people my best friend left me to move to hick-country.'

Pippa rolls her eyes. 'Come on, let's open the wine and I'll show you the rest of the B&B.'

Hannah coos over the bedrooms.

'Just one more room to go, and it's nearly done,' Pippa shows Hannah inside the Lavender Room, risking the fact that Grant is in there and probably smoking and swearing as usual.

For once, he's actually working, nailing tongue and groove panelling into the wall behind the bed that Pippa will paint sage green to contrast the lavender and white wallpaper. 'This is Grant,' she says, hoping to close the door as quickly as possible.

'Hello.' For the first time ever, Pippa sees him smile and stand up straight, making direct eye contact. His eyes linger on Hannah, looking her up and down. 'I'm Pippa's contractor.'

'"Contractor?"' she repeats in confusion, while Hannah introduces herself.

'Are you staying for the weekend?' Grant asks.

'Just tonight. Pippa's promised to show me a good time, haven't you?'

Grant smirks at Pippa, before turning back to Hannah.

'Only one place to go, then – The Trout. I'm usually there on a Saturday night with my brother.'

'I'm glad I brought my party dress, then,' Hannah says. Pippa, feeling horribly uncomfortable, terminates the conversation.

'We'll let you get on with the tongue and groove. Come on, Han.' She steers her friend out of there, two sets of eyes locked on each other.

'Oooh,' Hannah whispers as Pippa shuts the door. 'You didn't say he was super-hot.'

'No, do not tell me you fancy Grant. He's disgusting,' Pippa hisses in reply. 'And miserable. He's got to be at least forty! He's the worst person in the village. Besides, you're soon to be a fiancée.'

'You know I like a bit of rough,' Hannah giggles as they move along the corridor. Pippa shudders. She likes to think of Jake as rough-around-the-edges, not Grant.

'So, tell me why I haven't heard engagement news from you and Louis. I'm waiting,' Pippa says, pouring Prosecco into two glasses.

'So am I,' Hannah lowers herself dramatically onto Pippa's sofa. 'I'm starting to think it will never come. And since I've found the ring, I've become a mad woman. I'm waiting for signs of it every night. When's he going to do it? Is he going to do it? Last night we went to Pizza Express and I was nervous and jumpy between every course, waiting for him to get the ring out. I nearly had a fit at the end of the meal when he reached for his wallet. If you'd told me a month ago, I would have wanted Louis to propose in a Pizza Express I would have laughed at you.'

'That's insane,' Pippa laughs. 'He will do it, Han. He's probably just waiting for the right time.'

'He didn't tell you when he was planning it, did he?'

'No. And even if he did, I'm sworn to secrecy.'

'We've got nothing planned at the moment. No trips away. No fancy meals. I'm getting fed up.'

'On which fancy outing will my hot boyfriend propose to me with a gorgeous ring? It's a bit of a champagne problem, you have to admit.'

'Maybe,' Hannah says, although she pouts like she hasn't heard a word of what Pippa's said. 'He'd better hurry up.'

Pippa makes a mental note to message Louis to ask how proposal plans are going. He was meant to do it on Hannah's birthday, which has been and gone.

'Before you go running off with Grant, I think you should be patient. I'd love to be in your position.'

'You want a relationship?' Hannah instantly perks up. 'This is news.'

'I don't want a relationship . . . but I might have been on a date recently.'

'You sneaky thing! It's always the quiet ones. I thought you'd taken a vow of celibacy.'

'I'm still in the same position, don't get excited. And nothing's going to happen.'

'Tell me about him. Please!'

Pippa gives Hannah limited details about Jake before taking a big slurp of her Prosecco, feeling the bubbles go to her head. 'It's nothing long term, and the last thing I need now when I should be concentrating on getting my booking system and Pumpkin Cottage marketing on the road, but . . . you should see him, Han.'

'I hope I will. Social media?'

'He's not on it. I couldn't find him on Facebook or Instagram, and he's really not a TikTok kind of guy, unless I'm wrong.'

'So, you've checked. You luuurve him, don't you?'

'He's got a daughter.'

'Urrrgh. You didn't mention that.' Hannah gulps her Prosecco, pouring herself another glass without asking and topping up Pippa's.

They polish off the bottle and open another while Pippa makes food for them, chicken fajitas with home-made guacamole and so many toppings in little bowls they cover the whole kitchen island.

'I'll see you tomorrow, Pippa,' Grant comes through the kitchen. 'Nearly finished now.'

She frowns at him. She usually only knows when Grant's gone by the slam of the back door. He never gives updates. Pippa spots

Hannah wink at him and makes a fake-vomit expression when he leaves.

They eat in between giggles and mouthfuls of Prosecco, and Pippa feels her shoulders ease, the stress of setting up on her own leaving her body. It's been hard doing all this, making so many decisions, meeting so many new faces on her own. Pippa didn't realise how much she needed a night with her best friend. She feels like herself again, in an indefinable way.

'Oh my God, you will be totally overdressed in that,' Pippa says when Hannah comes out of her room, fully made-up in a slinky gold strappy top and black mini skirt. 'I told you to keep it casual.'

'But I didn't think jeans and a jumper,' Hannah says, checking out Pippa's ensemble. 'What's the point of living here if you can't get dressed up? Where's the fun?'

'Have you got anything else?'

'No, so you'll have to change too,' Hannah instructs her. 'Come on, I've seen plenty of your night-out clothes in London.'

Pippa is cajoled into changing into a black dress, but dresses it down with boots and a long green coat. She looks very modest next to Hannah still.

'Euuurgh,' Hannah shrieks as soon as they take a step on to the lane, and she clings to Pippa's arm. 'My heel,' she lifts her ankle to show leaf-mulch hanging off the heel.

'I warned you,' Pippa says, helping her pick it off.

'Remind me why you moved again? I think I just saw a bat.'

'It's refreshing! You don't get that in London.'

'Thank God,' Hannah laughs.

'You'll be able to watch the bats from the new hot tub I'm having installed,' Pippa's so excited at her news, her own stroke of genius. She decides not to tell Hannah about the cockroaches, though. A few weeks ago, she would have been like Hannah, but

Pippa feels she's started to adjust to the countryside. Started to love hearing the rush of the water rather than sirens and traffic. The fresh air through the windows. The falling leaves. She's not full Riverdean yet, but she's moved on from London. Between two worlds. Somewhere between Hannah and Jake.

They laugh at shared memories of nights out while they walk up the lane to The Trout. The Prosecco has definitely gone to Pippa's head.

'Remember in uni when we pretended to be Italian? Those two guys thought we were so exotic,' Hannah laughs, her arm linked in Pippa's.

'Or nuts. Our accents were awful,' she says as they round the corner to The Trout and Pippa spots Jake outside.

'Shit, that's Jake,' she says, grabbing Hannah.

'That's Jake?' she looks, eyes wide. Pippa's heart rate soars. She didn't expect to see him tonight. Didn't tell him she'd be at The Trout. Hannah looks back to Pippa now, a great beaming smile on her face.

'What?' Pippa asks, awkward and self-conscious.

'Okay, now I get why you moved here.'

Chapter Fourteen

Jenny

'Help yourself to more gravy, Grant,' Jenny offers. The man's a Neanderthal, she thinks, as a piece of dumpling slips from his fork. She's made beef stew for him, guessing a man like Grant isn't into exotic food. Jake said he'd be late tonight and Jenny's eyes keep sliding to the clock, wishing he was here. The conversation is drying up quickly. Phil has barely said a word all night and Archie is snoozing in his basket.

Of course, there is an ulterior motive for inviting Grant over. The miserable so-and-so isn't exactly batting off invitations to dinner in Riverdean. When Ruby first left him for another man, people felt sorry for Grant, but his sour demeanour usually meant he wasn't invited back. Still, it's all worth it if she can burst the balloon of Pippa Mason and her new ideas.

If Grant was surprised at her invite, he didn't show it. She had been taking Archie for a walk yesterday when she saw Pippa leaving with another girl. They set off in Pippa's black Audi, arms linked and laughing like hyenas. They certainly wouldn't be back for a long time. Jenny didn't know what came over her, but she seized her chance and walked into the house. Grant was inside so nothing was locked. He was playing Radio 2 loudly and didn't hear a thing.

She knew her way around the house as she had pored over the pictures on Instagram often enough. Jenny stood at the kitchen door taking it all in. Archie stood beside her, his tail wagging. It was smaller than it looked in the photographs and the island dwarfed the room. Breakfast plates with croissant crumbs were stacked on the kitchen counter, along with empty bottles of Prosecco. Pippa Mason obviously didn't care whether her guests saw a messy kitchen and her slovenly ways. Just as Jenny had suspected. She glanced around quickly and picked up a couple of notes pinned to the noticeboard next to the fridge. *Thank you, Pippa. We had a fabulous time and your breakfast was amazing. We're going to tell all our friends about Pumpkin Cottage.* Another read, *What a lovely weekend we spent in Riverdean! Your care and attention made the weekend for us. You're a superstar!* Jenny paled and couldn't face reading any more.

She wandered into the lounge, a cosy snug with a wood burner and a huge, fuchsia-coloured, velvet sofa dominated the room with cushions in rich jewel colours. Books and magazines were spreadeagled over the coffee table with a couple of coffee mugs. Moving back along the corridor, Jenny reached the bedroom. Archie followed dutifully behind her, his silence seeming to collude with Jenny's surreptitious mission. She paused outside Pippa's own room. Even she couldn't justify invading her space, but the guest rooms were surely open to public viewing. Yes, they all looked very fresh and inviting, Jenny had to admit. Three were completed already and Grant was working on the fourth one. Pippa hadn't messed about, that was for sure. Particularly on one room that had to have been extended, she's sure the wall had been knocked down.

Jenny stood at the doorway of the room Grant was in. He was kneeling on the floor, measuring thin planks of wood he was nailing to the wall. His jeans had slid down revealing the top of his buttocks and he was singing 'Hungry Eyes' in a ridiculous *falsetto* voice.

Suddenly, he looked up to catch Jenny watching him. 'Jeez, woman. You shouldn't creep up on people like that. You could give them a heart attack.'

'I did call out,' Jenny said, wide-eyed, 'but the music was too loud for you to hear me.'

'It's not against the law, is it,' he said, obviously smarting from being caught singing.

'I wanted to see you, Grant, as it happens and was going to call at your place.'

Hitching up his trousers, he stood up, nails perched in the corner of his mouth. He took them out and looked at Jenny, waiting for her to elaborate.

'I was wondering if you could do some work on the Lodge for me. I'm thinking of doing some alterations.' Until she said the words out loud, she had no idea her mind had formulated a plan. Perhaps it was seeing the renovations at Pumpkin Cottage. She needed to up her game. 'Jake is just too busy to help and Phil, of course . . .' She hadn't needed to finish the sentence.

'I have a few weeks' work here,' Grant said, already nailing some wood to the wall.

'Do you mind turning the music down for a second,' Jenny pleaded, reaching over herself to turn the volume down. She could barely think. Archie stood by her side, his head tilted as if he too found the music irritating. 'How much work have you got left here?'

'This bedroom will take the rest of the week. Then she wants me to do some clearing in the garden.' He balanced a spirit level on top of the wood he had just nailed. God, he was irritating, Jenny thought. 'Anyways, there's the hot tub to go in. I promised I'd help with that.'

'Hot tub,' Jenny spluttered. 'In Riverdean. I don't think her neighbours will approve of that. Noisy parties in a hot tub!'

'Don't get your knickers in a twist,' he said rudely. 'She's not planning Hugh Hefner-type parties, I shouldn't think. It's just for private use – for her and the guests, she told me.'

Jenny did not like this one bit. 'Look, Grant, I need panelling done in some of the bedrooms, a bit of painting.' She'd got the idea watching *Escape to the Country* the other day. Nicki Chapman was showing someone around a house in Gloucester. It was really effective. Would fit in beautifully with the genteel country look she wanted for Riverside Lodge and Nicki Chapman was positively gushing over it.

'Like I said, I've got at least a couple of weeks' work here.' He leant over and turned the radio up again, dismissing Jenny.

Jenny was not to be defeated. Turning the radio off, she said, 'I would be prepared to pay well, Grant. More than the job would be worth.' She had piqued his interest, she could tell. 'I tell you what. Come around tomorrow night at seven-thirty and you can have some dinner with us and I'll show you what I want done.'

Now, as she watches him dip his bread into the stew, she wonders if this is such a good idea. She has secured a date from him to start. Just as she had thought, the lure of money meant he was prepared to put the work at Pumpkin Cottage on hold until he finished her panelling. It meant that he would be around for a few weeks, though, getting under her feet and her skin!

'I'll go to the builders' merchant in the morning,' Grant says, 'but I'll need an advance.'

'Tell me how much and I'll transfer some money,' Jenny says. 'Will you go over to tell Pippa tomorrow?'

He says something under his breath that Jenny doesn't quite catch. 'She gets easily upset, I'd say,' he goes on. 'The cockroaches saw her screaming like a mad woman.'

'Cockroaches,' Jenny's nose wrinkles in disgust. 'The guests wouldn't like to hear that.'

'They're gone now,' Grant says, sipping his glass of beer.

'Have some more,' Jenny says, getting up and fetching another beer from the fridge. 'Has Pippa had planning permission for all the work she's had done?'

Grant puts down his knife and fork, 'Thank you, Jenny. That was nice.' He tops up his beer, 'She didn't need planning permission.' He belches. 'There's no extension or anything like that. Knocking down that internal wall was a different matter. There's all sorts of building regs to think about.'

Jenny sits forward in her seat, 'And did she sort it all out?'

'Between you and me, she might have skipped a few details.'

Suddenly, the back door opens and Jake enters, bringing a gust of wind with him. 'It's getting rough out there now.' He stops, seeing Grant at the table. Jenny can read him like a book. He's wondering why he's here for food when she's always complaining about him. 'Hello, Grant, mate. What are you up to?'

'Your mother invited me. Wants me to do some work on the bedrooms.'

'I didn't know you were planning any renovations,' Jake says, hanging his coat in the hallway.

Jenny laughs awkwardly. 'Hardly renovations, Jake. Just a bit of decorating.'

There's a tension in the atmosphere when Jake sits down and eats his food. Outside it's pitch-black and Jenny watches their reflection in the kitchen window.

Grant rises from the table. 'I'm gonna make tracks. I'll let you know how much I need as an advance tomorrow, Jenny. You coming to The Trout later, Jake?' Grant asks.

'Maybe,' Jake says.

When he leaves, Jake turns to Jenny. 'These renovations are all a bit sudden, aren't they? What about Dad?'

'What about your father?' They both look to Phil, who's stroking Archie's ears, oblivious to the tension. 'I'm always thinking of your father, Jake, so don't say that to me. It's time those bedrooms were done. I'll be here to keep an eye on everything, make sure there's as little disruption as possible. I don't have that many guests in over the next week or so. Grant can get it all done in that time.'

'Well, it's the first I've heard of this. I'm just surprised, that's all. Besides, I thought Grant has his hands full at the moment with Pumpkin Cottage.'

'It's fine. He'll sort it.' And then to take his mind off it, Jenny says, 'There's apple crumble to finish.' She hates any tension with Jake.

'Thanks, Ma,' he says. 'I can't be bothered to go out tonight. I think I'll just have a cup of tea and watch some telly.'

The river's swell is huge. There's been a high tide and heavy rain. Branches drift down the river, some quite big. As she walks Archie, he pulls on the lead and she slips. Archie bounds forward, the lead trailing behind him and he falls into the river. Jenny screams in panic. No one can hear her in the blustery winds. Then she hears a scream again, and Jenny realises it's a real scream, not from her dream. She sits bolt upright in bed, realising there's an empty space next to her.

'Phil,' she calls. Then she hears the scream again from down the corridor. One of the guest rooms. Oh Gawd, what's happened now? Reaching for her dressing gown from the hook on the door, she hastily ties it around her.

In the hallway, she meets Jake, looking as startled as she is. 'It's your father. He's not in bed. I think he's gone wandering again.'

'It was Room One or Two,' Jake says. He's dressed in his T-shirt and boxer shorts.

Jenny nods, putting the hall light on. 'Get some trousers on.'

Jake joins her in what seems like seconds. When they get to the guest wing, several guests are in the hallway. The Sweeneys from Room One, Colin and Cath Braithwaite from Room Three and an ashen-faced Diana Benson, the old lady staying for two nights whilst she visits her great grandchildren in Ross-on-Wye. Diana is sitting in the chair in the hallway.

'He's in my room,' she gasps. 'Completely naked.'

'I'm so sorry,' Jenny says, embarrassed.

'I'll get him,' Jake says. They emerge a minute or two later. Jake has wrapped his dressing gown around Phil.

'I was going to go swimming,' Phil says, looking confused. 'My mother said I could. But then I was so tired, I had to go back to bed.'

'Come on, Dad,' Jake says. 'That's not your room. I'll take you back to your own bed. Remember Mum told you not to go walkabout without telling her first.'

'The door must have been on the latch,' Diana says. 'I came back later than I thought. I can't have closed it properly. I had such a fright.'

'Can I get you a drink?' Jenny asks her, feeling grateful that only a few guests were disturbed. 'Tea? Something stronger?' She turns to Colin and Cath Braithwaite, the Sweeneys, 'And anyone else, would you like anything? He has dementia, you see. Honestly, he doesn't usually wander in the night. I can only apologise.'

When she's returning to the kitchen, it occurs to Jenny that it's not outdated rooms that's her biggest problem, but keeping Phil away from the guests. A naked night prowler is not good publicity.

Jake is sitting at the kitchen table. 'He's gone back to bed. I've made you a cup of tea.'

'Thanks, love,' Jenny says. 'I was hoping the medication might have settled him by now.'

'Perhaps speak to Maeve. She might have some ideas on how to handle it.'

'Maybe,' Jenny says, bleakly. 'I can't let this happen again. I might have to think about giving it all up, Riverside Lodge.'

'You love the business, Mum,' Jake says.

She nods. Neither of them mentions placing Phil in a care home, although it crosses both their minds.

'The look on that poor woman's face,' Jenny says. They both smile. 'I'm off to bed,' she says. 'I've had enough excitement for one night.'

Chapter Fifteen

Pippa

I stayed at Pumpkin Cottage last Saturday and have two words: never again. Pumpkin Cottage may sound charming but the rooms were cold and small, breakfast was underwhelming, and the icing on the cake was finding a cockroach next to my shoes in the morning! I recommend avoiding Pumpkin Cottage and its extortionate prices – I will certainly be finding somewhere else to stay next time I'm in Riverdean.

Pippa feels a sinking sensation in her chest as she reads the words over coffee. A few guests left this morning, with nothing but kind words of gratitude to Pippa, and one couple even filled two pages of the guestbook with praise. After the daily rush of changing sheets, spraying toilets and restocking tea trays, Pippa should be basking in the glow of satisfied guests and a job well done over coffee. But it seems not everyone has been truthful to her.

She reads over the Tripadvisor review again, the words stinging more this time as they sink in. Extortionate prices. Cold rooms. Which of her guests found a cockroach?! And why would no one mention that to her? None of her recent guests had complained about anything, at least that Pippa can remember. There was that woman last week who ran out of toilet roll, but besides the awkward enquiry for more the next morning, she'd seemed pleased enough. Who the hell has written her such a bad review?

Pippa doesn't know whether to be upset or angry about it. She wishes people would tell her if they are unhappy, rather than writing such a mean and potentially damaging review online. Luckily, most people could see through one bad review on Tripadvisor, but until she has a more positive one in the near future, this one will sit at the top of the page, warning others not to book Pumpkin Cottage. She feels tears sting her eyes. Pippa dealt with guest complaints every day at Mallory's, and was well versed in responding to them, but this feels more personal as it is for her B&B. Her B&B that she's worked so hard for. Her perfect Pumpkin Cottage.

She lets out an exhale, before logging in to Tripadvisor to reply. If there's one thing she's learnt at Mallory's, it's that a dignified and apologetic response never fails to ameliorate bad feelings.

She types, *I'm so sorry to hear your stay at Pumpkin Cottage wasn't up to standard. I work hard to ensure all guests have a comfortable visit, and wish I'd been able to improve yours with a simple tweak of the thermostat or offering breakfast alternatives. Please email* pippamason@pumpkincottagebandb.co.uk *with the name and date of your booking and we can discuss a refund and discounted stay in the future. Best wishes, Pippa.*

There. She rereads and posts the message, hoping it will counteract the negative words. She's purposefully avoided mentioning the cockroach, knowing it's the one aspect she can't help. She'd spent a small fortune on hiring pest control, and had closed the offending room for a week. Is it possible that one has slipped through the cracks? And does that mean there will be more?

Pippa shudders, hoping that isn't the case. Hopefully, they were just a one-off nasty occurrence, like the bad review. She'll chat to

Grant about it. He hasn't been around for a few days, brushing her off with an urgent job he's had to do.

Pippa starts to read it again. *I stayed at Pumpkin Cottage last Saturday* . . .

No one stayed at Pumpkin Cottage last Saturday. It was her night with Hannah, and she'd ensured the B&B rooms were free, partly so no one had to put up with drunken noises in the night as her and Hannah had returned from The Trout, singing tunes from the early noughties. In fact, Hannah had stayed in the Lavender Room that night, as it was the newest one, finished after the cockroaches were exterminated. No one had stayed in the room on a weekend yet. So, who had written this review? A real guest? Or someone hell-bent on bringing her down?

Pippa gets up from the table. She's just being paranoid now. No one in Riverdean is sabotaging her business, although the thought of her unpleasant conversation with the stranger comes to her mind, which is still puzzling Pippa. No. It's just one bad review. One bad review that she desperately needs to shake off.

The doorbell rings and Pippa runs to answer it. At least the excitement will take her mind off it.

'Pippa Mason?' A man in overalls checks.

'That's me,' the logo on the van behind him fills Pippa with joy.

'We have your order for the wood-fired hot tub Salzburg edition,' he says. Pippa smiles. This should boost any loss of bookings. Her B&B's very own hot tub.

She had the idea from *Country Hotels* magazine – the added touch of luxury that a hot tub or sauna could bring. And the views of the river from the rooftop balcony Grant and Joel are building on Pumpkin Cottage are perfect for it. They've reinforced the roof already, but need to install the glass balustrades Pippa has ordered for safety. Add a few fairy lights around the outside and a bar, and her miniature spa will be complete. Pippa is so excited she could burst.

'I'll show you up to the roof. My builder was meant to be installing the balustrades today but he's not here yet,' she explains as she leads the delivery men upstairs from the hallway, but she trails off. She's been so distracted with the review that she hasn't registered Grant is a no-show yet when he promised faithfully he would return for this. rant may be late to work more often not, but he's never gone totally AWOL before.Pippa decides to ring him once the delivery team are set to work and are busy carrying cedar wood panels upstairs.

'Hullo,' even his answer is grumpy, she thinks.

'Are you planning on coming to Pumpkin Cottage today?' She tries to keep the irritation out of her voice, but the emotions of the past hour are too much now. 'The hot tub team are here already.'

'Urrr . . . I've uh . . . I've got another job on today. Last minute thing. An emergency,' he says, detecting the panic in Pippa's voice.

'You didn't tell me,' Pippa says, unable to stay calm.

'No, I . . . didn't have time. I'll be here for a few days, I reckon,' Grant says. 'Owners needed the work doing immediately. I did explain the work at Pumpkin Cottage would be delayed to them, but they didn't mind.'

'I bet they didn't. You didn't explain to me, though,' Pippa says, really getting going now. If she has to be diplomatic to guests and reviewers, she's going to give Grant a piece of her mind. Surely, it's her role to give permission for Grant to take on another job halfway through hers, not the other way around. She's sure whoever these other owners are didn't give a shit about Pumpkin Cottage.

'Like I said, it was a bit of a rushed job, couldn't be helped. It's a small job, just some work on the bedrooms,' Grant says, sounding more sheepish now.

'Bedrooms?' Pippa asks.

'At Riverside Lodge, yeah. Jenny Foster needs them doing urgently.'

'I think it's pretty disgusting you haven't apologised or even warned me about this, Grant. I was prepared for you to miss a couple of days, but this is taking the piss.' Pippa is at the end of her tether now. She really doesn't want to argue with Grant but she's put up with enough from him.

'Mmm, yeah, sorry,' he practically grunts. 'I'd better go. I'll let you know when I'll be back at Riverside . . . uh Pumpkin.'

Unbelievable! Pippa leans back in her chair. She has so much anger, she doesn't know what to do with herself. Bloody Grant! He's been a nightmare from the start. And who do Riverside Lodge think they are demanding, Grant's time like this? No work updating bedrooms is that urgent, surely? It's times like this Pippa needs her mother. If she was alive now, Pippa would be able to call up and rant about her frustrations until it all seemed magically better. She knows she's nearly thirty and should be able to cope with this, but it really seems too much today after the review. Her mother always gave the best advice. She could handle any situation, with equal parts grace and forcefulness. What would she tell Pippa to do? Put up with it and wait for Grant? Or not take this lying down? The latter, definitely the latter.

Why should Pippa just put up with Grant's antics again? Why should she let Riverside Lodge take over the work on Pumpkin Cottage? They may have been around in Riverdean longer than her, but Pippa's going to assert herself – and Pumpkin Cottage – as on the scene to stay.

'Nearly done,' the delivery man tells her as he walks through the kitchen. 'We'll have to come back, though, once the balcony is finished to complete the installation. We can't release the cover or put the water in until it's a certified safe area. It's company protocol, and with no safety rail, it's just not done.'

'I'm guessing there's a cost with coming back.'

'Usually a two-hundred-pound call-out fee,' the man tells her. 'Sorry about that.'

'It's not your fault,' Pippa says. She knows exactly whose fault it is. And she knows exactly who should pay that fee. It's time to pay Grant Campbell, and Riverside Lodge, a visit.

Riverside Lodge holds an elevated position, with superb views of the river. The lodge itself isn't so pretty, though, Pippa thinks. It's like a bland conference centre or doctors' surgery. If she owned it, she would have the windows sprayed a pretty sage colour, maybe with little window boxes dotted along the building. Something to invite guests. Even the slanting font on the 'Welcome to Riverside Lodge' sign looks dated. No wonder the owners want it redecorated, if the outside is anything to go by.

Pippa bolsters herself with a deep breath, before going up to the front door and knocking. She doesn't want to go in all guns blazing, but she feels really mistreated.

After a few seconds, a man comes to the door. He looks immediately to be in his seventies, although is probably younger; there's something about his eyes, Pippa thinks. The cardigan isn't helping.

'Hello,' he says, ushering Pippa in the door. His smile disarms her. 'Are you the new childminder?'

'Uh, no,' Pippa hesitates, off guard now. 'I'm Pippa, I own Pumpkin Cottage.'

He frowns and squints at her. Pippa shifts her weight to her other foot, feeling deeply uncomfortable now.

'Well, we're waiting for the childminder. She's meant to be here at eleven,' he says.

'Phil, what are you doing?' A female voice calls. 'I'm sorry about this.' The owner of the voice catches up and Pippa draws in a surprised breath.

It's her.

The stranger who insulted her the other day. Who said her bookings were a 'novelty, no doubt'. She's the owner of Riverside Lodge. And now it all makes sense.

'Oh,' the woman says as she notices Pippa at the same time. The two women stare at each other for a beat, before she seems to regain herself.

'Phil, why don't you go and sit in the lounge?' She signals for the man to move, which he obeys, before she turns back to Pippa. 'How can I help?' The question is the most patronising thing Pippa has ever heard. How to put so much spite into one question.

'I'm guessing you're the owner of Riverside Lodge,' Pippa hopes she sounds just as insincere.

'Yes, I'm Jenny and the owner of Riverside Lodge,' the woman says without extending a hand.

'And I take it you've had some emergency that requires a builder?'

'Yes.' Where Grant sounded sheepish, Jenny is unflappable.

'Urgent decorations, I heard. I can see why now,' Pippa didn't intend to make catty comments but this woman really has her back up.

'If you've come to complain about Grant delaying your little project at the cottage, then I'm not the person you should be bringing it to. He agreed to work for me fair and square.' Jenny picks some fluff from her jumper.

'I agree,' Pippa says. 'It is Grant I should be speaking to. I'm sure you were very convincing in telling him about this *emergency*.'

'I think you'll find the work was ready to go on Riverside Lodge. I have all plans in place and formally agreed. Maybe something you should think about in future before having any work done.' Jenny shrugs.

What the hell does she mean? The hostility is radiating off this woman and Pippa suddenly wants to be as far away from her as possible. What is she suggesting about plans and formal agreements? Grant told her she didn't need any plans for the Pumpkin Cottage work. She hopes that was correct, but she can't show Jenny she's faltering now.

'You only had to wait a few weeks for Grant to finish if you wanted his help,' Pippa insists.

'And you'll only have to wait a few days,' Jenny says, an insincere smile across her face. Pippa isn't smiling. 'After all, a hot tub is hardly urgent building work. More an indulgence . . . and an eyesore at that.'

'An eyesore like Riverside Lodge, you mean?' Pippa is pleased with her comeback, but reeling at Jenny's attitude. She didn't come here to sling insults at the owner, but to get her builder back. 'Look, sorry, I shouldn't have said that. I don't want to create a rivalry between Riverside Lodge and Pumpkin Cottage.'

Jenny gives her a sceptical eye. 'Well, we'll see in the long run which is more popular. Who can retain their guests. And I think you'll find Riverside Lodge has already been running for fifteen years so I fancy our chances over some twee nonsense.'

'Okay,' Pippa holds her hands up, 'I'm going to go now.' There's no reasoning with Jenny. She's tried to be civil but there's no point. Jenny must feel intimidated by Pumpkin Cottage to act this way.

'Goodbye,' Jenny shuts the door before Pippa's fully out of it. Rude bitch. It dawns on Pippa that it was probably Jenny who wrote her bad review. Pippa resolves to speak to Grant over the phone. She doesn't want another showdown with Riverside Lodge, although she has the feeling that her problems are only just beginning.

Chapter Sixteen

Jenny

Jenny is shaking as she closes the door. What a cheek! Fancy coming to the door of a man who has Alzheimer's like some fishwife to argue over some work she wants done. The confidence and arrogance of the young. That Pippa Mason doesn't look as if she's had a day's worry in her whole life. She was the one to set up a rival business in Riverdean. What did she expect? For goodness' sake, all she wants is some bloody hot tub installed. How tacky! Jenny quells the niggly feeling that she did persuade Grant to abandon the work at Pumpkin Cottage, but it is only temporary, after all, and Riverside Lodge can't afford to lose customers as they head into the autumn and winter, when things naturally slow down.

When Jenny re-enters the kitchen, Phil is fidgeting in his chair. He always seems to pick up when there's any conflict.

'Fancy a cuppa, Phil?' she asks.

'When is she starting?'

'When is who starting?'

'The childminder, of course? Jake'll be in school soon. He can't look after himself. What are you thinking, woman?'

'Jake is all grown up now. He doesn't need a childminder, silly.' Seeing his scowl, Jenny realises that distraction is the only way forward, otherwise he'll get all frustrated, then angry. 'Will you give me a hand folding the laundry, darling? I've got to clear Room Three for Grant to start decorating today and I just haven't had time.' Before he can answer, Jenny puts the basket in front of him. 'Find the matching socks and fold them together. It will be a great help.' Maeve had told Jenny that simple tasks like this would make him feel useful and help with dexterity. He seems to be capable of less with every passing day. He's grown bored of the jigsaws he loved until recently, finding them too difficult to do and getting frustrated.

'Alexa, play Michael Bublé songs,' Jenny says. She needs to fill the house with music for her own sanity. 'Haven't Met You Yet' fills the kitchen. In moments like this, she can imagine everything is just fine and it's a normal day for her and Phil. They danced to this song at a wedding a few years ago over in Hereford. The reception was in a hotel by the river and fairy lights danced in the water. She was lightheaded with drinking champagne and as soon as the song came on, Phil stood up and grabbed her hand leading her to the dance floor.

'I've had too much to drink,' Jenny had giggled, 'and my feet are killing me.'

Phil laughed, pulling her to him. He was wearing his Dior aftershave, its masculine, woody scent filling her nostrils. She lay her head on his shoulder and he stroked her hair. It was just perfect.

If she could only go back . . . but what could she do? She couldn't stop what was happening. She couldn't stop time. In the background, fate had its plans for them. Was the decline happening then? He lost the keys that night and Jenny was fuming. Did it start then? Or was it later when he missed a meeting with those parents at school? He was teased mercilessly about that. Forgetting the name of George, his best man, made Jenny feel uneasy. Then there was that day he parked in the multistorey and he phoned Jenny distressed, telling her he couldn't remember where the car was parked. It still makes Jenny feel sick.

Phil is singing the words now, tapping his foot. Jenny smiles. Her old Phil is still in there somewhere. Unreachable at times, but still there.

'Hello, anyone in?' an impatient voice calls out.

Jenny goes to the front door. 'Sorry, Grant, I couldn't hear you. We were playing music in the kitchen. I've told you the back entrance is easier. It's what everyone uses.' The man really is insufferable at times.

He stands in the doorway, wearing his jeans, paint-spattered boots, and a T-shirt he's worn for the last three days.

Jenny catches a whiff of body odour and wrinkles her nose. 'I was hoping you might start on Room Three today after you finish Room Two. It won't take me long to clear.'

'Hmm, the thing is, I can only stay an hour.'

'Why on earth?'

'Well, Pippa Mason called to see me. She was saying all sorts about me abandoning her in the middle of the job.'

'Come on, Grant, you know I agreed to pay you over the odds for this job if you could get it done quickly.'

Grant pauses and inhales his cigarette. Jenny is about to say something about his not smoking but decides to let it go. She doesn't want to poke the bear.

'She told me the hot tub guys are back today and if I don't fix the safety rail, they're gonna charge her two hundred quid.' He stops to inhale again, 'I mean, if you're willing to pay it, I'd carry on here.'

Jenny deigns not to answer. 'Go and get the job done and come back tomorrow.'

'Well, the thing is, I promised to help the brother-in-law move house tomorrow. I'll be back the day after that.'

'Okay, okay, but just remember you promised to finish the work in ten days and that's why I agreed on the higher price.'

Grant turns on his heels and Jenny slams the door. Unbelievable! Fuck. She doesn't normally swear but Grant is enough to make the Pope swear. If only there was someone else she could call on to do some work for her. Jake has too much on his plate.

'Careful, you don't want to drop all that on the floor,' Jenny warns.

'I won't, Nanny,' Lola says, gazing up at her with her big, chocolate-brown eyes.

The table is covered with thick blobs of wet icing sugar and globules of raspberry jam. Taylor Swift is singing 'Shake it Off' and Jenny wiggles her bottom, making Lola giggle. Phil is snoozing in his armchair in the conservatory, wanting to be part of the action but always on the periphery, Archie, his faithful companion, beside him in his basket.

'Alexa, play "The Wheels on the Bus",' Lola says in a loud voice.

'Ooh, you naughty madam!' Jenny scolds, laughing. 'You'll wake Gramps. Come on, let's fill these with jam.'

Seeing a recent review of Pumpkin Cottage and the enthusiastic reception to Pippa's home-made shortbread has given Jenny food for thought. She often bakes and should try making personal touches like this the norm at the Lodge. Up her game a little. It's not copying exactly and making jammy star biscuits is more about pleasing Lola than her guests, but it can't do any harm, especially when she tells the three couples staying tonight that her granddaughter made them. How cute!

Having Lola over always makes Jenny happy. You can't be down in the dumps when a five-year-old is around, especially when she's in high excitement at staying over and Jenny's promise of setting a den in her bedroom.

'Will you come in the tent, Nanny?'

'Course I will. We'll get the torch and put all the lights out.'

Lola nods, but her wide eyes betray her fear.

'If that's too scary, perhaps we'll leave the lights on, and we can pretend we're camping.' Jenny pauses to squint at the biscuits. 'Oh dear, I think this one needs more jam. What do you think, Lols?'

'Will Daddy come in the tent, Nanny?' Lola asks, leaning her elbows on the table, losing interest in filling the biscuits, Jenny suspects.

'Daddy is going out tonight, but he'll be back later and he'll be with you all day tomorrow.' They hear a clatter outside. 'Talk of the devil. That'll be Daddy now.'

'Well, look who's here. It's Lola Cola,' Jake says, entering the kitchen.

'Daddy!' Lola squeals in delight and he reaches down and swings her around the kitchen.

'What are you two up to, then?'

'Making jammy stars,' Lola giggles, as Jake pretends to bite her stomach.

'I might eat them all up.'

'You can't, Daddy. Nanny and me are having some in the tent tonight.'

Jake catches her eye, 'Thanks for babysitting, Mum. Let me get out of this jacket and boots, Lola.'

'Anytime. I love having Lola, you know that. Are you off to The Trout tonight?' Jenny asks. Jake tends to stay at home when it's the weekend he has Lola.

'Might go over to Greenbrook tonight. There's a band on in The Swan.'

'Who's going, then?'

'Just some of the lads. Nobody you'd know,' he says.

Jenny wants to probe a bit more, but she knows how niggled he gets when she questions him and he is twenty-eight, after all.

'I'm going to get showered and changed.' He turns to Lola, 'Have you brought your wellies? I'm not going out for a while yet and we can splash in some of the puddles. We'll take Archie with us.'

'Yay!' Lola yells.

'Come on, let's finish these biccies,' Jenny says, 'and you can have one with some milk.'

Helping Lola to stand on the chair, Jenny asks, 'Are you looking forward to half-term next week? Has Mummy got any plans?'

'We're going to France with Ethan and Riley,' she says. 'For a whole week.'

'Wow! That's exciting.' Jenny suddenly feels uneasy. 'So, what are you going to do out there?'

'We are going to the beach if it's not too cold, Mummy says. And we're going to look at my new school.'

'Oh, I see, your new school. Does that mean you will be living in France?'

'Yes, silly. Mummy says I will have to learn to speak French so I can speak to the other children.'

Jenny wonders if Jake is aware of how far Amber has taken her plans. It sounds as if it's a done deal and not just toying with the possibility of moving to France. Jenny feels sick and she knows Jake will be heartbroken.

'Do you want to move to France?' Jenny asks.

Lola nods, and licks some jam off her fingers. 'Mummy says I might have to share a room with Riley.'

'Well, you like her, don't you?' Jenny pauses, 'Will you miss

Daddy?' She's not sure she should ask this and wonders how Amber has presented this to her.

'Mummy says Daddy can still come to see me. And you can, Nanny. You can stay with us.'

Jenny doesn't contradict her but can't imagine they will be very welcome in that house in France. It seems so unfair to her. Jake dotes on Lola. How can Amber take her away from him? When you have children, you are inextricably linked to that person, whatever happens in your relationship. Although not everyone felt like that, Jake's own father being a case in point. She'll sound Jake out about this move when she has a chance.

Lola is eating her biscuit when Jake comes into the kitchen. He whips a jammy star from the plate on the table.

'Come on, Lola Cola. I don't have long tonight. Let's get your Wellies on.'

'I've made a chicken casserole. Will you be eating some before you go out?'

'I might have a bite to eat later,' Jake says.

Jenny watches them go across the back lawn, hand in hand, Lola in her pink raincoat and lilac Wellies. She can't help worrying about him. He might be an adult, but she can't stop herself. It melts her heart seeing Jake and Lola together. What with Phil and his dementia, the stress of the business and now the prospect of hardly seeing Lola, the boy has got so much on his shoulders.

Jenny busies herself tidying up and seeing to the casserole. She wraps the biscuits in separate parcels of cellophane and ribbon. They look a bit rustic, but it's a nice thought. She'll put them in the rooms later. Why hasn't she done this for every guest? She loves baking and it's much better than those pairs of factory-wrapped Bourbons or Custard Creams. She has always perhaps taken it for granted. The location of Riverside Lodge, the magical views of the swirling River Wye and the valley dotted with sheep in Greenbrook opposite always seem to be enough of a draw for people in Jenny's mind. Later, when Lola's in bed, she decides she'll Google ideas for B&Bs. Think outside the box a bit. Rise to the challenge.

Later, Lola is in her little checked pyjamas with her hair newly washed sitting next to Jenny on the sofa, sucking her thumb.

'Are you sure you don't want to put the tent up tomorrow instead of tonight?' she asks the sleepy girl.

Lola shakes her head. She's watching *Encanto*, her current favourite Disney film. Phil is in the armchair, images reflected in his glasses, but Jenny has no idea if he's watching it.

'Right then, I'm off,' Jake says, entering the lounge.

Lola pulls her thumb from her mouth and reaches for a hug from her father.

'Hmm, you smell nice? Is that a new aftershave?' Jenny asks.

Jake deftly avoids answering. 'I shouldn't be too late tonight. We're off to the Butterfly Zoo tomorrow.'

'You're looking nice, Jake. Very smart. Are you sure it's just the boys you're out with?'

Flashing her a grin, he says, 'Now, wouldn't you like to know.'

Jenny hopes he does meet a nice girl. He deserves some happiness. She dreads the chat with him tomorrow about Lola and this move to France.

'Right, then, Lola, let's see about this tent, shall we?' Jenny asks, turning to her granddaughter.

Chapter Seventeen

Pippa

Pippa spies Jake as he approaches the door to Pumpkin Cottage. Even through frosted glass he looks yummy, she thinks, with his golden colouring.

'You look stunning,' he says when she answers the door.

'This swanky meal had better live up to expectations,' she says. 'I don't get my little black dress out for just anything,' *or anyone,* Pippa finishes in her head.

'Well, I appreciate it.'

Pippa feels the heat of Jake's gaze on her as she puts on her camel Borg jacket.

'You look good, too,' she says, although it is an understatement. Jake is a head-turner. He looks like he'd fit in on a red carpet as well as he does with the Riverdean tree-scape.

'You should have seen me an hour ago. Lola forced me to wear pink sparkly hair clips with her for our walk. I've got to be honest, I didn't hate it.'

Pippa feigns laughter although inside she feels horror on seeing Jake's car. The green Jeep is equally as mud-spattered inside as it is on the outside, no doubt permanently soaked from outdoor trips and transporting Archie around. He notices her hesitate before she gets in.

'Sorry, I didn't get a chance to clean it.' He hops into the driver's side.

'Uh, it's okay,' Pippa says, although she really doesn't want to get in.

'Hang on a second,' Jake says, getting out. She watches him fetch a blanket from the boot, before spreading it over the passenger seat for her. 'I should have warned you.'

'It's fine, I don't want to make a fuss.' Pippa places herself gingerly on the blanket, making sure no more of her clothes touch the car's interior than absolutely necessary. Thank God she brought her dainty clutch instead of her usual bulky handbag. Pippa thinks it must be the first time anyone has ever worn heels in this car, but then she remembers the gorgeous Amber, equally honey-coloured as Jake and perfectly groomed. She wonders if Amber would have flinched like this getting in Jake's car. No, she probably suited the outdoorsy lifestyle as well as looking like she'd stepped off the pages of a magazine. Before Pippa can feel too down about it, she remembers that Jake and Amber split up for a reason. She should enjoy spending this time with him. Especially once she's out of the grubby car.

'I'm guessing you're not used to transporting muddy wetsuits and life jackets in the Audi,' Jake says.

'Funnily enough it's more cakes and bakes I'm transporting at the moment,' Pippa says. 'It turns out Petro doesn't just make the best bread outside of the Ukraine, but his honey cakes are to die for. They're going down a storm with my guests – some have started putting in orders to take home. A nice profit for Petro and his family.'

'That's very kind of you,' Jake says as he shifts down a gear to get the car up the little hill out of Riverdean.

'It's a win-win for me,' Pippa smiles. 'And I need all the wins I can get at the moment. I've had the most awful week.'

'Right?' Jake asks, keeping his eyes on the road.

'You won't believe this,' Pippa begins to tell Jake the story of Grant defecting to Riverside Lodge. 'The first I heard of him leaving was when I had a team of hot tub deliverymen demanding two hundred quid to come back when the work was done! And that Jenny at Riverside Lodge – she was unbelievable! The woman must be threatened by Pumpkin Cottage, maybe because she finally has some competition in town and realises customers might want something more homely than the office block that is Riverside Lodge. She was vile to me,' Pippa shudders at the memory. 'I tried to call a truce but she wasn't having any of it. I've got a real bad feeling about her.' Pippa shakes her head, before noticing that Jake has been very quiet throughout her rant as he drives. Maybe he knows Jenny, or maybe he's one of those people that doesn't like to gossip about others. He looks very thoughtful.

'Errr . . . I should probably tell you—'

'Sorry,' she cuts him off. 'I just needed to get that off my chest. It's been a rough few days. I shouldn't moan.' She hopes she hasn't put him off with her monologue.

'Did you say hot tub?' Jake asks.

'I should have known that's all you'd hear from that,' she says, looking at his face. His expression changes from unreadable to that cheeky smile that turns her insides to mush.

'Is this hot tub for guests only?'

'Until it reaches the right temperature, it's for no one,' Pippa teases. 'But I might just test it myself next week, to make sure it's safe for guests. A secluded rooftop, glass of bubbly, view of the stars.'

'I think I could help, you know, review the experience,' Jake grins. 'Give you an unbiased view from a guest's perspective.'

'How helpful of you,' Pippa jokes. The thought of having Jake alongside her in a hot tub, wearing shorts, or even less, makes her skin tingle. All kinds of images come to mind, him kissing her neck, slowly pulling at the string on her bikini top. It suddenly feels a whole lot warmer and more comfortable in the car, all thoughts of Jenny gone. That would be one way to christen the hot tub.

'We're here,' Jake pulls up outside Barn 11, the closest thing the Wye Valley has to a Michelin star. Pippa has wanted to visit since her move, after reading great things about it online. She can justify another date with Jake as trying the local restaurants to recommend to guests. Barn 11 is in a town just a little way up the river from Riverdean, bigger and more popular with tourists. Pippa often hears guests talking about the independent trinket shops and cute cobbled streets.

'Do you come here much?'

'They have a great shop for fishing supplies,' he smirks. 'Probably not your thing, though.'

'Never assume,' Pippa says, again wondering if she and Jake would ever really work. They are polar opposites but those cobalt blue eyes of his make her think likes and dislikes are irrelevant.

'Welcome to Barn 11.' A waiter ushers them inside the low-lit, polished wood building. 'Would you like a drinks menu? Or we recommend the wine carousel if you're trying our three-course tasting menu today?'

'Wine carousel?' Jake raises his eyebrows at Pippa.

'I told you . . . high expectations.'

'I feel like we have to whisper,' Jake says, as they sit at the table. The dining room is indeed very quiet, the other diners speaking in hushed tones.

'And have intelligent conversation only,' Pippa nods.

'I imagine this is standard for London?'

'Well, I hardly had the time off in London to enjoy fancy

restaurants,' Pippa says, remembering the days she spent slogging away at Mallory's, the occasional meals out with Hannah in between. She'd worked hard after her promotion in the hotel, and even more so after her mother died, wanting something to fill the empty space in her days and heart. 'It used to drive my ex crazy.' She gulps. It's the first time she's mentioned her ex to Jake.

'He sounds like a lovely guy,' Jake says sarcastically.

'The best,' Pippa shrugs. 'Practically cheating on a girl a month after her mother dies.'

'My God, I was joking before but that's a real dickhead move. I'm sorry that happened to you.'

'It's okay,' Pippa smiles, even though it's not. 'If I'm honest, I was still grieving my mother so much, his wandering eyes didn't really make a dent in it. And I wasn't that into Ben, it was more just ease . . . it was easier to stay with him all those years than realise we never really suited.' Pippa hopes that isn't true with her and Jake. If they're not meant to be, then she doesn't want to waste time with him, time that she should be spending on her business, on finding out more about her mother's past.

'What was he like?'

'The total opposite to you. Tall, dark, handsome . . . of course, I'm joking. No, he was too into his looks, the gym, hanging out with his idiotic friends. He probably did me a favour in the end.' He was the opposite of Pippa, but also the opposite of Jake. Maybe she has more in common with Jake than she thinks.

'I was going to say it sounds like he's done me a favour, sending you here,' Jake smiles. They hold each other's eye contact for a few seconds before Pippa looks away. She could so easily fall for Jake. Too easily, it would be dangerous.

'The wine carousel.' The waiter perches a little wooden tray of wine glasses in front of them, numbered one to three. 'Number one is the Châteauneuf-du-Pape, which pairs with your starters of venison parfait, with a mushroom duxelle, pickled mushrooms, and a fig and turnip emulsion.' Two plates are placed between them.

'Well, this looks beautiful,' Pippa says.

'Too beautiful,' Jake agrees, 'although I'm slightly disappointed the wines didn't come on an actual carousel.'

'Vintage horses and fairground music?'

'Exactly,' Jake picks up his cutlery. Pippa tries to savour the rich umami flavours of her dish, although the word 'dish' is generous.

'I was kind of hoping it would be heartier,' Jake finishes. 'I think I ate that in two bites.'

Pippa giggles. 'It was a bit pretentious,' she concedes.

'Give me a craft ale and pie at The Trout any day.'

'Jake,' she chides. 'This wine is going down well.'

'Maybe that's the plan, get you so drunk you don't notice how underfed you are.'

'And overcharged,' Pippa adds. They both laugh.

'Would you like another glass?' The waiter asks, noticing they have finished.

'Yes please,' Jake said. 'It looks like it's a taxi back tonight.'

They clink glasses together when they arrive. 'I'm meant to be up early for the Butterfly Zoo tomorrow.'

'Good luck with that,' Pippa says, already dreading tomorrow's hangover. 'Lola seems to adore spending time with you.'

'I hope so,' Jake smiles a warm smile that makes Pippa like him even more.

'You must be a good father.' Something darkens in his expression then.

'Maybe. It seems it's not enough to keep Amber and Lola in the UK, though. She's playing it down, but I've got a gut feeling this move is all but decided.'

'That's going to be so hard for you when they move. France isn't that far, though,' Pippa says. She wants to say that it's been a while since Jake lived with Amber and Lola, but that would obviously be insensitive. France may not be far, but it's a whole lot further than Cardiff. Eurostar or not.

'True, and I will travel back and forth as much as I can. I just hope Lola doesn't forget that I'm her dad. It's going to be very cosy for them, living with Riley and Ethan. I'll just be someone that dips in and out of her life.'

'I think those are natural worries to have. But your relationship with Lola will be what you make it. I bet she will adore those visits from you, they'll be precious.' Pippa feels the wine bolstering her confidence, her ability to open up. 'As a child I longed to know my dad. I used to be so jealous of my friends, even the ones whose parents split up and they only saw their dads occasionally. Your love is all that matters.'

'That's kind of you to say,' Jake sighs and runs a hand through his sandy hair. 'I guess we'll settle into a rhythm in time.'

'It won't be easy for you. Or Lola.'

'I just feel so annoyed at Amber for taking her away from me. Not just me, but my parents too, Lola's grandparents.'

'You haven't told me much about your parents?' Pippa prompts. 'Are they still working?'

Jake seems to hesitate then. She watches as he shifts in his chair, takes a sip of wine, then another. 'My dad's retired,' he finally says. 'And my mum is . . . well . . .'

'Do you get on with them?' Pippa asks, before he's finished.

'Mostly. They can be infuriating, though, especially as I'm living with them. My mum treats me like a child. She gets so easily stressed over the smallest of things. It's hard for her looking after my dad with his Alzheimer's.'

'Families are never straightforward. That's one thing I've learnt,' Pippa says.

'Cheers to that.'

'Your second course.' The waiter produces two plates with a flourish.

'Okay this might be the booze talking, but I'm absolutely starving,' Jake says, putting his arm around Pippa as they leave the restaurant. The warmth of his body feels delicious next to hers.

'Agreed,' Pippa says. She has a feeling she will regret this in the morning, but decides to go for it anyway, 'Would it be a terrible idea to go for a kebab tonight?'

'Oh, Pippa Mason,' Jakes breathes. 'You are a woman after my heart. I nearly cried when I saw that main.'

'The parcel of beef? I think parcel was overselling it.' Pippa remembers earlier, getting in the car, how dainty and prissy she'd felt in her heels and pristine black dress. Now she wants nothing more than greasy food and a beer.

'Kebab and a beer it is,' Jake says. 'Then taxi.'

'Then wine at mine,' Pippa asserts. She feels Jake's eyes on her as they walk along, feels his pace slowing down. 'What?' she asks.

'I just really want to kiss you now.'

'That's the booze talking.' She laughs it off.

'It's not,' Jake says, and before Pippa knows what's hit her, he's kissing her, holding her head in both his hands. She kisses him back, feeling every inch of him against her, hard in places and smooth in others. Kissing Ben was never like this. In fact, kissing anyone has never felt this good before, this right. She sighs against him. This may not have been part of the plan in moving to Riverdean at all, but Pippa is absolutely powerless to stop it.

Chapter Eighteen

Jenny

'Goodness, Mum. What on earth are you doing sitting here in the dark?'

'I couldn't sleep. You're late. It's gone three o'clock. Where have you been?' Jenny shakes her head. 'Sorry, don't answer that. You're twenty-eight years old.' She puts the lamp on. 'I'm just nosy and I worry about you. I hope she's nice,' she smiles.

Jake flops down in the armchair. 'What's keeping you awake, then, Mum? Anything wrong?'

'Nothing particular. Well, other than your father. He seems to be getting worse and I don't know how much longer I'll be able to cope.' She closes her eyes. 'I don't want to burden you with this. You've got enough going on.'

'But he's my dad and I want to help.'

'I know.' Jenny smiles in the dark. If they were real father and son, could they be any closer? 'Realistically, I wonder how long I can keep the Lodge running. That business with wandering around the rooms naked. Whatever next? Then there's this new B&B Pumpkin Cottage run by that young girl Pippa Mason.'

'Yes, but that's no threat to the Lodge, surely? It's only a few rooms she has.'

'She called round here the other day shouting at me, saying I stole Grant from her. And she had the cheek to call this place an eyesore. I was fuming, to be honest.'

'Had he finished the work at Pumpkin Cottage?' Jake asks.

'How should I know? I think he was putting some hot tub in for her. Hardly an urgent job.'

'Still, Mum, it must be annoying if he'd promised her.'

'And whose side are you on?'

'I'm just saying. Grant is loyal to no one if there's money in it.'

She sighs. 'You're right. It's just Pumpkin Cottage has been having these great reviews and I just don't need another business, a complication, with your father as he is.'

'You're worrying too much. You never used to bother with reviews. Just keep doing what you've always done. You've got your regular customers. Things always quieten down at this time.' Jake stands up, 'Anyway, I'm off to bed. You look tired, Mum. You'll be shattered in the morning if you don't get back to bed soon. Have you got many in tonight?'

'Two couples, that's all.' Jenny yawns. 'I feel wide awake. I'll have a read for ten minutes and then go back to bed. Night, love.'

Jenny gazes at her reflection in the bathroom mirror of Room Four. That indentation in the middle of her forehead seems to have just appeared overnight and she has proper bags under her eyes. She's looking old, a lot older than her fifty years. The couple in this room, the Bagshaws from Leicester, are celebrating their anniversary. Jenny watched them holding hands as they left the Lodge after breakfast. She couldn't help but feel a bit envious of them. Linda Bagshaw must be around Jenny's age. Looks a lot more youthful, Jenny decides. Definitely had work done. Lip fillers, Botox. Jenny wonders if she should look into it. Might be somewhere in Ross or Hereford. Can she justify the expense?

Sleepless nights don't help. Maeve mentioned in her last visit that there was a day-care centre that offers respite once a week. She even spoke about volunteer sitters who come to your home. Jenny's not sure how Phil will take to a stranger sitting with him, but they visit when the carer is there for a while until the patient gets used to them.

Jenny's finding it hard to concentrate today. It's Abi's day off but there are only the two rooms to do. She empties the bathroom wastepaper basket into a black bag and then decides to tackle the dressing table. The Bagshaws are with them for the whole weekend and Jenny's lip curls at the state of the room. There's a bright red lipstick without its top, a grubby make-up bag. Siren-red, the lipstick's called. Jenny smudges some on her hand. Decides it's a bit too out there for her. She wipes the mirror and puts fresh coffee pods and teabags on the tray. Spick and span again.

Unlocking the door of Room Five, Jenny is suddenly stopped in her tracks as an ear-splitting scream fills the building. It takes her two seconds to realise it's the fire alarm. Oh my God! Oh my God! She rushes through the corridor and pushes the door into the main building.

Plumes of smoke are billowing from the kitchen. Where's Phil? 'Phil! Phil! Where are you?'

In the kitchen, she sees a pan on fire, bright orange flames spilling onto the hob. Hardly thinking, she runs the water and grabs a towel, before throwing it onto the pan. It dampens the flames, but they're not completely out. Seizing another towel, she soaks it and this time the fire is put out. It's only then she realises she should have used the fire extinguisher in the hallway.

Jenny collapses into a chair, her heart beating in her chest and her hands shaking. Opening the back and hall door, the smoke alarm finally stops. Tears spill down her face as she surveys the carnage. The wall behind the cooker is blackened with smoke and the hob is ruined. The units next to the cooker have begun to buckle in the heat.

In the living room, Jenny sees Phil in his armchair, looking at the television.

Jenny feels a mixture of relief and anger. 'Phil, what have you done? What the fuck have you done?' she yells. 'You could have killed us both!'

He looks at her, dazed, confused.

She sits next to him. 'What was in the pan? What were you cooking?' Her anger suddenly leaves her.

'I made some chips,' he says.

'I told you not to cook anything. It's not safe. You've just had breakfast.' She takes his hand, 'Oh, Phil, what are we going to do? What are we going to do?'

'Hello! Hello! Is everything okay?'

George, the hand-ferryman, is standing at the door.

'Come in, George. Yes, everything's fine now. I'm afraid Phil was cooking some chips and forgot about them. I was cleaning the bedrooms.'

George stands at the kitchen door, 'Oh, dear. I was just passing and could hear the commotion. It's quite a mess. At least you're both safe, that's the main thing.'

'Yes,' Jenny agrees, but she can't help feeling swamped, miserable with the hopelessness of it all.

'Let me make you both a cuppa.'

'That's kind of you,' Jenny says.

'It will be covered by insurance, no doubt. Have you called Jake yet?'

Jenny walks into the kitchen, her nose wrinkling at the smell.

'I'll call him in a bit. There's nothing he can really do here. The damage is done.'

George takes the tea into the living room for Phil and then hands Jenny her cup at the kitchen table. 'There's sugar in it,' he warns. 'For the shock.'

'Thanks, George. Look at him. He's none the wiser,' Jenny says, nodding to Phil.

'It must be so tough for you,' George sympathises. 'My mother died of Alzheimer's ten years ago. Bloody cruel disease. We kept her at home as long as we could. She used to go wandering. We were all terrified that she'd fall in the river.'

'I had no idea, George.'

'It's not something people talk about. There's much more awareness about it now, though. My father died years before, and my sister took the brunt of it. You need to accept as much help as you can, Jenny. You can't take this on your own.'

'I'll have to make a list of what I need to do. I'll ring the insurance first. Luckily, I've only got two sets of guests tonight. The cooker's ruined, though.'

'I can lend you a camping stove for breakfast tomorrow, if that's any help.'

'You are kind, George.'

'Like I said, never be too proud to accept help.'

'Oh, poor you,' says Louise. 'Mark has been a real liability in the house. One time he decided to paint the living room. I came home to find my sofa and carpets splashed with blue paint. I could have cried. I did cry,' she says, wide-eyed.

It's the evening for meeting the Wye Valley Choristers and it's just what Jenny needs. Even Phil has come round to the idea and enjoys the singing. Louise is one of the few people who seems to understand what it's like to live with someone with early onset dementia. The loneliness, the frustration, the sadness of it all.

'I was bloody livid,' Jenny says, 'and I shouted at him. Really swore at him. I feel so guilty.'

Louise tuts. 'You're not a robot or a saint. Trust me, everyone who cares for someone with dementia loses their tether regularly.'

'Come on, people,' Angie says to the choir. She has her back to the carers and Jenny watches her bottom jiggle, her voluminous skirt pulled tightly over her wide hips. 'One more time before we finish. From the third verse and this time with some enthusiasm.' The choir launch into 'Back For Good'.

'I love this one,' Louise says. 'I saw Take That at Wembley a few years ago. We got so drunk afterwards. Mark was running down the hotel corridor in his underpants. We felt like teenagers again.' She shakes her head, 'Fucking dementia. I hate what it's done to Mark. Every day I lose a bit of him.'

Jenny glances at Mark. He's silver-haired with bright blue eyes but his face is blank. That same look Phil has. Phil tonight is singing with abandon. It's good for him this choir, she thinks. Some colour in a world of black and white. It's good for her too.

'Do you think about the future?' Jenny asks her.

'I try not to. It doesn't do any good. I concentrate on now, today. Little moments that are precious. Sometimes he comes back to me. He brought me flowers from the garden the other day. Dahlias and begonias.' She sighs, 'It was precious.'

'After the fire, it's made me realise that I will have to look at winding down the business. I'll have to sell up and downsize.'

'Don't make any hasty decisions and speak to your Admiral Nurse. There are lots of aids and support to help. You'll know when the time is right.'

'And one more time!' Angie shouts from the front, launching into the chorus again.

'And in the meantime, take as many breaks as you can. See about respite care. The day centre in town.'

Applause explodes as the choir finishes their song.

'Why don't you and Phil come over for supper after choir sometime? The two of them are used to each other by now. It'll be nice for us to have a chat.'

'I'd like that,' Jenny says. 'It all depends what he's like on the day.'

'I know,' Louise nods.

'Right, if our choristers could all sit down for a moment. I have some exciting news for you.'

Jenny glances at Louise, 'Any idea?'

'Not a clue.'

'Jude, come and join me a moment,' Angie says. As he stands next to her, Jenny thinks how odd they look together, Jude thin and lanky and Angie, just over five foot and voluptuous. Her pink plastic earrings bob up and down as she speaks. Phil settles down next to Jenny and she squeezes his hand.

'Jude and I have managed to get us a gig over Christmas. The cathedral in Hereford has agreed for us to sing Christmas carols and some more modern songs on the seventeenth of December. In the next few weeks, I'll be listening carefully as we'll need some strong soloists.'

There's silence in the hall as everyone takes in the news. Jenny squeezes Phil's hand again.

'That's not all. The BBC might potentially be coming to film us that night as part of a new documentary. This is huge!' Angie says, smiling broadly. 'I know by your silence that it's a lot to take in, but this is good. This is great news! A real chance to show off what you can do.' Jude nods next to her.

Jenny doesn't know what to think. Phil doesn't like surprises and Louise seems equally ambivalent about the news.

'Anyway, take the lyrics with you tonight and practise over the week. "Back for Good" is one of the songs I'm hoping you'll sing. This will be a chance for you all to show off your skills,' she repeats.

Angie's voice is still going as Jenny and Phil, Louise and Mark head to the car park. 'This is a fantastic opportunity,' they can hear her say.

'I want what she's on,' says Jenny. 'Hereford Cathedral. Fair play, she's doing her best. I wonder how it will go.'

'Impossible to say. Mark loves coming here most times. On bad days, though, he's stubborn as hell and might just refuse to sing. He detests change.'

'Here's the car,' Jenny says, stopping at their battered grey Toyota Yaris. No one in Riverdean has fancy cars, not on those roads, she thinks, seeing Louise and Mark stop at their sleek Audi A3. Although Pippa Mason drives an Audi. No sense, that one.

'See you next week,' Louise shouts. 'Have a good one.'

'Well, singing in the cathedral, Phil. Wonders never cease,' Jenny says, starting up the car. 'Let's get home. The new cooker's arriving first thing in the morning, thankfully.' Jake painted the kitchen yesterday and it'll look as good as new. Jenny hopes she has a good sleep tonight.

Chapter Nineteen

Pippa

Pippa is relieved to get out of the house. She loves these autumnal days, when the sky is cloudless and endlessly blue and a carpet of tawny leaves skirt the river, which gushes below. This technicolour world is such a contrast to life in London. She barely had time for the gym and when she did, regimented lines of lycra-clad people pounded the running machines in front and behind her. She caught glimpses of a milky sky between the shoulders of runners, her landscape just acres of metal and glass. Here in Riverdean, her workouts are brisk walks on chilly October afternoons, which leave her face glowing and ruddy. The Maple Room, the last one at Pumpkin Cottage, is finished. She's spent the morning putting final touches to the room, with chenille throws and cushions in beiges, creams and taupes.

Her mind keeps returning to Jake and she touches her lips, thinking of the heat of that kiss on Saturday, which seemed to promise so much more.

She passes Riverside Lodge above her. It really is a rather ugly building, with its tired, mustard-coloured facade and steel window frames. It's in dire need of a facelift and lacks the cuteness and quirkiness of Pumpkin Cottage. She concedes the views must be lovely from its elevated position but that's all it's got going for it. Jenny Foster could do so much with the place if she invested more time and money. Shielding her eyes, Pippa looks up to see a couple knocking at the front door of Riverside Lodge. They look frustrated in an exaggerated way, the man looking at his watch and sighing like a character in a pantomime.

'Really!' the woman says. 'We're supposed to check in from three o'clock.'

'It's not on,' the man says grimly. Pippa's ears perk up.

Pippa walks past, trying not to linger, but she can't help wondering what's going on.

Suddenly the woman shouts out, 'Excuse me. Hello!'

'Yes,' Pippa says, stopping and turning towards them.

'We've booked in here for the weekend, but can't seem to get an answer. Are you local?'

'Um, yes,' Pippa says, 'but I've no idea where the owner is.'

'It's really frustrating,' the woman says. 'I don't know what to do. We've phoned a few times and knocked on the door. We've got a special dinner tonight and I was hoping to get showered and changed early.'

Pippa nods sympathetically. 'I'm sure they'll be back soon.'

'Perhaps we should book in somewhere else, Colin,' the woman says.

'I know of somewhere,' Pippa pipes up. For a second, Pippa wonders if she should do this, but she swiftly brushes away her conscience. If Jenny is leaving disgruntled customers, surely Pippa would be doing them a disservice not to offer. 'I run a bed and breakfast just a hundred yards away. It's not as big as this place, but I have a spare room tonight.'

'That sounds perfect,' the woman says. 'What do you think, Colin? They can hardly charge us for the room here when no one is around to check us in. We haven't paid a deposit.'

'Follow me,' says Pippa. 'There's not much room for parking, but a little further on, there's a car park at the pub. They're quite easy-going if you leave your car there.'

'I don't suppose they'll take too kindly if we leave it at the Lodge,' the woman says.

'No,' Pippa agrees, wondering if Jenny will find out that two of her guests have absconded with her. You can hardly call it poaching when Jenny Foster has abandoned the place with no word to her guests. It's not very professional at all.

'All right, ladies, what can I get for you? Pint of vodka?'

'Ordinarily I hate being called ladies, but I'll make an exception for you, Brett,' Monica quips with an exaggerated roll of her eyes. 'Baileys hot chocolate, please.'

'Same for you?'

'I think I'll have the craft cider,' Pippa orders, clocking Monica's look of dismay once Brett's left the table. 'What?'

'Riverdean's cracked you,' she says. 'Seriously, you're a different person now. It's finally happened. Ordering a cider. We've done it,' she laughs. 'You can take the girl out of London, and all the air pollution and expensive perfume just ebbs out of the girl.'

Pippa snorts. 'Shut up. Although I am wearing the Riverdean uniform, aren't I?' Pippa had opted for mom jeans and a checked shirt for this impromptu visit to The Trout, left her hair to dry in its natural wavy style. Besides, she didn't have a lot of time to get ready by the time Colin and Fay had checked in. They'd kept her chatting for ages, despite them saying earlier they wanted to get ready to go out.

Monica shakes her head. 'I would say Riverdean's converted you, but I think that's all Jake.'

'If you've called me here to quiz me about Jake,' Pippa laughs, 'then I'm keeping shtum.'

'I've called you here to catch up with my new friend,' Monica says. 'And if the rumours that you and Jake were seen kissing outside Barn 11 on Saturday could be confirmed, then that would be a bonus.'

Pippa's mouth drops open. 'This place really is the gossip mill.'

'Told you,' Monica says. 'Cheers, Brett.'

He drops off their drinks, pouring Pippa's cider into a small tankard. 'Brewed by your very own dating partner,' Brett says, causing Pippa to hide her face in her hands. 'Can't imagine his mum is best pleased, though.' Brett raises his eyebrows cryptically, before moving back to the bar.

'God, I didn't think about Jake's mum, that must be awkward,' Monica frowns. Of course, Pippa thinks, it hasn't occurred to her that Jake's parents will also have heard the rumours. Oh dear, meeting his parents will be embarrassing. Or not, they'll probably be as laid-back and adventure-focused as Jake. If she does meet his parents, that is. If things do get that serious.

Pippa's doing exactly what she vowed she wouldn't when she moved to Riverdean. She wanted to be on her own for a bit and here she is fantasising about meeting a man's parents. The date with Jake last week was so dreamy, though, Pippa's found herself reliving parts of the night: their flirty banter over dinner, giggling over takeaway food, kissing outside the restaurant, and again back at Pippa's. It hadn't gone any further, luckily, but Pippa had really wanted it to. And she'd found herself gazing at her phone since, lighting up whenever Jake sent her a message.

'Well, there are no plans to meet the parents any time soon,' she tells Monica firmly.

'When are you seeing lover boy next, then?' Monica asks, getting a moustache of chocolate cream from her drink which she hastily wipes off.

'He mentioned a walk next weekend, but he's busy with Lola and work, of course. And I'm busy too, I've got a TV crew staying at Pumpkin this week. They're filming a documentary about autumn leaf-peeping in the Wye Valley, you know, tourists coming just to see our autumn colours. Isn't that exciting?'

'Terrible attempt at a subject change,' Monica says. 'We get those documentaries every year. A few shots of the trees, dodgy tourists with binoculars and a comedy shot of a squirrel. What I really want to know is when you're going to show Jake the new hot tub? And when you're going to show me the new hot tub? Please do me first. I want that water to be clean.'

'Monica!' Pippa giggles. 'The new hot tub will remain sterile for my guests.'

'So how is it going at the B&B?'

'Well, besides the odd teething problem.' Pippa decides she daren't complain about Grant's defection, she doesn't know who's on which side any more. She's also reluctant to tell her about her extra guests this afternoon. Perhaps Monica would think it was mean to steal them from Riverside Lodge. 'I've opened The Maple Room,' she goes on. 'Just some landscaping outside to go.'

'Love the name,' Monica says. 'Do you feel like you've made the right move?'

'Well, working for myself is definitely . . . different . . . scarier. I feel like the business could be derailed at any second, and that would be catastrophic. At least when I worked for a big hotel, I could pack away any problems at the end of the day, enjoy my evenings. It feels like I'm always on the go here.'

'That must be liberating, though? I'm kind of jealous,' Monica says.

'You enjoy teaching?'

'I do, especially the little kids,' Monica says. She'd told Pippa a story about a little girl who walked in on her parents having sex. She told everyone in the class they were doing *naked gymnastics* on the bed. 'Plus, you can't beat the holidays. I've just always seen myself running my own business, selling candles. I've been doing it since I was a teen. Isn't that weird? Most kids spent their time snogging or drinking, I'd be experimenting with different scents. Probably why I'm still single.'

'I'd love to check them out,' Pippa says now, already envisaging home-crafted candles in the B&B. 'I can't promise any sales, but I'd be happy to display them in Pumpkin Cottage.'

Monica gives her a smile. 'I swear I wasn't saying it for that, but if you're sure, that would be great. You'll love the candles, perfect autumn scents. My latest is maple and vanilla.'

'Ideal for the Maple Room,' Pippa nods.

'You're like a breath of fresh air. I asked Jenny bloody Foster years ago if I could sample some for Riverside Lodge and she looked like I'd punched her in the face. She said *if I did that for you, I'd have to do it for everyone*. Like everyone in Riverdean is desperate to flog their wares. Of course, it's different with Jake's ciders.' Pippa didn't know Jake sold his ciders at Riverside Lodge. She makes a mental note to ask him about it on their next date.

Monica continues, 'They're so different those two, you wouldn't believe they're rel—'

'Monica? I didn't recognise you without a pint in your hands. Going teetotal, are we?' An older man wearing a baseball cap and flannel shirt moves in to give Monica a peck on the cheek.

'There's Baileys in this,' she indicates the cup, getting to her feet, then signals to Pippa. 'Pippa, this is my Uncle Richie. What are you doing in Riverdean tonight?'

'I've just been doing some work in the big house at the top of the hill. Needed the patio redone. Thought I'd pop into The Trout, see some old faces. I'd better be heading off soon, though, we've got friends coming over tonight.'

'You're not visiting Mum's? Richie used to live next door to Pumpkin Cottage, before the move to Hereford. Pippa's converted it to a B&B,' she tells her uncle.

'Impressive.' He's giving Pippa an odd look. 'You look the spit of someone I used to know, Suzy Miller.' His remark is casual but it makes Pippa's world lurch. She can hear blood rushing in her ears.

'That's my mother,' she says, astounded.

'No shit, you've got the exact same eyes. Fancy that,' Richie turns to Monica.

'Did you know Pippa's mum well?' Monica asks on her behalf. Pippa's told Monica all she knows about her mother's past in Riverdean. She was hoping to start asking questions soon, finding out more from anyone who might have known her mum, but the work at Pumpkin Cottage has been all-consuming so far.

'Knew her? We were mates back in the day. Same year at school. Next-door neighbours.'

'My mum lived next to you?'

'In the cottage with the ivy-covered porch and blue door. It looks exactly the same now,' Richie laughs. Pippa's too gobsmacked to speak. She never thought she'd get a lead like this. Her own mother grew up just a few doors down from Pumpkin Cottage. What are the chances of that? If she ever questioned why she bought the B&B, now it feels like fate to Pippa.

'I-I didn't know that,' Pippa stutters. Her mouth feels dry with the shock of it.

'I'm surprised she didn't tell you, she must have visited Pumpkin Cottage,' Richie says. His face drops when Pippa pauses.

'She died of cancer, earlier this year,' Pippa says, the words still able to knock the air out of her lungs.

'Poor Suzy. I'm so sorry to hear that, love.'

Monica gives her a sympathetic look too.

'It's okay,' Pippa says, fighting to keep hold of her emotions, 'I already feel closer to her, knowing she lived so close to me.'

'She was a proper firecracker your mum,' Richie shakes his head. 'You didn't want to be on the wrong side of her. Did she tell you once about her mischief in school? A girl in our class didn't do her homework, she had problems at home with her dad, I think. Suzy didn't want her to get in trouble so she got everyone in the class to give her their books, and then she dumped them all in the river! Right under the teacher's nose, it was brilliant!'

Monica and Pippa both laugh.

'Not surprisingly your mum got in more trouble after that.'

'That sounds like her,' Pippa says, relishing any morsel of information. 'I'd love to hear more stories about my mum.' Pippa wants to add *and my dad*, but can't yet.

'I'll have to pop over to Pumpkin one night. I'd better be leaving now, though. You could ask that old goat at the top of the hill, what's her name again? Your mum was thick as thieves with her, though I never understood why. Chalk and cheese, that was them. I've got loads of stories about your mum from when she was a little girl. Used to come over and pretend my garden was a pirate ship!'

Pippa wants to grab his arm, make him stay, find out who he's talking about. Who she could ask about her mum.

'Do you know anything about why she left Riverdean?' Pippa asks, knowing she should let Richie go but unable to.

'Uh . . .' Richie removes his hat, rubs the bald skin underneath. 'I think it was after all that business with . . . no, I'm speaking out of turn. I don't know the details, love, I'm sorry. We sort of grew apart once we got to secondary school. She wouldn't tell me about her romantic life and vice versa. And she left so suddenly.'

Pippa's itching to know what he was going to say. He must know something. He obviously does, she thinks, with the awkward look on his face.

'I'm sorry, I really have to get going or else your aunt will never speak to me again.' He nods to Monica. 'There must be a tonne of people in Riverdean who can fill in what I can't about your mum.'

'I hope so,' Pippa says, clinging on to what Richie has said. She can't wait to wander home soon, to peer at Ivy Cottage so close to hers, wonder about her mother. Maybe the new owners know more about her?

'Say hi to your parents,' Richie says, giving Monica's shoulder a squeeze.

'You'll probably see them before I do,' Monica says. 'I never seem to get the chance to call in, even though they only live a few doors down.'

Pippa nods and says 'mmm'. If her mother was alive and lived just a few doors down, she wouldn't keep away from there.

'Right, I'd better get back. I've got some clearing up to do,' she says, swigging the rest of the cider down. For one second, the crisp apple flavour reminds her of Jake's kiss.

Pippa takes a deep breath and another glance around looking for prying eyes. None. Total darkness surrounds her, with just the blinking fairy lights along the balustrade. It's time.

She slips her gown off, feeling the shiver of autumn against her bare skin. Her bathing costume feels totally inadequate with its cutouts and low neckline. Pippa gasps as the warm water envelops her body and she slips into the hot tub. A perfect forty degrees. Although she's outdoors, she feels totally hidden. The hot tub is perched on the rooftop balcony of Pumpkin Cottage, but the tree canopy above maintains enough privacy to slip in and out of the tub.

'Beautiful,' she sighs aloud. She nearly knocks over the glass of Prosecco she's balanced precariously on the side of the tub. Glass holders, they're next on her mental shopping list. Coat hooks, so guests can hang up their dressing gowns while they bathe in the tub. And maybe some kind of basket for communal slippers would be nice.

After a few minutes in the tub, the frenetic thoughts about shopping and the B&B simply ebb away and she begins to relax. Buying and installing this hot tub, though stressful as hell, has definitely been a good idea, Pippa thinks. From a pure logistics point of view, people are willing to pay over the odds for access to a hot tub, and aside from that the experience is gorgeous. Her guests will love it, a real unique selling point. She will open the hot tub for guest use tomorrow, but for tonight, the tub is just hers. Pippa is in a little private bubble, even though the rush of the river is just across the lane from her, and she can hear lively voices coming from The Trout. It's just Pippa, her thoughts, and her glass of Prosecco.

So, Pumpkin Cottage hasn't exactly been smooth sailing so far; what successful business venture is? Her mum used to say nothing in life worth having ever comes easy. She'd meant it about romance primarily, with her endless string of boyfriends. Her mother never did find true love, although she'd say Pippa was her soulmate. Pippa wonders for the umpteenth time what happened with her father, whether he was a true love or just another disappointment in her mother's life. Pippa feels closer than ever to finding out the truth. She can practically feel the spirit of her mother in the air, can even see the roof of the cottage where she grew up from her elevated position in the tub. Pippa has a good feeling about her quest to find out more.

And she has a good feeling about the B&B. It's been one problem after another recently, and the words of Jenny Foster have been ringing in her ears, whatever she implied about things being 'above board' and about Pippa's bookings being a novelty. And the cheek of the woman to try to steal her builder. She could feel real hatred coming from that woman, which had taken Pippa aback. Jenny deserved to lose a few guests for the way she had treated Pippa. She thought country villages would be all fêtes and picnics. Not catty games and sabotage. She doesn't need to rely on dirty tricks, though. Pumpkin Cottage can win on its own, especially with her new weapon.

She snaps a quick picture of the view from the hot tub, twinkly lights and steaming water included. That will go on Pumpkin Cottage's social media and is sure to draw customers.

She wonders what her mother would say about Jake. She'd definitely approve of his looks; the man could be a model. But her situation is so complicated, and after the year Pippa's had, a romantic complication is the last thing she needs. And she and Jake are so different, surely that means they're incompatible in the long run. If things end badly, then her life in Riverdean will be unbearable. *But what if it doesn't end badly . . .* her mother's voice says. She was always an optimist when it came to romance.

Pippa jumps as the message tone sounds on her phone. She leaves wet fingerprints on the screen as she leans out to read it. It's Jake.

So, I have a free day and a home-made cake ready for the weekend. If you ignore the fact it's made by my mother, then it could be a very nice picnic? Xx

Pippa smiles. *Currently trialling the hot tub. Despite the chemicals making my eyes itch, I may never get out. If I manage it, then picnic sounds great xx*

A reply fires back instantly. *Is it inappropriate if I bring my sleeping daughter for a walk down the lane? Irresponsible parenting but worth it to get a glimpse of you xx*

She sniggers. *The hot tub is very private. Also, I'm pruning. May need to adjust the chlorine. Enjoy your evening with Lola xx*

Enjoy the pruning. See you Saturday xx

Chapter Twenty

Jenny

'Unbelievable.' Jenny says. 'Unbelievable!' she says, louder this time, as she walks into the kitchen.

Jake is sitting at the computer in the conservatory. 'What is?' he asks, distracted.

'Colin and Fay Biggs, the couple who were supposed to stay in Room Four this weekend. I was ten minutes late from that appointment at the hospital with your father and they left. They're staying at Pumpkin Cottage.' Jenny pauses, 'She stole them!'

'Stop being so dramatic, Ma,' Jake says. He sounds annoyed. 'I'm sure she didn't deliberately steal them. You know what people are like. This Colin and May . . .'

'Fay,' Jenny corrects him.

'Well, people are impatient, aren't they? Don't want to wait.'

'They called me now. Didn't even apologise when I said I had gone to the hospital. Said they'd phoned several times. Even though I had only one missed call. Then she told me they'd booked in Pumpkin Cottage. Funny that.'

Jake shakes his head, 'You're reading far too much into this.'

'You always see the best in people,' Jenny says irritated.

'And you always see the worst.'

'I'm just saying it's odd that they checked into Pumpkin

Cottage when no one was here. How did they know there'd be a free room? They wouldn't have got a phone signal. It's too dodgy. I reckon that Pippa Mason called them over. She stole them from me!'

'You have an overactive imagination,' says Jake. 'Give it a rest, will you? You really need this night out.'

Jenny is unconvinced but goes to the bedroom to get ready. She appraises herself in the mirror. Where has her waist gone? She's definitely what the magazines would describe as apple-shaped. The green wrap dress she's chosen disguises her stomach a little, and the low-cut of the material draws attention to her boobs. She likes her boobs; they do hang a bit nearer to her belly button these days but they're fulsome and generous. Phil used to love them. 'I'm a boob man,' he used to say with a wink. Well, things in that department have definitely changed. It's been at least two years since they were last intimate and Jenny misses the closeness, the affection. Jake always moaned about it when he was a teenager and they walked hand in hand, or he caught them having a quick kiss in the kitchen. *It's disgusting*, he'd say, or *It's not natural at your age*. Jenny smiles at the memory.

'Right then, you two, I'm off. I won't be long, an hour or two at the most,' Jenny says, walking into the living room. Phil doesn't take his eyes from the TV.

Jake grins, 'Wow, Ma, be careful going out in a dress like that. Riverdean is a hotbed of debauchery, you know.'

'Very funny, Jake. Are you sure you don't want to go out tonight? It doesn't seem right that I'm going to Brett and Shaun's engagement and you're the one staying in.'

Jenny decides that she was being silly boycotting The Trout after seeing leaflets advertising Pumpkin Cottage. After all, it is the only pub in Riverdean and it's what you call cutting off your nose to spite your face. Something Jenny does rather a lot.

'I'm feeling a bit tired tonight,' Jake says. 'Might pop in later if I feel up to it. Besides, I've got a night of Monopoly and the footie with my dad. What more could I want?'

'It's just unlike you to miss an opportunity to go out,' Jenny says, 'especially to a party on a warm Saturday night.'

'Will you stop fussing and go, Ma.'

She sighs. 'There are plenty of snacks in the fridge. I should be back by ten.'

The air is unseasonably warm in the soft, pink dusk. Jenny strolls past the river, enjoying the warmth and the sound of the water mumbling gently below. Passing Pumpkin Cottage, she can see a small light inside the kitchen window casting an inviting yellow glow. The front door has been freshly painted and it looks as if Grant has started a bit of landscaping in the garden. Jenny grudgingly admits Pippa has transformed the place. She spots the hot tub, fairy lights twinkling on the canopy above it. Even though it's vulgar, Jenny knows that it will draw more customers to her.

Ever since Pippa Mason moved to Riverdean, it's as if she has brought with her bad luck. The bad reviews of Riverside Lodge, the fire in the kitchen, Amber and Lola moving to France. Okay, so it wasn't all Pippa's fault, but she is like a bad omen. Jenny can't wait for that girl to return to London, and she will. No doubt about it. What is there to keep her here in Riverdean? Far too tame and unsophisticated for the likes of that madam.

As the trees open up to reveal The Trout nestling closely to the river's edge, Jenny can hear the music, Madonna's 'Cherish', being sung rather badly on the karaoke, spilling outside. She sees Brett and Shaun's tabby, Taylor Swift, weaving between the crowds before disappearing behind the pub. Jenny jostles her way past those vaping outside to get to the front entrance.

'Evening,' Grant says, inhaling deeply. His eyes travel slowly over her ample chest and Jenny instinctively pulls the material closer together. She nods, practically stumbling over her feet to get inside.

The place is absolutely heaving and for once Brett and Shaun aren't ensconced behind the bar, but are mingling with their guests. Brett is in the corner by the karaoke machine, glancing at the playlist and gesticulating wildly, whilst Shaun is chatting to people Jenny doesn't recognise. Most of the village is here. Fi Clark is sitting in the corner by the fire and waves Jenny over. She glances at the elaborate cake on a table to the right of the bar as she passes. It's an ivory, five-tiered construction, with pink and lemon roses cascading artfully from the top. *Brett and Shaun's Engagement – He Said Yes!* is spelt out in ornate letters and there are even two little male figures depicting the happy pair perched in front of the cake.

'I'm the one with the good hair, obviously,' Brett says, resting his chin on Jenny's shoulder. He's clearly quite drunk already. 'I'm so happy you could make it. What would a party be without Jenny Foster in it?'

Jenny extricates herself. 'Well, perhaps I did overreact last time I saw you. Congratulations! I'm very happy for you both.'

'And where is that handsome son of yours? That cross between Chris Hemsworth and Ryan Gosling, who leaves a trail of broken hearts in Riverdean.' He gives a low whistle, 'If I didn't have Shaun, I'd . . .'

'You'd what?' Shaun says, creeping up behind him. 'Ignore him. He's had far too much already. Thank you for coming, lovely,' he says, kissing her cheek. 'There's free champagne at the bar.'

Jenny flops down at last next to Fi Clark and the table of other women Jenny knows. Fi gives her a warm hug. 'Glad you could make it,' she says.

Jenny sips the champagne and gazes about her. She's glad she came out now, but more often than not, she prefers to stay in. Phil hates crowds and the noisy atmosphere of the pub would just upset him. And she's reluctant to impose on Jake too much. It's not fair on him to look after his father so much at his age.

'How's things?' asks Rowena, who moved into the village ten years ago and whose children go to the school at which Phil taught.

'Oh, you know,' Jenny begins, with a shrug. How do you tell people how things really are? That the future you face is terrifying, that she loses a bit of Phil every day, that sometimes she just feels like running away. 'We're coping,' she says.

'We've put our names down to sing in the karaoke later,' Fi says. 'We're singing "Rehab". You've *got* to join us, Jenny.'

Jenny shudders, 'I'm a terrible singer and that's not the easiest to sing.'

'Well, it was either that or "Jolene". It's all the gay icons tonight. It's the rule,' Fi grins.

'I'm going to need more champagne.' Jenny swigs it down quickly and they all laugh. She feels herself relaxing.

Suddenly, Meghan Trainor's 'All About the Bass' is stopped and Brett and Shaun stand in front of the mic, which screeches noisily.

'Oops, sorry, folks,' Brett taps the mic and coughs. 'Shaun and I want to say a few words before the night properly starts.' Judging by his slurring, the night started a lot earlier, Jenny thinks.

'Thank you all for, uh, coming this evening to celebrate our very very special night. And it is a special night, a very special night.' He pauses for a moment as if he's forgotten what he was going to say. 'Not every day do I get engaged to the man of my dreams. And I had no idea when Shaun whisked me off to that cosy shepherd's hut that I'd find a trail of pumpkins with Marry Me carved into them.' There's a communal 'Ahh' from everyone in the pub. Brett hiccups before he continues. 'When I first set eyes on Shaun, I knew I'd marry him. Well, once he sorted his wardrobe out. I could *not* have been in a relationship with a man who wore that much polyester. Anyway, he has made me the happiest man in the universe and we're getting married next year, and you're all invited,' he says with a flourish, his arm indicating the whole room.

'I apologise for my fiancé,' Shaun says, taking the mic from Brett. The bar erupts at this mention of 'fiancé'. 'He's a bit the worse for wear, as you can see. He's right, though. We are grateful you are all here to share this momentous event with us. We've been so happy since we came to Riverdean, this quirky, dysfunctional, charming village, where everyone is related to or has slept with everyone else. Or both!' Everyone laughs at this. 'The champagne is free and flowing tonight and later we'll cut the cake. Thank you, Petro, you've done us proud.' He pauses, 'So, let's raise a toast. To happiness, love and friends, old and new.'

Jenny swallows the rest of the champagne and feels quite lightheaded. Fi tops up the glass from the bottle on the table.

'Come on, it's our turn on the karaoke,' Fi says and Jenny is nudged to her feet.

'Oh, I don't think I can,' Jenny says, and Rowena suddenly grips her elbow and directs her over to the mic. Jenny realises there's no getting out of this and she's grateful Jake can't hear his mother make a fool of herself.

There are four of them up there, Jenny, Rowena, Fi and Angela Bryant, who Jenny remembers is a singing teacher.

The start of the song is horrible with all of them coming in at different times. The crowd cheers, enjoying their discomfort. They start again, gaining traction this time but only Angela is able to hold a tune. Jenny hasn't got her reading glasses with her so struggles to read the lyrics. She's grateful she can barely see the crowds, as the bright lights shine in her eyes, creating silhouettes of the audience. Most end up chatting, growing bored of the karaoke. Jenny can't wait for it to be over, wondering what on earth convinced her to agree. As she hands the microphone back and emerges from the karaoke corner, she catches sight of Pippa Mason, sipping champagne and giving her the coldest, most venomous stare, she has ever seen. Pippa, sitting with Monica Riley, whispers something and both women laugh. Jenny has never liked Monica. She's a bit rough around the edges, a bad influence on Jake.

'Well, I don't think we'll be signing up for *Britain's Got Talent* anytime soon,' says Fi, giving an embarrassed laugh as they flop down in their seats.

Jenny sits with her back to Pippa and Monica, but she feels horribly exposed as she sips her champagne. Tonight is the first time in ages she's felt more her old self and it's good to have fun with her friends, but the spell is broken and she can't wait to go home. She knows that she upset Pippa, taking Grant away from her, but she is just as sure Pippa poached Colin and Fay Biggs this afternoon. She can feel it in her bones. Jenny does not trust this woman one little bit. This interloper, who just seems to cause trouble.

'I think I'll call it a night,' she tells Fi.

'But you've only just got here,' she protests.

'I'm not sleeping well lately, and you know . . .' No one argues too much, knowing Jenny's situation.

'I'll save you some cake. Bring it over tomorrow.'

Jenny slips out without saying goodbye to Brett and Shaun. It might be her imagination, but Jenny feels Pippa's eyes boring into her back as she leaves.

The chilly night air is a relief as she leaves the pub, the strains of Lady Gaga's 'Bad Romance' following her down the lane. A girl is on her knees vomiting into the river, her friend holding back her hair. The dusk has turned to darkness, but Jenny knows the path like the back of her hand. Tears prick her eyes and the colours of the fairy lights around the balcony at Pumpkin Cottage blur and dance before her.

Pull yourself together, she berates herself as she unlocks the door and lets herself into the kitchen. In the living room, she can hear the television is on.

'You're back early, Mum,' Jake says. 'Everything okay?'

'Very lively. It was packed out,' Jenny says. 'Brett is plastered already. How's your father been?' Jenny looks at Phil, struggling to keep his eyes open as he watches *Casualty*.

'I think I might just pop my head in,' Jake says, rising from his chair.

'Well, you've changed your tune. I thought you were tired.'

'Second wind,' he says. 'I'll just go and put something tidy on.'

'Have you ever spoken to that Pippa Mason?' Jenny asks suddenly. 'You know, the one who's bought Pumpkin Cottage.'

'No,' Jake says quickly. 'I mean, yes, I think I have spoken to her once or twice. Why do you ask?'

'You should have seen the way she looked at me in the pub. If looks could kill . . .'

'I'm sure you're imagining it,' Jake says.

'Maybe.' Jake knows she poached Grant from Pippa, but she didn't dare tell him about the reviews. He's too honest, too straight. 'Don't be too noisy when you come back in.'

Jenny eases her shoes off. 'I'm going to make a cup of tea. Do you want one, Phil?' When she looks over, he's drifted off. 'Come on, you. It's time for bed.'

Jenny helps Phil undress and gets him into bed. She's relieved to get out of her dress and take off her make-up. As she emerges from the bathroom, she's surprised to see Phil is still awake. Slipping into bed, she faces him. He reaches out and touches her face, gently places her hair behind her ear.

'I love you, Jenny Foster,' he whispers.

Jenny swallows and flicks the light switch.

Chapter Twenty-One

Pippa

'Lover boy's here,' Monica says, swigging down the rest of her beer.

'That's getting old already,' Pippa says.

Her smile is totally involuntary when she sees Jake, cutting his way through the crowd towards her. He's sidelined by a very drunken Brett on the way, who slurs something in his ear then gives him a kiss on the cheek, not unlike a dog greeting their owner. Jake laughs good-naturedly but pretends to wipe his cheek once out of Brett's eyeline.

'Sorry I'm late,' Jake says, shrugging his coat off and onto the back of a chair.

Pippa and Monica have a table by the window but it's so dark outside now, the river hidden in its October jacket. 'I couldn't leave my dad. He's having a good one tonight, was telling stories about when he worked in the local school.'

Monica gets up to go to the toilet and Jake gives Pippa a kiss across the table. Even though it's over in a second, it still manages to quicken Pippa's pulse.

'I wish you'd been here earlier,' Pippa says, 'I'm still reeling from seeing Jenny Foster. The woman completely ignored me, and I knew she'd seen me. I kept looking but it's like there was a force field around me saying *don't make eye contact*. That old witch probably can't look me in the eye after trying to sabotage me *again*.'

Jake shifts in his chair. 'What do you mean again?'

'She's leaving bad reviews on Tripadvisor for Pumpkin. It's been going on a while, but I had another one today. Complaining about cockroaches, which I know she's heard about from Grant. There's no one else who could have written it.'

'That seems a bit extreme,' Jake says after a beat.

'I wouldn't put it past her.' Pippa puts her wine glass down on the table a little too forcefully and Jake raises his eyebrows, probably thinking she's had too much. Pippa knows she shouldn't let Jenny Foster and her dirty games get to her, but it's hard when she's on her own and struggling with getting the B&B on its feet. 'After stealing my builder, anything goes.'

Jake looks around as if he wants to be anywhere but at this table, and Pippa feels a rush of emotion towards him. Jake is one of those people who can't say a bad word about anyone. Even Jenny Foster. Although she'd love to have a good old moan, Pippa has Monica and Hannah for that. She likes Jake's positivity. It shows he's a good, dependable guy. Pippa should be more like him. She was going to ask him about how long he's been selling his ciders at Riverside Lodge, but she decides against it now.

'Sorry, it's just been a rough week.'

'I thought you'd been lazing in the hot tub?' Jake grins. 'That review could have been anyone. You know how awkward guests can be over the slightest thing, wrong-coloured sheets, broken bulb, anything.'

'You sound like you're the one running a B&B,' Pippa laughs. She wants to believe him, but she has a bad feeling about Jenny Foster. 'Anyway, I was just about to go. I'm exhausted and I need my beauty sleep if I'm going to cooking breakfast for my guests in the morning.'

'That's what you call dedication! I thought Londoners were used to staying out all night,' Jake teases.

'It must be all this country air,' Pippa says, yawning on cue. She really is tired, and can see the crowd is starting to reach the wrong level of drunk. If Pippa stays for another drink, she'll be dragged into doing karaoke, and then there's no chance she'll be up making scrambled eggs and blueberry pancakes for the film crew.

'Leave me wanting more,' Jake gives a good-natured smile as Pippa leans over to kiss him again. He smells divine, like apple and woodsmoke.

'See you Monday,' she says, already excited about the picnic, then hugs Monica when she's back from the bathroom. 'Bye, Mon.'

'Incredible,' Pippa breathes, as she watches footage of a stag bathing in the river, shaking drips from its antlers which shimmer in the autumn sunshine. 'That must be, what, two hundred metres away from here?' Pippa is genuinely fascinated, never guessing that running her own B&B would mean she would meet such interesting guests. The film crew have stayed a few nights, proudly showing their shots from the day before.

'You'd never know it,' Ian, the cameraman staying with Pippa, clicks through the footage on his camera screen. 'They had this totally private cove, hidden from the village. We got so lucky to see it. There were five of them in total.'

'Hopefully the wildlife cameras will have caught some good stuff overnight too,' Josh, another crew member, complete with glossy locks and man bun, chimes in. Pippa knows the maintenance hair like that takes; she's heard the hair dryer going at five every morning from the Maple Room while he's been staying with her. 'Hopefully, they're still there where we left them at River's Rock.'

'I'm heading up there today, too,' Pippa says, that involuntary smile taking over again at the thought of Jake. She forces herself to stop, to serve the crew's breakfasts.

'Beautiful views of the valley,' Josh says.

'Mmm,' Pippa nods. 'Enjoy.' She leaves the crew to eat and busies herself with washing up and wiping the kitchen down. It's yet another of those glorious autumn days outside, sunny but cold. Perfect picnic weather, she thinks. She pictures herself and Jake, spread out on a tartan blanket, feeding each other quiche and drinking champagne with strawberries bobbing about. Mondays at Mallory's was mad. She loves having the freedom to go for a picnic like this, having no one to answer to. And Jake has no school parties to deal with today. Perfect!

Suddenly, her view of the river is blocked by a white van. Surely not Grant turning up to work early. Pippa watches a man get out, take a few steps backwards and look up at the property as though making an inspection. He frowns, muttering to himself.

Pippa hastily wipes her hands on a tea towel and moves to the front door.

'Can I help you?' she calls.

'Pippa Mason?' the man holds his hand out, his face solemn.

'That's me.'

'Andy Johnson. Herefordshire Council.'

'Pleased to meet you,' she says, feeling anything but pleasure. Is this a meeting she's forgotten about? Today's page in her mental calendar has one thing and one thing only on it. Jake.

'Can we step inside a moment?'

Oh no, Pippa feels a sense of foreboding here. Nothing good happens when official-looking people want to step inside.

'What's this about?' Pippa asks, leading the man through to the kitchen. She doesn't want her guests to hear this.

'It's a regulatory visit,' the man says, coughing at the same time. 'Standard practice after renovation works at business properties.'

'Yes?' Pippa's still confused.

'We understand that you've had some internal building work carried out at the property which hasn't been registered?'

'Well, nothing major,' Pippa says, feeling her cheeks redden. 'My handyman, Grant, has replastered some walls, the kitchen was refitted, a damp course put in.'

'And I understand there are four guest rooms?'

'Yes?' Pippa isn't sure why, but she feels this is the wrong answer.

'Ah,' the man nods. 'You're aware this was registered as a three-bedroom commercial property.'

'Well, yes, Grant's knocked down an internal wall, made another bedroom large enough to rent out.'

'And that's impacted on another wall?'

Pippa wants to ask *how do you know this*, but tries to maintain her composure. She can feel she'll be losing it in a moment. Why is he taking so long to get to the point?

'Yes, a doorway was knocked through,' she says, frowning. 'Grant said it wouldn't need planning permission.'

The man, Andy, looks at her as though she is stupid. 'It still needs approval from the building control team. Any change in layout, any steel erected, it all needs to be approved. I assume you've had a surveyor? Certificates? Structural engineer drawings?'

He seems to be enjoying Pippa's discomfort. She wants to kick herself. Or preferably Andy Johnson. Why did she trust Grant with that? He'd assured her nothing of the sort was needed.

Why didn't she bloody check herself? Pippa'd been too absorbed in the Pinterest ideal of her cottage, too eager to get the rooms ready for guests. She should have assumed the worst in Grant, should have checked herself.

'I'll speak to my builder,' Pippa says, plastering on a smile in the hopes it will hurry this meeting along. 'Let's say if we don't have the drawings or certificates . . . how do I go about getting them?'

'It can be sent retrospectively,' Andy says, and Pippa feels a great sense of relief. At least she can sort things out now.

'But you'll need to send photographs of the supporting steel, copies of the floor plans, and all structural engineering measurements to go to the board. And soon, otherwise there are penalties.'

'Great,' Pippa nods as though that is nothing. Her brain is working overtime, thinking of the time and effort that will take. The plaster will have to be taken off, redone, repainted. And she has paying guests booked into the Maple and Lavender rooms for the next two months. She's going to need to cancel bookings, to refund deposits, to pay over the odds to have this work sorted quickly. 'Well, I'll get right on that. If there's nothing more I can do for you?' She ushers Andy Johnson towards the door, wondering if his parents gave him such a boring name at birth as they knew he'd turn out to be the most boring man in Britain. Fancy doing this for a job, she thinks. Ruining people's days over technicalities?

How did the council find out about this when Pippa didn't even know about it herself? Andy Johnson seemed to know all too much about what work has been done at Pumpkin Cottage.

'Are you enjoying your breakfasts? Need anything else?' Pippa carries a fresh pot of coffee through to the film crew, but her mind is whirring. This reeks of Jenny Foster. Yes, that veiled threat she made, about things being above board. This is it. It has to be all her. Leaving bad reviews. Stealing Grant from her. Reporting her to the council is the next level.

Pippa is stunned she'd sink to such depths but there seems to be no stopping that woman. No wonder she couldn't look Pippa in the eye last night. Pippa's beginning to think she can't just ignore this problem. She needs to hit back. She needs to fight for Pumpkin Cottage. And if she has to play dirty, then Pippa Mason is going to play dirty.

She opens her laptop and finds the Tripadvisor tab. She knows just what to do.

'You didn't tell me we'd be hiking today?' Pippa says, sweating more than the wine bottle she's carrying in a cooler bag in her rucksack.

'Not much further,' Jake says, as if he is leading a school trip.

'Great,' Pippa's breath is laboured. *Not much further*, she repeats to herself. What does that even mean? This picnic had better be worth it, especially after the morning she's had. She tried telling Jake about the council visit when he picked Pippa up, but all he said was, 'You don't know she's reported you. Don't jump to conclusions.'

Jake might be too nice to see it, but Pippa isn't blind. She told Jake how she has half a mind to get revenge on Jenny and Riverside Lodge, which got a mumbled, 'Be careful', and an awkward silence afterwards. Pippa's going to call Hannah later; she knows she will react with more than silence.

Urgh, Pippa needs to shake off this mood she's in. Jenny Foster's already ruined her morning, she's not going to let her ruin her whole day with Jake.

'We could have driven up here.' Pippa spies a car park through the trees. Trust Jake to lead her the difficult way on foot up the mountain.

'The views are worth the walk,' Jake replies breezily. 'Plus, I plan on drinking a few glasses.'

'Not put off after the party Saturday night?'

'Brett tried his best, but I only stayed for one more,' Jake laughs. 'He did get me up doing karaoke, though.'

'Let me guess . . . "Wonderwall"?'

'It's a classic.'

'I thought it had to be a gay icon,' Pippa grins.

'Brett made an exception. I told him Oasis is the only band in my register. Monica absolutely murdered Lady Gaga, though. I knew then it was time for me to leave.'

'I have a rule against karaoke,' Pippa says. 'Never do it in the UK, only abroad. Then you can be sure no one will ever see you again. Saying that, my friend Hannah made friends with another couple on holiday once, got drunk together and made fools of themselves. She went to a job interview a month later and, lo and behold, there was the guy from holiday interviewing her.'

'Oh no,' Jake laughs. 'I can't wait to meet this Hannah.'

'I'm sure you will soon, she's dying to come down again,' Pippa says, thinking about how Hannah is still hanging on for her proposal. She's tried calling Louis a few times to find out his plans, but has had no answer. 'I haven't met any of your friends either, besides Monica,' Pippa says. She's also thinking about Jake's parents. Riverdean's a small place, she's probably seen them out and had no idea who they are. Although if they made Jake, then they're sure to be tall, sandy-haired, and gorgeous. Pippa wonders if Jake's thought about introducing her to them, although she knows his dad is ill. Meeting parents is a minefield and should probably wait until much further down the road. If there is a further down the road for them, of course.

'We're here, River's Rock,' Jake says, suddenly holding Pippa's hand and pulling her around the corner. The tree-lined path opens into a clearing, a dramatic plateau. The views are sweeping, expansive, taking in the valley and river bathed in a golden light. 'What do you think? Isn't it amazing?'

'Amazing is a bit of an understatement,' Pippa says. 'It's beautiful.'

It's clearly a tourist hotspot too, she thinks, taking in the informational plaque and overflowing bin nearby, complete with discarded selfie stick. Even if it was heaving with travellers, it would still be a stunning spot.

'You can see six counties from here,' Jake says. 'We bring lots of tours up to this spot. The jewel of Riverdean some call it.'

'I can see Pumpkin Cottage,' Pippa squeals, recognising the ramshackle roof and covered balcony holding the hot tub. 'It's funny, it really feels like home now.'

'I'm glad,' Jake says, and he slips an arm around Pippa. 'You've not got any plans to move from Riverdean, then?'

'If you're asking whether Jenny Foster's managing to oust me from the village, then the answer is a firm no. The opposite, in fact. I'm not going anywhere.'

'Good.' His expression is inscrutable, then he softens. 'Well, I'm really glad you've chosen Riverdean to set up home in.'

Inside, Pippa wants to burst. She turns and kisses Jake, ignoring a family with small children who have joined them at the top of River's Rock. 'Are we having this picnic, then?'

Jake lays out a small fleece blanket that has clearly had Archie's dog paws all over it, and fishes in his bag for the food. Two small supermarket sandwiches, two packets of McCoys crisps, and a Tupperware with two slices of cake inside. Pippa purses her lips. She's glad she thought to bring food herself. She's made canapé-style avocado toasts, home-made sausage rolls, and a roast vegetable tart. And thank goodness, she thinks. So, Jake is probably the type to let his mother cook for him, she can let that slide. Pippa's always enjoyed cooking, making others smile with her food. Her mum wasn't much of a chef and so Pippa had taken up the slack as a teenager, buying a cookbook and learning basic recipes. So far, she's loved doing the B&B breakfasts, making each dish a little bit special. Cooking for someone is caring for them, in Pippa's books.

'Wow, you've gone to a lot of effort,' Jake says, admiring Pippa's offerings.

'And you've been to . . . Tesco,' Pippa mocks.

'Okay, okay, I'm not much of a chef—'

'Clearly,' Pippa interrupts.

'Cheeky. But I can make up for it in other ways.' Jake looks Pippa straight in the eye.

'What other ways?'

At that exact moment, Jake manages to pop the cork on Pippa's wine, sending it straight up in the air in an arc, heading towards another family. It lands near their picnic, triggering their dog into a barking frenzy.

'I'm so sorry!' Jake shouts, sending Pippa into a fit of giggles. He looks back at her, red in the face.

'That was smooth,' Pippa teases.

'Nothing about me is smooth,' Jake laughs, before grabbing Pippa's face and pulling her in for a kiss. She loses her balance and shrieks, her knee ploughing into his packets of sandwiches, and they both descend into laughter again.

Jake may not know how to host a picnic, Pippa decides, but he can definitely do funny things to her heart.

Chapter Twenty-Two

Jenny

Jenny flips the eggs over and butters the toast as it springs out of the toaster. It's second nature to her now and she never gets too stressed. By October, the busiest season is well and truly over, and she only has three sets of guests in. The Martins, keen ramblers, left early this morning and just wanted bacon sandwiches, and the Petersons had requested a continental breakfast, taking it with them when they checked out. It's only Cynthia and Rob Lees, regular visitors to the Wye Valley, who sit in the dining room making their plans for the day.

'Here you are, large English breakfasts for you both with fried eggs and hash browns. Let me know if you need more toast.' Jenny places the breakfasts down. 'The honey is local, of course, and there's marmalade and strawberry jam.'

'Thank you, Jenny,' Cynthia says.

'Did you enjoy your walk to River's Rock yesterday?' Jenny asks.

'It was stunning,' Rob says. 'I can't believe it's the first time we've been there in all these years we've been visiting the Wye Valley.'

'We saw your son and his girl there yesterday. Young love, eh!' Cynthia laughs.

Jenny stops in her tracks, tries her best to cover her surprise.

'We're thinking of going to Tintern Abbey today. Is it far from here?'

'Only about thirty minutes,' Jenny stutters. 'A lovely place. You'd better check it's open, though. They're doing some conservation work. I think I've got a leaflet in the hallway.'

'Mmm, Jenny, this is delicious,' Rob says, talking through a mouthful. 'We were a bit dubious about booking here after all that on Tripadvisor but I'm glad we ignored it.'

'We thought the beds were very comfy too,' Cynthia says. 'Not rigid at all.'

Jenny frowns. All that on Tripadvisor? She makes her excuses and checks her laptop quickly. A glut of bad reviews plague Riverside Lodge's page on Tripadvisor, taking her star rating down to 3.2 now. Her eyes swim, unable to take it all in, from comments on the breakfasts, the rooms, the host . . . it's too much. Words jump out at her 'filthy', 'bedbugs', 'the host was borderline rude'. Jenny gasps. These can't all be real. The words are so spiteful. There's only one person who can be behind this. All for stealing a builder for a few days. It's ridiculous. Pippa can't know about her review and the call to Andy Johnson, an old friend of Phil's. What a petty way to retaliate, just for delaying her hot tub.

Jenny needs to think hard about what to do next. Reporting them to Tripadvisor seems an obvious choice.

When Jenny returns to the kitchen, Jake is sitting at the table. Dare she ask him about this new woman? She can't think why he's being so secretive. She feels a bit hurt. Especially after Pippa's reviews.

'I was wondering if you were getting up today,' she jokes. 'Did you enjoy your hike yesterday? Who did you go with?'

'Just some of the lads,' Jake says vaguely.

He's determined not to tell her, obviously. She'll have to leave it for now. 'Your dad took ages to get to bed last night. He thought the rug in the bedroom was a well. Honestly, no matter how many times I stood on it, he wasn't convinced.' Jenny starts clearing up. 'I've got that carer coming over today. The one Maeve arranged. Your dad has met her a few times now. I'm a bit nervous as it's the first time I've left him alone with her. She's great, though. Really patient. Cheerful. I could learn a lot from her,' Jenny smiles. 'The only thing is she's called Phyllis and likes to be called Phyl. Well, the confusion that's caused!' She pauses, scattering crumbs into the sink. 'Do you want some toast, Jake?' she asks. 'There's some bacon left if you want a sandwich.'

'No, you're all right.'

'Tea? Coffee?'

'Just leave it, will you?' Jake says irritably.

'Is everything okay?' Jenny pours a coffee and sits down. She doesn't push it, knowing she annoys Jake when she asks too many questions. He'll tell her in his own time if he's worried about something.

'Is Lola staying tomorrow night? Amber has that wedding, doesn't she? I might pop into town and get something special for us this weekend.'

'Well, take advantage of being with Lola as much as you can,' Jake says.

'What do you mean by that?'

Jake runs his fingers through his hair, pauses. 'Amber told me they're definitely moving to France and they've seen a house and they're hoping it'll all go through in the new year.'

Jenny is stunned into silence for a minute. 'Can she do that? Surely you have rights. You're her father!'

'Apparently she has to have my consent.'

'Don't give it!' Jenny says.

'It's not as easy as that, Mum. I can't really stop them. Ethan has some job opportunity out there and it pays much more money. They're all excited about it and have seen this house with a pool. It just seems as if I'm being vindictive and stubborn if I block it.'

'But when will you see Lola? When will *I* see her? I was hoping this was just some fantasy of Amber's and nothing would come of it.'

'You and me both,' Jake shrugs.

'Oh, Jake,' Jenny touches his arm. She doesn't know what to say. How can she comfort him? 'Have you noticed all the bad luck we seem to be having lately? Ever since that Pippa Mason moved into Riverdean, you should see the reviews she's—'

'That's pathetic,' Jake says sharply, standing up, his chair screeching across the kitchen floor. 'This rivalry between the two of you is ridiculous. You're as bad as each—'

Jenny flushes, embarrassed. 'I didn't mean it. It's just we seem to have had a run of awful luck these days.'

'I'm going. I've got a school group kayaking first thing.' He marches out of the kitchen and Jenny abandons the toast she's making, having lost her appetite.

At ten-thirty, Phyllis is at the door. She's wearing bright red lipstick and has tousled pink hair.

'Come in,' Jenny says. 'Thank you so much for this. I can't tell you how much just a couple of hours' respite means to me.'

'That's okay, lovely. I enjoy it. Morning, Phil,' she says cheerily in her strong Bristolian accent.

'He's watching *Rip Off Britain*. He loves it for some reason. Do you want a cup of tea?'

'No, I'm fine.' She sits down on the sofa. 'It's good this, Phil.

I watch it at home. It's unbelievable what some people get up to.'

Phil says nothing, doesn't take his eyes from the screen where Angela Rippon is talking animatedly about a romance scam. 'It turns out that this man was not a pilot . . .'

Jenny hovers at the living room door. 'You have my phone number, Phyl.' Both turn to look at her.

'Of course,' Phyllis smiles. 'Now, I'm not being funny, but you've only got a couple of hours to yourself and if you stick around here, you're not really going to have much of a break. I can phone you if I need to.'

'Point taken,' Jenny says.

'So, what are you going to do?' Phyllis asks.

'I was going to pop into Hereford, get a few things for the weekend. Maybe have a coffee.'

'That sounds nice, Jenny. Enjoy your break.'

Jenny feels like she's being dismissed and grabs her bag. Outside, the air is warm and she dithers, the car keys in her hand. She doesn't want to traipse around the shops. She could go and see Fi Clark, but realises she's working in the newsagents this morning. Jenny stands in the driveway, not having a clue where to go. She shouldn't just do her chores in this precious time, but she has devoted herself so much to caring for Phil recently, that she doesn't know what she wants to do any more. It's hardly as if she has any hobbies or interests. Or even friends! It hits her like a ton of bricks.

In town, Jenny spends fifteen minutes trying to find a parking space, aware the clock is ticking. She wanders into Boots and stops at the make-up aisle. It all seems rather intimidating. It's so long since she wore make-up. She hasn't the time or the inclination these days. She catches sight of herself in one of the small mirrors. Good lord! She looks so haggard, with dark rings under her eyes and she seems to have a permanent scowl from the lines etched from her mouth to her jaw. When did she develop those sagging jowls? Months of broken sleep and worry, as well as the menopause, are hardly conducive to a youthful glow. What about a bit of foundation, a good face cream. Hmm. She contemplates asking for help. The two girls on the beauty counter don't look too busy. One is tapping a long red talon on her teeth, looking bored, and the other is tidying some lipsticks. They spotted her when she came in, but she saw their eyes slide past as they do with every woman over a certain age. Nothing to see here. Just some old bid well past her sell-by date making a last-ditch attempt to be attractive. Jenny tries to shake off her low mood. She knows she shouldn't be so hard on herself.

She calls into Costa and buys herself a flat white and, feeling a sense of purposelessness, settles down with a magazine. She needs this and next week she'll be more organised and book a hair appointment. This is the start of Jenny reclaiming her life and finding herself again. She cringes, thinking it sounds like one of those self-help books. She could get used to this, she decides, biting into a chocolate brownie.

By the time Jenny reaches home, it's almost midday. Feeling butterflies in her stomach, she knows this means a lot. If Phil has enjoyed himself, she can do this again without guilt. If he hasn't . . .

At the kitchen table, Phyllis and Phil are playing a memory card game. 'Well done, Phil,' she says as he turns over a card with a motorbike on, pairing it with the other card. She manages to inject some warmth in her tone but without being patronising.

'Have you had a good time, Phil?' Jenny asks.

'Yes, I like this game.'

'I'll bring it over next week,' Phyllis says. 'I've got lots of puzzles and games to keep us occupied. Gosh, is it that time already? Time flies when you're having fun, eh, Phil.'

'Has everything been okay?' Jenny asks Phyllis this time.

'You are a worrier,' she smiles. 'Of course, it's been ok. Phil and I get on like a house on fire.' Phil nods in agreement at this. 'Did you enjoy in town?'

'Yes, I did. It was nice to have some time for myself.'

'You're looking a bit brighter. Right, then, lovely. I've got to make tracks. I've got another friend to see now in Ross. Same time next week?'

She's like the Mary Poppins for dementia patients, Jenny thinks, as she watches Phyllis get into her black Renault Clio.

'Let's have some lunch,' she says as she returns to the kitchen. She feels lighter and puts on some music as she warms up some soup. 'I'm still not used to this new hob,' she calls to Phil.

Hearing some clattering outside, she sees Jake going into the shed. What now? He looks unhappy about something as he kicks the door in irritation when it won't close first time. This is so unlike him. This move with Lola has really affected him and who can blame him?

'You're home early, Jake. I wasn't expecting to see you until this evening. How did the kayaking go with that school group?'

'It was a fucking disaster!' he says.

'Jake! Really!' He knows she doesn't like him swearing. 'What on earth happened?'

'One of the teenagers was mucking around. I knew he was trouble from the start and the teacher was a right knob, ignoring it.' Jenny refrains from telling him again about his swearing. It's so unlike him. 'Anyway, he kept using his oar to nudge his friend's kayak. I warned him but the silly bugger ignored me and there were fourteen hormonal and immature teenagers. It was impossible to keep control of them.'

'So, what happened?' asks Jenny, dreading the answer.

'He tipped right in and was carried downstream for about fifty metres. Thank God for that overhanging tree at Brookside. I went after him, and he did have a life jacket on. He had a helluva fright, though. The worst thing was the teacher was going ballistic. Shouting in my face that he was going to throw the book at me. He was going to consult the school's legal team. I shouldn't be running a business. Blah blah blah! I felt like hitting him.'

Jenny stomach lurches.

'I didn't, of course. I'm not that stupid.'

'Didn't anyone say anything?'

'Well, the other teacher showed a bit of common sense, tried to get this teacher, Tim Cavendish, to calm down. He was threatening to go to the papers, get the business closed down. I haven't got the stomach to go out this afternoon with the other group booked in.'

'It seems so unfair,' Jenny says, biting her lip.

'Sometimes these school groups are more trouble than they're worth, but they're fast becoming the biggest part of the business.'

'But if you're insured properly, Jake,'

'You'd think it would be enough, but bad publicity like this could mean other schools might not touch us with a barge pole.' Suddenly, Jake gets up, 'I'm off to The Trout.'

It's one thing after another, Jenny thinks as she watches Jake's retreating back. There was nothing she could do to help him with this or with the Amber and Lola situation. She hopes this new girl of his can give him some support. But why the hell he's being so secretive about her, she can't imagine.

Chapter Twenty-Three

Pippa

'Rude cow!' Hannah gasps down the phone.

'I know!' Pippa says, relieved to get the reaction she's been wanting all this time. 'I just know she's the one who told the council, probably dragged the information out of Grant when she was stealing him away.'

'How vindictive! It's like a TV drama down there. Who knew country life could be so spicy?' Hannah says excitedly. 'And I thought you'd ditched London for a quiet life making biscuits and stitching quilts.'

'I wish,' Pippa says, lying back on the sofa. She's been feeling guilty about writing those reviews on Tripadvisor, particularly with the effort it took to make separate accounts. It's nothing compared to what Jenny's done to her, though. And if Jenny wants to take Pippa down, then she's not going without a fight.

She usually avoided speaking to Hannah in the communal living room, not wanting her guests to catch wind of the Riverside Lodge drama. But Pippa's guests are out for the night, and now her work's done, she's putting her feet up.

'There has been a development with Jake, though,' Pippa's unable to hold the information back. She tells Hannah about their picnic date, how perfect the day had been once she'd got to River's Rock.

'Pipps, he's the one, I can feel it,' Hannah says.

'He is not the one,' Pippa fakes annoyance but she can't help herself smiling. 'He's the . . . one for right now. I don't know about the future, I mean, we're so different. Plus, the situation with his ex is . . . complicated. She was trying to call him towards the end of our date. And I should just be focusing on Pumpkin Cottage right now.'

'You know what they say, all work and no play . . .'

'You're right,' Pippa agrees, 'and with Jake I can definitely play.'

'I'm not sure I'm with *the one*,' Hannah says. 'Another dinner date, another disappointment last night.'

'Louis still hasn't proposed?'

'Of course not. I'm starting to wonder if he bought that ring for someone else,' Hannah sighs.

'Surely not,' Pippa says, but she is starting to sense Hannah's panic. Maybe she should nudge Louis along. She still hasn't managed to make contact with him.

Pippa manages to placate Hannah and move her on to another topic, but when the conversation has finished, she tries calling Louis again. No answer.

Pippa opens WhatsApp, scrolls to her last messages with Louis, which ironically were him sending pictures of ring ideas. It's odd he hasn't proposed by now. Pippa is about to send him a message when she notices he's currently online. *Any chance you could answer my calls?* she sends with a smiley emoji. She feels bad for cornering him but she has no choice.

Pippa! I'm at work at the moment, only have two mins. Busy night tonight. Will call tomorrow. It seems odd being at work at seven o'clock in the evening.

Buoyed by her conversation with Hannah, Pippa decides to call him anyway. This time he can't ignore her.

'Pippa, I really can't speak for long,' he says.

'I won't keep you. I just wanted to check in on proposal plans.'

There's an awkward silence where Pippa can sense Louis deciding on his next move.

'Well . . .' he hesitates, 'a bit of a disaster, I guess.'

'I thought you were planning to do it on her birthday?'

'I was but . . . oh, I don't know, Pipps, it's been weird lately,' Louis sighs. Pippa likes that he uses Hannah's affectionate name for her. 'You won't tell her this, will you?'

'No,' Pippa shakes her head, although she knows firmly where her loyalties lie. If Louis tells her something awful, then she will definitely tell Hannah. Oh God, she hopes he isn't about to tell her something awful. 'What do you mean weird?'

'Well, the last few weeks Hannah's been acting strangely. It's like something's flicked a switch in her. It's hard to put my finger on but it's like she's jumpy, really suspicious of me. She's just not herself.'

Pippa sighs. She wonders if the switch that's been flicked was finding the engagement ring. She wishes Hannah had never seen it. Hannah's been an open book since Pippa met her, it's one of the things she loves about her. She knows Hannah has been unable to hide her excitement at a proposal. No wonder she's been acting weirdly.

'She's been really quiet at home, too. When we get back from a meal or drinks, it's like she doesn't want to speak to me, she's really quiet and moody. I can't propose when she's like this – I don't think she'll say yes. I don't think she wants to be with me any more. You don't know anything, do you?'

'Urrrgh,' Pippa wavers, unsure how much to reveal. 'It doesn't sound like Hannah. She loves you, Louis. She's got a lot on her plate right now.' Pippa decides not to tell him about her finding the engagement ring.

'She has been pretty devastated since you moved away,' he concedes and Pippa's heart wants to burst.

'I think a proposal is just what she needs to pick her up,' Pippa says. She wants to bash their heads together, the pair of them. If only Louis would get on and propose, Hannah would go back to normal. She can't tell him this, though.

'I don't know, Pipps. I've never known her like this.' Louis sounds really exasperated.

'Trust me,' Pippa says. 'I may not be her future fiancé, but I've known Hannah a long time. She'll be delighted when you do propose and she will definitely say yes.' *Just pull your finger out and do it*, Pippa wants to yell.

'Maybe you're right.'

'Definitely I'm right,' Pippa says, triumphant. 'Do it soon. Or else I'll keep ringing you and distracting you from all that fake work that's so important.'

'Yeah, yeah,' Louis chuckles. Pippa hopes she's embarrassed him and hangs up.

'Pair of muppets,' she says aloud to herself. Their problems could be so easily solved if they just communicated. She suddenly thinks of Jenny Foster. Could Pippa just communicate with her? Lay her cards on the table?

No, the woman is totally unreasonable. She wouldn't listen to her.

Pippa is planning to host a little gathering at Pumpkin Cottage next week for Hallowe'en. She just hopes Jenny isn't planning any more acts of sabotage for it.

'Knock-knock,' Pippa hears a familiar voice call out from the hallway. She's surprised to see Jake standing there.

'I don't recall you booking a room for the night,' Pippa grins as she approaches him.

He gives her a weak smile. 'Sorry, I've just had a day of it. Could really do with seeing you. I'll go if you're busy, though. I don't want to keep you from your guests.'

'Please, I've only got one couple in tonight attending a wedding in Ross-on-Wye, Orles Barn.'

'Fancy,' Jake smiles, but Pippa can tell he's not his usual self.

'They'll be back late, I've given them a key. The place is our own.' She's not sure why she feels her cheeks heat at this. She wishes she'd had prior warning of Jake's arrival. Pippa doesn't have any make-up on, was planning a quiet night in with Netflix and a hot chocolate. She loves watching *Gilmore Girls* on a quiet night, and thinks Riverdean could give Stars Hollow a run for its money. Particularly dressed in its current autumn colours. Plus, Lorelai and Rory remind Pippa of her relationship with her own mother, their easy banter and constant closeness.

But now Jake is here, and sofa slobbing is far from Pippa's mind.

'Do you want a drink of anything? I've got a bottle of red I opened last night.'

'Perfect,' Jake follows her to the kitchen, and fetches two wine glasses from a cabinet ready for Pippa to pour. They both lean against the kitchen island and Jake rubs a hand through his short hair.

'You said you've had a day of it?' She prompts, before clinking her glass against Jake's. The Pinot Noir slips down easily, both smoky and earthy in Pippa's mouth.

'I took a school group out in the kayaks this morning, and this idiot kid fell in. Totally his fault but the teacher went ballistic, threatening to sue us and everything,' Jake gives a weary sigh.

'Ouch,' Pippa takes another sip of wine.

'I always knew something like this would happen one day. I

pulled him out within seconds, luckily.'

'Was the kid all right?'

'Not a scratch on him, thank God, or I wouldn't have heard the end of it. The teacher acted like I'd dunked him in head first, he was so unreasonable.'

'Arsehole,' Pippa said. 'He probably felt guilty himself, I bet he wasn't even watching him?'

'Too busy chatting to tell him off for fooling around and leaning out,' Jake shrugs. 'You're right. I just hope this doesn't spell trouble for the business. Things are quiet over the winter anyway. I can't stand to lose the bookings we've got.'

'You won't,' Pippa says. 'Was he wearing a life jacket?'

'Yes.'

'And you did your usual safety brief?'

'Yes.'

'And the teenager was unscathed?'

Jake nods, smiling.

'Then you did everything right.'

'It could have been a lot worse, though.'

'I've never met Negativity Jake before,' Pippa says. Jake's general sunny demeanour is one of the things she likes about him. 'Hi, I'm Pippa.'

'Hi, Sarcasm Pippa,' Jake jokes.

'Seriously, though, I've not seen you like this. Is there anything more going on?'

'Well,' Jake sighs and Pippa can tell she's hit the nail on the head. She's never felt this in-tune with a guy before now. 'I was having a shitty day anyway after speaking to Amber last night . . .' Pippa's heart lurches at the mention of his ex's name, but she forces herself not to react. There can't be anything going on with his ex or else he wouldn't be standing here with Pippa. 'The move to France is definitely going ahead. She's sold their flat and she and Ethan have found a place in Bergerac. She was a bit sheepish telling me, knowing my life's going to be destroyed.'

'Oh,' Pippa breathes, lost for words.

'I can't imagine not being able to see my Lola every other week.' He looks tearful, she thinks. 'God, sorry, I don't mean to get heavy like this. It just makes me so mad she's moving without a second thought for how I'll feel, how it will affect mine and Lola's relationship.'

Jake drains his wine glass and Pippa refills without questioning him. She doesn't interrupt, sensing Jake's need to get this off his chest.

'I know she's a good mum and I know she wants the best for Lola. And Lola will love France. Apparently, they've looked round the international school and Lola's already made a friend there. I guess I just feel like I'm being left out of the picture. How will I fit into Lola's life?'

'I guess . . .' Pippa starts awkwardly, 'France isn't that far?' She winces, knowing that's hardly what Jake wants to hear.

'That's what my mum says. And Amber's talked about alternating every school holiday. It feels about a million miles away, though, compared to Cardiff,' he says. 'Bloody Amber. I wanted you to meet Lola soon. She'd love you.'

Pippa feels astounded for a second. She had no idea Jake was thinking of her in that way. Meeting his child is a huge deal. It means he sees more in their future than Pippa's even thought about. Although, she wonders if that's true; she's been the one having to remind herself to hold back with Jake, to enjoy him *for now* without thinking about what's next. Could they really have a future together?

The way Jake is now, all vulnerable and honest, it makes Pippa want to dive in head first into the future.

'I'd love to meet her properly, whenever you're ready,' Pippa smiles. 'Hopefully, she'll remember that I found her doll.' Jake looks confused for a moment before remembering when they first met. Pippa doesn't know how she'd feel meeting Lola, she's guessing Jake's never introduced her to a woman he's dating before. And if she meets Lola, does that mean she'll meet Amber? Pippa's brain is working overtime thinking of different scenarios.

She needs to loosen up and tops up her own wine glass too.

'Anyway, I'm not sure if that'll happen now before they go to France. Apparently, Amber's *swamped* with all the packing and things they need to sort out before the new year. It's devastating for me, but I suppose I'll have to come to terms with it. Sorry, you must be wondering what you've let yourself in for.' Jake gives a weak laugh.

At this, Pippa hugs him. She can see he needs it. Jake holds her back tightly. It feels so familiar and comforting, somehow, being in his arms. Pippa can't believe she's found this just weeks into living in Riverdean. Maybe guiding Pippa here really was her mother's way of looking out for her after she was gone.

'Anyway, enough about my saga. Tell me about your day. Distract me,' Jake says.

An idea occurs to Pippa. 'Well, if you really want distracting, how do you feel about giving this hot tub a try?'

The glint in his eye meets Pippa's. 'I thought it was for guests only?'

'You're my guest for tonight. An uninvited one, true.'

'I haven't got my swimming trunks.'

'I could get you a pair from the lost and found,' Pippa laughs then, buoyed by the wine, grabs his hand. 'Follow me.' She takes another bottle with the other hand, and Jake brings their glasses.

Pippa flicks on the fairy lights surrounding the tub, then

realising that makes them visible from the street, decides against it. She busies herself with untying the cover from the tub.

'You seriously want me to strip off in this temperature?' Jake shivers.

'Pour us some more wine and you won't feel it,' Pippa instructs. She smiles at the steam coming from the tub again, inviting them in. It's a perfect night, the whole world quiet, including the river, which lies still and dormant, snaking a trail of silver through the night. Jake hands her a glass and they *cheers* again.

'Are you sure you want a hot tub, after, you know, everything that's happened today?'

'I think this is exactly what I want. Are you sure you want to do this?' Jake says, serious now, and Pippa knows he's talking about more than just the hot tub.

'I am,' she nods, then pulls him closer to her, kissing him. She thinks this way is better, unprepared, and the red wine has loosened all her inhibitions in the best possible way. So much so, she starts pulling Jake's shirt up. His body feels solid against hers, warm. Pippa sighs.

'Well, this isn't fair,' Jake says, 'why am I the only one shivering?'

He pulls at Pippa's top, and she slips out of her jeans. He's right, it really is freezing. 'Let's do this quickly.' Jake spins Pippa round so her back is against him and places a long warm kiss against her neck. It feels delicious, and Pippa nearly loses her balance leaning backwards in to him. He unhooks her bra, and Pippa without pausing to think about what she's doing, slips it off along with her knickers. She slides into the hot tub before Jake can see anything. She looks back up at him, taking in his bare chest, the shadows from the tub accentuating his lean musculature.

'It's your turn,' Pippa says, feeling like the luckiest woman in the world to have a front row ticket.

Jake smiles, embarrassed, which makes him even more attractive if anything, then takes a swig from his wine glass before handing it to Pippa. In one swift move, he removes his jeans and underwear, and Pippa catches a glimpse of his nakedness before he slips into the tub beside her.

The sound of the ripples he makes just subsides enough for Pippa and Jake to hear giggling in the distance. She looks around shocked, then the sound of more giggles leads her eyes to the lane outside Pumpkin Cottage. Brett and Shaun are stumbling away, holding each other's arms. Oh dear, perhaps the hot tub isn't quite as private as Pippa thought. The balustrade shields them from view, but perhaps their voices have drifted to the ears of passers-by.

'Oh dear,' Jake says. 'Brett's going to be a nightmare when I see him. Can I ever show my face in The Trout again?'

'Well, we can add indecent exposure to your list of sackable offences for the day now,' Pippa snorts. Jake's right, Brett will be a nightmare. For tonight, though, Jake's just hers.

'This is not how I thought today would end,' Jake gasps. Pippa kisses him, before sliding her body onto his, sitting on his lap.

'Who said anything about the day ending?'

Chapter Twenty-Four

Jenny

'I've finished in Room Five,' says Abi, 'and taken the rubbish around the back. Is there anything else needs doing?' She stands at the kitchen door where Jenny is stacking the dishwasher. Her hair is dishevelled and her mascara is smudged under her eyes. Caring for a little one on her own must be so hard. Jenny remembers when she and Mike first split and she had to look after Jake on her own for four years until she met Phil. Some days she was so desperate for sleep, she could have cried. She refrains from considering how similar it is caring for Phil. The tantrums, the sleepless nights and, even though Phil can feed himself, he forgets and Jenny has to prompt him to finish what he's eating.

'No, it's okay, love,' Jenny says. 'I'll see you in the morning.'

'Oh, would it be all right if I started a bit later on Friday, only an hour or so, and I'll work on, of course.'

'Yes, that's fine. The baby has an appointment.'

'Well, it's not that . . .' Abi hesitates. 'I've been invited to a Hallowe'en party and Mum has agreed to look after Storm for me. It's just that it's likely to be a late night and I'd rather say beforehand.'

Jenny smiles. Abi rarely asks for time off. 'In Ross, is it?'

'No, it's here in the village. Pippa Mason in Pumpkin Cottage.

Practically the whole of Riverdean has been invited . . .' She trails off as the penny drops that Jenny is clearly not on the guest list.

'That's fine,' Jenny says frostily. 'Just don't make a habit of it.'

Abi makes a hasty retreat, grabbing her coat from the coat stand in the hallway.

'Morning, Jake,' she calls as she leaves. 'Late night, was it?' Abi giggles. Jenny can't hear Jake's response and then the door slams.

'Morning. Coffee's brewing,' Jenny says as Jake enters the kitchen. 'You look like you need the caffeine. Good night at the pub last night?'

'Not bad. A bacon butty would go down well,' he grins. 'I've got a late start today.'

'I hope all this business with that tearaway teenager blows over.'

'Apparently, he was excluded from another school for his behaviour so he's got form.' Jake pours a coffee. 'Dad's quiet this morning.'

'I think he's in a mood. I've been trying to prepare him all week about going for lunch at Louise and Mark's. He hates any disruption to his routine. It really upsets him. Not that he'll remember that I've told him.' They both look at Phil who is staring at the garden. 'He's looking for that robin again. He gets so excited when he sees him. Come on, then, let's get you that bacon butty,' Jenny says, busying herself.

'You superhero,' Jake beams.

Jenny pulls up outside the house in the village of Thornbrook, just three miles from Ross-on-Wye. She had to switch satnav off earlier as it seemed to upset Phil and he kept asking 'Who's that?'

'Well, this is quite a grand house, Phil,' she says. The house is a substantial Georgian property set in about half an acre with sash windows and fronds of ivy creeping around the front door. 'It's a bit much for two people. Think of all that cleaning. Mark surely can't tend the garden.' Jenny often babbles to herself even though Phil has no idea of the thread of her conversation. She convinces herself it's reassuring that he hears her voice and it makes her feel less alone when Phil is so exiled from her.

'Come on, Phil,' she says, unclipping his seat belt. 'You remember Louise and Mark from choir? They've invited us for lunch. Isn't that nice?'

Louise is at the door, waiting for them, an apron tied loosely around her waist. 'Well, hello, you two. You've found us, then, and brought the sunshine with you. Mark's in the conservatory. Come in, come in.'

'What a lovely house, Louise,' Jenny says, looping her arm through Phil's and steering him inside.

Louise looks directly at Jenny, 'Everything okay?'

'Fine. It took some persuading to get him into the car and I've been talking all week about it.'

Louise nods sympathetically and leads them through the house. Like a meerkat, Jenny's head swivels as they pass reception rooms either side of the hallway, trying to catch a glimpse of the decor and furnishings inside. 'We always seem to gravitate to the kitchen and conservatory these days. The house is far too large for the two of us, but the thought of moving and all that entails.' Louise shudders.

'It's really impressive, Louise. My God, it must be worth a fortune.'

'Back in the day, we used to flip houses. This was meant to be our forever home. Here he is.' Mark is sitting at a large wooden table in the conservatory, which is drenched in light. 'He's doing a word search now, but he's helped me prepare lunch. Say hello to Jenny and Phil, Mark.'

'Hi Mark,' Jenny says, wondering if it's ever possible not to sound patronising with dementia patients.

'We went to tai chi this morning in Ross. It helps us both relax, to be honest,' Louise says, flicking her blonde hair out of her eyes. 'We're having quiche and salad. I hope that's okay. You stay with Phil and don't worry about helping.'

It's so easy with Louise, Jenny thinks. She completely understands how disorientating it is for someone like Phil to come into a new house. No explanation is needed.

'Why are we here?' Phil asks Jenny.

'To have lunch with our friends. Remember I told you in the car. I've been telling you every day this past week.' She rolls her eyes.

'These aren't our friends. I don't know who they are.'

'They're new friends from choir, Louise and Mark. You remember the choir.'

'Do you like word searches, Phil? I have another book of them here.' Louise gently distracts him.

'Phil used to be an avid reader. History was the subject he taught and he was a real history buff.' *Now, he struggles with word searches.*

'Mark used to run his own IT business. I was a Bed Manager in Hereford County Hospital. It seems a lifetime ago now. I had to give up two years ago when Mark finally had the diagnosis. It took seven years for them to tell us he has early onset Alzheimer's. By then, I could have told them myself.' Jenny moves to a stool at the edge of the island, where she can keep an eye on Phil. She watches as Louise starts cutting the quiche.

'That looks delicious,' Jenny says. In the conservatory, Phil's head is down, a look of intense concentration on his face.

'I enjoyed cooking this earlier. It's barely cooking but Mark has less interest in food these days.'

'All I seem to do is cook breakfasts. I do enjoy baking when my granddaughter Lola comes over, though. Phil likes his traditional food.'

'I don't know how you manage to run a bed and breakfast and care for Phil.'

'Well, I don't know how long I'll be able to continue. He tried to get into bed with one of our guests the other night and he was starkers. The poor woman almost had a coronary.'

Louise laughs, 'If you didn't see the funny side, I think you'd go mad.' She pauses and lowers her voice, 'I miss my old life. I can't even allow myself to remember it too much. It's just too sad.'

Jenny nods, 'It is. Phil was only recently diagnosed but we'd known for a long time. It was a relief in a way. It's odd how he has these moments of clarity, and he apologises so much. Like he's aware he's a burden. Sorry, a burden seems a terrible way to say it.'

'Don't feel guilty,' Louise says. 'That's one of the hardest things to come to terms with. You know, the way your relationship changes. Mark was one of these super-confident, charismatic people. Everyone loved him and we had lots of friends, dinners out.' The two of them look over to Mark, a pen in his hand as he scours the page. 'Now, I do everything for him, washing, dressing, feeding. And, Christ, sometimes he's so infuriating. Do you know one evening, when he threw his dinner on the floor, I completely lost it. I screamed that I hated him, and he cried. I was so ashamed of myself.'

'We're not saints, Louise.'

'I know. It was the pressure – it was too much. I need regular breaks. We've joined local groups and that helps. That support is everything. I get cabin fever in the house. And people in the same situation understand without saying the words.'

'I hate having to make all the decisions about every little detail in our lives,' Jenny says. 'It's lonely and I'm really conscious of putting too much on Jake. He's got his own problems with his business and the split from his girlfriend hit him hard.'

'I've made some lemonade. Do you want to pour it? I could do with a nice, chilled Pinot Grigio with lunch, but I daren't.' Louise grins.

'Are you and Mark still intimate?' Jenny says in almost a whisper, then flushes, aware that wasn't appropriate, 'Sorry, you don't have to answer that. It's just . . . I never get to talk about these things to anyone.'

'No, it's okay. You have to talk to someone about it. We used to have a fantastic sex life before he was ill and then there was a time when he lost all his inhibitions. Honestly, there was no filter. One time he said he was going to fuck me over the kitchen counter and how he wanted me to wear my heels. I wouldn't have minded but my daughter was here. It was mortifying.' She shudders. 'It dwindled then. I don't feel that way about him any more. It's hard to have sexy thoughts about someone when you're their carer. We still occasionally kiss and cuddle.'

Jenny nods, 'Yes, it's the same with us.'

'We're only fifty-four. It's hard to give up romance and sex at this age. Perhaps I need a lover,' Louise says, and Jenny is unsure if she is joking.

'Have you made any plans? For later, I mean.'

'Not, really. I will have to sell up eventually and move into something more manageable. I don't suppose I'll be able to look after Mark by myself forever.' Although the men are out of earshot, Louise speaks in an undertone. 'I have looked at care homes. It's inevitable he'll have to go into one eventually. He's not going to get better. A couple of weeks ago, when I lost my temper with him, he started shouting *Put me in a bloody care home!* I felt awful.'

'I suppose the time will come, won't it?'

'Leah and Martha, our daughters, help but they both have busy lives. Leah has two little ones and Martha lives in London. Mark frightened my grandson the other day. He didn't like his food and threw the plate. Poor Charlie howled his eyes out. How do you explain to a three-year-old that Grandpa has a bad head and can't help it?'

'Phil adores Lola, but his behaviour is unpredictable. I'd never leave him alone with her.' Jenny's never consciously acknowledged this before, but it's true. Phil can't assure his own safety, let alone Lola's. How did they get here? Sometimes the change in him has the power to wind Jenny.

Louise takes the food to the table. 'No one imagines a future like this, do they? Sorry, I don't mean to be so maudlin.'

'It's nice to get it off your chest. Sometimes I feel I have no one to talk to. I realised the other day that I barely have any friends. I'm so wrapped up in caring for Phil and we're hardly the most entertaining company. Let's just say we don't get many invites to . . .'

'Phil's gone in the garden,' Louise says, looking up.

Jenny gets up straight away, 'Oh lord, what now? He's confused. He hates going anywhere new.' She races into the garden. 'Where are you off to, Phil? You know you're not supposed to wander off like this.'

'I couldn't see you,' he says, irritated.

'Silly. I was only in the kitchen. Come on, Louise has made us a lovely lunch.'

'I don't want it. I'm not hungry. I want to go home.'

'Well, you'll have to wait for me as I *am* hungry. I've been looking forward to this.'

Phil has to be cajoled to eat his lunch. 'I'm so sorry, Louise. You've gone to so much trouble.'

'This is a real treat for me,' Louise says, brushing off her apology. 'Are you enjoying the choir, Phil?' Louise asks. 'What's your favourite song?'

Jenny can see she's distracting Phil; she's someone used to irrational and unreasonable behaviour.

'"Handbags and Gladrags",' he says, without hesitation.

Jenny sniggers, 'Gosh, the choir hasn't sung that yet. It would be a hard one to sing.'

'I wonder if Angela will pull off this concert in Hereford Cathedral,' Louise muses.

'If anyone can, she can,' Jenny says.

'It's really uplifting going to the choir. There's something about singing,' says Louise. 'Even if they sound like screeching alley cats sometimes.'

'That's better, Phil. I'm glad you're eating a bit,' Jenny says, relieved.

After coffees, Jenny says, 'We'd better make tracks. I've got a few things to finish at home.'

'You don't need to explain. It's been lovely having you both over.'

'Well, you must come over to us next time.'

Louise nods and she and Mark wave them from the door.

'That was a lovely lunch,' Jenny says, as they head out of the driveway. She feels rejuvenated. It was such a relief to speak to Louise and everything she'd said resonated with Jenny. 'Did you enjoy?'

Phil shakes his head, 'I don't like them.'

Chapter Twenty-Five

Pippa

'Thank fuck for that,' Hannah says, getting out of the car. 'I've been stuck behind a tractor for the last twenty minutes, travelling about half a mile an hour.'

Pippa comes around to hug her friend, 'Thanks for making the journey.'

'Please,' Hannah hugs her back, 'if my best friend is hosting a Hallowe'en party, even if it's in the middle of hick-country, I'm there. I told work I had to leave early for a gynaecology appointment. Before I'd even finished the word *gynae*, my weirdo boss had signed the paper. Probably afraid I'd start talking about periods.'

'I told my boss I wasn't feeling well. She didn't believe me,' Pippa jokes.

'She's a real arsehole, that one,' Hannah laughs, carrying a suitcase over the gravel towards Pumpkin Cottage.

'Ooh, it's looking decidedly spooky in here.' Hannah admires the kitchen. Pippa has draped cobwebs across all horizontal surfaces, and has laid out a table with biscuits in the shape of bats, witches' fingers made of marshmallow, and fake syringes of blood, which really hold strawberry gel.

'It's taken me all afternoon,' Pippa says. 'I was made up when I found this bunting, though,' she indicates the black lace. 'Charity shop in Hereford.'

Hannah decants several bottles from her case into the fridge, then pours herself a glass of Prosecco. 'I'm in the mood for a party tonight, I need it after all this proposal stress with Louis. Seriously,' she practically downs the glass, 'I've given up. Maybe he's had cold feet, maybe it was never my ring in the first place, whatever. If he doesn't want to propose, that's fine. It's his loss.'

Pippa bites her lip. Hannah doesn't look very *fine* at all; she's clutching her glass like it's the handlebar of a white-knuckle ride. She's been urging Louis to do it all week and still nothing. She doesn't know what to say now to encourage Hannah without giving the game away.

'Don't give up on him, Han, he might surprise you one day.'

'Urgh, I don't even want to talk about it. I've given enough mental energy to the situation,' she shakes her head. 'Let's go and get ready. How many are you expecting to turn up?'

'No more than about twenty,' Pippa says, 'I've basically invited all Riverdean residents between the ages of 25 and 35. Plus Brett and Shaun. Lots couldn't make it. I don't think it'll be too rowdy.'

Pippa's heart flutters when she sees the kitchen rammed with people.

'Sorry,' she says, squeezing past Abi and her friend. It's her first night out without the baby in a long time, and she seems to be making up for it in alcohol consumption.

There are already more than twenty people here, and Jake hasn't even arrived with his friends yet. It seems everyone she's invited has brought someone extra with them. Pippa's surprised to see her hallway filled with faces she doesn't recognise.

Pippa refreshes a few glasses, including her own, then forces herself to leave the kitchen. Although she's hosting, she wants to enjoy her own party without worrying about the numbers or whether people are having a good time. She trusts the friends she's made in Riverdean so far, no one's going to damage the kitchen or get ridiculously drunk. It's the countryside, after all, she thinks.

The cackle at the start of Michael Jackson's 'Thriller' rings out through the speakers. 'I'm worried my playlist has peaked too soon,' Pippa says as she gets back to the living room where Monica is chatting to Hannah. '"Thriller" should be on later when everyone's dancing.'

'So that was five weeks ago, still nothing.' Hannah doesn't seem to have heard Pippa, and has been filling Monica in on the Louis situation.

Pippa was worried Hannah and Monica wouldn't get on as they have totally opposite lifestyles and nothing in common, but they both seem absorbed in talking about relationship dramas, she needn't have stressed about it. A new group of people edge their way into the room, led by Fi Clark from the newsagents. The shuffling of bodies that occurs sends a lamp off the edge of Pippa's coffee table and onto the floor.

'I'm so sorry,' Fi starts saying, scooping up the lamp.

'It's okay,' Pippa smiles, inspecting the object. 'Not a scratch on it.' But she hides the offending lamp and a few other possessions on the window sill. Pippa catches her appearance in the mirror. She and Hannah have dressed up as black cats – not the most original Hallowe'en costume but definitely the easiest. Pippa just hopes Jake arrives to see her while she still looks semi-decent. She has stuck two black felt ears onto a hairband, and stuffed one leg of a pair of tights with newspaper to make a tail. It's dragging Pippa's little black dress down at the back and is definitely a tripping hazard with the number of people in here.

On Pippa's next trip to the kitchen, she notices more of Abi's friends have arrived, along with some people she's seen in The Trout once or twice. They all smile at her sheepishly, as though she's going to kick them out, and for a minute Pippa feels like doing just that, before considering what that would do for her reputation in Riverdean. Besides, there's no sign of Jake yet and it's nearly eleven. Pippa doesn't want the party to be over before he's arrived.

One of Abi's friends looks younger than the others, wearing an asymmetric white mini dress with a veil and smudged lipstick that she's guessing is meant to be a zombie bride. She also seems much more drunk than the others, given she's the only person dancing and shouting over the music. Pippa tells herself to keep an eye on her.

As Pippa edges out of the room, she collides with a familiar face.

'Grant!' she says in surprise.

'Hi,' he mutters, looking over Pippa's shoulder. 'Thanks for the invite.'

She wants to say *I didn't invite you.*

'Is that your friend, Hannah, I just saw?'

'Yes,' Pippa sighs.

'She down for the weekend?'

'Yes,' she crosses her arms. Grant flirting with Hannah is the last thing she needs.

'Which room is she staying in?'

'Gross,' Pippa says, no longer having the energy to make pleasantries, and moving away from him. Grant gives a dirty laugh.

'Are you okay?' Monica stops her. 'You look a bit stressed?'

'I'm fine,' she says. 'The house is just starting to feel a little cramped with everyone in here. I'm sure I don't know half these people.' In the corner of her eye, she sees Grant making his way over to Hannah, her friend hugging him, then doing a hair flip and overexaggerated laugh. Oh well, it seems Pippa's powerless to stop that pair talking.

'Let me know if it gets too much,' Monica says, placing both hands on Pippa's shoulders. 'It seems like everyone's having a good time, though.'

'You're right, besides, it's the country. It's not like a city party, is it? People won't get too rowdy.'

An odd look crosses Monica's face. 'Sure,' she says, not sounding totally convinced. 'Come on, let's go and get a shot – I love the pumpkin juice and vodka one.'

'I didn't make shots,' Pippa says, confused.

'Then maybe Brett and Shaun have brought them.'

'Sorry we're late, Pipps,' Brett says. Pippa's pleased her nickname is catching on Riverdean. 'Shaun wouldn't let us leave until all the punters had gone. I thought this old couple were going to move in.' He is clearly well-lubricated and dressed like Madonna in the Blond Ambition days, complete with conical pink bra. Shaun has chosen a more eighties Madonna look.

'I love it! Well, it seems I have you to thank for the pumpkin shots,' Pippa eyes the trays of shot glasses Brett and Shaun have brought. They hand her one and she clinks with them before downing her shot. Pippa's drunk enough that she should be feeling the relaxing effects of the booze now, but she still feels tense watching the guests stumbling around. The floors feel sticky to Pippa, probably after a few pumpkin spillages.

'Where's your man?' Brett asks now, breathing fumes of vodka into Pippa's face. 'We've only come to get another glimpse of those abs, those shoulders, and that massive—'

'It was definitely a welcome sight in the middle of a dreary

Riverdean night,' Shaun says, pulling his fiancé back.

'Don't tell him that. Jake will never live it down,' Pippa says.

'Precisely why we *will* tell him that,' Brett cackles. 'It was *quite* the show.'

'Don't listen to him,' Shaun says. 'We didn't see a thing. We heard a lot, though.'

Brett chips in. 'You are one lucky girl. Ooh, I love this song.' He immediately grabs Shaun's hand and starts dancing to 'Monster Mash'.

A pair of sturdy hands grasp Pippa's waist. 'Surprise!' Jake whispers in her ear. She turns round to see a very normal-looking Jake.

'Where is your costume?'

'This is it,' he holds his arms out, 'I'm a North Face advert. Literally head to toe.'

'That's rubbish. You wear this stuff all the time,' Pippa says. He's in a fleece, jeans and walking boots.

'Not true!'

'Yeah, Pipps, he wasn't wearing it in the hot tub last week,' Brett squeals. She can see Jake flushing red as she knew he would. She lets Jake greet Brett and Shaun before he comes back to her.

'I've got half a mind to squirt some strawberry gel over you, then at least you can be a zombie North Face advert.'

'I'm sorry I'm so late,' Jake kisses her cheek. 'Amber was an hour late picking Lola up. I wasn't meant to have her today but apparently Amber had to do some *France admin* as she called it.' Pippa can tell he needs to talk about it. Later, when they're in private.

'Did you bring the guys?' Pippa's question is answered by a roar as three burly men that Pippa knows to be Jake's mates walk into the kitchen. If testosterone had a sound, this would be it, she thinks. She's met them in The Trout and they are exactly what she'd expected – outdoorsy, alpha male, big drinkers.

'They were waiting for me in the pub, and I think it's safe to say they started without me,' Jake explains.

'All right, Pippa?' The group come over and Pippa finds herself in the middle of drunken male in-jokes. She fears for the future of her house, which is being used and abused by the guests, especially as she hears another smash and an awkward laugh from the next room.

'Where are you sneaking off to?' Jake asks.

'I thought I'd find Hannah. Do you want to meet her?'

Jake follows Pippa, holding her hand the whole time, but there's no sign of her. The drunkenness level of the crowd seems to have increased by the time they've done a loop of the house, with lots of dancing in the kitchen. Someone has a pumpkin on their head, the face Pippa carved into it barely recognisable now. The upside-down smile seems to jeer at her.

'I don't know where she's got to,' Pippa says, thinking that she hasn't seen Grant either.

'Maybe she's gone out for some fresh air,' Jake offers.

'Maybe,' Pippa admits weakly.

'Pippa, are people allowed in the hot tub?' Shaun asks her.

'No, no, definitely not,' Pippa says. She'd locked the door leading to the balcony.

'I think it might be a bit late for that.' Shaun leads her outside to where Abi is sitting in the middle of the tub, music blasting and coloured jets bubbling away. The younger woman is with her, with the other friends cheering them on. How did they get the keys? Pippa had hidden them away, hadn't she?

Pippa is about to go over and ask them nicely if they'd mind stepping out, her hospitality background kicking in, when the younger one stands, leans out, and proceeds to vomit over the side of the hot tub. It's like a horror film as Pippa watches dark sick cover her beautiful wooden balcony, before the girl flops back in the water and wipes her mouth.

'I'm so sorry,' her friends start apologising profusely.

'It's okay,' Pippa forces herself to say. 'As long as we get it cleaned up.'

'We'll help,' Pippa's grateful to the woman who says this.

'I'll get cleaning supplies. In the meantime, can you get her out?' She gestures to the hot tub, wanting to say *and take her home*. The last thing Pippa wants is vomit in the house. She thought this party would be a bit of fun, something nice for Riverdean locals to enjoy and to get to know each other. But this is turning out to be a nightmare. Maybe Pippa was wrong about country parties after all.

As she rushes inside to the kitchen, elbowing past people she's never seen before, Pippa notices a swish of black hair that she'd recognise any day. Hannah, pulling Grant along by the hand, and into the Maple Room where she's staying.

Pippa feels her heart sink as though plummeting in a very fast lift. How could Hannah do this to Louis? And how could Pippa let her? She's been so focused on her own issues tonight, she's ignored her friend. Tonight has all been a mistake, a big mistake.

'Woohooo!' she hears a loud male shout from the next room. The revelry of her partygoers feels insulting at the moment. Pippa's of half a mind to go and pull Hannah away from Grant, when she trips and stumbles on an empty beer can, falling forwards into her own side table. On the floor with bruised knees, Pippa feels superbly sober.

'Are you all right? Bit too much to drink?' A voice she doesn't recognise calls. Pippa turns to see a woman in her forties. She's not offering assistance, and so Pippa heaves herself up, righting the side table as she does.

'Fine . . .' Pippa says. 'Not had much.' The stress is ironically making her sound quite drunk, she thinks.

The woman frowns. 'The apple doesn't fall far from the tree there,' she mutters, before walking away.

It takes Pippa a second to realise what the stranger said, not that she's sure at all. 'Excuse me,' she starts, but the stranger is lost in the crowd now. *The apple doesn't fall far from the tree . . .* Is that a barbed comment about Pippa's mum? She needs to find out what that means, but is stopped by Monica.

'Mike, from Greenbrook, is getting in the river starkers,' she says, excitedly.

'What?' Pippa's too distracted by the apple comment to process Monica's words.

'He lost at beer pong, so he's going to jump in, swim across to Greenbrook.'

'Oh my God, he'll drown,' Pippa says, imagining the headlines about her party. 'This night is a disaster.' She just wants to turn the music down, which has been creeping up and up in volume all night, and get everyone out. There are loud chants and whistles coming from the lane outside Pumpkin Cottage, and guests are filtering out to watch the commotion.

One of Jake's friends, Mike, is standing in boxer shorts, while others cheer him on. He seems to be encouraging others to strip off, but is failing. He pushes one guy too hard, who then gives him a shove. Mike shouts, and the excitement of the crowd turns to aggression as he pushes back.

With dismay, Pippa catches sight of Jake's head in the middle of the brawl, although she can tell he's trying to break them up. He's shouting, 'Stop!' at the top of his voice, to no avail.

There's a forward surge of the crowd, and in one deafening crack, Mike hits the water. A few shouts are emitted from onlookers, before Jake follows him in, fully clothed. Pippa hears more retching from behind her, as Abi's friend is pulled out through the front door. She doesn't turn to look, her eyes glued on the black water of the river. She watches as Jake pulls Mike in, utterly relieved Jake was there and not drunk.

She'll have to go inside, find a blanket or a towel for him. Or is this the kind of situation that calls for a foil blanket? Or does that cool you down? She's seen people in them after a marathon. Pippa isn't thinking straight; she just wants everyone to leave.

As the excitement of the crowd dies down, the sound is replaced with a very distant siren, followed by a flash of blue lights in the trees covering the road above Pumpkin Cottage.

'Fuck! Who called the police?' one of Jake's friends says.

There is much booing and complaining amongst the crowd, but for the first time tonight Pippa feels totally relieved.

Chapter Twenty-Six

Jenny

'Have you thought about going a bit shorter?' the young stylist at Prime Cuts asks Jenny. She can't help but think the name sounds like dog food rather than an upmarket salon as this one is trying hard to be.

'I don't know,' Jenny says hesitantly. She had a restless night last night with Phil back and forth to the toilet, and one time she narrowly avoided him peeing into their wardrobe. Then that party of Pippa Mason's that must have gone on at least until two o'clock in the morning.

'Just above the chin and some layers. It would really flatter your face shape,' she insists. Jenny catches a waft of her cheap perfume as Lottie, the stylist, crouches down to demonstrate what she means, and it stings her eyes.

'Okay, why not?' Jenny says, feeling daring for once. 'Go for it.'

'Follow me,' says Lottie.

Jenny notices that all the staff seem to be tall gazelles, who wear black leggings so tight they leave nothing to the imagination and polo-shirts with Prime Cuts embroidered into them in gold letters.

Jenny was more organised this week when Phyllis came over. She had booked into the hairdresser and was going to enjoy coffee in town. She settles in her seat and leans back in the sink.

'Tell me if the water is too hot for you,' Lottie says.

'Hmm,' Jenny mumbles. Sometimes she feels like she's a coiled spring. Perhaps next week she'll book a massage. She stops herself from thinking about what's going on at home. This is *her* time.

Having lunch at Louise and Mark's the other day made her think about the future. Louise seems to be planning her life for when she doesn't have to look after Mark any more. Even thinking about a new partner makes Jenny feel guilty. She knows that she won't be able to carry on at Riverside. Perhaps, one day, she could work in a bookshop or coffee shop.

'Did you go on holiday in the summer?' Lottie asks.

Jenny tries not to roll her eyes at the banality of the conversation. 'Um, uh, yes. My husband and I went to Malta.' God, why are these words coming from her mouth? She just can't face telling this young girl about her life and Alzheimer's.

'Ooh, I've never been there. What's it like?'

Jenny dredges up her faded memories from a holiday years ago. 'Well, it was very hot and there are some lovely bays and beaches. The history is fascinating . . .'

Lottie's concentration is already drifting, and their conversation dries up. Jenny can daydream and enjoy her escape from the house.

Afterwards, she catches glimpses of her new hairstyle in shop windows and she likes her reflection. Lottie was right: the new hairstyle suits her. The layers are flattering, although she's not sure she can replicate the way Lottie has styled it. She picks up a few things in town before heading back to Riverdean. It's a bit blustery and the river gushes and gurgles below, making Jenny worry that she'll spoil her hair. As she pulls into the drive, she sees Fi Clark passing with her chihuahua.

'Hi, Fi. I thought you'd be at the shop now.'

'Ooh, I like your hair, Jen. Sadie is holding the fort today. I thought I'd bring Gigi for a quick walk to clear my head.'

'I know just what you mean. I took ages to get to sleep last night. There was some wild party going on at Pumpkin Cottage and you must have heard it. They were so rowdy and there was a big commotion down by the river. I was furious, to be honest.' She shakes her head, 'That Pippa Mason is dragging Riverdean into the mud with her partying and newfangled ideas.' Jenny's lips tighten. 'I called the police in the end. I had no choice.'

Fi is silent for a beat. 'I knew it was you. I knew it.' She shakes her head, 'I said to the others, I bet it's Jenny Foster who's called the police.'

Jenny feels as if she's been slapped in the face. 'Were you at the party?'

'Yes, I was. A lot of the village were and perhaps you need to consider why you were not invited. Rowdy, indeed. There were high spirits, no doubt, but it was all under control. People just enjoying their Hallowe'en celebrations and you have to rain on their parade. You used to be fun, you know. Now, you're just a vicious old bitch and no one likes you, Jenny Foster.'

Jenny is so stunned she can barely speak. 'I was thinking about Phil. Anything noisy upsets him with his Alzheimer's.'

'Yes,' she nods, 'but you're not the only one with problems, Jenny. I've got my mother living with me, who also has dementia as it happens, but do you ever think to ask how I am coping? Do you hell! That's because you're too wrapped up in your Jenny pity-party.'

'I, um, I'm . . .' Jenny stutters.

'People would have more time and sympathy for you if you were just a little less obsessed with yourself and a bit nicer. What's Pippa Mason done to you? She's trying to make an honest living here. On her own, I might add. She's embraced village life, tried to help Petro by finding work for him. Everyone likes her bar you.'

'I had no idea you felt like that,' Jenny says.

'I'm going to go now, before I say something I really regret. There's a reason why you haven't had any real friends since schooldays. My mother always told me when I was younger that if I had nothing nice to say, then say nothing at all. Gigi, come on,' she says, tugging on her lead.

Tears smart Jenny's eyes and she waits a moment or two before going into the house. She can't let Phyllis see her like this. How ridiculous, she thinks, wiping the tears away with the back of her hand. Catching sight of her reflection in the back door, she sees the layers in her hair have sagged in the gusty weather.

'He's been good as gold,' Phyllis smiles as Jenny comes in. Phil is doing a 'Spot the Difference' exercise in some puzzle book Phyllis has brought with her.

Jenny kisses the top of Phil's head, but he ignores her. What she would give to feel his arms around her now, for him to tell her everything will be all right. Like he used to.

'Have you thought about taking Phil to the day centre on Friday afternoons?' Phyllis asks. 'They have all sorts of craft activities, lots of social events, like quizzes and bridge, photography. There are quite a few people of Phil's age there.'

Jenny's mind conjures up pictures of elderly men and women sitting in armchairs at the mercy of the forced jollity of the staff. Wild horses wouldn't drag him there. She's had enough trouble getting him to choir.

'It's worth a thought,' Phyllis says. 'Keep him socialising and active. Anyway, I must be off.'

Alone with Phil, Jenny sags when she sits down at the table. It's too early to start cooking dinner. She leafs through the post

Phyllis has placed on the counter. Amongst the bills and junk, she spots the November issue of *Riverdean Ramblings* at the bottom of the pile. Flicking through, she sees the columns of events for the month, Bonfire Night at The Trout, a craft fair in the church, the annual raft race against Greenbrook. That's why she loved this place when they first moved to Riverdean. The sense of community, like a warm hug in an increasingly busy and stressful world. It was a bit like stepping back into another era, the 1950s, where there was an innocence about people and everyone was prepared to help each other. She can't face socialising with people from the village, especially if she's disliked as much as Fi Clark told her.

There's the usual requests for gardeners and cleaners. Then Lynnie Townsend, who fancies herself as some top-notch journalist because she's got a degree in English literature, has written about river pollution. There on the back page is a piece on Pumpkin Cottage and Pippa Mason. There are shots of the inside of the cottage and her renovations and a rather artful image of Pippa with her halo of blonde hair and a wide smile. There's even a recipe for lavender shortbread biscuits that Pippa leaves in her guest bedrooms. 'Riverdean is close to my heart,' Pippa says in the article. 'My mother grew up here and passed away very recently.'

Jenny drops the magazine. Can she ever escape from Pippa Mason? As if this shitty day could get any shittier.

In the evening, Jenny has regained her composure, but she still feels out of sorts. She busies herself making a cottage pie and when Jake comes in, he obviously approves.

'Something smells good,' he says. 'I'm absolutely starving. I've barely touched a thing all day, it's been so busy.'

'You're in a good mood,' Jenny says, relieved. She does worry about him. 'How did it go with Amber last night?'

'Now you've managed to dispel my good mood. There's nothing I can do about the situation, but it's her lack of understanding that gets me. She's so selfish. I wish she could be in my shoes for a second and think what it will be like not seeing Lola every week.'

'Look, get washed up and I'll put dinner out.'

When he returns to the kitchen, Jenny asks, 'Jake, can I ask you to be honest with me?'

'Oh no, I hate it when people say that,' he grins, but then stops when he sees the look on her face. 'What is it?' he says, sitting at the table.

'Do you think people dislike me? In Riverdean, I mean.'

'Why on earth would you say that?'

'It's something Fi Clark said earlier. She told me that no one likes me. She said a lot worse, in fact.'

'What prompted that?'

Jenny hesitates. 'I told her about not being able to sleep last night with that party at Pumpkin Cottage. I don't know what time you got back last night but you must have heard the racket. Anyway, Fi just lashed out saying I felt sorry for myself and I was too self-absorbed. She said her mother has dementia and I never ask about her. I mean, it is slightly different when it's your husband, somehow.' Jenny can feel herself getting worked up again. 'When you're looking after a parent, well, it's the natural order of things. I didn't sign up for this.'

Jake stands up and gives her a hug. 'Listen, Mum, I think you're doing a fantastic job of looking after Dad.' He pauses, 'But do I think you're under a lot of stress? Yes, I do. You haven't been yourself lately. You mustn't pay too much attention to what other people say.'

'And ever since Pippa moved in—'

Jake interrupts. 'Can I give you some advice? Let this rivalry with Pippa Mason go. It won't do you any good.'

'Yes, you're right,' Jenny sniffs.

'So, what's a guy got to do to get fed around here?' Jake grins.

Jenny smiles. He always knows how to make her feel better and she has been under such a strain with Phil and all this business with Amber and Jake.

But he's wrong about Pippa Mason and Pumpkin Cottage. She doesn't fall for the girl's wide-eyed innocence and forced cheeriness. There's more to that one than meets the eye. Well, Jenny is not prepared to roll over and let Ms Mason steal all her business from her, as well as her friends and good name.

Chapter Twenty-Seven

Pippa

The apple doesn't fall far from the tree . . .

Those words have haunted Pippa ever since the night of the party.

Who was the woman that said that to her? And what did she mean? She must be talking about Pippa's mother, which means she must have known her before, but what on earth did she mean by that?

Why didn't she just tell her straight? Why did she have to speak in riddles? That can't be a good thing, surely?

Pippa dons rubber gloves, takes a deep breath and begins scrubbing.

The wooden balcony is clean already; Pippa scrubbed it and scrubbed it the night of the party after everyone had left, knowing whatever alcohol was left in her system would make the job of cleaning vomit a whole lot easier, even if she did gag and heave throughout it. The balcony smells of bleach already, but in today's bright November sunlight, she's convinced she can see a faded outline, the remnants of that night taunting her just like those words.

The apple doesn't fall from the tree.

Weird. Pippa ponders on it as she scrubs, her skin heating up despite the chill in the air. After a while she pauses and leans her back against the balustrade, gazing out to the river and Greenbrook on the other side. The autumnal canopy of trees is beginning to look a little bare, with a few skeletal branches poking through the scarlet and mauve leaves. Soon Riverdean will be lined with fairy lights ready for Christmas, which Monica has promised Pippa will be 'magical'. But Pippa isn't feeling in such a whimsical mood.

Ever since the night of the party, she's felt a little off. Hannah rushed away early the next day, not even staying for breakfast as she'd planned to, and so Pippa still doesn't know what happened with Grant. Luckily, the party disbanded as the police arrived, and so as soon as they realised Pippa was sober, she was left alone pretty quickly. Jake had had to go with Mike to make sure he got home safely and dry, and Pippa had spent the whole night and the next day restoring order to Pumpkin Cottage.

It's nearly back to normal now, ready to receive a full complement of guests tonight. Miraculously, she still has all her glasses and cutlery, and the place looks almost like new, bar a few scuff marks in the hallway. Ironically, the worst of them is from where Pippa fell and knocked the side table, just before she saw that woman.

The apple doesn't fall far from the tree.

It's no use wondering and wondering about it. If there's anything Pippa has learnt so far this year, it's that taking action is what works. She needs to find out who this woman is and track her down. And Pippa knows just who to ask.

'Hot mulled cider?' Brett leans over the bar as he sees Pippa approach.

'Hot chocolate please.'

'Ooh, still hungover?' He makes a face.

'No,' Pippa protests. 'I just need to avoid you and anything containing pumpkin for a very long time.'

He busies himself with the hot chocolate machine, back turned to Pippa.

'Wait until you try my pumpkin eggnog on Bonfire Night. It's a Riverdean tradition. You'll eat your words.'

'Uhh . . .' Pippa falters. She'd worked up the courage to ask Brett or Shaun about the mystery woman on the walk over to The Trout. But now she's here and Brett's back is turned, Pippa feels a little embarrassed. She doesn't want to shout it across the bar, even though The Trout is quiet today. If she's honest, Pippa was hoping Shaun would be here instead of Brett, being the more discreet of the two.

'Whipped cream? Marshmallows?' He interrupts her thoughts.

'Need you ask?' Pippa smiles. 'Although, I'm not just here for the hot chocolate.'

'I'm intrigued,' Brett turns to her. 'Give me one second.' He garnishes Pippa's drink with cocoa powder and a small pumpkin made of tempered chocolate. 'Well, we needed a reason to charge people what we do for these. Go on, you have my full attention.'

'At my party, I spoke to a woman who I'm pretty sure I've never seen before,' Pippa pauses, unsure how to continue. 'She said something potentially . . . interesting . . . and I need to speak to her again.'

Brett raises an eyebrow and Pippa realises she needs to give more explanation than this. 'I think she thought I'd had more to drink than I had, and she made some comment about, oh I don't know, the apple not falling far,' as if Pippa hadn't heard those words in her dreams every night. 'I don't know what she meant but she seemed like she knew my mother.'

'Or your father,' Brett chips in. For a second, Pippa is taken aback. Why hasn't she thought of that herself? Pippa's been so focused on finding out about her mother's background that she hasn't even considered someone might know her father. She thinks back to everything her mother has told her about him, tiny morsels Pippa has stored up over the years. 'He hurt me,' her mum would say, before taking a deep breath. She never felt she could ask more, could never probe in the way she wanted to. She made comments about him being 'useless' and 'drifting', although Pippa never understood what she meant at the time. Her mother said he didn't want to be a father, had discarded her as soon as he knew she was pregnant. After giving birth to Pippa, she'd sent him pictures, small updates for a short time, but he never responded and she stopped making contact after a while. As painful as it was for Pippa to hear initially, she was grateful for her mother's candidness. Her father was like a closed door, one she would never open. Still, Pippa can't help but retain a morsel of curiosity about him. Maybe this one throwaway comment was about him?

'Yes,' she says, taking a sip of her drink to give herself a moment to think.

'What did she look like?'

'That's the thing,' Pippa says, 'maybe I was more drunk than I thought. I don't really remember.'

'How don't you remember?'

'I didn't exactly think, "*Hold on, let me memorise your face just in case you say something profound and life-changing.*" She disappeared as soon as she'd said it.' Pippa grips the bar. Brett raises two eyebrows this time.

'Touché. Stressed much?'

'Sorry,' Pippa concedes. 'It's just been a busy few days.'

'Jenny Foster calling the police didn't make it easier,' Brett says.

Pippa sips her hot chocolate. 'It's not just me that thinks it was her, then?'

'It was definitely her. She admitted it to Fi Clark,' Brett shakes his head. 'Don't get me wrong, I like Jenny, known her for years. But lately she's changed a lot. I think it's all the stress with her husband.'

Pippa thinks back to the man she saw at Riverside Lodge. 'What's going on with her husband?'

'He's not very well,' Brett says, then mouths '*in the head.*'

'Oh dear,' Pippa says. That makes sense. Caring for a husband with mental illness, must be difficult for Jenny alongside running Riverside Lodge.

'It started a few years ago when he was deputy headteacher. Started losing the car keys, things like that. I think one day he turned up to parents' evening in pyjamas, that sort of thing.'

'Oh,' Pippa says. It sounds like hell. Still, she can't feel too sorry for Jenny. Everyone has their stresses and she's been vile to Pippa. There's no excuse for that.

'What are you gossiping about now?' Shaun walks behind the bar.

'Pippa needs our help identifying someone at her party,' Brett fills him in.

Pippa shuts her eyes, trying to remember the moment. 'She was about my height but definitely older, brown hair.'

'Short brown hair?' Brett asks, 'Trying to pull off a *Rachel*?'

'No, longer, kind of shoulder length.'

'Damn, I was going to say that sounded like Fi's friend.'

'What was she wearing?' Shaun asks.

'I can't remember,' Pippa groans. 'It's futile, isn't it?'

Brett looks sad on her behalf. 'Come on, I'll make you another hot chocolate.'

* * *

For one awful second, Pippa thinks Hannah isn't going to answer the phone, but after a while her face appears on screen.

'Hey, Han,' Pippa smiles, light and breezy, although she feels slightly awkward speaking to her friend. It's odd, she and Hannah usually share everything, but there was something strange about the way Hannah left after the party. She wasn't involved in the commotion outside, but Pippa knows she was inside with Grant, a thought that makes Pippa feel sick. She doesn't know what happened, although with the way they were giggling, Grant's arm resting on Hannah's waist as she unlocked the bedroom door, Pippa suspects the worst.

'Hi Pipps,' she gives a thin smile. 'I'm just with Louis at the moment, cooking dinner,' Pippa clocks the way she name-checks him, as if Pippa's going to start asking questions. 'Actually, I need to pop to the corner shop, do you mind stirring this while I go and speak to Pippa?' She calls over her shoulder.

'Right, I'm free,' Hannah says. 'I'll buy a tin of tomatoes or something.' Pippa can see the evening sky behind her head, pastel blue.

'I guess I just wanted to check you're okay,' Pippa launches straight into it. 'You left quite abruptly yesterday.'

'Yeah, I kinda did,' Hannah smiled sheepishly. 'I guess I was embarrassed. The party was chaos and I just sort of left you to get on with it. I should have been more supportive.'

'I don't care about that,' Pippa says, surprised. 'It's more what you were doing while I was getting on with it. With Grant?' She feels icky even saying his name aloud.

'I hoped he wouldn't come up,' Hannah says. 'Believe me, Pippa, nothing happened. I would have told you if it did.'

'It sort of looked like something happened.' Pippa probes. She feels Hannah's trying to play it down.

'Well, Grant wanted it to,' Hannah says. 'Oh, I don't know, Pippa,' she sighs. 'I'm embarrassed with how I acted. I was so hung up on Louis not proposing and feeling really *meh* about it all. Then Grant gave me all this attention, and he's a good-looking guy.'

'If you say so.'

'I did kind of welcome his flirting. Probably a bit too much,' Hannah admits.

'Well, that's fine, everyone enjoys flirting. As long as it's harmless,' Pippa feels like her mother for a moment.

'I thought it was, but once we were in the bedroom, he started getting creepy and trying to get close to me and I came to my senses. I don't think anything would have happened, I mean, I love Louis. I'd never do that to him, engagement ring or no engagement ring.'

'What were you doing in the bedroom, Han?'

'Grant wanted to show me the woodwork he'd done with the window seat. I thought it would be fun.' Hannah laughs.

'Oldest line in the book.'

'I feel like I led him on a bit. It was just nice to feel like some guy wanted me.'

'Louis wants you too,' Pippa says, frustrated that this pair still haven't sorted things out.

'Not as much as Grant. Believe me, if there was no Louis in the picture . . . Oh shit,' Hannah's face turns to stone.

'Han?' Pippa asks.

'Did you just hear that?' Hannah's talking to someone off-screen. Pippa hears a man's voice. Her stomach flips for her friend.

'I've got to go Pippa, Louis is here. I think he just heard our conversation.'

'Oh, shit indeed,' Pippa says as the phone call cuts out. That would not sound good for anyone overhearing. Poor Hannah.

She hopes Louis will listen to her explanation. Those two. This engagement ring has really seemed to put the pressure on their relationship. They were perfectly fine before it.

Let me know if you're OK? Pippa messages Hannah, imagining the argument going on outside Hannah's flat in Finsbury Park at the moment.

She sighs. She wonders if Jake would ever want to get married, or whether his fingers have been burnt by Amber. Things definitely seem complicated between those two as well, although the more Pippa tries to tell herself to keep it casual for his sake as well as hers, the more she falls for Jake. The doorbell rings. Pippa hopes it's her parcel. She's hired a special wood cleaner from a furniture shop in Greenbrook, hoping to take another pass at the balcony.

'Hello,' she answers the door, 'oh.' Standing there, holding Pippa's wood cleaner, is the woman.

The apple doesn't fall far from the tree.

Chapter Twenty-Eight

Jenny

Jenny watches as Amber and Lola walk away from the house, the little girl's curls bobbing as she skips down the path whilst clutching her mother's hand. Being a grandmother seems at times the only joy in her life. For those few hours on the weekend, the mood in the house lifts. Even Phil seems to perk up, laughing at Lola's antics. With a teachers' training day, Lola has stayed with them a day early. In France, it will be Ethan's parents filling in the gaps, which makes Jenny feel sad.

Jake closes the back door and comes into the kitchen. 'Well, the house is all going through, by the sounds of it. Amber is so excited. She can't wait to move and begin her new life.'

'Have you told her how you feel?'

'Of course, I have, Mum. She just doesn't bloody care. She started lecturing me about how it's a great opportunity for all of them. Then she accused me of being selfish for trying to stop them going.' He sighs in frustration. 'I'm not stopping her going. I'd never stand in their way, but I'm going to miss my daughter.' Jake flops down into the chair, runs his fingers through his hair. 'I just wish for once she saw things from my perspective.'

'She is insensitive,' Jenny says in sympathy. 'Perhaps things won't be as bad as you think. You'll still get to see her in the holidays.'

That's what Pi—everyone says,' Jake mumbles. 'It won't be the same, though.' Jenny can see he's getting emotional. 'Do you know what I really worry about?'

Jenny says nothing, waits for him. He rarely opens up to her.

'I'm worried that she'll see Ethan as her father, that she'll not need me any more.'

'Oh, darling, that will never happen. You'll always be her dad. No one can ever change that. She adores you.'

Jake pinches his nose. 'Maybe.' He doesn't look convinced. 'Look at me and Dad. I've never wanted to know my real father because Dad has been more than a father to me. I've always felt loved by him. There's been no place for Mike.'

'That's totally different,' Jenny says. 'You know that Mike was never really interested in being a parent. He was always too selfish. Never bothered to get in touch and I tried, honestly. I wanted you to have a relationship with him. Lola knows how much you love her. You'll always be in her life.'

Jake shrugs and Jenny wishes she could do more to help him. It's agonising seeing him like this.

'Are you out tonight?' Jenny asks. 'We've got an extra choir practice tonight, although Dad is really out of sorts today.' They both glance over at Phil, who is sleeping in his usual armchair, his puzzle book draped over his lap.

'I thought he's quieter than usual. He didn't want to read to Lola earlier, even when she took her book to him. Normally he can't resist.'

'I wish he could just say what's wrong. He seems depressed.'

'Perhaps you should get in touch with that nurse who comes over, the Admiral nurse.'

'Maeve. Maybe. I'll see how he gets on in the next few days.' Jenny pauses. 'You could invite this new girlfriend of yours over sometime. I'd love to meet her.'

Jake reddens, 'What new girlfriend?'

'Come on, Jake, I know all the signs. The eagerness to go out, the aftershave . . .' Jenny grins, 'Why all the secrecy?'

'Can't you just leave it?' Jake says, his irritation rising. 'You never let things go. I'm twenty-eight, for God's sake, not a teenager.'

'I didn't mean anything, Jake,' Jenny stutters.

'No, you never do. Except you manage to offend every single person you speak to.' He stands up, suddenly. 'It's time I looked for somewhere else to live. I'm fed up of twenty questions every time I go out. Where have I been? Who did I see? What time did I get back? It's suffocating. It's never going to work – this. Me living here.'

'Oh, Jake, don't say that.'

'It's hard for me coming back to live at Mum and Dad's. And the stick I get for it in the pub!'

'But that's just silly . . .'

'No offence, but it is time I moved on. I've got enough for a deposit, and I'll start looking straight away.'

'Just because I asked about your new girlfriend?' Jenny feels a lump in her throat.

'It's not just that. I need my own space. You can appreciate that, Mum. I'll still come over all the time, help you with Dad.'

Jenny nods, not trusting herself to speak.

'I'm going to have a shower,' Jake says. 'I won't have anything tonight. I'll eat when I'm out.'

'Me and my big mouth,' Jenny mumbles to herself when he's out of earshot. He's right. That's all she seems to do is offend people. Is she overbearing with Jake? She doesn't think so. Is he just being oversensitive because of everything that is happening with Amber and Lola? Can't he see that she's on his side? Why does everyone misinterpret her intentions? When her tears fall, she doesn't attempt to stop them. What did Fi Clark call it? The Jenny pity-party?

Phil stirs in his chair. 'Mum, where are you? Don't leave me, Mum.'

Jenny gets up. 'I'm here, Phil,' she says, kneeling in front of him. 'It's just a bad dream. We'll have something to eat soon and we're going to choir tonight.'

'I'm not fucking going, woman. How many times do I have to tell you?'

Jenny knows she shouldn't have come. She's had a knot in her stomach all day – like a sixth sense. Phil has been out of sorts and uncommunicative. He didn't touch his dinner, refusing to come to the table.

'Phil, please come and sit at the table. I've made lasagne and a lemon cake.' He wouldn't look at her.

'Come on, darling. Are you not hungry tonight?'

Phil sat in his armchair, with the television off, and ignored her repeated requests.

'You'll be starving. I'll have to cover it and heat it up when we get back.' This stress she did not need. 'I wish you'd just bloody tell me what's wrong.'

Now, they sit in the car outside the church hall. She's practically dragged him here with a combination of threats and bribery, 'I'll make a roast dinner tomorrow and we'll have some profiteroles for dessert.' That's all she has in her arsenal. What do you bribe a dementia patient with? A wild night of hot sex worked a few years ago, but now all he really enjoys is eating and watching television.

As the rain dribbles down the window, Jenny feels overwhelmed with misery. The sky is inky black, clouds swamping the stars, and there's a feeling of winter in the biting, knife-like cold. Inside, the yellow glow of lights and life makes Jenny desperate to escape the claustrophobia of the car.

She looks at him. 'You're a real pain in the arse, you know. No arguments, you're coming in.'

Phil says nothing but opens the car door and follows Jenny, dragging his feet, and showing his reluctance in a scowling face.

A blast of warm air and noise greets Jenny, and Angela's voice carries above the chatter. 'I expect everyone to be perfect tonight.' Jenny spots Louise, who is rolling her eyes. 'This is an important gig and tonight I want to choose who is going to take the lead in "Back for Good".'

'Lord, give me strength,' Louise says. 'Anyone would think it's the Royal Albert Hall. Is Phil okay?'

Jenny looks behind her. Phil's head is bowed. 'He's really strange today. Didn't want to come tonight. Nothing new in that, but he didn't eat his dinner.'

'He's looking a bit flushed. Perhaps you need to get him checked out.'

Angie says, 'Right, everyone. Let's begin.' She's a very animated speaker and her coloured beads bounce up and down on her ample chest. 'Jude, let's start with a warm-up and then we'll practise our *pièce de resistance*, "Back for Good". Written by the multitalented Gary Barlow, who also happens to be very yummy.' She grins.

Embarrassingly, Phil refuses to sing or even stand up and join the choir, despite Jenny's cajoling. There's no judgement here, though. Everyone knows the score.

As the choir rehearses, Jenny contemplates leaving. There's no point if Phil is not engaging at all. Then she decides to stand her ground. If they go now, she'll never get him to come here again. Everything she's read of Alzheimer's points to the importance of continuing to socialise, get out and about, keep the mind stimulated to halt a speedy deterioration. The trouble is she never knows when he's genuinely not well or just being plain stubborn.

Then it happens really fast. As the choir stands for yet another rendition of "Back for Good"', Phil slumps in the seat beside her. It catches Jenny completely off guard and she shrieks. The choir stops and Lucy Rowberry, the daughter of one of the older Alzheimer patients, is beside her.

'I'm a GP,' she says reassuringly, checking Phil's pulse. 'How long has he been unwell?'

Jenny's heart pounds in her chest. 'Just today, really. He's been off his food.'

'Let's lie him on the floor. Jenny, put your coat under his head.'

There is a moat of silence around them.

'Call an ambulance,' Lucy says.

In a side room on the ward, Jenny and Jake sit either side of Phil. Jenny holds Phil's hand as she watches him sleep.

'I feel so guilty,' she says.

'You weren't to know he had a urinary tract infection, for goodness' sake.'

'I know, but I should have been able to see that something wasn't right. I'm his wife. I'm with him all the time.'

'Stop this, Mum. It won't do you any good. Dad doesn't tell us when he's not well, and we're not mind readers.'

'He weed the other night in the wardrobe. I should have noticed how often he's going in the day, too.'

Jenny catches sight of herself in the reflection of the window. Her hair hangs in damp curls after being soaked earlier when she got into the ambulance. It gives her a wild look. The ambulance journey had seemed surreal. The siren, the blackness of the countryside, the concerned faces of the paramedics. The bright lights in the hospital hurt her eyes and Jenny felt sick to the stomach.

'Did they tell you how long he's likely to be in?' Jake asks.

'Just a day or two to monitor him. They've started him on a course of antibiotics.'

'Well, that's good. He'll be fine, Mum. You need to go home to rest.'

'Yes, you're right. Will you take me back to the church hall in Ross to pick up my car?'

'Come on,' Jake says, and Jenny kisses Phil on the forehead.

As the lights shift past the car window, Jenny is wracked with guilt. She's relieved to leave the hospital and sleep in her bed alone tonight and not have to worry about Phil. She can visit him tomorrow and have a day off from all the responsibility.

She replays the conversation with Fi Clark. She told her she's no fun any more. But how can she be the life and soul of the party when her life has imploded. They don't go out, go for walks, take holidays. Life has become narrower, that house, that living room, that chair with just her and Phil. What kind of monster is she to harbour such selfish thoughts?

She just wants to run away.

Chapter Twenty-Nine

Pippa

Pippa walks down the lane towards The Trout at five-thirty in the morning, the darkness of the night just starting to retreat to make way for autumn sunlight. She's had many a sleepless night since moving into Pumpkin Cottage, but has never actually been outside at this ungodly hour. Riverdean seems sleepy, cocooned in its autumn foliage.

'I must be mad,' she says to herself, also realising she's never been in sports gear at this time of morning. 'Just like the rest of this village.' She spies the group of people dressed similarly congregating outside The Trout. She spots Jake in the crowd.

'Good morning.' He gives her a wide smile, pulling her in for a kiss. 'I've got you a number.'

'Great,' Pippa tries to muster some enthusiasm. 'Remind me again why I'm doing this.'

'Because you want to be part of the Riverdean community. And you can't get more community spirited than the annual raft race.' Jake pins a laminated number in green on Pippa's lower back.

'I know, I know. But when my alarm went off at five, community spirit was the last thing I was feeling.' She sees Monica and Jake's friend Mike wearing matching green numbers, their team of four. Jake explained the rules to Pippa yesterday like it was gospel: entrants to the annual raft race had to be in teams of four, they had to be ready for a 6 a.m. start, and would be given four hours to assemble their rafts using only natural supplies they could find in Riverdean. After an hour's break, the village would assemble to watch as teams set off on their rafts from Pumpkin Bridge, all the way down the half-mile track to the finish line outside Rushmore Corner. Teams that made it to the end with all four team members dry and onboard were the winners.

'Sorry if I seemed a bit off yesterday,' Jake says. 'My father isn't very well.'

'That's okay,' Pippa says, wondering when she'll meet his parents. 'Are you sure you're in the right frame of mind for this?'

'No getting out of it that easily,' Jake smiles. 'I'll be fine, it's nice to have the distraction to be honest. Morning guys,' he greets Monica and Mike. Pippa sees a few faces she recognises in the crowd, from Petro and his family, to Abi and her friends. She smiles at Brett and Shaun, who are handing out hot chocolates. Pippa goes to get some for her fellow teammates.

'I wanted to put vodka in it, but Shaun said I wasn't allowed,' Brett says.

'Anyone up at this time needs a stiff drink,' Monica agrees.

'Come see us after the race and we'll sort you out.'

Pippa rejoins the others. 'So, these are my plans.' Jake starts showing them drawings of a raft. 'I'm thinking Mike, Monica, you collect twine for the fastenings. Pippa and I will go logging, I spied some strong potentials in Kenaston Wood yesterday.'

'I'm just reeling from the fact you've made technical drawings.' Pippa admires the sketches Jake's made, from multiple angles. 'I've never seen this side of you before.'

'He does this every year,' Monica chips in. 'Every time the plan gets more and more elaborate. It's taken more seriously here than the Oxford–Cambridge Boat Race.'

'Buoyancy aids,' Jake says, keeping a straight face. 'Anything that you find will help, especially if we can tie them to the underside of the raft.'

'Geez Louise,' Pippa breathes, 'I'm already regretting my decision to participate. I could be watching from the bridge with a cocoa and a blanket.'

'Just be glad it's not raining,' Mike says.

'We're grateful you've taken over from Adam, anyway,' Monica says. Jake's colleague is usually the fourth team member, but Jake told Pippa he was off with a toe infection.

'Contestants,' Shaun calls through a megaphone, 'your four hours start now!'

'What can I do?' Pippa asks, very much aware that she is getting in the way at the moment, as Jake selects logs in the forest.

'If you can carry the logs I cut onto the loader, that would be great,' he instructs.

Pippa picks up one log, expecting it to be much lighter than it is. She tries not to show how much of an effort it is as she slings the log onto Jake's loader. She hopes he can pull this along, as Pippa's back will be crumpled by the end of the morning.

Jake is busy measuring, marking, and then sawing through another set of logs. He's told Pippa it's better to cut the logs to size here, so they aren't dragging unnecessary wood to the start line.

'So, tell me about what happened with that woman,' Jake says, without looking up.

'Fern Cooper,' Pippa says. 'She runs the furniture shop in Greenbrook, hence why she was making the delivery to Pumpkin.'

Pippa gave Jake the story about the comment she'd made to her at the Hallowe'en party.

'How did she end up at the party?'

'It turns out she knows Tom, at the post office. I got talking to him the other day and invited him along. He must have taken that to mean bring a date with you.'

Jake chuckles. 'So, what did she say to you?'

'Well, she was a bit sheepish when she saw me again. I wasn't missing my opportunity, though, despite how much shock I was in. I said I'd been thinking about her comment the other day and wanted to know exactly what she meant.'

Jake looks up and stops sawing. 'And?'

'It turns out it was about my mother. She apologised for the comment, said she was drunk at the time, but talked about my mum being a party girl, liking her drink, hence the apple not falling far.'

'How did she know your mum? And how did she know who you are?' Jake pauses working for a moment.

'She grew up in Riverdean, but was a few years younger than my mum, so they weren't close or anything. She said she remembers her at school, even remembers the books in the river incident. She said she found my mum on social media years ago and saw pictures of me, so there was no mistaking it, despite our different surnames. It's odd, as my mum never posted much on Facebook, but it makes sense.'

'Could she tell you anything more about your mum?'

'Well, one thing she did say was that my mum had a best friend in the village. She couldn't remember her name, but she said she thinks the woman still lives here now.'

'I wonder who that is,' Jake muses aloud. 'It's a bit of a useless lead, though, without any clues.'

'Exactly,' Pippa sighs. 'I can't question every female around my mum's age in Riverdean, it would be impossible.'

'Did she say anything about what happened before your mum left Riverdean?'

'She said that my mum had lots of different boyfriends, which doesn't surprise me. Poor Mum was always searching for love. She married three times,' Pippa explains, getting sidetracked. 'But she did say one seemed more serious than the others. She couldn't say more, though.'

'I'm sorry, Pippa,' Jake says, rubbing her shoulder with a big, gloved hand.

'Don't be,' she tries to smile. 'It is frustrating that I still don't know what happened with my mum. Fern said she was with this guy for a year or so, then she left suddenly. Some people thought they'd run away together but Fern was adamant that wasn't the case.'

'People's memories can't always be relied on,' Jake says. 'There must be someone in Riverdean who knows what happened.'

'Hey, have you tried asking your parents? They've lived in Riverdean forever, haven't they?' Pippa wonders why the thought hasn't occurred to her before. Unless Jake hasn't mentioned her at all to his parents, which would be embarrassing.

He looks awkward all of a sudden, shakes his head and clears his throat. 'No, I haven't really asked, to be honest. They bought the Lodge fifteen years ago, but Mum was brought up around here.'

Bollocks, Pippa thinks. He's probably had too much on his plate with his dad. How insensitive of her.

'Don't worry,' she breezes. 'How are you getting on with chopping?'

'Four more to go,' Jake says. He looks relieved to have another topic of conversation.

Pippa tries to busy herself, to distract from the pain of talking about her mum. She misses her so much, her quick wit, her fearless nature. Jake must sense Pippa's upset as he suddenly comes over and puts his arms around her.

Jake's arms feel so comforting around her, like home. She wonders if he feels the same way.

'Is everyone ready for the seventy-fifth annual Riverdean raft race?' Brett shouts through the megaphone.

'Sorry, someone's had a little too much to drink,' Shaun takes over. 'He means the seventy-sixth annual raft race.'

The waiting crowd laugh but Pippa's stomach flips. The team and their raft are ready after hours of hard graft. She has literal dirt under her fingernails, a first for Pippa. What her former self would have thought of her now, standing at the edge of the river in sports gear and a life jacket, about to take the plunge in a rather impressively sturdy-looking raft. How far she's come!

The raft is constructed from logs, fastened together parallel and diagonally, which Jake was convinced would make it sturdy. They've attached six water drums to the base, which has raised the base of the raft to a height Pippa isn't too happy about.

'Are you sure we're not going to fall in?' she asks Jake, semi-joking.

'I'm sure,' he says. 'Never fallen in before.'

'But you've never had me on your team before. I'm not particularly good on water.' Pippa's only experience rowing has been on a machine at the gym.

'Just follow my instructions,' he says.

'Contestants, move your rafts onto the water,' Shaun calls.

Oh God. She looks at the four other rafts in the race. Jake's definitely looks the most sturdy, with others making use of branches, plastic and netting. Pippa fiddles with the strap on her life jacket, taking a quick glance at the crowd of Riverdean and Greenbrook locals. The race is a fight between the two villages, with Riverdean teams wearing green numbers, and Greenbrook teams in blue. The locals are gathered on the bridge, all blanketed in big coats and cheering loudly. There's a buzz in the air, the excitement of the race. The river even stirs with it, sparkling in the November sunlight.

Jake and Mike push the raft onto the water from the Riverdean bank. Pippa's pleased to see it floats. Another raft next to theirs disintegrates immediately, half of it floating ahead of them down the river. The team boo and laugh. Pippa can't help but feel a stab of envy, knowing they'll get to stay dry and safe.

'Contestants aboard,' Brett calls. 'Wait for the starting klaxon!'

Monica and Mike quickly hop onto the raft. It doesn't seem to bother them that it lurches and nearly tips over in the water. They both sit side by side at the rear, and Mike leans to hold on to the bank.

'See, solid as a rock,' Jake says to her. He must sense Pippa's fear. 'You don't have to do this if you don't want to.' He lowers his voice so the others don't hear.

Pippa feels her emotions split in two. She'd love to back out now, to stay warm, drink another latte. But that's what her London self would have done. And look how far she's come – hiking with Jake, making friends with the villagers, assembling a bloody raft out of twigs with her bare hands. Riverdean Pippa is here to challenge herself. She's here for the new experiences. Even the freezing-cold wet ones that cause her fear.

'I'm going to do it,' Pippa says, 'for my mum.'

Jake winks at her, and Pippa takes a deep breath. She climbs aboard, ignoring the rocking motion that feels precarious, and tucks herself in front of Monica.

'Go Pippa, go Pippa!' She turns and sees Petro and his family shouting for her.

In a flash, Jake is aboard too. Pippa's glad for the water drums, as they sit higher off the water than the other teams, but not as high as she thought they would when the raft was on dry land.

'Ready . . . Steady . . . Go!' The klaxon sounds, and Pippa focuses her mind on Jake's words, pulling her oar through the water like Jake showed her in the break. She doesn't look up, ignores the other teams, ignores the rocks either side of the river that spell imminent danger. She concentrates only on the oar, on co-ordinating with Jake's shouts of 'one, two, pull, one, two, pull.'

'We're in the lead,' shouts Monica, and Pippa squeals with the effort and excitement of it all. Jake was right, the raft is damn sturdy. She doesn't care when the spray from Monica's oar soaks the side of her face and hair.

'Well done, team,' Jake calls. 'One, two, pull!'

As they progress down the river, a new crowd greets them at Leafy Bridge, waving green flags as they pass to cheer for Riverdean. 'Booo!' a few onlookers shout, clad in blue.

'We're miles ahead of the others,' Monica calls.

'Right, we're approaching the bend,' Jake says. The bend with the rapids, Pippa remembers his briefing. 'Remember, the river will do most of the work, we just need to focus on stability.'

The familiar twist of fear strikes Pippa again. She and Monica will be on the outside of the corner. She looks up just quickly enough to dodge a low-hanging branch from a willow at the edge of the river, and sees the bend quickly approaching.

'Jaaaake!' Pippa shouts as the speed of the raft picks up.

'It's okay,' he calls, but before he can finish, a rapid carries the raft quickly. Pippa struggles to keep her eyes focused on anything, they are moving so quickly, the boat swept along in a blur. Something doesn't feel right to Pippa. The distribution of the weight. She can feel herself sliding towards Jake before she even knows what's happening.

Pippa realises she's about to hit the water a split second before it happens. She's pulled down by the moving water, enclosing her whole body, an arctic plunge that feels like it's piercing her skin all over.

Her adrenaline is already sky-high, but she waits until her face is above water again before she takes a breath, doesn't fight it, and lets the river carry her. She sees the crowd waiting at Rushmore Corner, just after the rapids, where the river becomes calmer and more shallow. The finish line.

Pippa scrambles upright, confused about what's just happened. She gasps, then sees Jake, Monica and Mike just behind her. All soaking wet and standing.

'Are you all right?' Jake is shouting, moving quickly towards her. 'You didn't hurt yourself?'

'I'm fine,' Pippa laughs, and she really is. She's fallen in, but she's okay.

'Fucking raft,' Mike calls.

'The raft was fine,' Jake says, and as if it's mocking them, their perfectly intact raft glides past them, calm as a swan.

'I told you I was a bad luck charm for the team,' Pippa says, giddy with excitement, or is it exhaustion?

'I didn't believe you,' Jake says. 'The first time I've lost in eight years. Come on,' he pulls his teammates in for a hug. 'Let's go dry off at Pippa's then hit The Trout.'

Pippa holds her hands up to clap for the winning team, whose raft is barely intact but has carried them all this way, and is pleased to see it's a green team made up of guys in their forties. The four of them are cheered as they make their way through the crowd and up the lane back to the start line.

Pippa begins to shiver despite the sun beaming down on them. Her clothes are clinging to her, soaked through. Her hair hangs in rivulets. Her stomach aches with laughter and adrenaline. What a change, she thinks, from the groomed hotel girl who came to Riverdean just two months ago. She likes this one more.

As they approach The Trout, Pippa sees a familiar face in the crowd of people. 'Oh God, there's Jenny Foster,' Pippa says to Jake. 'I hope she doesn't see me.'

Jake looks dumbfounded for a moment.

'Are you all right?' she asks him.

'Yes,' a sharp nod of the head. 'Listen, you three go on ahead. I just need to speak to someone quickly. I'll catch up.' He ducks into the crowd, before Pippa can stop him.

She frowns. She's always thought Jake is straightforward, an honest guy. And still she has a feeling there's more to him that she's yet to understand.

'Do you want to wait for Jake?' Monica asks.

'No,' Pippa says. 'A hot shower is calling my name.' It's true, but Pippa really wants to get away from Jenny Foster. She wonders if *she* was the bad omen for their race.

Chapter Thirty

Jenny

Jenny watches as the flames hungrily lick the kindling and logs on the outer edges of the bonfire. The night is so still. She has never known a November night quite so mild. Wearing a thin jacket, she feels her face flush in the heat of the fire. There has to be eighty to a hundred people here. There are so many faces she doesn't recognise; perhaps they have come from Greenbrook, drawn by the promise of a party and an exciting and expensive fireworks display. Every year Brett and Shaun seem to become more extravagant in their plans and the bonfire is about ten times the size it was when they first arrived in Riverdean. She was going to opt for a hot chocolate with habanero chillis, but decided to push the boat out and she's now sipping her third drink – no, fourth – mulled pear and cranberry punch. It's so delectable and moreish that she keeps on drinking and now feels quite light-hearted.

Children play with sparklers away from the bonfire, weaving figures of eight in the blackness. Jenny's eyes search for Jake. She had missed him in the raft race. He must be here somewhere. He has never missed Bonfire Night in Riverdean. His spicy cider, infused with caraway, aniseed and fennel, usually goes down a storm. Jenny watches as the 'guy', a crude effigy which looks remarkably like Vladimir Putin in a neon green mankini, is spreadeagled across the top and everyone watches and giggles as it curls and bubbles in the increasing heat.

'How's Riverdean's favourite sourpuss?' Brett asks, putting an arm around her shoulder and resting his head on her.

'Oh, not you as well. I think I need to move. I seem to have more enemies these days than friends,' Jenny pouts.

'Don't take it to heart. Your bark is worse than your bite. Everyone knows that.' He grins, 'Besides, it makes you interesting. You're not one of these bland, blah, vanilla people. You're spicy, hot-headed, authentic. People know where they stand with you.'

'Those are just euphemisms for saying I'm a bitch.'

'Gosh, my dear, you are on a downer. Come on, tell Uncle Brett what's up.'

'Well, Phil is being kept in hospital for a couple of days. He's got a urinary tract infection and he was rushed in on Saturday night.'

'Oh, darling, I am sorry. I hadn't heard.'

Suddenly, there's a surge of cheers from the crowd as Putin is consumed by the flames.

'He's okay. He'll probably be out Tuesday or Wednesday, depending on how he responds to the medication,' Jenny says.

'Then you must take full advantage of a few days' rest, my lovely. When was the last time you had a break? Two, three years ago?'

'Longer,' Jenny concedes.

'Drink up. That's an order! Watch the fireworks and get steaming drunk.' He removes his arm from her shoulder. 'Right, I'd better go and start these fireworks before Shaun blows us all to smithereens. That man is like a bull with horns in a china shop.'

Jenny watches the silhouette of the crowd lit by the amber flames. He's right, of course. She should take advantage. What she didn't tell him was the relief she felt when the ward sister told her apologetically that Phil would be in for the rest of the weekend and beyond. Jenny was euphoric. Excited at the prospect of time to herself. She was tempted to stay in tonight and watch television, something that wasn't a quiz. She loves detective shows but can't watch them because Phil wouldn't understand them, or worse, be upset by them. She had terrible FOMO over *Happy Valley*, getting to watch only one programme of series one and being left out when the conversation in the newsagents turned to Catherine Cawood and her antics.

This morning, she had luxuriated in the warmth of her bed. She stretched out, her toes reaching the bottom and then, like a scissors, had crossed over her legs this way and that. The bliss of a double bed to herself. She didn't have to get up and check for damp patches on the carpet or puddles in the wardrobe. She showered and then made herself a croissant and some fruit, a strong coffee, and sat at the table gazing at the river below, the willows brushing their locks into the water, the fields opposite and the clear sky. It was like being reborn, but then she felt immediately guilty, as if people could read her mind and see just what a horrible person she was.

Visiting Phil in the hospital had assuaged her guilt. He was asleep when she got there, and this reassured her that he was comfortable. He'd already eaten lunch just before twelve, the hospital being typical of most and following the most bizarre timetable for meals.

'He was asking after you this morning and did plead to go home, but Avril, the health care . . . Well, she's brilliant with them, you know, dementia patients,' the young nurse coughed awkwardly at this.

Jenny sat there watching the television, but only horse racing was on. Feeling bored, she picked up a newspaper and waited for the bell to ring. She was relieved when it did. She kissed his forehead as she left, telling the nurse, 'Will you tell him I called?' The nurse nodded but looked as if to say, 'He'll never remember that.'

Jenny can hear Brett tell Shaun, 'Careful, you fool. You'll blow your hands off.'

It's a funny tradition, Jenny thinks. Celebrating a foiled terrorist plot. Phil loved history. Told her all about Guido Fawkes and how it was Robert Catesby who was the actual leader of the plot. She used to tell him that he was a mine of useless information. Where did all that information go when your brain cells disintegrated?

She takes another sip of her pear and cranberry punch, enjoying the warmth down her throat. She feels the presence of a man next to her and is suddenly self-conscious about being alone at this public event.

'I think the fireworks are starting,' he tells her. 'About time.'

Jenny takes a surreptitious, sideways glance. He's tall and broad and has salt and pepper hair. She doesn't recognise him.

'Well, you'll have to be patient,' she tells him. 'Brett and Shaun do nothing quickly. This usually goes on for hours.'

'Oh, I know only too well. I went to many of their parties when they lived in London,' he laughs.

Jenny notices the tattoos on his hands. She can't read what they say. She hates tattoos but he carries them well.

A rocket flies loudly into the air and explodes in a myriad of colours. It catches Jenny off guard. She stumbles backwards and feels strong arms around her.

'Steady on, there. Are you okay?'

'I'm fine,' Jenny mutters. Gosh, she really shouldn't have had that third, no fourth punch. His arms hold her for a beat longer than necessary.

'So, are you one of the locals?' he asks. 'I'm Elliott, by the way. I feel I should introduce myself, seeing as we got a bit personal there.' He laughs at this.

My God, is he flirting with me? Jenny asks herself. She's so rusty at this, she's practically seized up. 'Yes, I am local. I own Riverside Lodge, the B&B, just a couple of hundred yards away.'

'Ah, I think I passed it on the way in. It's a gorgeous place. I admire anyone who has the commitment to run a business like that.'

Jenny doesn't know what to say to this, what to say to a handsome stranger. They watch in silence as a Roman Candle fizzes and then splits the sky like lightning.

'So, you come here often?' Jenny asks.

He laughs at this. Jenny laughs too, with embarrassment. 'Yes, I do, when I can, at least. You know what Brett and Shaun are like. Any excuse for a party.'

'What do you do in London?'

'I sell vintage motorbikes in East London. Honda Rebels, Triumph Scramblers – Harley Davidsons, of course. That's the only one most people have heard of.'

Jenny grins. She feels she's having an out of body experience. This man couldn't be more different to her than if he told her he was a Tibetan monk or an alien from Mars. Yet, he's strangely attractive. There's something so masculine, so charismatic about him.

'There you are,' someone calls out, encircling an arm around Elliott's waist. 'I've been looking everywhere for you, you old dog.' He kisses Elliott on the lips.

He turns to Jenny. 'This is Brendan, my partner. Jenny is a local,' he says. 'I was hoping to get all the gossip from her.'

Well, that's a surprise. She really is out of practice and she feels foolish. It's time to go home, Jenny thinks. She slips off as everyone's gaze is held by a Catherine Wheel as it whizzes frenziedly in a shower of gold.

She feels a lot tipsier as she stumbles along the path. She hasn't felt like this in a long time. A hangover and caring for a husband with Alzheimer's is not a good combination. The night is starry and still, the moon glittering on the river. What a romantic setting she thinks, dreaming of walking hand in hand with a good-looking man, a silver fox. Hmm, a Pierce Brosnan or Patrick Dempsey lookalike. Perhaps even Jeff Goldblum, although he is a bit quirky. Jenny hiccups. She's glad she can have a lie in again tomorrow. She's got guests coming late afternoon, but tonight is free. Free. She giggles to herself.

Up ahead, she sees lights on in Pumpkin Cottage. Pippa Mason, her nemesis, is at home. Jenny wonders if she has guests in tonight. As she passes on the path below the cottage, she can see fairy lights twinkling from the balcony above and music, Ed Sheeran, drifting from the open window.

'Don't forget to bring the ice,' she trills.

She's bloody there in the hot tub, Jenny thinks, as she stops outside. Perhaps if she hides behind the hydrangea bush, Pippa won't know she's there. Jenny can't see the hot tub, but Pippa's voice carries down to the lane.

'Oops, I think my bikini top just dropped off.'

Hussy! She's got someone with her. A man. It didn't take her long to get her claws into some hapless fool in Riverdean. Probably sleeping her way through all the eligible men in the village. Jenny hears someone call from inside the house but she can't catch the words. Does that woman not care who can see or hear her? She clearly intends having sex in that hot tub for all the world to see. Okay, Jenny is halfway way in the garden and craning her neck, but Pippa Mason is doing little to hide what she's up to. Anyone passing might see this little tryst, Jenny convinces herself.

'Oh no, I think the bottoms have slipped off too,' Pippa giggles. 'Are you coming to rescue me or are you going to make me stroll across my balcony naked so the whole of Riverdean can see me?'

Jenny catches a glimpse of Pippa's blonde hair, usually caught up in a ponytail, cascading over her shoulders. She seems to be struggling with a bottle and then suddenly there's a loud pop.

'Woohoo! I've got it open and I am going to drink it all myself.' There's no sound from inside. 'All myself,' Pippa repeats.

Jenny stumbles backwards. 'Shit.' Her shoe is trapped in the mud.

'Hello,' calls Pippa. 'Hello? Is anyone down there?'

Jenny holds her breath. If she looks over the balustrade now, she will definitely see Jenny. But then Pippa sinks back into the tub, starts pouring her Prosecco. Relieved, Jenny lets out a sigh.

'At last!' she hears Pippa say. 'What were you up to in there? I was tempted to start without you.'

Jenny grimaces. Then she sees strong, muscular shoulders and short blonde hair. 'I was trying to get that bloody ice machine to work,' says the male voice. That. Recognisable. Male. Voice.

Oh my God! Oh my God. It can't be. It can't be Jake. Surely not.

'Are you getting those boxers off, Jake, or do I have to rip them off you?'

'Is that an offer?' he laughs, tearing his boxers off and slinging them over the balustrade. They hang suspended amongst the hydrangeas, just by Jenny's shoulder. She hears a lot of splashing and laughter and then silence.

Jenny feels sick.

Chapter Thirty-One

Pippa

Pippa leisurely washes up the few dishes left over from the breakfast she made for herself and Jake. Pancakes with maple syrup and bacon, Canadian style. The perfect post-sex breakfast.

Jake left a few hours ago, as he's spending the day with Lola. Pippa doesn't mind. It's the first morning she's not had B&B guests for a while and Pippa wants to languish in the peace and quiet. Unfortunately, she has another meeting with Grant planned later to discuss what needs to be done to get the council approval for the building work, but until then Pippa wants to enjoy some alone time.

The radio presenter is introducing 'Go Your Own Way' by Fleetwood Mac on the radio in Pippa's kitchen, and she starts humming along. Even though they didn't go to the bonfire celebrations last night, with Jake insisting you could see the fireworks from anywhere in Riverdean, Pippa can still smell woodsmoke in her hair. She inhales, enjoying that very specific scent.

Jake was right, you could see the fireworks from anywhere, particularly well from the hot tub. He'd joked about fireworks outside and fireworks under the water. It was cheesy but Pippa liked it, and it really did feel like fireworks between them; the sex was amazing. As much as she wanted to heed all the warnings and protect her heart, Pippa had developed very strong feelings for Jake. How could she not? The whole village was practically gaga seeing him dripping with water after that raft race. But he is hers, and only she got to see him dripping with water in the hot tub.

She smiles to herself, realising she's been washing the same dish for two minutes. Get a grip. Pippa has enough to do today without mooning over Jake.

There is a knock at the door. Pippa feels her good mood failing, as she quickly dries her hands on a tea towel. No one ever knocked on her door before she moved to Riverdean. Between the B&B guests and the host of quirky locals, the door never stops here. She likes it, but sometimes Pippa wouldn't mind some alone time.

'Coming!' she shouts.

Pippa opens the door to the last person on the planet she expected to see. 'Jenny.'

Her good mood has definitely plummeted now. Jenny stands looking sombre at the doorway. 'Can we speak a moment?'

'Urrr, yes,' Pippa says, off her guard a minute. She wishes she'd known Jenny Foster was going to pay her a visit. Pippa would have prepared more; burning sage seems appropriate.

Jenny leads her through her own kitchen to the living room, and Pippa realises she's been here before, is familiar with the cottage.

'Take a seat,' Pippa says, a moment too late as Jenny is already placing herself on the sofa. She seems to perch as though wanting the least amount of contact with the sofa possible. Pippa feels acutely aware of the power and age imbalance between them. The experience Jenny has that Pippa's lacking, the knowledge of Riverdean. Jenny has all the power here, the ball is in her court. Pippa tries to take some of it back.

'You can sit back you know, Jenny,' she says.

'Well, I don't know if this sofa's clean.' She wrinkles her nose. 'You could have had anyone here, for all I know.'

'What?' It takes Pippa a second to compute what Jenny's saying. 'That's rude. I'm going to ask you to leave if you continue to insult me like this,' and out of nowhere too. What is Jenny implying?

'Fine, then, I'll keep it brief,' Jenny sniffs. She taps her nails on the handle of her handbag, square on her lap. 'You can't keep seeing Jake any more.'

Pippa feels like she's been slapped in the face. Blindsided by Jenny's words.

'Wha—?'

'If you do, then I'm going to make sure Pumpkin Cottage is closed down forever. I know people on the council panel who will block the approval of the rather unorthodox work you've had done.' She talks quickly, casually, as though she's reading out a shopping list, not threatening to destroy Pippa's future and livelihood. 'I can call health inspectors, who won't take too kindly to the cockroach infestation. And, also, I've been reading about hot tubs on balconies, which can pose a damp risk.'

'Why would you do this?' Pippa asks. Jenny simply looks at her, tight-lipped.

'You've also got an outhouse with an asbestos roof. That's a risk with paying guests. All these details, Pippa, that you're just too young and too naive to understand. Anyone with a modicum of experience would have secured all of this before ploughing on ahead and opening, taking over the village, taking over Jake.' She gasps then, as though she's said too much.

Jenny's words spiral in Pippa's mind, an evil echo. She's so confused she doesn't know where to start.

'I don't know why you're threatening me, Jenny,' her voice

wavers now, a struggle to stay calm. 'Perhaps it's Riverside Lodge that's threatened by me. Ever since Pumpkin opened, it's been nothing but problems with you. Are you scared I'm going to steal your customers? Bring Riverdean into the modern world? Run a better B&B than you? Because I've got news for you Jenny, I'm already doing it.' Pippa feels she's on a roll now. It's not like her to make jabs like this, but she's under attack with Jenny. Pippa's just laid down and taken her hostility so far, it's time she fought back. And she must be right, Jenny *is* threatened by her. But how does this relate to Jake?

'You're just a stupid little girl. Pumpkin Cottage might be all shiny and new now, but you don't have the sticking power, you'll see,' Jenny says with unshakeable confidence.

'Time will tell, and I've got more news for you, Jenny,' Pippa takes a deep breath, 'I'm not going anywhere. You can't scare me away. Your jealousy and threats won't get anywhere. In fact, they just spur me on.'

Pippa stands, ready to usher Jenny out, but she stays firmly planted on the sofa, even sits back a little.

'You're not right for this village, you're not a local. Novelty's got you so far, but your true character won't be enough. It's the same for my Jake too, you're not right for him.'

'What does this have to do with Jake? Why do you care so much? Jake doesn't belong to you. He's nothing to do with you.' And then Pippa clocks it. *My* Jake.

'He's my son,' Jenny says, watching Pippa closely. 'You didn't know?'

'No,' Pippa shakes her head, too astounded to say more.

'He's deceived both of us, then,' Jenny picks at a thread on her jacket.

Jake Taylor is Jenny Foster's son. No. That can't be true.

'But . . . his surname?' Pippa asks, still trying to figure this out, to find a loophole. Anything to stop it being true.

'I remarried,' Jenny says. 'Phil's been like a father to Jake, even though his real dad is elsewhere.'

Jake's dad has dementia. Jenny's husband is ill. It all clicks into place now. Pippa is too shocked to speak, even to move.

'Why didn't he tell me?' It's all Pippa can think.

'I don't know why Jake didn't tell us,' Jenny says, 'but I'll find out, and when I do, I'll be having serious words with him about continuing to see you. I don't know what sort of relationship you have but it can't carry on . . .'

Jenny is talking but Pippa's stopped listening. All those times she talked to Jake about Jenny, all those times she's bad-mouthed her, all along it was his mother. And all those awful things Jenny has done to her, Jake has just allowed her to do it. How can Pippa be expected to believe this?

The level of deception cuts Pippa deep. She knew Jake was too good to be true. And there she was thinking about what an honest man he was. All this time he's been playing her. No wonder he avoided Pippa meeting his parents. He clammed up every time she mentioned them. No wonder he never invited her to his place, not wanting her to see his mother. All along it was Jenny Foster?

It doesn't make sense to Pippa, and yet at the same time it makes perfect sense. Of course, Jake has deceived her. Just like Ben did. Just like every other man she's met. Why would Jake be any different just because he's from the countryside?

Pippa can feel tears threaten to fall, but the last thing she can do is cry in front of Jenny Foster.

'I think you've said enough, Jenny,' Pippa says. 'I don't need to listen to this any more. Coming into someone's home and making threats and insults, I'm pretty sure it counts as harassment.'

'Harassment,' Jenny gives a dry laugh. 'Listen to you. You think you're so right and special. Jake will see after a while, there's nothing special about you.' Pippa just wants her to stop talking, to leave. All she wants to do is sit and cry.

'Jenny, I'm warning you—'

'Don't worry, I'm leaving.' She clutches her handbag and Pippa sees her hand is shaking. 'I think I've made my point.' As they get up, a startled look crosses Jenny's face. She seems to have noticed something on Pippa's coffee table. Pippa's eyes follow Jenny's gaze but before she can understand her expression, Jenny's moved on.

Pippa finds herself following Jenny again, out through the kitchen, wanting to make sure she leaves. When Pippa thinks she's free, just before Jenny opens the door, she spins round again.

'I meant what I said about going to the council,' Jenny says. 'Don't you think about going near Jake again. He's already got enough going on with poor Lola and that mother of hers taking her away from him.' For a second Pippa can see real anguish in Jenny's face, concern for her granddaughter and son. 'He doesn't need you causing problems as well.'

As much as Pippa wants to shout in Jenny's face, to do the exact opposite of what she's telling her, Pippa knows it's over between her and Jake. She can't have a relationship with someone who would deceive her like this. She can't imagine why he did it, other than to be cruel, to play her, to make her feel an idiot. She was going to find out one day, what did he expect? In a village as small and tightly knit as Riverdean, it's incredible she hasn't found out sooner.

Pippa feels devastated. She was falling in love with Jake. She knew all along she shouldn't, but it happened. It wouldn't hurt like this if it wasn't love.

'I don't think you need to worry . . .' Pippa starts, her voice wobbling.

'Good,' Jenny says, although she sounds just as upset as Pippa. She looks like she is about to say something else, then decides against it and turns around. She's about to open the door when it opens anyway.

And there on the doorstep is Jake.

Chapter Thirty-Two

Jenny

Jenny was shaking when she came in from Pumpkin Cottage earlier. She could barely get the key in the lock. Seeing Jake standing there had given her the shock of her life and he looked just as startled to see his mother in his girlfriend's kitchen. He couldn't have heard anything of their argument but the look he gave her as she walked out. She'd never seen him look at her like that before, like he hated her.

Now, Jenny keeps replaying the conversation with Pippa in her head. Perhaps she was a bit petty hinting that her sofa wasn't clean, that she slept around. It was just seeing that smug face of hers, like the cat that got the cream. Pippa implied that Jenny's nose has been put out of joint by her, that she was threatened by her business, that she would lure her customers away. That was all very well, but Pippa didn't play by the rules and flew in the face of planning regulations. She was a cheat and her sort was not fit to date someone like Jake. Jenny dreads Jake coming home, though. He will have heard Pippa's side of the story and no doubt that one will have blackened everything she's said.

Jenny finishes the rooms, busies herself, anything to take her mind off what happened earlier. When she's sorting out the recycling, she hears the back door slam and her stomach flips over.

She makes her way down the hallway, dreading what Jake will say.

He's sitting in the kitchen chair, bent over, taking off his shoes and doesn't look at her. She stands at the doorway, hesitant.

Jenny wades in, feet first. 'Do you want to talk about it?' She puts down the recycling with a clatter.

He looks up at her, pauses. 'What is there to say? You've gone and ruined one of the few good things in my life.'

'Oh, Jake, you can't be serious. How long have you known her? Two months? Three months?'

'What's that to do with you? Are you saying you can't have feelings for someone unless you've been going out for longer.' He sounds exasperated with her. 'Six months? A year? How long would you say?'

'I'm not saying that, but you hardly know the woman.'

'The problem with you is that you're bitter. You begrudge anyone else being happy because you're not.'

Jenny fiddles with the sleeve of her cardigan.

'She told me you'd threatened her,' Jake says. 'Told her she had to finish the relationship between us or you'd go to planning, tell the council on her. Is it true?'

Jenny flushes at this. 'I-I, uh . . . I was trying to protect you.'

'From what exactly? I'm not six years old.' Jake stands up. 'It's none of your business, anyway.'

'Don't be like that, Jake.' Jenny reaches out to touch his shoulder, and stops mid-air.

'Just tell me. What have you got against her? What has she done to deserve your venom?'

Jenny's hackles raise at this. 'She's been taking business away, bad-mouthing this place.'

'That doesn't sound like her. It's more your style, Mum.'

Jenny is shocked at the sharpness in his voice. 'Not telling either of us didn't help matters, Jake. You've got to take some of the blame for this. Wouldn't it have been easier for you to admit you were seeing her? It was sneaky of you. Quite devious, really.'

'You know what? You're right. I should have said something.' He leans against the kitchen counter. 'I regret that I didn't say something sooner. But you were so against her. It got to the point where things had gone too far for me to say anything. It was cowardly of me, I realise that now.' He shrugs. 'Not that it matters any more. I'm going to look for somewhere else to live.'

'Oh, Jake . . .'

'Don't *Oh Jake* me. Pippa has finished things between us. Says she can't trust me because I lied to her. I can't say I blame her.'

Jake picks up his shoes. 'I need my own place. I'll obviously be back to help with Dad. I won't visit today, but he's coming home tomorrow, anyway. Let me know what time you want me to come and pick him up with you. Right, I've got a few invoices to sort out, so I'll get out of your way.'

When Jake leaves the house, Jenny watches his back retreating down the pathway, his shoulders hunched in misery. She's made a mess of things, she can see that now. Jake can be stubborn as a mule at times, and he obviously has feelings for this girl.

Why did things have to be so complicated? Catching sight of that photo in Pippa's living room had given her such a jolt. She'd recognise that blonde hair, those grey eyes anywhere, even if it had been decades since she last saw Suzy Miller. It was the surname that threw her. Ironic, really, as Pippa hadn't clocked the connection between her and Jake because of the surname and she had made the same mistake. Pippa was so much like her mother, though, a carbon copy. Those intense grey eyes. She had that determined jawline too. A strong sense of justice. It was Suzy Miller who led the strike at Larkfield's School for Girls when they were served mash, liver and onions three days in a row. She can hear her say it now as if it were yesterday, 'It's just not right and I for one am not putting up with it! Let's go on strike. Who's with me?' Jenny can remember the photo of the girls brave enough to back Suzy, and she was one of them. She still has that photo from the front page of the *Hereford Post*. The girls with their heavily eye-liner-rimmed eyes, their fat ties and short skirts, every inch the epitome of teenage rebellion. Jenny's parents were livid. Then the books in the river incident. That was legendary. Suzy always seemed to be at the centre of controversy, any trouble.

She was outspoken, confident and independent and Jenny was awestruck by her. She was always a conformist, longed to be like the rebellious Suzy. She even had a cool name, a proper rock chick like Suzy Quatro. Jenny was a good girl and went to Sunday school, and being with Suzy made her hope that some of her glamour rubbed off on her. To this day, she doesn't know why Suzy chose her to be her best friend, they were nothing alike.

That school visit to Normandy was magical for Jenny. For the first time ever, she escaped the surveillance of her parents. They'd stayed in a youth hostel and had visited the Bayeux Tapestry and historical sites by day, but had smoked cigarettes and sneaked out at night. Suzy had snogged a French boy called Jean-Luc. He was tall, with floppy dark hair and chocolate-brown eyes. She came back one night with a purple bruise on her neck, much to the admiration of the other girls. She definitely had a thing about dark-haired boys.

All the boys in Riverdean wanted Suzy, and she liked the attention. She remembers Suzy turning up to an end-of-year party with an older guy. No one knew how they met but of course someone like him – rich, film-star good looks – liked Suzy. They looked like they'd leapt from the pages of a magazine together. Suzy would tell Jenny everything, all the details of her dalliances, but she was strangely quiet about him. And then she got pregnant, and everything changed. Jenny remembers Suzy in tears, on her doorstep, telling her she was leaving Riverdean. She had no choice. Her pregnancy would start to show soon, she'd be the talk of the village, her parents would never allow it. She told Jenny she didn't know who the father was, but Jenny wasn't sure if that was true. She never saw Suzy again.

Jenny doesn't know how to feel about Pippa being Suzy's daughter. She'd heard Suzy had died a few months ago, but they had lost touch when Suzy left for London. Being pregnant out of wedlock was frowned upon in those days. The stark reality of bringing up a baby alone was frightening. Suzy Miller served as a warning to others. Rebellion could go too far. Look where it got you. She was shunned, as if her condition was catching. She did think about her now and again, when Radio 2 occasionally played 'Stumblin' In' or a young girl passed her in town with smoky, winged eyes and a mini skirt.

Jenny catches sight of the time and realises she'll be late for visiting if she doesn't leave now. Outside, the sky is the colour of charcoal and the wind whips up the leaves in a swirling frenzy. The mildness of Bonfire Night has been replaced by a biting, cruel wind. She hates leaving the house in this weather, hates driving out of Riverdean with its vertiginous drops and winding paths that can barely be described as roads. Carol Kirkwood had warned of the impending storm today, wrapped up in her warm camel coat on BBC Breakfast, and grinning wildly as if delivering to the nation a particularly longed-for gift.

'Expect high winds and some structural damage.' Giggling, she went on, 'The torrential rain will make things seem very miserable indeed.'

Well, Carol wasn't wrong! Jenny's fringe clings to her forehead in wet tendrils by the time she reaches the car. She has a new puzzle book for Phil and some grapes. Not very original. Phil has seemed to retreat further into himself in the last few days. He's exiled from her, buried somewhere deep inside and unreachable.

The water bounces off the tarmac, pooling dangerously at the sides of the road, and Jenny is almost fifteen minutes late when she arrives at the hospital. Not that Phil will notice.

'You're late.' he says unceremoniously, when she reaches the ward.

Kissing him on the cheek, Jenny says, 'The weather is awful, Phil.' She points to the window. 'I had to drive really slowly and then I had to wait ages for a parking space.'

In the bed opposite, a large family is gathered around the bed of a frail, old man and their conversation is punctuated by loud laughter, going off like machine gun fire. Adjacent to Phil, the curtains are pulled around the bed and the patient is using the commode, the laughter opposite at least saving his dignity.

'Couldn't Dad come today?' Phil asks. 'Where's Dad?'

Maeve had told her not to contradict him when he says something like this. He obviously thinks she's his mother.

'He promised to take me to the fireworks.' This is typical – he has some grasp of the time of year. 'I want to go home,' he wails.

'The doctor said you can come home tomorrow,' Jenny says patiently. 'Jake and I will come to get you.'

'Who's Jake?' he asks, genuinely bewildered.

'Our son, Jake.'

'He's not my son. I don't have a son.' Jenny winces. Is this acknowledgement that Jake's his stepson or just part of the melee that is his brain?

'I've brought you a new puzzle book,' Jenny says to distract him.

Throughout the visit, Phil calls her 'Mum' and keeps up the refrain, 'I want to go home.'

'He should be ready to leave mid-afternoon,' the sister says as Jenny leaves. 'It's hard to be precise because he'll have to be seen by Mr Carney, the consultant, and then we'll have to wait for Pharmacy to send the meds. The wheels turn slowly in the NHS.'

Jenny wonders how on earth she'll cope when Phil comes home. The rain and wind are still battling outside when she takes in gulps of fresh air, a relief after the stuffy ward. Perhaps she can look at some respite care. It all seems overwhelming, especially with Jake not at her side. He was so upset when he left, Jenny doesn't know if he'll ever forgive her. Does Pippa being her old friend Suzy's daughter change things? This woman she was hellbent on disliking. It is all so confusing.

Chapter Thirty-Three

Pippa

Pippa sits in Hannah's flat, a steaming mug of instant coffee in her hand. It tastes flat to Pippa, now she's used to the proper coffee she makes in a cafetière in Pumpkin Cottage, but she doesn't care.

She looks out of the window at the ubiquitous grey streets of London, rain lashing at passers-by as they huddle underneath umbrellas. It's such a familiar sight to Pippa, the wet concrete of the city. The streets she grew up on, and yet she knows in her bones this isn't her home.

It hasn't stopped raining since Pippa last saw Jake, that horrendous morning, which had started so well. She's still reeling from the shock of it all. Finding out he lied to her, that Jenny Foster is his mother, that he was stringing them both along . . . it's unbelievable. How did he think he was going to get away with it? How *did* he get away with it for so long?

Pippa thinks back to their argument, the look on Jake's face when he was confronted with his lies, his girlfriend and his mother in the same place at the same time. He looked like he wanted to be sick. Jenny made a hasty getaway, leaving them to talk it out.

'How could you, Jake?' It was all Pippa could say.

'I never meant to lie to you,' he said. He'd looked distraught as he told Pippa the number of times he tried to tell her, how awkward it was when his mother and Pippa were talking about each other, how he waited so long that it was too late, just became worse and worse the longer things went on between them. As much as Pippa hates him for lying, she remembers the times she bad-mouthed Jenny in front of Jake. It would have been pretty hard to turn around and tell her it was his mother. Then again, he should have done that from the very beginning. 'It snowballed, Pippa, the lie snowballed. You were asking about my parents, my family, and I just couldn't say. It's been agonising. I've spent so many nights wondering how I could tell you, planning to just sit down and come clean. I never meant for you to find out like this.' He shook his head, distressed.

'That's exactly what you should have done, been a man and told me straight,' Pippa bit back, making Jake wince.

'I know,' he said. 'I was a coward, I waited too long. But it hasn't been easy for me . . .'

'Aww, poor Jake,' Pippa had said, sarcastically, 'stuck between his girlfriend and his mum.'

'You don't need to get nasty like this,' he'd said, just escalating the row between them. Pippa was angry but hurting.

'Like your mum has been to me. God, the things she's done to me that I've told you about and you just let her do it again and again. No wonder you never said a bad word about her. I thought it's because you were a nice person, but no, she's your mother.'

'It's been awful, Pippa, I've tried to stop her so many times.'

'You were too late. Again!' Pippa could hear the anger in her voice, bordering on tears. Each new revelation, each memory of when she spoke to Jake about Jenny, felt like a new blow to Pippa.

'It's over between us,' she said eventually, the only conclusion she could come to. Even though it hurt her heart more than it had ever hurt before, she knew it was over.

'No, don't do this, Pippa. You don't have to.'

'I do,' she said firmly. He knew it, deep down. 'I can't be with someone who lies like this.'

Pippa can still see the look on Jake's face. Devastation. Was that a lie too? If he did care that much about Pippa, surely he wouldn't have lied like this? Wouldn't have jeopardised their relationship for the sake of an awkward conversation?

She just can't forgive him for hurting her like this.

'Hello,' Hannah's voice calls out, interrupting the negative spiral of thoughts Pippa's dwelt on over and over. As soon as Jake left, Pippa had packed her bags for London, knowing she needed a break from Riverdean, needed to clear her head and see her old friend. She arrived earlier in the day, let herself into the apartment while Hannah was out at work like she told her to.

'Hey,' Pippa says with a weak voice. This isn't how she wanted to catch up with Hannah, but her friend is her rock. She knows she'll be there for her.

'Come here,' Hannah holds out her arms. She looks impossibly glamorous with her jet-black hair and expensive-looking silk shirt. Pippa used to dress like this once, before she traded it for muddy boots and checked shirts. For Jake.

Pippa hugs Hannah close to her. She feels tears brim in her eyes. 'Are you sure Louis won't mind me staying?'

''Course not,' Hannah says, muffled through Pippa's hair. 'Although things are in a weird place between us.'

'Still?' Pippa follows her through to the kitchen where Hannah opens the fridge and wordlessly pours two glasses of white wine.

'I think he believes me that nothing happened with Grant,' Hannah rolls her eyes, 'but he's just not the same. All since finding that bloody engagement ring. I wish I hadn't looked for it.'

'You could just talk to him about it,' Pippa says.

'I've tried. I just get the silent treatment,' Hannah takes a gulp of wine worthy of an immediate top-up. 'Anyway, I need to know about you. I'm sick of thinking about me and Louis. What happened with Jake? Tell me everything.'

She tells Hannah the full story now. The whole sorry tale.

'What do you think? I just can't believe he kept it from me,' Pippa moans as they flop back on the sofa.

'Do you know what? I think I can,' Hannah says. 'Remember in sixth form, when I told everyone I went to that open day at Oxford, but really I'd stayed in a hotel with Damien?' Hannah's secondary school boyfriend was bad news all round, one of those older guys.

'Miss Roberts was so on to you,' Pippa says. 'I think Jessica Klein told her.'

'And remember Miss Roberts grilling me the next day, about which college I went to, who did the lecture, what the accommodation was like. I lied through my teeth and after a while, I just wanted it to stop. The endless questions. I wish I'd come clean in the first place, but it was too late.' Hannah shudders at the memory. 'Then Miss Roberts said she knew all along. How embarrassing!'

Pippa sees where Hannah's going with this, 'I think a sixth former lying in school is a bit different to a grown man lying to his girlfriend about something as fundamental as his family.'

'Maybe, but that feeling was awful. I wanted to come clean but I just couldn't. And you and that Jenny woman have both been pretty psycho about each other. Putting myself in Jake's shoes, I can imagine it was a bit of a nightmare.'

'I just feel like I can't trust him again,' Pippa says, the tears coming again.

'I've never seen you this hurt over a guy,' Hannah says, watching

Pippa. 'Even with Ben, and what he did was way worse.'

'Mmm,' Pippa mumbles through tears.

'I really thought Jake was the one, you know,' Hannah says.

'That's not helping.'

'I know. I just think you might see things differently in time. Once the dust settles.'

'I don't know,' Pippa sighs. 'He's hurt me so much. I don't think I can get over that. I told myself not to get involved, to protect my heart. Pathetic me, I didn't listen to my own advice. And here I am, crying and hurt, over a man *again*.'

'But Jake's not just any man,' Hannah says. She leaves a pause. 'And the fact you haven't contradicted me means you feel it too.'

Pippa doesn't want to admit that Hannah's right.

'Oh, Han. I just wanted to moan and get drunk. Can you let me have that tonight?'

Hannah smiles smugly. 'Okay. We'll get drunk tonight. You can admit I'm right tomorrow.'

Walking down Oxford Street in the rain, Pippa feels like a tourist in her own town. She used to walk this way for years as part of her commute to Mallory's. Now her commute is from bedroom to kitchen, with an occasional walk under Riverdean's autumnal canopy on the way to the village centre to pick up supplies. It couldn't be more different, she thinks. She doesn't know why she's doing this but she feels the need to go, the draw towards her old workplace. As though she needs to confirm that she made the right decision moving to Riverdean.

She passes shop windows, some displaying their Christmas ranges already. How quickly things turn from autumn to Christmas. The big flagship Marks and Spencer on Oxford Street is showing off Fair Isle jumpers, knitted coats and leggings. And yet the weather is mild and wet. Pippa's jeans stick damply to her thighs. For a second, she longs for Pumpkin Cottage, snuggled up next to the Aga with a slice of Petro's honey cake, and the radio on in the background.

She spies the golden curled 'M' on black background up ahead, Mallory's. Pippa hangs back, unsure what to do now she's here. She isn't going to go in, just wants to see what she's missing. She doesn't recognise the doorman; he must be new. Pippa can't see much inside through the revolving doors and potted plants in the lobby.

Gosh, the number of times she's donned a black shirt with Mallory's embroidery, along with pencil skirt and heels. She doesn't miss the uniform, just like she doesn't miss working for someone else, running entirely on their schedule. Pippa has loved being her own boss, even if it is at times intimidating and terrifying. She loves Pumpkin Cottage too, although now she can't seem to think of it without seeing Jenny Foster sitting there on her sofa, or herself shouting at Jake in the kitchen. Then there was sex with him in the hot tub, cuddling on the sofa, leisurely breakfasts in bed, acting like Pippa's own hotel guests. Can she really go back now with those memories haunting her?

'Pippa Mason?' A familiar voice sounds behind her.

'Robin?' She turns to see her old boss, deputy manager of the hotel. 'How are you doing?'

He hugs her tight, despite carrying a bag of pastry in one hand and a coffee in the other. Pippa always worked well with Robin; he was the ultimate professional in public but loved to gossip like no one's business when the office door was closed.

'Just grabbed lunch quickly before the youngster they got to replace you is in my office.'

'Tuesday target meetings. I don't miss those,' Pippa shakes her head.

'Tell me all about Hereford, then. Is it wonderful?'

'Riverdean,' Pippa corrects. 'And yes, it's beautiful.' She fills him in on Pumpkin Cottage, the renovations and guests she's had.

'Sounds like you're living the countryside dream,' he says.

'Maybe,' Pippa smiles, although inside her heart sinks again. She *was* living the dream. Now, not so much.

'Well, I'm glad and gutted in equal measure,' Robin says. Pippa frowns. 'The boss is leaving. Yep, Nigel's going next week. There's gossip about an affair with a woman on reception, new girl. Barely nineteen, if you ask me.'

Pippa gasps. 'That's a shock. Where's he off to?'

'Don't know, he's being very hush-hush about it all. Guess who's being promoted, though?'

'Congratulations!' Pippa hugs him again, 'I always knew that would be you one day.'

'You're too kind,' Robin says. 'God, it's a nightmare sorting out staffing, though. If you were still here, the deputy role would be yours in a heartbeat. You don't fancy coming back, do you?'

Pippa laughs, uneasy. 'No. You're joking, aren't you?'

'I'm bloody serious,' Robin says. 'There's no one else who's up to it. We could be partners again. God, it would be so much easier than getting anyone else. I was thinking of calling you the other day to float the idea, but I thought, no, I'll never see her back here, and now here you are.'

'Oh,' Pippa says, weighing up what to do. 'I'm just . . . visiting. I'm not coming back.'

'Not even for deputy manager? With me as a boss? Come on, that's what you wanted back in the day. Enough of this Butternut Cottage stuff.'

'Pumpkin Cottage.' Pippa doesn't know what to say. 'Can I think about it?'

'Yes, but don't take too long. It's like fate, seeing you here today. You're meant to be at Mallory's, Pippa.' Robin smiles but Pippa doesn't feel so jovial herself. Go back to her old job? Her old job with the promotion to end all promotions? The one she dreamt about one day? She knows she shouldn't, but a part of her can imagine it, her Mallory's name badge back with the gold lettering, Deputy Manager. No stress about renovations. No stress about bookings and cancellations and Jenny Foster reporting to the council. No stress about Jake.

'I'll think about it,' she says, before she can stop herself. Is that the right move? Has she been foolish going to Riverdean?

Pippa feels more confused now than ever.

She says goodbye to Robin and carries on down the street, but her mind is elsewhere. What is she going to do?

She needs to get a grip, get back to Hannah's flat. As Pippa pulls out her phone to get an Uber, she sees a message from Monica.

Hope Pumpkin's holding up all right in the storm. Any damage so far? Have you got enough sandbags? X

Pippa hasn't had a chance to speak to Monica since the fight with Jake. If anything, she feels a bit weird about Monica. She must have known about Jake's identity, and yet she didn't say anything either when Pippa was telling her about Jenny Foster's antics. What was her excuse? Was she in cahoots with Jake?

I'm in London at the moment. Back tomorrow.

A reply comes through straight away.

I think you need to get back now. Riverdean's at risk xx

Chapter Thirty-Four

Jenny

Jenny pulls back the curtain and gazes at the world outside, the battling winds and the river boiling below. The trees bend and wail like something out of a gothic horror story, as if presaging some apocalyptical event. She hates this weather. Turning back to the kitchen, she looks at Phil sitting in his chair in his pyjamas and slippers. The sight should bring her comfort. He's here at last where he belongs, but he seems further away from her than ever.

Jake had brought him back. He'd picked Phil up in the Jeep earlier.

'The roads are too bad to take your car,' he warned her. 'I'll go. You stay here.'

When he returned with Phil and his holdall, he'd been curt with her. He dropped a green plastic bag on the table. 'Here's his medication. The list of everything is inside.'

He and Phil were both drenched from simply coming from the car. 'I've got the fire on. Come and dry off,' she'd urged.

'No, you're all right,' he'd said, hovering at the door.

'You're surely not going out again.'

'I've got to. I'm going to check on Pippa and Pumpkin Cottage. She's so close to the river, it'll be a miracle if there's no damage.

She's not used to this. She might not want me there but . . .' he shrugged, 'she has no one else.'

He was right, of course. Pippa needed help and it was typical of Jake to be the Good Samaritan. That's how she'd brought him up. She swallowed her guilt, feeling a bit ashamed. Could she say that of herself?

'Let's have some dinner, Phil,' Jenny says. 'You must be starving after all that hospital food.' She kneels in front of him and takes his hands in hers. 'It's so lovely to have you home at last,' she says.

Phil looks directly at her, removes his hands from hers. 'When can I go home?'

'You are home, Phil darling.' She sits on the edge of the sofa. 'I was going to make us fish and chips tonight, seeing as it's a special occasion.'

Outside, the wind groans and Jenny gets up to close the curtains.

'When can I go home?' Phil asks again, rubbing his hands along his pyjama bottoms, a habit of his when he's stressed.

'You are home, Phil,' she sighs. 'I'll go and put the oven on.'

'When can I go home?' Phil asks.

'Soon,' Jenny tells him. 'Come on, let's put the telly on, shall we?' She finds the remote and the screen lights up. 'Richard Osman is on this one. You like him.'

Suddenly, there's a loud pop and they're plunged into darkness.

'Oh shit,' Jenny says. 'That's all we need. Don't worry, Phil, the electric has just gone out. It's the storm.' The blackness is thick in the living room and Jenny rummages for the torch in the top drawer of the Welsh dresser. She switches it on, relieved the batteries still work.

'Right, that's better.' Phil's eyes are wide in fear, just like a child's might be. 'I'll get some candles from the pantry,' she says. 'It looks like we'll have to have a picnic for dinner.' She tries to keep the cheeriness in her voice. She lights the candles and the place looks cosy, a haven from the warring winds and pounding rain outside. It reminds her of the days when she first went out with Phil and they ate beans on toast by candlelight to save money and because it was so romantic. 'I hope Jake's all right,' she wonders out loud. She'll have to sit it out, though, as the Wi-Fi is down and she can't ring him with the electric off. She tries with her mobile, but it doesn't ring, goes straight to voicemail. She feels a knot in her stomach. Come on, Jenny, keep yourself busy, she thinks.

She perches a candle on the kitchen counter and cuts some bread. She watches Phil's silhouette against the living room wall, a strange, twisted, eerie shape. Like his fear manifested in this other-worldly creature. She's being fanciful now, the storm getting to her. Phil hates anything that disturbs his routine.

Jenny keeps up a running commentary, as much for herself as Phil. 'We'll have cheese sandwiches and we've got some of those fancy sweet chilli crisps. We could even stretch to some carrot cake.' Jenny thinks about taking some to Pumpkin Cottage tomorrow, when all this storm dies down. A peace offering, perhaps.

As she lays their feast on the coffee table, Jenny considers opening a bottle of wine. Better not. It's Phil's first night home and with this storm, she needs a clear head. Thankfully no one is in tonight. There are no guests booked in for a couple of weeks. That's the way it is in hospitality.

As Jenny sits down, there's a loud crash from outside.

'What on earth was that?' Jenny says out loud. Peeping out the window, she can see one of Jake's kayaks, propped up against the shed, has crashed through the window. 'Well, that's careless of him. He has his craft ciders and all sorts in there.' She sits back down and nibbles a sandwich.

'It's no good,' she says. 'I can't sit here when there's things to be done. I'll have to do something about that window. I'll be ten minutes.' She wonders if she should lock Phil in, but he seems engrossed in the game show, his hand in the crisp packet.

Jenny reaches for her cagoule and wellies, unlocks the front door. The fierceness of the wind shocks her as her hood is wrenched from her head. She lays the offending kayak on the boggy grass. Unlocking the shed door, she weaves the torch into the blackness, searching for something to cover the gaping hole in the window. The glass is jagged, its transparent teeth in a grimace. She can imagine Jake will moan at her tomorrow for braving the storm for something that can be fixed later. She lays the torch down on a rickety old table and picks up some wood propped up in a corner of the shed.

The first piece she picks up is quite heavy and is too long to wedge in the window. This is hopeless. She'll never be able to wedge wooden panels in. Who is she kidding? Then she has a brainwave. If she could place something in front of the window, it might offer some protection. Eventually, she pushes an old chest of drawers that holds some empty bottles against the window, not before a couple crash to the floor. What a bloody mess, she thinks. Oh well, it'll have to do and she can sort it in the morning.

'Phil!' she calls, 'I'm back. What a mess, and this weather is horrible.' She's been gone half an hour. 'Phil?'

Fear grips her chest. Where the hell is he? She shouldn't have been gone so long. Checking the toilet and bedrooms, Jenny tries not to panic. The back door was still closed when she came in. Jenny makes her way to the guest wing, the fear burgeoning inside her. As she reaches the first four bedrooms at the top of the L-shaped hallway, she hears a door bang further down. She races towards the noise, then sees the fire door swinging open as the wind catches it.

'No, no, no. He can't have gone out there,' she wails, knowing that is exactly what has happened.

She bursts through onto the lawn and the darkness swallows her up. He was disorientated. What if he's gone to the river?

'Phil!' she yells, the wind trapping her voice in her throat. She'll have to find him. Frantically, she races down the bank, not bothering with the path, and she slides onto her back. The sobs take over now as she struggles to her feet. She's dropped the torch and her back feels sore.

Without street lights, the paths so familiar, are alien to her. Even Greenbrook is in darkness. It would be so easy for someone to fall into the river, even for someone who knows the paths and lanes of Riverdean like the back of their hand. It's a challenge for anyone with their wits about them. For someone who hasn't . . .

If only this rain would stop, Jenny thinks. Branches litter the path and she falls and stumbles a few times, righting herself awkwardly. She sees candlelight flickering in the first cottage she reaches, Belle View, Brian and Meryl Turner's place.

Jenny hammers on the door as loudly as she can.

'Jenny, what on earth are you doing out in this weather?' Brian asks.

Cutting him off, Jenny asks breathlessly, 'Have you seen Phil?'

'No, no,' Brian says. 'Come in. Is he missing?'

Meryl sits in her armchair, a dressing gown wrapped around her, and she covers her mouth with her hand.

'I went to fix a broken window in the shed. It was stupid of me to leave him alone in the house. When I came back, he'd gone.' She collapses into a chair and gives in again to her sobs.

'Have something to drink,' Meryl says.

'Where's Jake?' Brian asks, handing her a glass with amber liquid inside. Jenny winces as she sips the brandy.

'He's at Pumpkin Cottage. Helping Pippa.'

'It's flooded, I heard,' Brian says gravely. 'I would have helped but I'm unsteady on my feet these days. Come on, I'll grab my coat and we'll get Jake and call the police. He's a vulnerable adult.'

The guilt envelopes Jenny. What kind of wife is she to let her husband go missing? He shouldn't have been out of her sight.

'Don't blame yourself for this,' Meryl tells her, sensing her guilt. 'You can't have eyes everywhere.'

When Brian joins Jenny outside, they head to Pumpkin Cottage. He loops an arm in Jenny's. The path is submerged in rainwater and debris from the river. They have to climb the bank to reach the cottage. Jake is at the front door, hunched over and hammering wood across the threshold. He doesn't hear Jenny and Brian until they are almost upon him.

'What are you doing here?' he asks, startled.

Falling into his arms, Jenny says, 'Your father is missing.'

Chapter Thirty-Five

Pippa

Pippa hears a hysterical voice outside, wailing. It takes her a beat to recognise it's Jenny Foster, usually so calm and collected. It's typical of her, though, to turn up when Pippa's at her lowest.

Pippa arrived back in Riverdean an hour ago, after a hellish drive back from London. What is it about heavy rain that makes people forget how to drive? There were people on the motorway crawling along at ten miles an hour, and others determined to plough ahead at their usual speed, kicking up rainwater as they passed so that Pippa's vision was completely obscured for a few seconds. The blackness didn't help and Riverdean seemed so alien with the storm raging through. Adrenaline has pumped through her body for the last few hours, but Pippa at least hoped she could relax with a cuppa when she got to Pumpkin Cottage.

The damage is so much worse than she expected, though. The few measly sandbags she had have done nothing to stem the rain from puddling under her door, a pool of water that has snaked its way around her kitchen, leaving her floor and units sodden. A tree has fallen into the Lavender Room, leaving shards of glass over the bed. Pippa's potted plants have blown over outside too. It's going to take a while to recover, but Pippa has a horrible feeling the damage is not complete yet.

And then Jake showed up, a solemn look on his face, demanding he help Pippa. It took all of her resolve not to melt into his arms, to allow him to hold her, to take the stress away. He'd worked in silence next to her, clearing up the glass in the bedroom, boarding up the window.

'There's an emergency window fitter in the village, I'll give you his number tomorrow, but he'll probably be inundated with calls after the storm,' Jake said awkwardly, after a while.

'Thanks,' Pippa said, serious. 'I can move my guests to another room tomorrow, that is if they're still coming.'

'The storm's meant to clear tomorrow.'

And that was that. Conversation over.

There was so much Pippa wanted to say to Jake. To tell him that she understands why he covered up his mother's identity, but that it still hurts. To tell him that she's had a job offer in London, but doesn't know where she stands in Riverdean. To tell him that the last couple of days she's felt lonelier than ever, and that she's missed him and being without him felt wrong. But Pippa just continued in silence. Pippa peeks out now from the kitchen window, sees Jenny out there, with another man she doesn't recognise. Despite the torrent of rain and blackness of the unlit street, Pippa can see Jenny's crying. Jake puts his arm around her. When he turns round, Pippa can see he looks panic-stricken, too.

She feels drawn outside to Jake. She's still wearing her coat and boots, and heads out.

'Dad's gone missing,' Jake says to her. 'He went wandering.' Pippa gasps. She understands now, of course, that Jake's dad is the same man she saw at Riverside Lodge that one time.

'Well, where could he have gone?' Pippa asks, then realises it's a stupid question. She feels the need to say something practical, something helpful. 'He hasn't gone in the car?'

'No, the car's still there,' Jenny says. 'He's definitely on foot. Oh God, he was in pyjamas before he left.'

'He's probably freezing,' Jake says, looking desperate.

Okay. Pippa needs to look at this practically. Jake and Jenny are too blinded by emotion. She needs her managerial head on, the one Mallory's want so badly. She can do this.

'First of all, someone needs to tell the police.' She looks questioningly at the other man present.

'I'll do that,' he says, taking the hint.

'Thanks, Brian,' Jake says.

'The rest of us will start looking. Jake, you have the Jeep, so it makes sense you drive around. I'll go on foot. Where does he usually spend time? Old work? Hobbies?'

Jenny and Jake both look at each other. 'The Trout,' they say simultaneously.

'Maybe the school,' Jake says, 'or River's Wood.'

'He could be at the post office. Anywhere, really,' Jenny says.

'He can't have gone far on foot,' Pippa says, trying to reassure Jenny, 'and you know everyone in Riverdean. If someone sees him and recognises him, they're bound to help bring him back. Why don't you go home just in case he comes back there on his own?'

'I can't just sit there.' Jenny looks pleadingly at Jake.

'It's a good idea, Ma. He just might come home, and it would be awful if no one was there.' It's odd to hear Jake call her Ma so openly, so casually. Pippa can see Jenny relies on him, that he's clearly a calming presence. The kind of guy you'd want around.

'I'll weave my way up to the square, look down all the cut-throughs and alleyways,' Pippa starts.

'But what about Pumpkin?' Jenny nods to the cottage, the damage.

'There's not much I can do about that now. Finding Phil is more pressing.'

'Thank you,' Jake and Jenny both say, and Pippa catches it. Tiny, but there. A smile from Jenny.

'The police said they'll send someone, but there's a fallen tree on the A road. Riverdean's currently cut off from the rest of Herefordshire,' the man reports back after ending his phone call.

'Oh God,' Jenny cries.

'That's good,' Pippa says. 'It means he can't have left the village.'

'Come on, let's move,' Jake commands.

Pippa goes back to lock Pumpkin Cottage but wonders what the point is. No lock in the world could stop the storm tonight.

'Phil!' Pippa calls out to no avail. The wind is screaming louder than her voice, and her hair whips around her face, muffling any noise she makes. Her torch light only shines so far, the rest of the street pitch-black. Pippa is up in the village but the river could be right next to her, the water rushing with such fierce force.

She's checked everywhere Jenny and Jake listed, but there's no sign of him. Pippa can't help but fear the worst – a vulnerable man like him, out in this storm, wearing pyjamas of all things. He'll be hypothermic now, and that's if he hasn't met some other danger like a falling tree.

She checks her phone again, hoping Jake will message to say he's been found, but there's no signal anyway. Pippa sighs in frustration. Her hood is blown down again, rain soaking her already wet hair.

It's no use. He's not around in the village centre, or any of the residential streets Pippa's checked. Jake is scouring the outskirts in his Jeep. Maybe Pippa should check the pedestrian parts of Riverdean, the footpath along the river. Although it will be a miracle if Phil's there and hasn't come to any harm; it's so close to the river and is lined with overhanging trees.

Pippa joins the path down at Mustard Cottage, named literally after the autumnal colour of the wood. The path looks deserted, like something from a horror movie. She doesn't want to walk it alone, but thinks of Phil, who must be terrified, wherever he is.

'Phil!' she calls, and shines her torch straight ahead, although it only illuminates the tree branches above, overhanging spidery fingers that seem to be trying to claw at Pippa. She forces herself to walk on. Around one corner, Pippa feels water soak into her boot. The river has burst its banks here, and water is collecting in deep puddles on the path. *Oh God, what if this has happened outside Pumpkin too*, she thinks.

The path clears ahead leading to the car park of The Trout. No lights are on inside, just like the rest of Riverdean, although Pippa spots a torch light swinging through the rain. Two figures are huddled in raincoats. They look ominous, watching Pippa, but it's only once she's closer she sees it's Brett and Shaun.

Pippa gasps with relief. 'Thank God it's you two!'

'Pippa,' Brett grabs her arm, 'what are you doing out on your own in this?'

'Looking for Phil,' she says.

'Same,' Shaun nods, 'Jake called in to check he wasn't here. We couldn't just sit around doing nothing.'

'Thank you so much,' Pippa says. The more pairs of hands they have the better.

'You're helping too?' Brett scrunches his nose. 'I thought you and Jake had broken up?'

News really does travel in Riverdean. 'It's . . . uh, complicated,' Pippa says, because as she's about to agree with Brett, she realises she doesn't want to say it aloud. She doesn't want them to be broken up. She doesn't want to be Jake's ex. *Oh God, now is not the time to consider this.*

'Whew, I haven't seen a look that confused since I told my parents I was gay,' Brett laughs. 'You can sort your story out another time.'

'You look drenched,' Shaun comments. 'Do you want to go home and change, and then come back and search with us?'

Pippa's about to protest, knowing the more search teams they have the better, but she really doesn't want to walk on her own any more. She's tired and wet and cold.

'Yes please, that sounds like heaven,' she sighs.

'Go on, then. We'll come meet you at Pumpkin in two mins.'

Pippa continues down the lane, but is startled when she sees her beautiful cottage, and the water rushing at the door from the river. This is now a full-on flood, with Pippa unable to see the gravel driveway beneath the water. She can see damage to the hot tub balcony as well, more branches and broken glass. She wants to cry so desperately, in fact maybe she is crying but she doesn't feel it against the wet of her skin. Her precious B&B, ruined. Her relationship, over. Her life in Riverdean, so precarious.

Everything seems so pointless, Pippa thinks, as she trudges towards the cottage. Why did she ever bother coming here? She's learnt nothing about her mum. She's done all that work on the cottage only for it to be ruined in the storm. She's added another failed relationship to her total. What was the point?

Just as Pippa's about to push through the knee-deep water to the door of Pumpkin Cottage, she catches a movement ahead. The lane is deserted so where was it coming from? Did she imagine it?

The movement happens again, suspended over the water. Pippa squints through the black, realising it's on Bobbin Bridge. There's someone on the bridge, moving back and forth. She can tell whoever it is is frail, the way they're huddled against the weather.

Pippa knows instantly it's Phil.

All thoughts of Pumpkin Cottage are immediately gone. She runs towards the bridge, further down the lane, before it's too late. Phil looks so unprotected, so waif-like up there. It seems like one gust of wind could blow him off, into the river.

'Phil,' she shouts again, hoping he can hear. 'Phil!' She's on the bridge now. He turns to Pippa and, for a second, he looks like a frightened animal, his eyes wide and shaking. 'Don't be frightened, Phil, it's okay. You must be freezing.'

'No, I'm not,' he says, still wary of Pippa. The little stone footbridge is only wide enough for two people, and so Pippa keeps her distance, not wanting to startle him.

'Do you want my coat?'

'No,' he says, but Pippa can see he's shivering, his fleece pyjamas soaked through.

'Here,' she offers and he does take the coat. At least that will keep him warm enough to get him home. 'Where are you going to?'

'I have to get home,' he starts. 'My mum will be worried about me.'

Oh, Pippa realises just how confused he is. Jake had told her how he sometimes says things like this, thinks Jenny is his mum, or talks as if he is a child. Jake said he used to contradict him but now he goes along with it. *It's easier, gentler on Dad*, he'd said.

'Okay,' Pippa says, channelling Jake. 'Where does your mum live, Phil?'

'In Greenbrook.'

'Is that why you're on the bridge?'

'Of course, keep up,' he says. Pippa can see his frustration. It must be exhausting, being spoken to like a child all the time. 'I can't remember which side is Greenbrook.'

That must be scary, Pippa wants to say, but stops herself. She wants Phil on her side as much as possible if he is to walk home with her.

'It's this way,' Pippa says pointing to Riverdean.

'I don't think so,' Phil says, and her heart sinks just a little.

'It is, I know where your home is,' Pippa says.

'Who are you?' Phil asks now.

'I'm Pippa.' She doesn't know what to say to get him to come with her, but she senses that keeping him talking is the best thing to do. 'I live in the village. I run a B&B.'

'My wife runs a B&B,' Phil says.

'Really? Let's walk and talk about it.' She nudges him along and to her relief, he starts to move with her. 'Do you have any children?'

'There's Jake, who's ten,' Phil explains. 'He's learning to kayak. I hope he's not on the water now.' He starts to turn back towards the bridge, but Pippa manages to steer him away.

'I'm sure he's at home now, safe from the storm.' She spies Brett and Shaun outside Pumpkin Cottage, who both cheer when they see she's with Phil.

'I'll go and get the car,' Shaun motions. Brett comes over with an extra jacket for Phil. Pippa is relieved for the extra help. Between them they manage to bundle him into the car and drive him up to Riverside Lodge. In the back of the car, Pippa can see his slippers, thin and wet through. The poor man's been through the mill, and so have Jenny and Jake. Pippa wants to be there for Jake in future. Just like he was for her, silently helping with Pumpkin earlier. They need to talk it out in the light of day, to see if there's a way they can make things work.

As they pull up to Riverside Lodge, Pippa sees the front door opening before the car engine's stopped. Jenny must have been waiting like a coiled spring. She looks like she's going to collapse when Phil's door opens.

'Phil! Thank God for that. Thank you so much Brett,' she says, breathless.

'No, no, Jenny. It was all Pippa. She's the one who saved Phil.'

Chapter Thirty-Six

Jenny

There's a calmness in the air, a raw freshness. The sky is a crystal blue with thin, wispy clouds soon burnt off by the morning sun. But the land is scarred and battle-weary after the storm. What was this storm coined? Storm Josie, as if giving it a friendly name lessened its impact, like monsters given cutesy monikers in children's books. Trees lie prone and the paths are littered with branches. The river glitters benignly but the water is a muddy brown and the flotsam and jetsam of the storm float downstream. Phil is still in bed sleeping off his 'adventure'. She had wondered last night whether he needed to go to hospital again, but thankfully he wasn't out there that long. He was disorientated and confused, but there was nothing unusual in that. Physically, he was bruised and had scratches on his arms and legs. She and Jake decided he was better off at home. He needs more care, that is becoming increasingly obvious, but she can't think of that right now after the relief of finding him in one piece last night.

Jenny sips her coffee and swallows two paracetamol. The stress of these last few weeks has been almost intolerable, driving her to the edge. As Jenny gets up to pour another coffee, she hears a tap at the door. She's surprised to see Pippa Mason there, with sunglasses on and her hair pulled into a messy bun.

'Can I come in?' she asks tightly.

Jenny opens the door wide. 'Please do.' She hopes she sounds welcoming. 'There's some coffee left in the cafetière.'

Pippa shakes her head.

'How's the cottage looking this morning?' Jenny asks.

'A mess. Chaos.' When Pippa takes off her glasses, Jenny can see dark rings under her eyes. 'A tree has damaged a window and there's extensive damage to the plaster in one of the guest bedrooms. The worst is the flood, though. Inches of water in the kitchen. All that money on renovation, months of work.'

'You have insurance?'

'Yes, of course.' She shrugs, 'I don't know if I've got it in me to start again. I'm exhausted by it all. I had such hope coming here. I was so naive.' Her phone buzzes in her pocket. Pippa takes a brief look at the message, clicks it off. 'That's the insurers. They're over at two o'clock.' She puts the phone back in her pocket. 'Anyway, I'm here to say you've won. You've managed to drive me out.' There's a bitterness in her voice and Jenny winces. 'Your dislike of me, no, your *hatred* of me, makes it impossible for me to stay.' She bites her lip. 'I have no idea what I did to you to make you feel like you did. That's for you to answer. It certainly worked, this vendetta of yours.'

Jenny stares ahead of her, swallows hard. Silence hangs in the air.

Pippa says briskly, 'I've had a job offer. My old job back, in fact. Some might think it's a step backwards, but I don't think so.' Jenny is unconvinced and she can't help but think that Pippa feels the same. 'It's pretty clear I'm a city girl at heart,' Pippa goes on. 'I'm certainly not cut out for running a bed and breakfast in the country. I don't know what I was thinking.'

She lapses into silence again. This time, Jenny is the first to break it. 'Don't go,' she says in a small voice.

Pippa looks at her curiously, as if wondering what the trap is, what's coming next. Jenny can't blame her.

'Don't go,' Jenny says more firmly this time. 'You *are* suited to country life. You are great at running a bed and breakfast. Much better than I am, and I've had fifteen years of practice. You were quite right in what you said before. I was threatened by you.' She shudders, 'And I was horrible to you – tried to put a spanner in the works. The bad reviews, the complaint to the council, the police – all me.'

'The police? I guessed it was you.'

'I was jealous of you as you seemed to sail right in and everyone liked you immediately. Just as I was more alienated, more isolated from everyone. Just as my life was narrowing, it was Pippa Mason this, Pippa Mason that.' She looks steadily at Pippa. 'I'm sorry. I'm deeply ashamed of my behaviour. All I can say is that it's not usual for me to be like this. I have got a lot on. Phil, I mean, and I've been incredibly stressed. There's no excuse for the way I've behaved, I know that. And I wish I could turn the clock back, I really do.'

'Well, it's too late,' Pippa says. 'I've been through a lot, and I haven't exactly been an angel either.' She shakes her head. 'I can't stay here. It would be too difficult with things as they are, with Jake and—'

Jenny interrupts, 'Jake is miserable without you. Heartbroken. He loves you. I've never seen him like this, not even when he and Amber broke up.' Her words come in a rush.

'But he lied to me,' Pippa says. 'He lied to you, too. I'm not sure I can be with someone who could do that.'

'I know my son and he hasn't a deceitful bone in his body. I made him lie. I made it impossible for him to tell the truth. And I know how much lying would have cost him.'

Pippa nods slightly.

'I can only tell you the truth, Pippa. He's in love with you.' There's a pleading note in Jenny's voice.

Pippa looks doubtful at this. 'I don't know,' she says. 'I've been hurt in the past. I can't risk it again.'

'You are brave, Pippa. I admire you. Coming here all alone. You have a good heart, a genuine one. Everyone saw it before I did. I will be forever grateful for what you did last night, going out like you did to help a woman who has been so awful to you.'

Pippa gives a small smile at this.

'I'm putting fresh coffee on,' Jenny says. 'Do you take sugar and milk?'

'Just milk,' Pippa says. She hasn't taken her coat off, Jenny notices.

When Jenny puts the coffee in front of her, she says, 'I want to make it up to you. I'm going to roll up my sleeves and help repair Pumpkin Cottage. One thing you'll find in a community like Riverdean is that everyone rallies around. You are never alone. I'll be there when you meet with the insurers this afternoon,' Jenny says. 'Two heads are better than one and they often take advantage of a young woman.'

Pippa nods, 'Petro has been around and Brett and Shaun. I left the two of them bickering in the kitchen when I came here. Even Grant called earlier.'

'Wonders never cease!' Jenny smiles. 'Seriously, I'd like to help you organise it all. It can be so overwhelming. I'm also a dab hand with a sewing machine and can do some upholstering. I went on a course a few years ago.' She smiles wryly, 'When I had more time.'

'Look,' Pippa says. 'I'm going to be straight with you. I don't know how I feel about staying. I'd set my mind on leaving

Riverdean after everything that's happened. Then I got the job offer and the storm . . . It's almost as if the stars are aligning to tell me I should move on.'

'Pfft,' Jenny dismisses. 'Besides, there's more.' She puts down her cup, 'I have something to tell you.'

Pippa sips her coffee, looks intrigued. 'It was when I came to see you last time. When I came to warn you off Jake.' She swallows. 'Those photos on your coffee table. You and your mother. And your mother when she was young. Suzy Miller was your mother.'

Pippa nods. 'You knew her?'

'Yes,' Jenny admits, 'I knew her very well. She was my best friend in school. I had no idea. Well, the surname threw me.'

'Mum married three times. She was never very lucky in love. It's the same reason I didn't connect Jake Taylor with Jenny Foster.' Pippa pauses. 'So, you're the best friend everyone's talked about. Tell me about her. I'm desperate to know. It's one of the reasons I came to Riverdean. It's a part of Mum's life I know very little about.'

'You're like her,' Jenny says. 'You remind me so much of Suzy when she was younger. She was very feisty, spirited, but she had a heart of gold.'

'Did you grow up together?'

'Suzy joined the school late. Form two or three, I think. She was very popular. People were naturally drawn to her. She had soft, wavy blonde hair, just like yours, and long dark lashes framed her grey eyes. Boys fell at her feet and she knew it.'

Pippa smiles at this.

'Your grandparents thought the countryside would tame her, away from the temptations of the city. Not that she was wild or anything. Just free-spirited. I was in awe of her, if I'm honest.'

'It's funny hearing someone talking about Mum like this.' Pippa's eyes shine. 'She did love to travel, and we'd go on these wild adventures with hardly any notice. I got in trouble at school once as she whisked me off on a trip to Morocco – Casablanca and Rabat, Fes and Marrakesh in a battered old camper van she'd hired. It broke down twice.'

'That sounds like Suzy. I could never imagine her settling down in one place. It would be like caging a bird.'

'We did move around a lot,' Pippa says, 'but I want to lay down some roots.'

Jenny sighs inwardly with relief at this. Jake needs someone who is steady and reliable, not someone who flits off at a moment's notice.

'There's lots I can tell you about your mother,' Jenny smiles. Pippa does too.

'That's exactly what I've come to Riverdean for.'

'Did she ever tell you about your father?' Jenny asks tentatively.

'No,' Pippa replies, 'she didn't. Just that he didn't want to be involved. I have wondered about him, I don't know who he is. Unless . . .'

Jenny hears what she thinks is a hopeful note in Pippa's voice. 'I'm sorry, I don't know either. Suzy never told me.'

She doesn't know how she expects Pippa to react, but she seems to take it in, frowning a moment. 'It's okay,' she says. 'It's my mother I want to know more about. She's the one that raised me, gave me everything. She was always there for me.'

Jenny looks at Pippa and her heart goes out to her. The young girl who has no one in the world.

'I can see why Jake has fallen for you,' Jenny says. 'Please don't give up on him.'

Pippa flushes, says nothing.

Suddenly, Phil appears at the door, startles them both. He's wearing just a T-shirt and pants.

'For goodness' sake, Phil, get dressed,' Jenny scolds. 'You'll give this young lady the fright of her life.'

Pippa laughs. 'Anyway, I'd better go. Lots to do.' She rolls her eyes.

'I'll be there before two o'clock to meet those insurers,' Jenny says, and Pippa realises there's no arguing with this.

Pippa pauses at the door, 'Thank you for telling me about my mum.'

'Thank you for bringing Phil back.'

They smile shyly at one another and Pippa leaves, bringing in a draft of the fresh, chilly autumnal air into the kitchen.

Chapter Thirty-Seven

Pippa

'Well, that went well,' Jenny says, after the door is closed on the insurers.

'Do you think I'll get the full amount needed?' Pippa asks.

'I should think so,' Jenny says. 'The guy with the moustache was dodgy . . .'

'Trying to claim that the tree could have fallen before the storm . . .'

'But hopefully we talked him out of that,' Jenny says. And between the pair of them they had been firm, telling him not to be so ridiculous. Pippa was glad to have Jenny at her side for the meeting. It really did feel nice to have backup. And Pippa knows there are no flies on Jenny.

'We make a good team,' Pippa says. Jenny gives her an odd smile.

'I was just thinking that myself.' If only they hadn't wasted so much time bickering and backstabbing. 'It's funny how women are often pitched as rivals. Riverdean's big enough for two B&Bs. I should have helped you instead of working against you. Instead of being enemies from the start.'

'We adopted that role a bit too easily,' Pippa says now. 'Men are meant to be the competitive ones, but I think women are worse.'

'There's so much pressure on us,' Jenny pauses. There really has been a lot of stress on Jenny lately, Pippa can see that.

'How's Phil today?'

'Better,' she says. 'Maeve, the dementia nurse, is with him now. He mentioned the storm and I thought maybe he remembered it, but then he was talking about getting the kids inside off the yard.'

'How do you do it, Jenny?'

'I don't.' Her voice is brittle. 'I don't do anything these days. I can't help him. In fact, me being around seems more of a stress to him sometimes, and he's always snapping at me. It makes cleaning him, getting him dressed, everything impossible.'

Pippa sighs. 'Let me get the kettle on. I know you've probably thought of this, but could you get any help? Or respite care?'

Jenny's shoulders raise. 'I have, but I feel so guilty. He needs more help than I can give, really – I know that. This storm's just confirmed it. I can't keep the doors locked all the time, not with paying customers coming in and out, and yet it's not safe for Phil. I found him in the hallway this morning putting his coat on, trying to get out, still in his slippers. I'm sure he would have gone if the door wasn't locked. Turns out having a husband with dementia and running a B&B is not really compatible.'

'Oh God,' Pippa says. She busies herself with making tea, not knowing what to say.

'I'll speak to Maeve, see what she suggests.'

'I'm sure you'll figure it out, Jenny. I've always thought you had it so together.'

'I always thought that about you. I don't have a clue.'

'Well,' Pippa hands her a mug. 'Cheers to being clueless.'

'Cheers.'

* * *

After Jenny leaves, Pippa leans back into her sofa. She has so much to do with the clean-up now, she doesn't know where to start. Grant's coming over later with another handyman to help with the windows and plastering. He's offered to do what he can for free, which has surprised Pippa. Brett and Shaun have brought some kitchen supplies to help while her own kitchen is out of action. Paula and Abi have brought a tray of cakes to cheer her up as well. Even Monica turned up first thing this morning, with a dustpan and brush, ready to clear up any glass and dirt before she went to work. When Pippa tackled her about saying nothing about Jake and Jenny being mother and son, she was full of apologies. 'I thought you knew,' she'd said. 'How could you not in a place as small as Riverdean? When you were complaining about her, you were just doing what everyone does. Let's be fair, she's a right pain in the arse!'

Pippa's glad Jenny didn't ask her about whether she's staying in Riverdean or not. Pippa doesn't have an answer. The last twenty-four hours have been confusing on an enormous scale.

Pippa has thought about taking her old job at Mallory's, the exciting promotion to deputy manager. It is tempting to slip into that black uniform again, a brand she knows so well, no more risk, no more relying on her business. A city and job she knows so well. And the idea of selling Pumpkin and not having to start afresh with the work is definitely appealing.

But could she really leave it all behind? Leave behind months of hard work? Leave behind a community that's rallied round her at her lowest point? She can't imagine that ever happening in London. Pippa would be leaving behind her dream.

And then there is Jake. Pippa doesn't know how to feel about him. The initial shock of finding out he'd covered up the truth about his mother was so painful, but the shock has gone now. And Jenny said she made it impossible for him to say anything. He was definitely in an awkward situation. But Pippa feels so uneasy now. Where does she fit in with his family?

Leaving Riverdean would be so easy. Back to her comfort zone. Back to the familiar. No more risks.

But you know what they say, with no risk comes no reward.

Pippa's never been a quitter. Just like her mother, according to Jenny. Her mother stood up for what she believed in and what she wanted. And if Pippa's learnt anything from being in Riverdean, it's that community is everything. How could she walk away from her community? From her home?

Her mother was unlucky in love, but Pippa doesn't have to be. She knows in her heart Jake is a good man. Jenny's right, he is loyal and dependable. Pippa knows he's giving her space right now, letting her make her mind up, but she needs to see him.

Pippa grabs her bag and keys, decisive, before she can think too hard and back out of it. She's going to find Jake.

She's pretty sure he's in work today, although she doubts any groups will be up for adventure today after last night's damage.

The November air is biting, but the sky is blue and hopeful. Pippa walks along the lane, ready to make her decision. She nods to a group of tourists, passing in brightly coloured cagoules, seemingly oblivious to the havoc wreaked on Riverdean last night.

She doesn't know what she's going to say to Jake when she sees him, but she isn't going to think too hard. Just speak her heart, say the first thing that comes to her.

Just before Pippa rounds the corner past The Trout, she notices a kayak, moored on the side of the river. It's one of Jake's, flamed-red, printed with his logo on the side.

It's odd to see it empty like this, and Pippa goes over to inspect it. Maybe it's been left by a group. Someone given up on their kayaking trip?

There's an envelope inside, with her name on it. Pippa's heart begins to pound.

She feels the need to check around her, make sure she's not being watched.

She begins reading. *Pippa, I've been an idiot of enormous proportions. I'm not sure I'll ever be able to say sorry enough, and I don't know if you'll ever forgive me . . . but maybe, just maybe, I'm hoping you will. If there's a chance, then please find the next letter in the place we first met.*

A smile crosses her face. Where did they first meet? It was in some random lane in Riverdean, just round the corner from here, when Jake was with Lola and she lost her doll. Does he mean there? Or at the autumn festival?

She walks up the lane, quickly now. Her thighs begin burning as soon as she hits the incline. Pippa thinks she could live in Riverdean her whole life and still never make it up the hill without losing her breath.

She spies the flash of red up ahead. Another kayak. Tied to a lamp post in the lane. It looks incongruous on dry land but Pippa smiles. When did Jake have time to do this?

She knows there'll be an envelope inside and sure enough, there it is.

Pippa, I'd never met anyone like you before. This beautiful, intelligent, determined stranger was moving to Riverdean? It was like all my dreams coming true. I felt we clicked right from the start, even with nothing in common! If you felt the same, please carry on to the site of the pumpkin toss.

That's an easy one. Pippa practically skips up the hill to the village hall, and there, tied to the railings is another red kayak. As she stoops down to pick up the envelope, a stranger smiles at her curiously.

So much has happened since that night we first spoke at the pumpkin toss, some good, some bad. I hope that the good outweighs the cowardly. If I could go back in time, I would have told you there and then about my mother. I guess I was scared you'd want nothing to do with me. And now I'm scared you won't want anything to do with me in the future . . . Although if you've made it this far, then I'm hoping there's a chance you will. Either that or you're as much of a big kid as me and just love a treasure hunt . . .

Pippa laughs at this.

Please forgive me, Pippa. I want us to have a future together. I'll be waiting in our favourite place, with two drinks and a hope that you'll show up.

Pippa pauses. Their favourite place? Two drinks? She grins. Try the *only* place.

Pippa wants to break into a sprint on the way. She lets her legs carry her down the hill, her heart pounding, her scarf flapping wildly behind her.

She pushes open the door to The Trout.

And there at the table in the window is Jake. Waiting. With two drinks. He sees Pippa at the same time she spots him. Pippa has never seen Jake look so nervous.

She makes her way over to the table, not looking up at the other diners. All she sees is Jake. All she wants is Jake.

'Here,' he says, as she approaches. 'It's the last kayak.'

He hands Pippa a tiny red kayak, a Christmas decoration, complete with his logo on the side. She takes it and grins. 'I couldn't fit an envelope inside this one.' He hands her another envelope. Pippa notices the slight shake of his hand.

She opens it up, turns the paper over and sees his words.

I love you.

Pippa looks up at Jake. 'You've gone to a lot of trouble.' She pictures him carrying kayaks around the village, writing his notes.

'Well,' he shifts uncomfortably, 'I just wanted you to know I mean it.'

'I think I'd like to hear it,' she says, winding him up. 'Aloud.'

Jake takes a deep breath, smiles self-consciously, then says, 'Pippa Mason, I love you.'

She decides not to keep him waiting long. Things feel right between them. She's made her decision.

'I love you too, Jake Taylor.'

Chapter Thirty-Eight

Jenny

Four weeks later . . .

Jenny gazes up at the monolithic structure of the ceiling. It's awe-inspiring, giving the performance of the Wye Valley Choristers a gravitas she hadn't expected. Angie is wearing an emerald green velvet dress and a black cape draped over her shoulders as if she's stepped out of a Harry Potter movie. Her oversized, gold drop-earrings flash and glint in the light as she steps towards the front of the nave.

'Oh my God!' Louise nudges her. 'She's clearly hoping for stardom.'

On cue, the cameras click and whirr behind them, reminding everyone that they are being filmed for the BBC. A presenter Jenny recognises from breakfast television stands beside Angie, waiting for the fidgeting to stop. She's a pro, Jenny thinks.

The presenter paints on a smile before beginning. 'Welcome everyone to our last destination on our whistlestop tour of the Alzheimer's Choirs of Britain. What a fitting place Hereford Cathedral is, home to the famous treasure, the Mappa Mundi, a medieval map of the world created in approximately 1300 by Richard of Holdingham.' She pauses for the congregation and viewers to take in her words. 'Tonight, the Wye Valley Choristers will be singing two songs, Take That's "Back for Good", followed by the traditional and much-loved Christmas carol, "Silent Night". Nothing could be more Christmassy than that. I'm going to leave you in the capable hands of their singing teacher, Angela Bryant, who has worked with the choir for two years, following the passing of her own father to Alzheimer's. She is ably assisted by pianist, Jude Sinclair.'

Angie was interviewed this afternoon, but this segment of the show is going live. The lights from the hundreds of candles placed strategically around the nave twinkle amongst the wreathes of green holly and the scarlet berries. The cameras whizz and hum and the tension in the congregation is palpable. Jenny stands next to Phil, Louise and Mark next to them and the people who have become so familiar to them in these past few months, have become friends, gaze at the crowds in the filled cathedral, ready to sing.

'Oh, please, God, let him join in tonight,' Louise whispers to Jenny, as the first bars of 'Back for Good' start up. 'Please let this be the night when he doesn't throw a tantrum.'

Jenny knows exactly what she means. Last week, Mark started crying as rehearsals began and Louise had to take him home. The week before, Phil sat on the floor and refused to sing.

Jenny looks across at Jake and Pippa in the congregation holding hands. Pippa's blonde curls spill out of her striped beanie and she's biting her lip, almost as if she's as nervous as Jenny. Jake gives her hand a reassuring squeeze. They look at each other and smile. Ah, that look of love. Pippa's a great girl: kind, bubbly and totally reliable. A typical girl-next-door, but strong, too, and will stand up for what she believes in. They are perfect for each other and Jenny wonders why she ever thought otherwise.

The singing starts, a little uncertain at first and then the choir settles and gives it their all. Phil is singing. Mark is singing and Jenny's shoulders sag in relief and, like a Mexican wave, the relief spreads through the entire congregation.

The shenanigans of the storm have been a wake-up call for Jenny. Maeve has arranged carers to come in twice a day to help Phil in the morning, when Jenny is at her busiest, and in the evening to help get him ready for bed. She's left some brochures about care homes. Everything is so expensive, but Jenny knows the inevitable is coming soon.

As the first song comes to an end, there's rapturous applause and one of the BBC crew holds up a card saying 'Clap' on it, which they all follow dutifully by bursting into applause again.

Tears sting Jenny's eyes as the choir starts singing 'Silent Night'. When Jake was young, she, Phil and Jake had spent one Christmas skiing in Mayrhofen in Austria and it was a snowy and magical fairyland. They were all exhausted by the skiing in the day and Jenny remembers the fairy light-bestrewn, cosy cafés and bars serving mulled wine and hot chocolate. She and Phil had imagined a retirement filled with Rhine cruises, Icelandic adventures and Norwegian getaways to see the Northern Lights. It was snatched away before their very eyes and her emotions oscillate between anger and desolation.

Louise kisses Jenny on the cheek as they leave the cathedral, the thunderous applause still ringing in their ears. 'We'll meet up in the new year,' she promises. Angie had told them that the choir starts back on 8th January and she has 'big plans for the Wye Valley Choristers.' Both Jenny and Louise had suppressed a groan.

'Have a good Christmas,' Jenny says, then takes Phil's arm to lead him to Jake's car.

* * *

Jake pulls up outside The Trout later. 'Shall we have one for the road?' he grins. 'Dad's not too tired?'

'Why not?' Jenny says. 'It is Christmas Eve.'

Jake leads them inside, holding on to Pippa's arm, where a roaring fire greets them and the noisy chatter of the Riverdean locals.

'Well, look what the cat's dragged in,' Brett winks. 'The Montagues and Capulets. "Two houses both alike in dignity, In fair Riverdean where we lay our scene."'

'Give over, will you,' says Shaun. 'Ignore him. He's had too much to drink. Again!'

'If you're quick,' Brett says, 'you can grab a seat by the fire as a group is just leaving now.'

'Perfect,' Jenny says, grabbing Phil's arm. Across the bar, she spots Fi Clark. She hasn't seen her since their argument weeks ago. Jenny nods and smiles and Fi raises her glass to her. She'll see her in the new year. An apology to Fi is long overdue.

Pippa joins them at the fireside, carrying a plate of mini mince pies.

'Not more mince pies!' Jenny groans in mock exaggeration.

'I know. Brett insisted. Petro's made hundreds of them, apparently.'

'I'll have one,' Phil says, and Jenny and Pippa laugh.

'Phil always has an appetite,' Jenny says.

'My mum was the same,' Pippa grins.

'That used to drive me nuts about Suzy, she'd eat and eat whatever she wanted and still stay supermodel slim,' Jenny says. They've been swapping stories about Pippa's mother since their truce. It's been nice to reminisce, and Pippa always seems grateful for any memories Jenny shares. Last week they'd got Jenny's old photo albums down from the loft, flipped through them with a glass of Baileys. Pippa is the spit of her mother, and they'd laughed at Phil's old haircuts in one of her albums.

'Well, Mum was always the same. Sadly, she never passed that gene on to me,' Pippa takes a sip of her drink. 'Jenny, it's been so nice hearing about my mum, I feel closer to her somehow. And coming to Riverdean, finding you, well . . . I kind of feel like I have a family now.'

Jake envelops Pippa in his arms. Jenny feels quite choked. No one speaks for a few minutes.

'I don't think I've ever seen a quiet night at The Trout since I've moved to Riverdean,' Pippa says, nibbling a mince pie.

'Wait until the new year. It'll be packed to the rafters.'

'My friend Hannah is coming from London to stay with her boyfriend, I mean fiancé, Louis. He's proposed to her, at last.'

'At last?' Jenny raises her eyebrows.

'It's a long and infuriating story,' Pippa says.

Jake returns from the bar carrying a bottle of champagne and four glasses.

'Ooh, what's the occasion?' Jenny asks. 'Dad shouldn't have champagne with his medication.' Then she kicks herself. 'Perhaps a small one.'

'It's a celebration,' Jake says. 'First, for Dad's superb performance at the cathedral tonight. It was a blinder, Pa.' Jake hands Jenny a glass. 'And I heard today that Amber and Lola are not going to France. She and Ethan have parted ways.'

'That's wonderful news, Jake,' Jenny says. 'Not the break-up, of course.'

'Ethan seemed a decent guy,' Jake agrees, 'but I'm so relieved they're staying.'

'I wonder what happened,' Jenny thinks aloud.

'You know what Amber is like,' Jake rolls his eyes. He squeezes

Pippa's knee, obviously keen to get off the subject of his ex.

'Well, I have some news,' Jenny announces. 'Well, more of a proposal really.' She stops, the noisy chatter from the bar and the music from Slade's 'Merry Christmas Everybody' making her wonder if now's the time to tell them what she's thinking.

'Well, go on, Ma, don't leave us hanging,' Jake says, laughing.

'Ok, ok. You know how your father is and how Riverside Lodge is getting more difficult, well, impossible, really. Anyway, I'd like, I *need* a smaller place and with Pumpkin Cottage still having repairs done, I was just wondering if you and Pippa fancy taking over the Lodge and Dad and I could move into Pumpkin Cottage once the work is finished. It's a much more manageable size for the two of us. I could give up working. Perhaps have just one or two guests.'

There's a silence as Jake and Pippa take in what Jenny has said.

Jake whistles, 'Fucking hell, Ma!'

'Jake,' Jenny admonishes. 'Look, I'm not expecting an answer straight away, of course. But it would be a way out for me. And you and Pippa could have a bigger place.' Jenny had wondered if this was pushing the two of them faster in the relationship than they wanted to go, but Jake had practically been living at Pippa's since the storm.

Jake and Pippa look at each other as they sip the champagne and smile.

'There's a lot to work out, legally, and it won't be easy, but you two would be great running the Lodge, what with Pippa's experience in hospitality and you've got a real eye for interior design. The place could do with a makeover and I haven't got a clue where to start, if I'm honest. Jake, you've got a good business brain. I'm not sure how it would work with your current adventure business, but we can hammer out the details.'

'We'll have to chat about it,' Jake says, and Pippa nods.

'Don't say anything now,' Jenny says. 'We'll chat about it over Christmas.'

Pippa leans over and kisses Jenny's cheek.

'It's a Christmas miracle,' Jake teases.

The closest they'll get to a happy ending, Jenny thinks.

Suddenly, Michael Bublé's 'It's Beginning to Look a Lot Like Christmas' bursts out and everyone sings along. Phil reaches for his champagne glass and it smashes on the floor.

'I'll clear it,' Pippa says, heading to the bar.

'Time to go,' Jenny sighs. 'You and Pippa can come around about two o'clock for your Christmas dinner.'

Jake kisses her on the cheek, 'You're a star!'

As they leave The Trout, snow starts to fall, a light confetti swirling before them and landing softly on the path and the willow trees fringing the River Wye.

Anna Burns is a psychiatrist and Jacqui Burns is a lecturer. Mother and daughter write their novels while living over two hundred miles apart, emailing chapters back and forth, focussing on strong but relatable women at the centre of families and communities. *Love at Café Lompar* was shortlisted for the RNA Debut Novel Award and with *Poles Apart* and *Escape to Pumpkin Cottage*, they have been writing stories set in their native Wales.

@annaandjacqui
annaandjacquiburns.com